Adrian Howell's

PSIONIC

Book Five

Guardian Angel

Cover Design: Pintado (rogerdespi.8229@gmail.com)

ISBN: 1482521490
ISBN-13: 978-1482521498

CONTENTS

INTRODUCTION

Imagine a person with a strange tattoo, eyes that don't match in color, only one ear, and scars all over his body. A person who thinks nothing of killing people. A person who would kill his own family… who would take his own blood. And you might think, *That's not a person. That's a monster. A person would never do that.* Perhaps you're right. But that's the thing about monsters: the only real ones are the ones we become.

My name is Adrian. I don't know if I'd agree with scars "all over" my body, but the rest of it's true. It's also true that once, long ago, I honestly believed that I could change the course of history, if only a little. Whether or not I succeeded… well, that's also debatable.

I admit that the motives behind my actions were, for the most part, selfish in nature. But I swear I never wanted to become a killer. Sometimes I lie awake all night, my face hidden under my blanket, remembering the lives I have taken. Sometimes I can see their last moments even in the daylight. I may be crazy, but I do know the difference between right and wrong. I know the difference between self-defense and cold-blooded murder. I know because I have done both.

In the end, we are all products of our environments, and I won't ask for forgiveness for the wrongs that I've committed. Judge me as you see fit.

But just remember that it could have been you.

1. HOME SWEET JAIL ON WHEELS

I stopped screaming the moment my eyes snapped open. The chilly dawn light filtering through my thin curtain gently brought my senses back into the waking world. Fingering the small amethyst pendant around my neck, I carefully steadied my breathing until the memory of my nightmare faded into oblivion.

Telekinetically sliding open the curtain, I squinted out at the deep orange sun steadily rising over the grassy fields that were rushing past my little rectangular window. The summer was officially over, October just around the corner, but it looked like we'd still have a few more mildly warm days ahead. The country road was straight for miles in both directions here, and aside from the low humming of the engine and constant, slight vibration, I could hardly tell that we were in motion.

I gingerly stepped down from my upper bunk in the midsection of the motorhome and stretched my arms up over my head until I felt my body begin to recover from another restless night on a hard mat.

I noticed that the lower bunk, where Alia usually slept, was empty, as was the bunk on the other side of the aisle: the one that belonged to Ed Regis. It was Ed Regis's shift to drive, and I could pretty much guess where my sister was.

Unaffected by my wake-up cry, James Turner was snoring up a storm on the bunk above Ed Regis's. I quietly slipped by him and made my way to the tiny kitchen, if it could even be called that. Though I didn't drink it, making the morning coffee was my job. So was breakfast, but that could wait a bit. It was still the crack of dawn.

The rear bedroom door opened, and Terry, by way of greeting, said brusquely, "Coffee." She was wearing a typical morning scowl and nothing else. My combat instructor, in addition to missing her left arm, had absolutely no sense of modesty.

"Couple minutes," I replied through a yawn. "Get dressed."

Terry disappeared back into her room.

The coffee drinkers among us were Terry, James and Ed Regis. Alia was still on chocolate milk, and most mornings, so was I.

While waiting for the coffee to drip, I too changed out of my nightclothes and into a dark gray shirt and a pair of navy-blue sweatpants. Psionics like myself rarely wore jeans or other clothing with metal parts since it interfered with our powers.

Terry reappeared just as I was pouring the morning drinks. Though properly clothed this time, she was still visibly lopsided since she hadn't strapped on either of her two left-arm attachments. After she lost her old hook at the Historian's mountain, Terry had purchased a prosthetic hand to help her blend into crowds, and Ed Regis had fashioned a new battle-oriented hook attachment for her. Terry's new hook was essentially a very curved, extra-sharp double-edged blade. Neither attachment was very useful on a normal day.

Terry took her mug of coffee without so much as a please or thank you, and sat down at the miniature lounge next to the kitchen. I was used to that from her. I telekinetically levitated one more mug of coffee and two glasses of chocolate milk in front of me as I made my way to the front of the vehicle.

Ed Regis was at the wheel, and as I expected, so was my sister. Alia, still in her nightclothes, was sitting in Ed Regis's lap, her hands tightly gripping the steering wheel and carefully keeping the big motorhome between the lines. Ed Regis, arms loosely around Alia's stomach, was just handling the pedals.

"Good morning," Ed Regis said pleasantly as I passed him his coffee. "Thanks."

"Good morning," I said. "Alia?"

My sister's concentration was such that she didn't even glance at me. As she guided the motorhome around a gentle curve in the road, the morning sunlight glinted off the little horn on her unicorn-shaped bloodstone pendant.

"She's a natural," Ed Regis informed me. "I haven't touched the wheel for more than an hour now."

I placed our chocolate milks in the cup holders and plopped myself down in the front passenger seat next to them. Rolling down the window, I let the cool morning air blast my face to freshen me up.

"Is Terry awake?" Ed Regis asked me.

I nodded. "Yup."

Ed Regis gave Alia's shoulders a squeeze. "You got this, right?"

"I think so," Alia mumbled uncertainly.

"Good girl. Here, let me out. I want to talk to Terry."

Ed Regis set the cruise control and then carefully got out from under my sister, leaving her to handle the motorhome all by herself. Even with the power steering, cruise control and wide, empty, backcountry road, I felt that this was a bit premature. My eyes met Ed Regis's for a moment. He gave me a slight smile and nod which I took to mean "Watch out for her." I didn't need telling. Pretending to be looking out the windshield at the passing scenery, I kept one eye on my sister and my telekinetic power ready to grab the steering if she lost control.

Her focus on the road notwithstanding, Alia let out a loud yawn. Terry had suggested that we teach Alia how to drive sometime soon, and I guessed that my sister had gotten up at 2am with Ed Regis this morning. An oversized motorhome wasn't the ideal practice vehicle for an undersized eleven-year-old, but it was all we had, and I had to admit that Alia was keeping us safely on the road. I relaxed just a little.

Not Terry, not Ed Regis, not even Alia had mentioned my morning scream. It might not have been that loud, but they would have heard it. I woke up screaming every few days so they were used to it by now, and they knew that I didn't want to talk about what was haunting me at night.

After a few minutes, I asked my sister as casually as I could, "How are you doing?"

"I'm okay, Addy," Alia replied telepathically. *"You?"*

"I'm alright," I said quietly, giving my pendant a light tap. "I'm fine."

I took a sip of my chocolate milk, and Alia, catching me through the corner of her eye, said into my head, *"I'm thirsty too."*

"Keep your hands on the wheel," I told her. "Both of them."

"Can't you hold it for me for a minute?"

"The wheel or the glass?"

My sister thought about that for a moment. *"The glass, please."*

I levitated Alia's glass to her mouth so she could sip her drink without using her hands. It didn't work, and she ended up dribbling more chocolate milk down her pajama shirt than she got down her throat. Even so, Alia kept her hands firmly on the steering wheel and her eyes on the road.

Home sweet jail on wheels. That's what James had once called our modified motorhome, and it was an apt description. It wasn't quite as long as a bus, but pretty big as far as motorhomes go. Terry and I had "acquired" it about five months ago, shortly after our return from the Historian's mountain. Consequent modifications to the vehicle pretty much guaranteed that it wouldn't be recognized by its previous owner, who, by the way, we had killed. I felt no remorse about that. He was an Angel, after all.

In the weeks that followed, Terry and Ed Regis had gutted the main bedroom in the back and turned most of it into a storage room where we kept an ample supply of emergency rations and water in case we suddenly had to become scarce for a few weeks. They had also added a layer of steel siding all around the body that not only made us impervious to most bullets, but also helped hide my psionic power from enemy finders. Mine and my sister's. But a little steel shielding wasn't enough to keep us completely hidden, especially in the countryside, so we kept moving, often driving all day and all night. We never stopped for sightseeing. It made me feel like I was living in the tiger cage of a traveling circus that never actually performed.

Our mobile jail housed five inmates. There was my obtuse combat instructor and one-armed leader, Terry Henderson. There was James Turner, the boy that we had rescued last year and later trained and took with us to the Historian. There was Major Edward Regis, former Wolf, now one of us, enough said. There was my second sister, psionic healer Alia Gifford. And me, Adrian Howell, the cook. It would have been wonderful if that was my only role here, but it wasn't.

Because we were on a mission.

After being deadlocked with the Guardians for more than seven hundred years, the Angels had finally come out on top. Not only were they the single largest psionic faction on the planet, they were the last faction headed by a master controller: a powerful mind controller who could semi-permanently bend people's loyalties to their cause. And with that power, they were growing ever more powerful as they absorbed scattered, leaderless Guardians and other, lesser psionic factions into their ranks. If left unchecked, the Angels would soon have complete control of not only the psionic world, but of people everywhere.

Ever since I turned psionic, I had a personal stake in this conflict. My first sister, Catherine "Cat" Howell, had been abducted by the Angels when she was just ten years old. Aligning myself with the Guardians, I had made it my personal mission to find her and free her from her enslavement.

But when I was briefly reunited with Cat at the gathering of lesser gods last year, it was at gunpoint. Cat was the one holding the gun, and she called the Angel queen's nephew, Randal Divine, her father. Cathy Divine, as she called herself now, had found a home among the Angels in the same way that I had found my place with Cindy Gifford and the Guardians, and there was nothing I could do to bring my sister back.

And that should have been the end of it, but it wasn't.

During the gathering of lesser gods, the Guardians had succeeded in assassinating the Angels' last known master controller, Queen Larissa Divine, and we all thought the Angels' conversions would quickly wear off and their faction would fall apart. But that didn't happen. Soon afterwards, the Guardians' capital city of New Haven was brought down in a single night by a hoard of newly converted Angels who had been bound to the service of Randal Divine. Despite the conventional understanding that master controllers were always female, Cat's adoptive father proclaimed himself the Angels' new "king"—a legendary male master controller that appeared only once every millennium.

The night New Haven fell, Terry, Alia and I fled the city with a crowd of lost children in tow while Cindy Gifford was taken by the Angels along with the rest of the New Haven Council, and we hadn't seen her since. Taking refuge in the small Guardian settlement of Walnut Lane, Terry and I started giving combat training to the children we had rescued, including James, in the hope that we could use their strength to help get us to the Historian, a 3000-year-old psionic who might be able to tell us the location of Randal Divine. It didn't work out quite as we planned it, but nevertheless this spring, with the help of some Wolves we rescued from an Angel outpost, we finally made it to the Historian's mountain.

But when we got there, the Historian taught me just how much the truth could hurt.

Randal wasn't a psionic king at all. In reality, Cat was the one doing the converting. My own sister was the Angels' new queen, the female wild-born of a once-lost master-controller bloodline. But not even the Angels knew that. Randal was using his power as a mind-writer to make the new converts believe that he was their master. Cat was still fourteen years old, and Randal Divine, her "loving father," was protecting her with this outrageous lie until she was old and wise enough to rule the Angels, and later the entire planet.

And so now I had a new mission.

In return for his assistance, the Historian had demanded that I help restore equilibrium to the rapidly deteriorating balance of power between the Guardians and the Angels. He had asked me to put an end to my own bloodline.

It's a strange world we live in. A world of consequences for both action and inaction. Consider this: If you were to destroy a tyrannical government at the height of its power, you would be forever remembered as a great hero who saved millions from cruelty and oppression, but you could not bring back to life those who had already perished under the tyrant's rule. If you could somehow kill the same tyrant *before* he came into power, then you would save millions more from a horrible future and no one would have to suffer, but you yourself would be nothing more than a murderer.

I wanted to be neither hero nor villain, but master controllers were the greatest enemies of free will, and by unhappy chance my sister was the world's last. Catherine Divine and her faction couldn't be allowed to rule this world. Thus I had promised both the Historian and myself that I would do something absolutely horrible: I would hunt my sister down and kill her.

And it was *because* Cat was my sister that I couldn't turn away from my mission. There was no way I could let a stranger do this in my stead. As her brother, as her family, I owed it to Cat to end her life myself. I know that's crazy. You really have to be there to fully understand it.

The day the Historian told me that Cat was the new Angel master, I already knew what I had to do about it. But knowing and accepting are two different things, and five months later, it still gnawed at me. Out of consideration for my feelings, everyone on my team was careful never to refer to Catherine Divine as my sister. Unless we were talking about Alia, "sister" was a taboo word around here. Instead, we called Cat the "Angel master" and the "target." I was grateful for that, but it didn't really change who the target was. She was my own flesh and blood, and there was simply no getting around that fact.

Hence the nightmares.

As for the Historian's precious "equilibrium," I cared for it only in-so-much as it brought Cindy (who we learned had been converted into an Angel) back to Alia and allowed my part in the faction war to be over once and for all. To that end, I didn't care how many people we hurt or killed. Over my years as a psionic destroyer, I had crossed many lines, and I was used to it by now.

All summer long, we had been moving from hidden Guardian settlement to god-forsaken hidden Guardian settlement, some places just a tiny collection of psionics living in fear of capture and conversion. Though the Historian had given us the true identity of the Angels' last master controller, he knew nothing of her location. At the Historian's suggestion, we were asking the leaders and elders of the scattered Guardian groups for any and all information that might lead us to the Divines.

But it wasn't easy gathering information. No one yet knew that Catherine was the new master of the Angels. Daddy Divine was still parading himself as a psionic king, and would do so for as long as he could. The Guardians believed him too, and we couldn't tell anyone the truth without revealing that I had master controller in my blood. At the present, the only people alive who knew my family secret were Randal, Catherine, the Historian and my team. Eight people. We wanted to keep it that way, as there was no telling what would happen if this got out. Thus it was with carefully guised hints and roundabout questions that we dealt with the remnants of our own faction. Everywhere we went, we were given much sympathy, but little help.

Still, in all this time, we had been extremely fortunate in that we hadn't been waylaid by Angels. We were constantly on guard, but so far no contact. At least, not unless you counted the pair that we accidentally ran into several weeks ago. But they weren't even Seraphim, and Ed Regis shot them both before they could get away and report our location to their master. All I remember of that encounter is how impressed I was, once again, with Ed Regis's skills. And also how entirely emotionless I had been when we disposed of the bodies. I sort of wished that I could feel bad about what we did, but I didn't. I knew that the pair of Angels might have been victims themselves, their minds converted against their wills, unable to keep themselves from serving Randal and Catherine's twisted cause. But that didn't change the fact that if we hadn't killed them, our lives, and more importantly, our mission, would have been compromised. We did what we had to. There was no shame in it.

The only thing that really bothered me about our run-in with those Angels was that they recognized me. Not that I was a particularly inconspicuous person, but apparently my name and face were now known to more than just the Seraphim. When he discovered that I had returned from the Historian's mountain still breathing, Randal Divine had put a price on my head. And it wasn't for me "dead or alive." It was specifically for my capture. Alive. That's what really scared me.

Though only females could become master controllers, the potential for this power was passed exclusively down the male side of the family. That meant that Catherine's future daughters would never become master controllers, but mine could. In fact, according to the Historian, I was the world's last male psionic capable of passing the power of master controllers on to the next generation. Thus Randal Divine wanted me alive, turned Angel… for *breeding purposes.*

But in order to keep his own secret safe, Randal couldn't allow anyone, not even his own people, to learn what I was, so his bounty on me didn't detail the true reason he wanted me brought to him in one piece. Nor was I the only one on Randal's most wanted list since there were still plenty of other important Guardians at large. But as my infamy grew, I feared that it would only be a matter of time before someone figured it out.

"Addy," said Alia, breaking into my thoughts, *"is there any more chocolate milk?"*

"I could go make some," I replied, and then asked with a grin, "Do you want it in your mouth or down your shirt?"

"Could you hold the wheel so I can go change?"

"Sure."

"And shower."

"Make it quick."

Alia disappeared into the back. Too lazy to switch seats, I telekinetically held on to the steering wheel, keeping us steady.

I could hear Ed Regis and Terry talking in the lounge space behind me. James had woken up and joined the conversation too. They were discussing our next destination: yet another breakaway Guardian settlement. But this one was very special to us. Though recently renamed the Wood-claw Guardians, they were none other than the former residents of Walnut Lane, led by Mrs. Harding.

We had visited thirteen Guardian settlements already, staying with them for anywhere from a few hours to several weeks, trading what little information we had for whatever they were willing to offer. So far, however, we had no real leads on Randal Divine. These scattered Guardians were, for the most part, simply trying to survive, and weren't actively fighting the Angels anymore.

However, we did hear several rumors from them about an underground resistance network hidden within the former Guardian city of New Haven—now occupied by the Angels and renamed Lumina. If such a resistance movement really existed, then we wanted to be a part of it. The Historian's only advice to me regarding how to find Randal Divine was to get that information from people who were "closer to this war," as he put it. Guardians in Lumina would certainly be a step in the right direction. But no one we had talked to so far could confirm these rumors or help us make contact.

Not that we were expecting someone to simply give us Randal Divine's home address, but our utter lack of progress over the past months was frustrating, especially for Terry. With each fruitless visit, Terry pressed us harder toward her alternate plan, which was to attack an Angel outpost and gather information directly from the Angels. Ed Regis and I were skeptical about the merits of this approach. For starters, it was downright dangerous. Most psionic settlements would be much too large to take down with only five people, even with people like Terry and Ed Regis. Furthermore, the Angels themselves had just about as much chance as the Guardians did of knowing where King Randal Divine lived. Only the very top Seraphim, members of

Randal Divine's personal guard, would have that information. We would have to identify one, capture, and finally extract Randal's whereabouts from him. Not an easy task even with Guardian support, and impossible without it. But Terry insisted that we might get lucky, and anything was better than just driving around. The pair of Angels that we had bumped into last month would have gotten away had Ed Regis not shot them, but Terry was furious that we didn't get them alive.

Then, on our thirteenth stop—just a single house shared by three psionic families—we finally got a lucky break. Their leader knew the location of Mrs. Harding's Wood-claw settlement. Back when we parted with Harding's faction in Walnut Lane, we all knew that there was a fair chance we would be caught by the Angels before reaching the Historian. Thus Mrs. Harding hadn't told us where she was planning to relocate to, and we knew better than to ask. Mrs. Harding was a master at keeping her people hidden, and we had spent much of the summer wondering if we would ever see our refugee kids again. Now, finally, we had found them.

Our visit to Mrs. Harding's had multiple purposes. Even if we were going to go with Terry's plan, we would still have to pick our fights carefully. Old Mrs. Harding, with her years of experience leading her breakaway faction, could probably supply us with some useful information. She might even know something about the Guardian Resistance in Lumina. We also needed reinforcements. We desperately needed a hider and finder if we were going to do anything covert against a psionic settlement. If Mrs. Harding was unwilling to part with her own Knights, we hoped to at least take back some of the kids that we had rescued from New Haven, especially the hider, Rachael Adams. Lastly, we needed to retrieve the Wolves' psionic database that I had left in Scott's care before heading to the Historian. As incomplete and outdated as it was, this database would still come in handy when dealing with our target Angels.

But my personal best reason for visiting the Wood-claw Guardians was that I could see Candace again. I'm sure my sister felt the same way about Patrick and baby Laila.

We were now only half a day's drive away from the city where Wood-claw was hidden, and Ed Regis was planning out a safe approach. Aside from the name of the host city, nobody knew the exact location of the settlement.

It was protected by hiding fields which kept potential aggressors from sensing Wood-claw's psionic population from afar. Once inside the city, we would have to wait for the Wood-claw finders to locate us by homing in on Alia's and my psionic powers. There was no guarantee, however, that other psionic factions, namely Angels, wouldn't find us first. That was what Ed Regis wanted to go over with Terry. Those two were the real soldiers among us, so they were our leaders. Unlike James, I didn't concern myself with the details. Whatever they decided would be fine.

Terry called up to me, "Hey, Half-head, how about some breakfast?"

I was getting hungry too. "Alia," I called back, "get back up here and drive so I can whip something up for the alligators."

"In a minute!" Alia replied aloud.

I rested my elbow on the open window, gazing out at the passing farm fields along the road. Leaving a corner of my mind to telekinetically manage the steering, I thought about what I might make for breakfast. I wasn't in the mood for fried eggs, and we were too low on milk for cereal. Did we still have some bagels left?

"Hey, Alia, what's keeping you?" I called again, but my attention was on the side mirror, where a car seemed to have suddenly materialized out of thin air.

Then I did a double take. It wasn't just any car. It was a black and white police car! It was already less than a hundred yards behind us, and in my surprise, I lost my telekinetic focus on the steering.

This was the first of two major mistakes I made that morning.

Before I could re-establish contact with the wheel, the motorhome had crossed over the centerline, and then rocked wildly as I overcompensated, this time taking us dangerously close to going off-road.

"Adrian!" shouted Terry.

"I got it, I got it!" I yelled back, physically grabbing hold of the steering from the side and steadying our swerving vehicle.

I had been expecting it, but I swore under my breath when I heard the blaring police siren behind us. Ed Regis appeared in a flash to take the driver's seat. Looking in the mirror again, I saw the cop car closing the gap, red and blues flashing.

"What are you doing?" I asked as Ed Regis disengaged the cruise control and carefully pulled us to the side of the road.

"We can't outrun them," replied Ed Regis, cutting the engine. "Not in this tub. Get out of sight."

I ducked back into the lounge space where I saw Terry strapping on her hook attachment. She glared at me and mouthed, "Idiot."

James and Alia were there too.

"Good morning, James," I deadpanned.

"Good morning," said James, grinning. "I guess we're off to an early start today."

Thinking quickly, James had drawn the curtains over all the windows in the cabin. Now he was checking his pistol. Alia, hair still dripping from her morning shower, was looking at him anxiously.

"You don't need the gun, James," said Alia.

"It's just a precaution," replied James, refusing to put it down.

Alia shook her head.

I shared my sister's dislike of firearms—mainly because I had an innate talent for getting myself shot. Ed Regis had shot me in the back once, the Slayers had put a bullet in my leg, and the Angels were responsible for my missing ear and the messy scar on my upper right arm. No, I didn't like guns, but I was more tolerant of them than my sister. And James was right to be armed. He hadn't come into his power yet, and even if he did end up a psionic destroyer like his Knight parents, modern weapons were usually more effective than psionics anyway.

"Everybody stay calm and quiet," said Ed Regis from up front. "They would have radioed us in already. Let me see if I can't talk our way through this."

The police siren had gone quiet. We heard footsteps approach the driver-side window. We all held our breaths.

"Good morning, Officer," Ed Regis said pleasantly.

We couldn't see the policeman from here. I wondered if he was alone or if he had a partner.

"Good morning to you, sir," the officer replied in an equally friendly tone. "May I see your driver's license, registration and insurance, please?"

"Yes, of course," said Ed Regis, pulling his fake documents from the glove compartment and passing them out the window. They were expensive, professional forgeries, but I wondered if they could really fool a policeman.

The officer's voice carried no suspicion as he said, "Well, Mr. Reese, do you know why I pulled you over?"

"I can pretty much guess."

"You seemed a little tipsy there."

"I haven't been drinking, Officer."

"What happened back there?"

"It's been a long night and an endless road," Ed Regis said submissively. "I'm afraid I dozed off a bit."

"You must be in an awful hurry if you're driving an RV like this through our beautiful countryside and couldn't stop for the night."

"I'm sorry, Officer. It won't happen again."

Ed Regis obviously understood the importance of being polite to the police. And it worked. After a moment's silence, the officer said, "Well, you weren't speeding, I'll give you that. So if you can prove to me that you're not my first DUI today, then I just might be persuaded to let you off with a warning. How does that sound?"

"That sounds real good, Officer. Thank you."

"Alright, I need you to step outside for a moment."

"Yes, sir."

Ed Regis got up from the driver's seat and gestured to us to move to the back of the cabin so we wouldn't be visible when he opened the side door. We moved quietly, and Ed Regis gave us a confident smile before stepping outside and closing the door behind him. I breathed easier. We were going to be just fine.

Outside, the cop asked Ed Regis, "Where are you headed?"

Ed Regis gave him the name of the next town, which wasn't all that far from our real destination anyway.

"You look a little familiar," said the cop. "Have I seen you around here before?"

"I don't think so, sir," said Ed Regis. "I'm just passing through."

"Is anyone else in there?"

Ed Regis hesitated for a moment before answering, "Yes. Two boys, one girl."

"Your children?"

"My nephews and niece."

"How old are they?"

"Uh, fourteen and seventeen, and about nine, I think."

"Eleven," Alia said crossly into my head. I smirked at her.

Actually, Ed Regis had missed my age by two years, too. I was sixteen going on seventeen next month but, like Alia, I was small for my age. I envied James and Terry, who had turned seventeen and eighteen over the summer and actually looked like it.

We heard the cop say to Ed Regis, "Could you have them all come out, please?"

"Certainly." Ed Regis opened the door and stuck his head into the cabin. "Jason, Adam, come on out. Alice, you too."

Ed Regis had left Terry out on purpose. A teenage girl amputee would be conspicuous enough to raise unwanted questions. Besides, if things went sour, it would be better to have someone with a gun hidden in the shadows. I just hoped that the policeman wouldn't try to look around inside.

James silently passed his pistol to Terry, and then exited the motorhome. Alia took hold of my hand as we followed, carefully stepping out onto the side of the road.

Squinting a little in the morning sun, I saw that the police officer was a middle-aged man with a white, bushy mustache. And he had a partner standing nearby: a slender man who looked young enough to still be on his first year of duty. Their squad car was parked about ten yards behind our motorhome, its red and blue lights still flashing. I realized that we were probably being filmed by its onboard video camera, and though it was already too late, I turned my face away from it.

Not that being videoed by the police was a major problem. I looked very different from the kid who went missing from his house four years ago, and the only government organization that could identify me as a psionic was the Wolves. Still, it was always better to be safe than sorry.

Keeping a tight grip on my hand, Alia looked nervously up at the senior officer. He gave her a reassuring smile and said, "It's okay, kid. Just stretch your legs a bit. I just didn't want anyone inside at the moment. Is your name Alice?"

Alia nodded silently.

"Had a bit of a scare this morning, huh?"

She nodded again.

"This won't take too long, honey," said the senior officer, and returned to his conversation with Ed Regis.

The younger cop approached us. "Good morning, kids," he said, his tone just as cordial as his senior. Then he looked down at Alia and asked, "Are these your brothers?"

Though not blood-related, Alia and I both had brown hair, and though Alia's hair was a touch lighter than mine, we could probably pass for siblings. James, on the other hand, was blond and had a much stockier build than me, much like Ed Regis, and no doubt the officer had noticed.

Alia still didn't speak, so I explained to the young cop, "I'm her brother. Jason is our cousin."

James gave the man a little wave. "Hi."

"Hey there, Jason," he said to James. Then he looked back at me, asking, "So, your name is Adam?"

I nodded.

The young cop looked curiously at my eyes for a moment, having noticed that they weren't the same color. My right eye was brown and reddish purple, my left was yellow-green, and I was used to people staring at them by now. I just smiled up at the man, who didn't comment.

He said instead, "Your sister's awfully quiet, isn't she?"

"She's scared, that's all," I said.

Alia had long since overcome her fear of strangers, but a pair of uniformed, armed cops was an entirely different matter. They made me feel pretty nervous too, especially considering the load of illegal weapons we had stashed in the back of our motorhome.

The senior officer, who had been explaining something to Ed Regis, stopped and gave Alia a sympathetic look. "Don't you worry, dear," he said reassuringly. "No one's going to hurt you. You can go back inside if you want."

Alia let go of my hand and disappeared into our motorhome, slamming the door behind her.

The senior officer asked Ed Regis, "Is she going to be okay by herself?"

"She'll be fine," replied Ed Regis.

"Well, all the same, I think we'll let your boys go on back inside."

In stark contrast to cops in movies, these guys were true gentlemen. I was glad that we wouldn't have to kill them.

Ed Regis said to us, "Jason, Adam, wait inside."

James and I turned to go. Before we reached the door, however, the senior officer called my name.

I obediently stopped and turned back toward him, and that was my second big mistake of the day. One second too late, I realized that he hadn't called me Adam. He had called me Adrian.

James and I froze on the spot.

The senior officer's hand went to his belt, and in a blink his gun was pointed at Ed Regis's chest.

"Keep your hands where I can see them!" he said sharply, all the friendliness gone from his voice. "Now I remember where I've seen you before, sir. I'm placing you under arrest for kidnapping and murder. Get down on your knees. Slowly."

Ed Regis complied.

Keeping the pistol pointed at him, the officer commanded, "Lie down flat on the ground with your arms stretched over your head and your legs spread wide."

As Ed Regis lay facedown on the ground, I could sense James bristling at my side. But James had taken a bullet on the way to the Historian this spring, so he knew what it felt like, and he was smart enough not to rush an armed policeman.

"Please don't do this," I said to the cop. "No one has been kidnapped, and my name isn't Adrian. This is a big mistake."

"Stay there, boy," he said. "I don't care what your name is right now. Your eyes match the description of a missing child and the man you're riding with matches the description of your abductor. We're going to have to take you all in. If this really is a mistake, we can sort it out at the station."

Keeping his eyes and gun on Ed Regis, the senior cop said to his partner, "Hank, go radio it in. Call for backup."

"You really do not want to do that," I said quietly.

I knew I had only seconds, not to save ourselves, but to save the police officers. No doubt Terry was about to shoot them both from inside the motorhome.

The senior officer still had his gun on his prime suspect, Ed Regis, and that might have been the correct way to deal with a normal arrest situation. This, however, wasn't normal. I made sure of it.

Thrusting my arms forward, I released a telekinetic blast, knocking the man onto his back. The gun flew out of his hands, and I focused my power on it, catching it before it hit the ground. Made of metal, the gun was hard to levitate, but within my power, and I pulled it into my right hand. The moment it touched my hand, however, my power instantly dissipated due to the draining effect that metal contact had on psionics.

Alia's panicked voice cried into my head, *"Please don't hurt them, Addy!"*

The younger officer, recovering quickly from the shock of what he had just witnessed, was going for his gun.

"Don't!" I shouted, sighting him down the barrel. "I don't want to kill you but that could easily change. Take your hand away from your belt!"

His hand gripping the pistol in its holster, the officer seemed undecided on the matter. He must have seen the hesitation in my eyes, though. He decided to chance it, and a split second later, we were pointing our pistols at each other's hearts.

"Addy, don't!"

Neither of us fired.

"Put it down!" the cop shouted. "You don't want to do this."

He was right: I didn't want to kill him. And not only because of Alia's plea. These guys were just policemen, not Wolves, not Slayers, not Angels, not even random psionics. They weren't a part of our war.

"Put it down, kid!" the young officer shouted again. "Right now!"

He was only seven yards away, and I was confident that I could telekinetically disarm him as easily as I had done to his senior. The problem was that as long as I was being drained by the pistol in my own hands, my psionic power was completely useless. The answer was simple.

"Alright," I said slowly, "I'm going to put the gun down. Please don't shoot me."

"Nice and easy, boy," said the young officer, keeping his pistol leveled on me.

I complied, gently placing the gun on the dirt.

Then I telekinetically flipped the safety on the young officer's pistol before yanking it out of his hands. The officer's jaw dropped as he watched his pistol fly into my right hand. Quickly flipping the safety off again, I pointed the pistol at his head.

"Jesus Christ, kid!" cried the cop, wide-eyed. "What in God's name are you?!"

"I ask myself the same question every day of my life," I replied, reaching down to pick up the senior officer's pistol with my left hand. "Now get down on your knees."

Ed Regis got up, lightly brushed the dirt off of his shirt and gave me an embarrassed smile. "Thanks, Adrian."

I nodded and mumbled, "Don't mention it."

I tossed my two pistols to Ed Regis and James, who took over for me, taking the handcuffs from the officers' belts and cuffing their wrists behind their backs.

Our motorhome door opened, and Terry lightly hopped out.

"We're not going to kill them," I said to her. "Alia's orders."

"Yeah, I heard her too," said Terry, rolling her eyes. "Why do you think I didn't shoot them from the window?"

Alia stepped out from the motorhome too, looking shaken but relieved. She quickly put her arms around me, burying her face in my chest.

Gently patting her back, I joked, "For a moment there, Ali, I thought you were more afraid for the cops than you were for me."

Releasing me, Alia silently shook her head and smiled.

The senior officer wasn't wounded, just winded. I had carefully adjusted the intensity of my blast to ensure this, but Alia nevertheless insisted on checking to see if there were any physical injuries that she needed to work her healing power on. Once my sister was satisfied that the man was okay, Terry, Ed Regis and James marched both cops to the side of their squad car. Alia and I followed.

"Alright," said Ed Regis, forcing them to sit on the ground, "how the hell did you recognize us?"

The men didn't reply.

Since I had already used my telekinetic power on them once, there was little point in hiding it. I levitated a few pieces of gravel from the side of the road and flew them around the officers' heads. It had the desired effect in that both cops looked terrified.

"Answer him," I growled.

"You're on our files," mumbled the younger officer, his eyes fixed on the gravel orbiting his head.

"Physical descriptions?" asked Terry. "Mug shots?"

The young officer nodded silently.

"On a *police* file?" Ed Regis asked incredulously. "A regular police file?"

The officer nodded again, and Ed Regis swore loudly.

The young cop's frightened eyes were still silently tracking the gravel zipping around his head, and I couldn't resist saying to him, "You're awfully quiet, aren't you?"

Alia nudged my side. *"Addy, stop scaring him."*

James asked Terry, "If we're not going to kill them, now what?"

The road was currently deserted, but there was no telling how long it would stay that way. We couldn't be spotted here with two handcuffed police officers, and someone was bound to call them on their radio at any moment. What we really needed right now was a mind-writer to modify their memories of what they had just seen. Unfortunately, we had no such luxury.

"I guess we'll have to let them go," Terry said resignedly.

"Yeah," I agreed. "And maybe in return they'll be nice enough to let us go."

Ed Regis looked at Terry and me, asking, "You want me to talk to them?"

Intimidation was a poor substitute for psionic mind control, but I figured that it might work coming from the mouth of our burly ex-Wolf. I let the gravel fall to the ground, saying, "Be my guest."

Ed Regis looked down at the cops and said coolly, "Alright, now I'm going to give *you* a warning. This boy could have killed you both today, but he didn't. Against our better judgment, we are going to let you live. So listen to me very carefully. There are powers in this world far beyond your understanding, and believe me, I'm not talking about us. I'm talking about the people who will silence you, and erase your families, if you ever speak about this to anyone. What happened here was a routine traffic stop, nothing more. Does that sound like something you gentlemen can handle?"

The officers looked at each other for a moment, and then nodded silently.

Ed Regis tossed them the keys to their handcuffs. "Then radio it in and be on your way. And don't forget to destroy your car video."

We got back into the motorhome and left.

Ed Regis drove, keeping us nicely over the speed limit. The rest of us gathered in the lounge space.

No one spoke for a few minutes. James was looking out the window, his mouth wired into a tight frown. Terry was staring down at the hook attached to her left stump. Alia was the only one smiling.

Knowing my sister's visceral dislike of hurting people, even our worst enemies, I suspected that she was basking in her personal victory of having prevented unnecessary bloodshed. And she certainly had the right, since things could have turned out very differently today. I had no desire for a fifth gunshot wound, so when that young cop drew down on me, it took every ounce of my wits not to shoot him dead right there. But the cop didn't owe me any favors. It was mostly Alia's voice in my head that had stayed my hand.

Eventually, James turned his head from the window and said to me, "I'm sorry I didn't help you back there, Adrian."

I smiled and shrugged. "Don't sweat it. There was nothing you could've done. Besides, I was the one who fell for the cheap trick. I'm just glad no one got killed today."

"I never guessed those cops would recognize you, though," said James, shaking his head in disbelief. "To think the Angels would stoop so low as to register us with the police..."

"Randal must be pretty desperate," I said mildly.

Not even the Wolves' psionic database had information about the color of my eyes after my operation, so there was no question about who was responsible for passing our physical descriptions to the police. Those two cops might have only recognized Ed Regis and me, but it was a sure bet that all of us, Alia included, were now wanted by the law for some false reason or another. The world had suddenly become a much more dangerous place for us.

Ed Regis called from up front, "Hey, Terry, what do you reckon are their chances of keeping silent?"

Terry looked up from her hook. "Fifty-fifty, tops."

"I was thinking about the same," said Ed Regis. "We're going to have to ditch this vehicle at the next town. Maybe sooner."

"Yeah, thanks to Half-head here," said Terry, narrowing her eyes at me.

I grinned back at her, countering, "You could've ignored Alia and killed them if you wanted to, Five-fingers. Do not blame me for your exceptionally rare acts of mercy."

"I'm talking about losing control of the steering!" said Terry, hitting me in the arm hard enough to guarantee mild bruising. "That's what caused this mess, you idiot!"

"Hey, go easy on him, Terry," said Ed Regis. "I think we just dodged a real bullet back there. Imagine if we had been stopped in the city."

"I'd rather not," said Terry.

"At least we know the police are on the lookout for us, so we can be more careful next time."

"That doesn't change the fact that Half-head lost us our home," said Terry, hitting me again, though not very hard.

James said jokingly, "Well, this life of total luxury couldn't last forever."

I glanced at my sister sitting next to me. She was still grinning from ear to ear.

"Please don't hurt them, Addy!" I mimicked sarcastically. "Is that going to be your standard attitude every time someone pulls a gun on me?"

Wiping the grin from her mouth, Alia gave me a sheepish look and mumbled, "Sorry."

I ruffled her hair. "You're even worse than Cindy, you know that?"

I fully agreed with Terry and Ed Regis that the cops were unlikely to keep their mouths shut. Perhaps we should have killed them when we had the chance, but I was still glad that Alia had stopped us. For all the terrible things we often hear and say about the police, these were the people who had sworn their lives to protecting the innocent. They were heroes in ways we could never be. Sparing them helped me feel just a little more normal.

And normal is so hard to come by sometimes.

2. THE CAUTIOUS APPROACH

Within an hour, we had reached the outer limits of the last town we had to pass before moving on to Mrs. Harding's Wood-claw Guardians. But our plans had changed. We couldn't afford to be spotted by the police in a lumbering motorhome, no matter how bulletproof.

The problem was that there was no way to properly hide or dispose of a vehicle this large. We needed to get it done quickly and move on. Thus, after swapping our license plates with spares that we carried for just this sort of occasion, Ed Regis drove us to a recreational campsite where we ditched our motorhome in plain sight.

"I'd give it a week, tops," said Ed Regis as we packed up our things. "Someone's bound to notice it's been abandoned and call the police."

We were taking just the bare essentials: money, pistols, spare clothes and basic camping equipment. Not that we had much more to begin with, but downsizing is never comfortable.

James gave the table a light pat, saying, "I think I'm actually going to miss this cozy little jail."

"Unfortunately, it's going to get a lot cozier," warned Ed Regis as he slid our last legally safe pair of license plates into his backpack.

A public bus took us from the campsite into the town's commercial center, and a rent-a-car shop there accepted Ed Regis's forged identification as readily as the police had. Terry and James quickly swapped out the license plates on our new stolen car: a dark blue four-door sports sedan. Alia watched this silently but with Cindy's disapproving frown.

We then stopped by a supermarket to buy some road food for the journey ahead. Most of the stuff we had in our motorhome needed a kitchen to prepare, so we had left it behind. My days as the camp cook were officially over.

James suggested we buy some hats and sunglasses to help disguise us, but Ed Regis pointed out that there wasn't enough sun these days to justify that, and we would stand out more than we already did if we dressed like secret agents.

"We'll just have to stay alert," said Ed Regis.

A little before noon, we managed to leave the town without incident.

Ed Regis drove with James riding shotgun, while Terry, Alia and I shared the back seat. Terry had wanted to sit up front, but Ed Regis insisted that Terry, with her bright red hair and prosthetic hand, would be too conspicuous.

"This car is tiny," I complained, rolling down my door window. Our bags were packed in the trunk so we weren't particularly cramped, but after months in a motorhome, it felt like a coffin. "I would have preferred a van or at least an SUV."

"Yeah, but our pursuit would be expecting that," explained Ed Regis. "This car blends in better, and it has a better ride too."

Ed Regis had disabled the car's navigation system so that we couldn't be tracked by satellite. Though Terry was still our best fighter, the ex-Wolf had years of training and experience in military, security and anti-psionic operations. We trusted him to keep us safe.

We were still headed for Wood-claw, but no longer in a straight line. Instead, Ed Regis took us on a one-week roundabout tour far and wide from our target city, making sure at every step that we weren't being followed. It was tedious but we all agreed that the precaution was necessary. We had already uprooted Mrs. Harding's faction once. We weren't going to be responsible for them having to move again.

But days of long-distance travel in a sports sedan were decidedly uncomfortable. We couldn't stand up or stretch easily and there was no entertainment aside from the radio, which we mostly used to check for possible news about fleeing kidnappers. I felt especially sorry for my sister, trapped between Terry and me all day long, but not sorry enough to trade places with her.

Nights were no better. Despite the danger of being spotted by psionic finders, we stopped every evening so that our driver could sleep. Ed Regis had an extra set of forged documents which he planned to use if we got pulled over by the police again, but that wouldn't work if he wasn't the one at the wheel. We used our tent when we could, and slept in the car when we couldn't, but Alia and I were always left in the car regardless.

"The more metal shielding the better," insisted Terry.

"It's bad enough that we're being drained all the time," I grumbled. "We should at least be able to stretch out at night."

"Tough luck for you," was Terry's unsympathetic reply.

Since losing our armor-plated motorhome and constantly-in-motion lifestyle, in order to keep our psionic presence to a minimum, Alia and I were each wearing a steel ring on our fingers all day and all night. This was basically the same trick Catherine Divine employed to help keep her power hidden from members of her own faction. Queen Divine did it with a silver chain that once held the amethyst pendant I wore.

Draining did more than mask psionic powers, though, especially for me, since I still couldn't balance my power half as well as I wanted. Wearing the metal ring made me constantly drowsy and prone to motion sickness, hence my attachment to the window seat. I envied Alia: Aside from her inability to speak telepathically, Alia's draining hardly showed on her. Though I had much better power balance than when I first turned psionic, I doubted I would ever be as good as my sister.

Terry, James and I were in charge of the night watch, staying awake in shifts while Ed Regis slept. Alia was exempt, but she always kept me company, sitting beside me in the back seat of the car and making sure I didn't fall asleep on the job.

"You can take it off for a while, Addy," Alia whispered to me one night when everyone else was asleep in the tent. "I won't tell."

"No," I said. "Terry's right. It's too dangerous."

Only a proper hider could conceal psionic powers completely, but draining was a pretty good substitute, especially against long-range finders. We were camping in open country, and removing my ring when we weren't even in motion wasn't prudent to say the least.

"Are you sure you're okay?" Alia asked worriedly. She had caught me yawning more than once already.

"I'm fine," I insisted. "Besides, I think wearing this thing is making me better at balancing my power."

Alia said seriously, "Cindy once told me that the better you are at balancing your power, the longer you live."

"That's probably true," I said with a shrug.

"Then you should get better at it, Addy."

I chuckled. "Do you honestly think we're going to live to be old?"

"Who knows?" said Alia, frowning. "But we might."

We sat silently for a while, huddled under our blankets, listening to the wind in the trees.

I had promised the Historian that I would try. I had said nothing about succeeding. The Guardians had spent years working to assassinate the last Angel queen. They were the second largest worldwide network of psionics, and it was only by a series of lucky breaks that they succeeded. In comparison, we were just five people cut off from most of the psionic world. Though we rarely said it out loud, we all knew, Alia included, that this was essentially a suicide mission. Still, my sister had a point: to assume failure would make trying meaningless.

I asked Alia, "When this is all over, and when we get Cindy back, where do you want us to live?"

"I don't know," said Alia, staring out the window. "Somewhere where it's quiet. Somewhere where people don't fight. Somewhere without guns."

I grinned. "How about the moon?"

"Anywhere is okay," said Alia. Then she looked at me sadly. "But I hope it's soon. I miss Cindy. I miss her so much."

"I know," I said quietly. "I miss her too."

Alia shook her head. "Sometimes... sometimes I can't remember her, Addy. I mean, I can remember what she's like, and I can remember the things she said to me when everything was dark, but..." Alia stopped to brush away a tear. "I can't see her. I just can't see her in my mind."

"Don't even try," I told her. "Your mind isn't important. Remember her here," I said, lightly poking her in the chest. "That's the only place it matters."

Alia wiped another tear. "Do you really think we'll see her again?"

In fact, we already knew exactly where Cynthia Gifford was. The Historian had told us that Cindy was now Lumina's primary psionic hider. Being the world's only psionic capable of covering an entire city in a single hiding field, Cindy was as valuable to the Angels as she had been to the Guardians, and she still lived in our old penthouse at the top of what used to be the New Haven One building. But we couldn't just go in and take her back. Even if we could somehow beat the Angels' security measures which included armed guards, bulletproof windows and an armored safe room in her penthouse, Cindy had already been converted, and her primary allegiance was to Randal Divine and the protection of Lumina. To forcibly remove her from the Angels could destroy her mind. The only way to safely break her conversion was to kill... the target.

"You want to know something?" I whispered to my sister. "I can remember Cindy very, very easily. I can see her anytime I want."

"How?"

I smiled. "I just look at you. And yes, Alia, I'm absolutely sure we'll see her again."

Alia put her arms around my neck, and I rubbed her back until she stopped sobbing. It had been stupid of me to let Alia think that I doubted our chances. Sometimes, even false hope was better than none.

I heard tapping on the door window and turned to see James peering in at us. "Hey, let me in," he said.

Alia let go of me, and I opened the door.

"Your shift isn't for another hour, James," I informed him. "Go back to sleep. I'll wake you when it's time."

"It's alright. I'm already up," said James. Then he noticed Alia wiping her eyes. "Hey, kid, what's the matter?"

Shaking her head, Alia managed a weak smile. "I'm fine, James. I'm alright now."

As James got into the back with us and closed the door, I said to him, "Well, if you're willing to take an extra hour, then I'm going to sleep. You keep my sister company."

I carefully squeezed my way into the driver's seat and tilted it back as far as it would go. Pulling my blanket over my chest and gazing up at the ceiling, I suddenly found myself face to face with Alia, who was crouching on the seat behind me and peering into my eyes. For a moment, she just hovered there, smiling serenely down at me. I was relieved to see that her eyes were at peace.

"Addy," she said softly, "Cindy says goodnight."

"Goodnight," I whispered back, closing my eyes. "We'll get her back, Alia. I promise."

Two days later, Ed Regis decided that we had been on the road long enough to be certain there was no pursuit. We were once again headed for Wood-claw. Alia tortured Ed Regis with the "Are we there yet?" routine for six straight hours.

The approach was pretty much the same plan Ed Regis and Terry had agreed upon before our detour. We would find a hotel at the edge of the city and await discovery by Wood-claw's finders, keeping a cautious lookout from a defensible position for unwanted guests.

But to get to this hotel, which was on the northern side of the city, we had to carefully circumnavigate the outskirts. Ed Regis insisted that we couldn't drive straight through just in case we accidentally drove into Wood-claw. If our psionic powers were to suddenly flicker out as we passed through a hiding bubble, we could be inadvertently giving away Wood-claw's location to enemy finders. Considering the size of the city that Wood-claw was hidden in, the possibility of this actually happening was truly minuscule, but Ed Regis was taking no chances.

"You're really starting to think like a psionic, you know that?" I said to him teasingly.

"Know thy enemy," Ed Regis replied tartly.

We arrived in the early evening. As we approached the hotel's parking lot, Ed Regis said to us, "Okay, you all remember your new names? Let's hear them."

"Jack Tyler," said James.

"Richard Anderson," I called.

Alia chimed in, "Alyssa Anderson."

"Tiffany Hendricks," said Terry.

"Tiffany!" I laughed, remembering Terry's new identity.

Alia started laughing too.

Terry glared at me. "How many fingers would you like broken, Richie?"

"Hey, kids, knock it off back there!" said Ed Regis. "Now, what's my name?"

"Edmund Tyler," we called in unison.

"Wrong!" laughed Ed Regis. "It's Uncle Ed. Or Dad if you're name is Jack."

I was glad that we had done away with our old Guardian call signs, which I always considered embarrassingly stupid. Ed Regis had us pick out common names that started with the same letter as our real ones so that they would be easy to remember. After our run-in with the cops, I couldn't keep Adam so I swapped it with my father's name, which didn't start with an A but would be easy enough to use. Alice became Alyssa, and Jason became Jack. Terry had been going by Tess, but even though the cops hadn't heard that name, Ed Regis insisted that it had to be changed. But *Tiffany?!*

The hotel Ed Regis had chosen for us turned out to be a white concrete five-story with an outdoor pool behind it, though it was closed this season. The parking lot was to the hotel's left side, with two exits, one on each side of the block. Ed Regis considered this important in case we needed to make a quick getaway.

Parking just inside the rear exit, Ed Regis said to Alia and me, "Okay, time to take those rings off and get noticed."

"With pleasure!" I said, ripping off my draining ring.

"Ooh! That feels so much better!" said Alia, breathing deeply.

"You're telling me!" After a week's draining, the telekinetic power coursing through me was truly exhilarating. I felt ready to fly non-stop around the world.

Ed Regis handled the check-in while the rest of us stretched out in the lobby.

"I can't wait to take a good long bath," said Alia.

My sister wasn't the only one. I felt really grimy after so many days on the road.

"Alright, I got us three twin rooms on the second floor," said Ed Regis, returning from the check-in counter, "so that's Richard and Alyssa, Jack bunks with me, and Tiffy can have her own room."

As Ed Regis tossed me my room key, I grumbled, "Let the girls bunk together, and let me have my own room for a change. Why does Tiffy always get her own place?"

Terry grinned at me. "Because I'm older, taller and stronger than you, Half-head."

"Yeah, well, I've got more bones."

Terry was wearing her decorative prosthetic hand, but the hotel staff had already noticed her shortage of real limbs. They were too polite to comment, of course, but I wondered if they were also polite enough to mind their own business and not talk to anyone who might cause trouble for us.

Ed Regis said to me, "Sorry, Richard, but the bait stays together. Anyway, we're all going to stick close in one room for most of the time, so it hardly matters."

Picking up our dusty backpacks, we headed up to our rooms. It was still too early for dinner, so we decided to get settled and cleaned up. The longer we stayed here, the greater the chance of being found. That was our objective, of course, but a risky one nevertheless. It made sense to take it easy while we still could.

Our second-floor rooms were side by side, balcony windows overlooking the parking lot. Aside from this essential feature, they were pretty ordinary twin rooms with small kitchens, wooden tables and mildly soft single beds: certainly no luxury resort. Still, it wasn't every day that we got to sleep on real mattresses.

Alia lost no time running the bathwater while I opened up the windows and checked our escape route. As the tub filled, we went through our backpacks, pulling out all our clothes that needed to be washed.

"The bait stays together," I muttered. "Why are we always the bait?"

Alia laughed. *"I liked it better when we were Hansel and Gretel."*

I didn't, but life was simpler back then. Not much simpler, but simpler.

"How long are we going to stay in Walnut?" asked Alia.

"Wood-claw," I corrected. "And I don't know, but it'd sure be nice if we could stay for a while."

"You miss Candace," Alia said teasingly.

"Well, sure I do," I said freely, knowing that denying it would only encourage her. "Just like you're in love with Patrick."

Alia threw a dirty sock at me. *"I am not! He's just a friend."*

"Oh yeah?" I grinned. "Then why are you changing color?"

Alia decided to change the subject. *"Can I take my bath first, Addy?"*

I telekinetically tossed her sock back. "Think you can keep it short?"

"No."

"Then I get to go first."

Alia moaned loudly. *"Please? I'll keep it under an hour, okay?"*

"Fine. Whatever."

There was a knock on the door. Alia got up and opened it to Terry, who promptly slapped her on the head, saying, "You have to ask my name before you open it, Alyssa!"

"What's up, Tiffany?" I asked mockingly.

Entering, Terry closed the door behind her and scowled at me. "You're really asking for it, Half-head. Anyway, I just wanted to check out the view from your window."

All three of us stepped out onto the balcony where, looking down, we saw Ed Regis getting into our car.

"What's he doing?" asked Alia.

Ed Regis started the engine, pulled out of his parking space, and then re-parked the sedan right under our balcony.

"It's almost like he's expecting trouble," I mused.

"The major's right, though," said Terry. "You can never be too careful, especially since you're openly showing your powers now."

"Wood-claw will find us first," I said confidently.

Child psionics gave off a unique signature that any adept finder would be able to identify, and how many kid-healers were traveling around with a flight-capable telekinetic these days? I was certain that the Wood-claw finders would instantly know who it was. The only real question was how soon the cautious Mrs. Harding would be willing to come and collect us.

As Ed Regis got out of our car, a white van quietly pulled into the hotel's parking lot from the rear entrance. We saw Ed Regis tense up slightly as he watched the van approach him, but then he calmly strolled over to its driver-side window. Ed Regis was well trained in blocking mind control, but we couldn't see the driver from here so I probably wasn't the only one holding my breath.

Ed Regis pointed up at us, and the driver stepped out. It was too dark to see him very clearly, but we recognized him. It was Scott, our eldest refugee soldier from Walnut Lane.

"Scott!" I called down. "Hey, Scott!"

"Adrian! Terry!" Scott shouted up to us. "Alia? Is that you?"

Alia, never one to raise her voice if she could help it, replied telepathically.

Ed Regis whispered something to Scott, who nodded and got back into the van. Scott parked next to our sedan, and then he and two others stepped out. One, I recognized as his girlfriend, Rachael. The other was a stocky, middle-aged man who I didn't know by name, but I remembered as one of Mrs. Harding's Knights.

Ed Regis led them around to the hotel's entrance, and a minute later we were all gathered together in Ed Regis's room.

"It's so good to see you guys again," I said, shaking Scott and Rachael's hands.

The Knight didn't greet us, keeping a mild distance and silently watching us with a cautious frown. I noticed that he was armed with a pistol holstered under his long jacket. Though we were all standing inside Rachael's psionic hiding bubble now, at this distance, I would have sensed the Knight's destroyer powers if he had any. But this man wasn't a destroyer. Perhaps he was a controller or had some other power, or maybe he was entirely non-psionic.

"How did you find us so quickly?" James asked Scott.

I was wondering the same thing. We had all assumed that we would be here at least one night.

"I've been tracking you guys for a week," replied Scott. "Ever since you got close to us and then disappeared."

"You've been tracking us?" I asked. "You personally?"

"That's right," said Scott, grinning. "I came into my power just after we arrived at the mountain camp. And I'm actually pretty good with it already. I can do long-range and pinpointing."

"That's amazing," James said with a touch of envy in his voice.

"It wasn't easy following you, though," continued Scott. "You guys went hundreds of miles out, and I'm guessing you were draining yourselves too, weren't you?"

I nodded.

"I kept losing you when you were moving, but I could still spot you during the nights."

"So much for caution," I said wryly.

"Where's Merlin?" asked Scott.

"Dead," I told him quietly. "He didn't make it to the Historian."

We never really found out what happened to Merlin, so for all we knew, he could still be alive, but the chances were next to nil.

"And the Wolves?" asked Scott, glancing at Ed Regis.

"The Wolves, too," I said. "It's a long story."

"I'm sorry," said Scott.

Ed Regis just nodded.

"We had a feeling about Merlin," said Rachael, "since your powers weren't hidden."

We observed a moment of uncomfortable silence. I hated being the bearer of bad news. Merlin had been Scott's psionic blocking instructor, and he was a good friend to everyone in the old Refugee House.

James asked Scott, "How is everyone at Wood-claw?"

Scott was about to answer, but suddenly the Knight stepped forward and cut across him, saying brusquely, "Let's save the chitchat for later. I don't want to stick around here long."

"Yeah," said Scott, "you're right, Hammer. Let's bring them in."

But the Knight called Hammer said warningly, "Scott..."

Scott turned to him and said in an exasperated tone, "Oh, come on! They're all here. There's no danger. Let's just bring them in."

Hammer shook his head. "Mrs. Harding's orders."

"What's going on?" I asked.

Scott looked at us apologetically. "We can only take two of you right now. Once Mrs. Harding is sure that this isn't some kind of trap, we'll come back for the rest. And whoever we take will have to be blindfolded on the way in. You know how Mrs. Harding is."

"Yeah," I sighed. "So, who gets to go?"

"You choose," said Scott.

As our leader, Terry was the obvious first pick. As to the second, I didn't want to leave Alia behind, she didn't want to go without me, and the former Wolf wasn't Mrs. Harding's favorite. Thus we decided that James would accompany Terry.

"Alright, let's go," Hammer said impatiently.

"Wait," Rachael said to him, "I need to put hiding bubbles over these rooms so that Adrian and Alia can stay here till we return."

"Make it quick," ordered Hammer.

"Sure thing," replied Rachael, entirely unperturbed by Hammer's blunt manner.

"Actually, Rachael," said Ed Regis, "if you can, would you mind giving them individual protection so that they can move about?"

"Okay," said Rachael, shrugging.

Rachael started with Alia. Kneeling, she put her palms on Alia's chest and back, working her hiding protection into my sister's body so that her healing and telepathy would remain undetectable wherever she went.

Watching, I wondered why Ed Regis had asked Rachael to give Alia and me individual hiding protection. Was it just a precaution, or was he already planning to move us to a different location?

Rachael took about five minutes for my sister, and Hammer looked on with an impatient scowl.

Releasing Alia, Rachael came over to me next. "Excuse me," she said, gently placing her hands on me. This was simply how psionic hiders created personal hiding bubbles, but it felt a little awkward in Scott's presence.

"How's Candace?" I asked Rachael.

"Candace is fine," she replied, smiling. "You'll see her soon."

Ed Regis cleared his throat and said, "Alright, let's all pack it up. We're relocating as soon as Rachael is done with Adrian."

Alia was flabbergasted. "But I just finished filling the tub!"

"We'll find another one," Ed Regis said crisply. "It wasn't smart for you all to shout your names outside like that."

Alia looked at me accusingly. "I didn't shout anything."

"Sorry," I said, cringing.

As Rachael continued working her power into me, Alia stomped back to our room to repack our bags.

Ed Regis told Scott where we would be holed up until he came back for us. It was a recreational campsite a little outside of the city, which meant cold showers and no bathtubs. My sister was going to be in for an unpleasant surprise.

"Okay," said Rachael, releasing me. "That's good for about sixteen hours."

"And we'll be back for you well before it wears off," Scott assured us.

Now that Alia and I were properly hidden, we could relocate without anyone tracking us. Any Angel finders converging on our last known location were just going to find a bunch of empty rooms with "Do Not Disturb" signs hanging from the doorknobs. We didn't bother checking out.

The Wood-claw van, carrying a blindfolded Terry and James, left via the back exit. Ed Regis drove our stolen sedan out the front, Alia and me in the back seat.

"Where are we going?" asked Alia.

"You'll find out," said Ed Regis.

"Will there be a bath there?"

"You'll find out."

3. DISCOVERY AND THE FALL

We were already at the city's edge, so it took only minutes before Alia figured out that we were headed away from civilization and the amenities it provided. She groaned in frustration.

"It's just another day," I promised her. "You can bathe for a week once we get into Wood-claw."

Suddenly Alia gave me a worried look. "Scott didn't tell us if everyone was alive."

I smiled. "I'm sure they're all just fine."

Alia stared out the window for a moment before saying, "Rachael said Candace was okay."

"Hey, cut it out, Alia!" I snapped. "I'm worried about them too, you know!"

Alia gave me a wounded look. "I didn't mean it like that, Addy. I just meant that I wanted to see Candace too."

"Candace?" I repeated. "What for? I thought you'd be more interested in seeing Patrick again."

"Well, sure," said Alia, looking down at her knees. "And baby Laila. But Candace is my friend, too. We used to talk a lot back when we were living in that old house."

"Yes, I know," I said dryly. "You're a big blabbermouth. You didn't have to tell her everything you knew about me."

Alia laughed. "I didn't tell her *everything.*"

"Hey," called Ed Regis from the driver's seat, "are you two wearing your seatbelts?"

"No," Alia and I said together.

"Put them on. Now."

Alia had caught the tension in Ed Regis's voice too. "What's going on?" she asked.

"I think we're being followed," Ed Regis replied quietly. "Don't look back. Just buckle up and sit tight."

I helped Alia tighten her seatbelt. Then, buckling myself in too, I gave her arm a little tug. She looked at me and nodded quietly. All of her playfulness, her little upsets and worries, all instantly gone, replaced with a warrior's calm. I never fully understood how my sister managed it, but I was glad that she did.

"You want me up front?" I asked Ed Regis.

"No," he replied. "Not yet, anyway. I see one car, one driver only. Let's just watch what he does."

We were only about halfway to our campsite, speeding down a narrow asphalt road that ran along the foot of a steep hill to our right. The left side of the road was mostly flat, grassy fields, with an occasional clump of trees here and there. It was too dark to see much else. I occasionally caught the headlights of the car behind us in the rearview mirror. I couldn't see it well, but it looked like a light truck or SUV.

"Is he really following us?" I asked.

"Honestly, I'm not entirely sure," said Ed Regis.

"Maybe it's someone from Wood-claw keeping an eye on us," I said hopefully.

Suddenly the headlights behind us disappeared completely, as if the driver had turned them off.

"Hang on!" shouted Ed Regis.

The engine roared as he floored the gas pedal, and Alia and I were pressed hard against our seats.

"Hey, slow down!" I said. "He's gone, isn't he?!"

The front windshield exploded. Our car rocked wildly, spinning around once as it flew off the road and into the grassy field. My seatbelt cut painfully into my waist and I bashed the side of my head against my door window.

When everything finally stopped moving, we hadn't turned over, and nothing appeared to be on fire.

"Addy?! Are you okay?" Alia asked frantically. "Ed? Are you hurt?"

"I'm alright," groaned Ed Regis.

"Addy?" cried Alia. *"Addy?!"*

"I'm fine," I said, holding the throbbing side of my head, ears ringing. I knew I wasn't seriously injured because if there was any blood on my skin, the iron in it would have drained my psionic power.

I looked over at my sister, who was panting heavily but appeared uninjured and alert. Ed Regis was clawing his way out of an airbag. Through the shattered windshield, I saw that the hood of our car had been torn to shreds, bits of metal sticking up at odd angles. We had been shot at from the air!

I saw dark metallic shapes in the night sky, and then we were hit by an all-too-familiar spotlight from above.

These weren't Angels.

"Don't run, Adrian," warned Ed Regis. "Just stay in the car. They'll kill us if we move."

I was furious but I knew that Ed Regis was right. There was no escaping a military gunship, let alone many.

The spotlight stayed right on us as two other helicopters landed in the field. Our car was buffeted by the wind from their rotor blades, and I squinted in the dust swirling in through the broken windshield.

Alia shouted into my head, *"Addy, I can't go back there! I can't go back!"*

"I know, Alia," I breathed. "Just—just stay calm. We're not going back."

Uniformed soldiers were closing in on us, weapons drawn.

Ed Regis sounded strangely calm as he said, "Slowly put your hands together on the back of your head. Alia, you too. Do it now. We'll live to fight another day."

"That's easy for you to say, Ed Regis," I said, putting my arms up in surrender. "They're probably your old war buddies anyway."

"Hey, at least they have reason to keep you alive."

Doors were opened at once, and everything was chaos for a while. Several hands roughly pulled me out of the car and shoved me facedown onto the ground. I heard Alia screaming. I felt thick plastic bracelets being locked around my wrists, and in an instant I was being drained as small metal rods extended from inside them, pressing against my skin. They were psionic control bands, designed to drain and, when necessary, incapacitate their wearers with high-power electric pulses. I knew better than to resist.

The Wolves stood me up, and one of them shined a powerful flashlight right into my face.

"I'll be darned," said a deep voice. "It's really him, isn't it?"

A hand grabbed the left side of my sweatshirt's collar and pulled down hard, revealing the P-47 tattoo on my upper left arm.

"Adrian Howell, what a pleasure."

Someone punched me hard in the gut, and I doubled over, gasping.

Alia was shouting my name but I couldn't see her. She let out a high-pitched squeal as someone probably did something very painful to her, and then she was silent.

I found myself being pushed alongside Ed Regis, who had his wrists handcuffed behind his back. I remembered his words back in the basement of the Angel outpost that we had rescued him from: "The Wolves never take a captured soldier back because that soldier could be converted or worse." Was Ed Regis about to be executed?

And where was Alia? Had they knocked her unconscious?

Ed Regis and I were pushed aboard one of the helicopters. As the side door slid shut, a black cloth bag was slipped over my head.

The ride felt short—probably about half an hour, though it's difficult to have an accurate perception of time when you're panicking.

We landed at what sounded like a large airport or military base. With the black bag over my head, I couldn't be sure if Ed Regis was still with me. The Wolves silently marched me across a long stretch of pavement, and then we stopped as one of the soldiers talked into a phone or radio.

"No, sir, they're not going to the detention center," said the Wolf soldier, who sounded young and a little flustered. "We were told to skip the interrogation completely. We have orders to transport all three immediately to the RG. I understand it's irregular, sir, but all three were requested to be transported together, ASAP. No, sir. The order came directly from the top. I understand, sir, but we have our orders, too."

I tried to make sense of this, but I didn't get far. The Psionic Research Center had been completely destroyed, but I knew there was a place somewhere called "Site-B," which was another research facility for psionics. What was the "RG"? And why weren't we being interrogated for the whereabouts of other psionics prior to transport?

The soldier continued talking. My control bands felt heavy on my wrists, the draining effect making it difficult for me to concentrate on his words. But I heard the next thing he said loud and clear.

"Yes, sir, it's Adrian Howell, sir. No question about it. Yes, sir. King Divine will have him by sunup, sir. Thank you, sir."

King Divine?!

The soldier hung up. A sturdy hand grabbed my upper right arm and forced me up a metal ramp. By the sounds around me, I guessed that it was the rear loading ramp of a cargo plane.

I was pushed down onto a hard chair.

"Move and you die," said a female voice as hands pulled a seatbelt around my waist.

Even with the bag over my head, I could tell that there was someone sitting next to me. I carefully slid my right hand over and discovered a small set of fingers.

"Addy?" Alia whispered into my mind.

"I'm here," I said, grasping her hand. She was wearing control bands on her wrists too, but apparently they weren't draining her. "Are you hurt?"

"I'm okay. Where's Ed?"

"I don't know. I think we got separated."

I heard the grinding sound of the ramp closing, and the airplane started taxiing forward, its noisy propeller engines drowning out every other sound. After a few turns and stops, we were thundering down the runway and up into a steep climb. I could tell by the angle that we were sitting with our backs against the left side wall of the cargo hold.

"What's going to happen to us?" Alia asked anxiously.

What indeed? Was I right in assuming that the Angels now had control over the Wolves? How powerful had Randal's kingdom become? I had originally feared that the Wolves were taking us to another research prison, but this was far worse.

"Addy?"

"I don't know, Alia," I whispered back. "Just stay with me."

As the plane leveled out, I heard boot-wearing footsteps approach, and suddenly the bag was removed from my head. I squinted a little in the cabin light, but it wasn't very bright here and my eyes adjusted quickly.

I found myself looking up into a familiar face. It was Jodie Decker, ex-cop, ex-Raven. She was dressed in a Wolf's uniform, complete with the wolf-head patch on her upper right sleeve, but she was armed only with a pistol at her side.

"Hello, Adrian," she said pleasantly.

I glared at her, but she calmly reached over and undid Alia's head bag next.

Against the other side wall sat another head-bagged figure: Ed Regis. His handcuffs had been removed. He wasn't moving but I could tell he was conscious, listening.

There were four other Wolf soldiers in the otherwise empty cargo hold, all dressed in military uniforms, carrying assault rifles strapped over their shoulders and sporting fragmentation grenades on their vests. To my left, I could see the entrance to the cockpit, which was open, but from this angle the pilots were out of sight.

"Would you like something to drink, dear?" Ms. Decker asked Alia.

Alia didn't reply, staring defiantly up at her.

Ms. Decker fingered the unicorn-shaped bloodstone pendant around Alia's neck. "This is really pretty," she said warmly.

Still Alia kept her eyes on Ms. Decker, refusing to even twitch.

"I'm so sorry we scared you like that," said Ms. Decker, "but it was for your own safety."

"What is this?" I asked quietly. "What's going on here?"

"This is the future," said Ms. Decker, turning to me. "The bright future of our world, unfolding before our eyes. Would you like something to drink?"

I had to know for certain. "Do the Wolves work for the Angels now?"

"The Wolves work for the government," replied Ms. Decker.

I narrowed my eyes. "So who does the government work for?"

Ms. Decker smiled broadly.

I glanced around at the four uniformed soldiers. I couldn't tell which of them were Wolves and which were Seraphim, if there was even a difference anymore. I didn't sense any destroyer powers, but the way they were armed, it hardly mattered.

"Accept it, Adrian," Ms. Decker said in a cheerful tone. "Soon this country will be but one in the grand alliance we are creating. The day is fast coming when King Divine will bring peace to all of humanity. That is our destiny, our great and noble work which you now have the privilege of sharing."

I shook my head in disbelief. "Listen to yourself, Ms. Decker. You're talking about things like *destiny* and you think you're still sane?"

Ms. Decker merely nodded. "You will soon be a believer yourself."

"Don't count on it."

"You don't know how fortunate you are, Adrian. The king has asked for you personally, alive and unharmed. This is truly a great honor. And I might also add that, thanks to your VIP status, you and your friends have been spared a most painful interrogation today."

Under the circumstances, that was very small consolation. We were being shipped directly to Randal Divine, and to Catherine, so that we could be converted into Angels. So that we could mindlessly serve them for the rest of our lives. I had promised Alia that we would be reunited with Cindy. But not like this.

Ms. Decker noticed me eyeing the cargo loading ramp at the rear of the plane. "Please don't get up," she said. "You are a top-level VIP, but don't think my boys won't kill you if you try anything at all."

My control bands' rods were still extended, but draining no longer affected my physical strength so much that I couldn't move when I really needed to. "Fine," I said, swiftly unbuckling my seatbelt and jumping clear of Ms. Decker's reach. "Kill me."

I instantly had the attention of four assault rifles, but as I suspected, nobody fired.

"You can't kill me!" I shouted furiously. "King Divine's orders!"

Ms. Decker recovered quickly from her surprise. As an ex-cop, she was quick on the draw too, and suddenly the barrel of her pistol was pressed against Alia's forehead.

"I like a boy who knows how to call a bluff, Adrian," she said, "but do consider that the king's order is just for you."

Though Ms. Decker had her pistol on Alia's head, her eyes were fixed on me, so she didn't notice it when Alia reached forward and carefully plucked a little white remote control out from one of Ms. Decker's pockets. Miraculously, the other soldiers missed it too.

"Come on," said Ms. Decker. "Don't play with your life like this. You are much too important." Then she added in a mischievous tone, "I can make you sit down if I have to." She reached into her pocket with her free hand, searching for something that was no longer there.

My control bands snapped open, falling to the floor.

"No! No!" cried Ms. Decker as she saw a grenade pop off of one of her soldiers' vests and fly into my right hand.

There was a sudden, short burst of gunfire, and I felt a searing pain tear through my lower right side. In his surprise, the soldier I had taken the grenade from had accidentally fired several rounds from his rifle, and one of the bullets had nicked me. The force of the impact made me lose my balance, and I fell onto my knees, but I kept a tight grip on the grenade.

"Don't shoot him!" shouted Ms. Decker.

It hurt like hell, but it was just a flesh wound, probably less than half an inch deep. Besides, my telekinetic power had already drained the instant I touched the grenade so I hardly noticed the difference as my blood seeped into my clothes. Pressing down on the wound with my left hand, I forced myself to stand back up. Then I brought the grenade in my right hand up to my mouth and pulled out the pin with my teeth.

I noticed Ed Regis had removed his head bag.

"Ed Regis," I said, spitting out the grenade pin, "get up and lower the ramp."

"Major Regis," Ms. Decker said warningly, "if you stand up, you'll die."

"He dies, I drop this," I said, holding up the grenade and trying not to let my pain show. "We all die."

Ms. Decker smiled. "I'd die for my king any day."

"This could be the day, then," I replied evenly.

Ed Regis decided to chance it, cautiously standing up and walking over to the ramp control. The soldiers seemed to be at a loss as to what to do. Perhaps these four weren't converted, but merely stumbling along under Ms.

Decker's fanatical command. The ramp slowly opened, revealing a pitch-black night sky. I desperately looked around for parachutes, but saw none.

"I can't let you go, Adrian!" shouted Ms. Decker. "Come on, you had your chance. You're bleeding. You can't fly. Give it up!"

The pain was getting to me, and I couldn't help wincing a little.

Ms. Decker said in a calming tone, "Come on, kid. Just hand me the grenade and let this little girl heal you. You don't want to die here."

Kid? Little girl?

My eyes met Alia's for a brief moment, and then I looked at Ms. Decker again. "Do you know why Alia and I are still alive, Ms. Decker?" I said slowly through clenched teeth. "It's because people like you keep underestimating us."

I tossed the grenade into the cockpit.

Once you release its lever, a grenade explodes in about four seconds. Alia used a quarter of that time to knock the pistol out of Ms. Decker's hand. The soldiers, distracted by panicked shouts from the cockpit, didn't notice Ed Regis bash Ms. Decker's head against a wall or see him pull Alia out of her seat. By the time we heard the explosion, we were in freefall.

"Addy! Addy, where are you?!" Alia yelled into my head.

"Here!" I shouted hysterically over the howling wind. "Alia! Close it! Close it! Close it!"

But I couldn't see her anywhere. Nor could I see Ed Regis. I was alone, and I wasn't even sure which direction was up. All I knew was that I was falling, drained by my blood and unable to fly.

I felt Ed Regis's firm hand on my right arm. He pulled hard, and I found myself next to Alia. Ed Regis kept the three of us close together as my sister, hair whipping about her face, healed the gash in my right side. How she managed to focus her power as we wildly spun around and around in midair is something only she would know, but soon I felt the pain in my side disappear.

I was still being drained by the blood on my body. I tore off my sweatshirt and used the clean part of it to wipe myself until I felt my power return. The freezing night air was biting into my skin, but the pain helped me focus my telekinesis as I saw a sea of lights below, rapidly approaching.

We were over a city! There were buildings below us!

"Hang on!" I screamed, grabbing Alia and Ed Regis by their shirts.

They didn't need telling.

For a fleeting instant, I had a wild, insane image of us splashing down into some expensive hotel's rooftop pool, but that didn't happen. We instead smashed into an open dumpster in a back alley. I did all I could to telekinetically break our fall, but add Ed Regis's weight to Alia's and my own, plus the fact that I had just recently been shot and was still being slightly drained by some dried blood left on my skin...

"You both alive?" moaned Ed Regis. "Alia? Adrian?"

"Addy?"

"I think so," I mumbled feebly.

We took our time in the dumpster. I had completely exhausted my psionic power in our semi-controlled crash, and for a while, I felt so faint and dizzy that I couldn't even sit up. Fortunately, the plastic garbage bags we had landed on had been filled mostly with kitchen leftovers, probably from a nearby restaurant. Several of the bags tore open when we hit them, which was disgusting, but at least the food scraps were soft and yielding enough to keep our bones intact. We had a few odd bruises and Ed Regis had twisted his right ankle pretty badly, but we were otherwise alive, which wasn't so bad considering that we had just fallen out of an airplane.

Once Alia healed his ankle, Ed Regis got out from the dumpster and then carefully lifted Alia and me out, setting us on the cold, damp concrete in the dumpster's shadow. Ed Regis sat down beside us, removed his jacket and put it around my shoulders. I had lost my sweatshirt somewhere in midair. I could tell Ed Regis was impatient to put some distance between us and our crash site, but I still felt too weak to stand.

"I hope that plane didn't fall in the city," I breathed.

"There's no telling," said Ed Regis, glancing up at the dark sky, "but it had a fair amount of altitude. Lucky for us. And lucky we landed in the garbage."

That wasn't entirely luck. I had guided us into the dumpster at the last second, but I didn't feel like bragging. Alia was gingerly picking spaghetti noodles out of her hair.

"You need a bath," I said to her mildly.

Alia glared at me. "That's not funny, Addy!" she said dryly. "That's not funny at all! And could you please, please, *please* stop getting shot?!"

"I'm working on it, Alia," I said apologetically, "but no promises."

Alia quietly drew herself closer to me and I put an arm around her shoulders. I noticed that she was still shivering a little as her adrenaline slowly ebbed away. Mine had instantly dissipated along with my power, leaving me spent but calmer. It was never easy reorienting your emotions after something like this. Even Ed Regis still looked a little shaken. We sat silently, listening to the distant sounds of people and cars on the busy road at the end of the alley. Alia eventually stopped shivering.

Ed Regis asked me if I was ready to try standing up. I still felt lightheaded and my legs were a bit wobbly, but I found that I could walk without falling over.

"You need to drink something and replenish your fluids," said Ed Regis. "I think you lost a fair amount of blood there."

"I'm fine," I said as I buttoned up Ed Regis's jacket, which was much too big for me but better than being shirtless on a cold night. "Let's get moving."

"Here," Ed Regis said to Alia, "let's get these things off you first."

Alia still had her control bands clamped onto her wrists, and although the draining rods were retracted, the bracelets looked heavy and uncomfortable on her. They would also be a dead giveaway to anyone on the lookout for us.

Ed Regis looked around for something hard to break the plastic casings with. Alia reached into her pocket and pulled out Ms. Decker's remote control. Studying it for a second, she pressed a few buttons, and her control bands snapped open.

I asked Alia in wonder, "How did you know where Decker was hiding that remote? How did you even know she had it?"

"She used it on me once," replied Alia. "To shock me. It really hurt, but I saw where she put it afterwards."

Never underestimate my little sister. I had learned that lesson more times than I cared to count. Tough luck for Decker.

Ed Regis was staring at me. "If you didn't know that Alia was going to get your control bands off on the plane, what was your original plan?"

"I didn't have one," I admitted embarrassedly. "I just figured that we didn't have much to lose anyway."

Ed Regis laughed. "Terry's right. You really are crazy."

By the way my sister was eyeing me, I could tell that she agreed.

"Hey," I said to her softly, "if we can survive something like this, Alia, we just might live to be old."

Alia looked like she was about to say something, but then just let out a resigned little sigh and smiled.

We soon discovered that we were in the same city as Wood-claw. Apparently the Wolves' helicopters had taken us away from the city once, but then the plane had flown us back over it. If only we knew which direction it had been flying when its cockpit exploded, we might have gained a clue as to Randal Divine's whereabouts, but no such luck.

Ed Regis kept us to the back alleys as much as possible as we made our way to a public park several blocks from our crash site. He had been right about me lacking fluids, and I felt immensely better after taking a long drink from the park's water fountain. Alia took care of our remaining bumps and bruises, including the nasty one I got on the side of my head when our car was shot up by the gunship.

"Sixteen hours, right?" said Ed Regis, referring to the hiding protection Rachael had given Alia and me. "It should wear off well before noon tomorrow. We just have to stay out of sight until then, and Scott should be able to find us."

"How hard can it be?" I said.

We had no money, no weapons, no change of clothes and nowhere to go. It reminded me a little of my first days on the run as a child psionic, but there was an all-important difference here, which was that I wasn't alone.

It wasn't quite midnight yet. Ed Regis ruled out staying the night in the park as there were no decent hiding spots and someone might deem us suspicious enough to call the police. I suggested my old fallback of climbing a building's fire escape and camping out on the roof, but Ed Regis pointed out that we could be spotted from above and that we wouldn't have a viable escape route.

"What we need to do right now is blend in," said Ed Regis.

We joined up with a small group of homeless people living out of some abandoned, broken-down cars. They probably saw right through us, but didn't question Ed Regis's claim that we were a family and that we had been recently evicted from our house. Ed Regis made it clear to them that we would only be there one night, and they kindly shared their food and drink, which was meager but much appreciated.

We were prepared to sleep out in the open, but one elderly man offered to let us stay in the van that he called home. He cleared out his clutter of cans and other junk so that there would be room for three in the back. Then he himself took the driver's seat, which was broken and couldn't even be tilted back.

"We can't thank you enough," Ed Regis said to him.

He smiled in the rearview mirror, showing a mouthful of chipped, yellow teeth. "Everybody falls down sometimes," he said sympathetically. "You look like a nice family. I'm sure you'll be alright in the end."

That night, we stuck close in the van and slept very little. There was no telling when another team of Wolves might shine flashlights into our hiding place and drag us out like they did just hours ago, and while we might be just as powerless to stop them, we still had to be awake. Just in case.

4. A RAPIDLY CHANGING WORLD

We wanted to leave the homeless group at first light, but they insisted that we share their breakfast. One man even gave me an old sweatshirt which, though a little loose on me, was warm, comfortable and moderately clean.

As touched as we were by their generosity, I was relieved when we finally parted company. They had next to nothing, and yet they would help complete strangers for no reason at all, and here I was on a mission to kill the last surviving member of my own blood. Something just didn't feel right.

We made our way back to the park. I returned Ed Regis's jacket and we cleaned up as best we could at the water fountain.

Lifting up my sweatshirt, Alia carefully examined her latest work in the daylight. The gash in my lower right side had come back together pretty sloppily, leaving a long and messy scar.

"Sorry, Addy," said Alia, running her fingertips along the uneven line. "The wind was really just too much."

Alia wasn't a reconstructive healer, but she nevertheless prided herself on precise healing. Personally, I didn't care. It was just another scar.

We found a table at the end of the park's picnic field. We didn't have anything picnic-like to spread out, but at least it wasn't a school day so we didn't look too out of place here now that the sun was up.

"Just a couple more hours," Ed Regis assured us. "Scott's team is probably already out at our original rendezvous point. They'll know something went wrong, and once your hiding bubbles fade, they'll be here in a flash."

That did little to alleviate my fears. Now we knew why we had been put on the police database. The Angels had taken control of our government, which was something we hadn't expected for several more years at the earliest. This was no longer a war between two psionic factions. The longer we stayed in the open, the greater our risk of capture.

Ed Regis helped pass the hours by telling us stories of his youth. He had grown up on a farm, the oldest of three brothers, and he had some funny stories to tell, including one that involved riding a horse into his living room. I wasn't sure I believed everything he said, but at least it was entertaining.

Ed Regis also told us how lucky we had been on the cargo plane. He strongly suspected that none of Ms. Decker's soldiers were trained Wolves. They were probably just Angel Seraphim playing dress-up. It might have only been due to my VIP status with King Divine that Ms. Decker didn't properly restrain us, but real Wolves would have certainly had us in chains and possibly drugged unconscious. They would have kept Alia drained regardless of her age or lack of combat powers, and they wouldn't have been wearing grenades like that on an airplane. Thus, at least according to Ed Regis, our escape had been comparatively easy.

"I have a hunch the Angels don't yet have complete control over the Wolves," said Ed Regis. "Your Ms. Decker probably didn't trust them enough to let them fly with us to Randal Divine's location."

"I hope that's true," I said, unable to keep myself from looking around nervously every few minutes.

Noon came and went, but Scott didn't appear. Alia finally voiced the thought I had been too afraid to say out loud. "Something happened to them, too," she said quietly. "They're not coming for us."

"Faith, Alia," said Ed Regis.

Psionic hiding protection is neither visible nor tangible, and Ed Regis suggested that perhaps Rachael had given us a slightly conservative estimate on our time. But even he agreed that our protection must have worn off by now, and as the deep orange sun slowly slid behind the cityscape, Ed Regis announced that we would have to find another place to spend the night.

"But we're no longer hidden," argued Alia. "If Wood-claw isn't out looking for us, then someone else is."

"I know," said Ed Regis. "If Scott doesn't find us by sunup, we'll have to start thinking about other options."

Alia huffed. "What other options?"

"We'll think of something."

"Ed Regis is right," I said to my sister. "One thing at a time."

Alia looked as unconvinced as I felt, but we needn't have worried. The moment we stood up to leave the park, we saw Scott and Rachael coming our way.

Alia let out a cry of joy in my head. I sensed she was about to break into a run, so I grabbed her arm and kept us at a slow walk. Scott would know by our powers that we weren't Angel shape-shifters or anything, but we could still be part of a trap. I suspected that there were hidden Wood-claw Knights watching us, and it wouldn't be safe to do anything that could be misinterpreted.

Once we closed the gap, Ed Regis asked Scott, "Do you trust us or would you like to ask a security question?"

"We trust you," Scott said calmly. "Do you trust us?"

Ed Regis nodded. "Not that we have much of a choice right now, but yes."

"Where's your car?" asked Scott.

"We lost it," Ed Regis replied simply.

Rachael said, "Well, our van is parked just outside, and it has a hiding field so let's not stay here."

As we walked together toward the exit, I asked, "What took you guys so long?"

"I'm sorry about that," said Scott. "We had some trouble getting Mrs. Harding's permission to bring you in." Then he glanced at our dirty clothes and added, "But I guess you guys had some trouble, too."

"Let's hear yours first," I suggested as we left the park and headed to Scott's white van, which was waiting for us on the curb, engine running.

Hammer, the snappish Knight from yesterday evening, was at the wheel. He looked even crankier now, and silently started driving as soon as we closed the doors. Scott rode beside him and Rachael sat with us in the back, putting cloth blindfolds around our eyes.

"Please don't take those off until we're inside the building," said Rachael. "Especially Alia, since you're still too young for mind-writing."

"Okay," said Alia.

"So why did Harding want to keep you guys from coming for us?" I asked, closing my eyes and leaning back into the seat.

Scott explained, "There was a plane crash last night. You might not have heard about it, though. It wasn't on the news. It was a military transport, and Mrs. Harding thinks that it might have been carrying Wolves. She put Wood-claw on high alert: no one in or out for a while."

"Where did the plane crash?" I asked.

"Nowhere near Wood-claw," said Scott. "But it's still a serious issue for us."

"I meant did it crash inside the city?"

"Oh, no, if that had happened, the press would have been all over it. Mrs. Harding said it crashed somewhere just outside the city limits. We don't know much more about it, though. Mrs. Harding thinks there's going to be a surge of Wolves in the city until they finish dealing with it."

"She's probably right," said Ed Regis.

"The whole thing is just a big nuisance," said Scott. "So, anyway, what kind of trouble did you guys run into?"

I wasn't sure I wanted to answer that within earshot of Hammer. "Nothing serious. We'll tell you later," I said lightly. I quickly changed the subject, asking, "So how is everyone doing? Still alive and kicking?"

"Pretty much," said Scott.

Alia asked hesitantly, "How's Susan?"

Susan had been on my mind too. Her older sister, Felicity, had been killed when the Angels raided our house to kidnap Alia. For all of their frequent and loud arguments, Susan had been very close to her sister. Susan's outrage at being forced to evacuate early had been partly from her fear of being separated.

"Susan is alright," said Scott, and added, "I mean, she is now."

Rachael explained, "Susan was really down for a few months, kind of hollowed out after... you know. She was a bit like Max, just sitting around all day and hardly talking to anyone."

"I'm sorry to hear that," I said. Sorry, but not surprised. That's just what happens when someone you love suddenly dies.

Rachael continued, "But then a really nice family adopted her. Recently, she's pretty okay."

"Does she..." Alia started to ask, but her voice quickly trailed off.

Rachael asked curiously, "Does she what, Alia?"

My sister couldn't bring herself to say it, so I did, asking, "Does she blame us for what happened?"

"Blame you?" Rachael repeated in a surprised tone. "Of course not! Susan's a fighter. She understands."

Scott said, "Hey, Alia, you know those little kids you used to teach combat to? Rachael and I took over the classes after you left, and we still have them twice a week."

Rachael added, "And since about mid-summer, Susan's been helping out almost every class. It's been really good for her too."

"A lot of things have changed," said Scott. "I think everyone has pretty much forgiven us for what happened at Walnut. They're really nice to us now."

Sure they are, I thought to myself wryly, *now that you guys are helping to protect them.*

I couldn't say that out loud since our driver would hear. I hoped Hammer's attitude was the exception to how we would be treated at Wood-claw.

A few minutes later, I heard Alia yawn loudly. I couldn't help following suit.

Rachael said, "We're just about there, but remember you can't remove your blindfolds until we say so, okay?"

I felt the van make a sharp left turn down a steep ramp, and then slowly back into a parking space.

Exiting the van, I could tell by the sounds and the air that we were in an underground parking lot not unlike the one under New Haven One. We held hands, and Scott and Rachael guided us to an elevator. As we got in, Rachael explained that we were in a seven-story apartment building, and that all of the apartments from the first floor up belonged to the families of Wood-claw.

Scott said, "We managed to kick... I mean, *convince* the last of the former residents to move out before the summer started. Everyone got a fair price for their troubles."

"We have two guest houses on the second floor, but they're kind of like prisons," Rachael said apologetically. "The windows are all boarded up so you can't see outside."

The elevator stopped. We were guided along several yards of carpeted corridor. A door was opened, and we stepped into what I assumed was one of the apartments.

"Can we take these off now?" I asked.

Instead of an answer, I suddenly felt a pair of lips touch my own. I jumped a little and almost released a telekinetic blast in my surprise, but as I felt her arms around me, I hugged her back, and found her lips again.

Candace lifted up my blindfold. "Welcome home," she whispered.

"I missed you," I said, gazing into her deep blue eyes.

Rachael was having trouble suppressing a laugh as she undid Ed Regis and Alia's blindfolds. Candace was three years older than me and noticeably taller, and I discovered that I was levitating myself to compensate. I quickly set my feet back onto the floor.

Once her blindfold came off, Alia instantly jumped into Candace's arms.

"Oh, you got so big!" said Candace, picking her up. "We were all so worried about you!"

I looked around. We were in a modestly furnished living room. The only window was covered by wooden boards, painted the same off-white as the walls, but otherwise it was a perfectly normal and livable place. Rachael had no idea what a prison was like.

James was there too, sitting on a long sofa, but not Terry.

"Terry's taking a shower," James said unnecessarily. We could hear the water running.

Letting go of Candace, Alia said weakly, "I'm really hungry."

"Me too," I said. We hadn't had anything since breakfast with the homeless group.

"You'll be dining at our place tonight," announced Scott, smiling.

"Your place?" I asked.

Scott explained, "Rachael and I, we have our own apartment now, right down the hall, actually."

"This is getting serious," I commented. "You guys married?"

"Not yet," said Rachael, blushing.

Scott laughed. "But we already got kids."

I raised my eyebrows. We hadn't been away *that* many months.

"Walter and Daniel," explained Rachael.

Candace told us that she and her friend Heather, like Susan, had been adopted into the Wood-claw families. Both Walter and Daniel had been offered homes too, but they had refused, preferring to stay with Scott and Rachael.

"Where do you live now?" I asked Candace.

"Up on the fifth floor," said Candace. "I live with this elderly couple and their daughter, Kate. She's in her forties but she's more like my sister than my mother." Candace giggled and added playfully, "But don't think I'm going to invite you over to meet my family until after our first real date!"

I heard the shower shut off, and a minute later Terry appeared, properly clothed but hair dripping, and without her arm attachment.

Noticing our lack of baggage and my unfamiliar sweatshirt, Terry asked brusquely, "What happened to you guys?"

My sister decided to get straight to the point. "Addy got shot."

Terry's jaw dropped. "Again?!"

"Yes, again," I said wearily, knowing I wasn't going to hear the end of that one for a while.

Candace asked in alarm, "What happened to you?!"

"It's nothing serious," I insisted, not wanting to worry her. "Alia healed me in seconds."

"Literally," agreed Alia.

Terry narrowed her eyes. "Don't tell me you guys had something to do with that plane crash."

"You won't hear it from me," I assured her.

Terry smacked her forehead and groaned. "You did..."

There was a knock on the front door. Scott opened it to Mrs. Marjorie Harding.

The leader of the Wood-claw Guardians was a dignified gray-haired old woman whose grandmotherly appearance was offset by the calculating, no-nonsense manner of a breakaway faction leader. A former Guardian Knight herself, Mrs. Harding still had a fairly powerful telekinetic focus, though I suspected that mine was stronger now.

"Adrian! Alia!" exclaimed Mrs. Harding, stepping into the living room.

Without commenting on our appearance, she shook my hand and hugged Alia. Then she caught sight of the ex-Wolf. "Ah, Major Regis," she said, forcing a smile. "Welcome to our settlement."

Ed Regis nodded to her and said pleasantly, "Thank you."

Mrs. Harding quickly turned her attention back to Alia and me. "I do apologize for the delay in your pickup. Perhaps Scott has already told you of the Wolf plane."

I smiled and said lamely, "He did."

"I had to be sure it was safe for Scott to leave. I have more than a hundred people in my care at the moment, and these are very dangerous times."

I nodded. "We understand, Mrs. Harding. Thank you for having us here."

Terry was scowling at me. I knew that I should hurry up and confess to Mrs. Harding my involvement in the plane crash, but by now, news of our arrival had reached the rest of the building. Daniel, Walter, Heather and Susan came down to greet us, along with several of Alia's former kiddie-combat students and their parents.

There were many more hugs and handshakes as everyone crowded into the living room. I was happy to see that Susan, at least outwardly, was in very good spirits. Like Alia, I too felt some responsibility for Felicity's death. Felicity had been one of our charges, after all. But Scott was right about Susan: at thirteen years old, she understood and accepted this war.

We also met Thomas and Sally Richardson, the two psionic sparks who had helped us retrieve Alia from the Angel outpost. Their young son had been one of Alia's students, and he was there too, quite delighted to see his former instructor.

My sister was a bit of a living legend among her young trainees. Though a few years younger than her, most were slightly bigger, and at first they had been reluctant to learn combat techniques from a frail-looking healer girl. But the youngest-ever Honorary Guardian Knight soon showed them that size is no measure of strength, and now she had returned from a death-defying journey to the great Historian's mountain. The kids instantly bombarded her with questions about our travels. Alia brushed them off, citing hunger and fatigue, and promised them the story another time.

Then my sister said something that made everyone stop.

"Where's Patrick?" she asked. As an uncomfortable hush fell upon the crowd, Alia peered around at their faces. "Where's Laila?"

Mrs. Harding looked at her sadly. "The Lands no longer live here, dear."

"Where did they go?"

No one seemed to want to answer. Finally, Candace said, "They've turned Angel, Alia. They went to Lumina."

Mrs. Harding quietly explained that the Angels had abducted Dr. Land's wife and baby Laila back when they were living at their temporary mountain retreat following the evacuation of Walnut Lane. Several weeks later, Dr. Land and Patrick decided that they were willing to accept Angel conversion to be reunited with their family.

"I'm really sorry," said Candace, putting her hands on Alia's shoulders.

Alia refused to cry in front of her students. She just nodded silently.

We had heard stories like this at other Guardian settlements all year. Taking advantage of the fact that Guardian morale was at an all-time low, the Angels frequently targeted children and non-psionics in an attempt to divide families and entice surrender.

Mrs. Harding cleared her throat and said to the crowd, "Okay, I think it's time we let our guests get settled and rested. There will be plenty of time to see them again tomorrow. Let us leave them for now."

Mrs. Harding ushered the crowd out and, after reminding Terry to explain to us the conditions of our stay in Wood-claw, left us too.

Only Scott, Rachael and Candace remained.

"Alia..." began Candace.

"It's okay," said Alia. "I'm just really tired right now. I just want a bath and a bed, and maybe some dinner."

"Dinner will be in an hour," promised Scott. Then, after a quick glance in my direction, he asked Candace, "Would you like to join us too?"

Candace smiled. "I'd love to come."

"We'll set another plate," promised Scott. "It's going to be a feast tonight."

Gesturing toward Ed Regis, Alia and me, Rachael said to Candace, "These three lost their luggage. I think we can spare some clothes for Adrian and Mr. Regis, but we don't have anything Alia-size at home. Think you can go borrow some?"

"Sure," Candace replied confidently. "I'll go ask around your combat kids."

Then Candace gave me a quick peck on the cheek and said, "And you can tell us over dinner how you got shot, Adrian." She looked at Alia and asked, "Um, how many times now?"

Rolling her eyes, my sister put up a hand, all five fingers.

Candace shook her head in wonder.

Scott, Rachael and Candace left us. As soon as the door closed behind them, Terry rounded on me like a cobra. "Okay, Half-head, talk."

I told most of the story, with bits of help from Ed Regis and Alia. Terry and James looked intrigued, shocked and mildly amused by our account of last night from our capture by the Wolves to our plunge into the dumpster.

"Harding is going to blow her top when she discovers what we did over her city," I concluded, laughing nervously.

"It's worse than that," said Terry. "Harding suspected already, but this proves that the Angels are in control of the government now. Or at least bits of it." Terry had quickly realized the significance of what we had seen and heard on the cargo plane. "Jodie Decker was a top-level Guardian. She was the Raven Knights' second-in-command. Even converted, the Angels wouldn't have entrusted someone like that with the location of the Divine family unless they were seriously trying to heal the break between the two factions."

"Maybe King Randal just trusts his daughter's power," I suggested.

"No," said Terry. "They're planning to do it. Soon. And if they really have control of the government, then what's to stop them? We need to go tell Harding right now."

"Sorry, Terry," I said, "but I'm with Alia on this. All I want is a meal, a bath and a bed. Everything else can wait till tomorrow."

Terry let out a loud huff. "Okay, okay, you big baby! I'll go talk to Harding myself. She won't be too mad at us, I hope. This is going to be a real game-changer, and it's good that you found it out before the Angels made a public announcement."

"Oh, so this is a good thing now?" I said sarcastically.

"Well, we could all be dead before the year is out," said Terry, grinning, "but aside from that, sure."

It had taken a lot of time to tell Terry and James the story of our capture and escape. We now only had a few minutes left till dinner and we still hadn't even washed up. Before heading up to Mrs. Harding's place to report our discovery, Terry very quickly explained the conditions of our stay to us.

We had been given two guest apartments: the one we were in now and the one across the hall. Ed Regis and Alia were restricted to the second floor, Ed Regis because of his ex-Wolf status and Alia because her age prevented safe memory alteration. Terry, James and I were permitted access to the other floors on the condition that if we accidentally saw the neighborhood from the windows, we would submit to mind-writing to erase our memories of it. Technically, James and I were still under the safe age limit, but Terry had vouched for us.

As Terry left, Candace returned to our apartment carrying three small duffle bags packed with donated secondhand clothes for Alia, Ed Regis and me. She had also driven out to a nearby store to get us clean underwear, socks, towels and toothbrushes.

"We can't pay you for this," I said apologetically. "We lost all our money along with our car."

"Don't worry about it," said Candace. "Everything's on the house for now. But how did you lose the car?"

"We'll tell you over dinner," I promised.

Pressed for time, Ed Regis, Alia and I settled for two-minute showers to make ourselves presentable before heading to dinner at Scott and Rachael's.

But we weren't as fashionably late as we thought we'd be. Scott was still finishing up in the kitchen and Rachael was setting the table, so Walter and Daniel took us on a short tour of their apartment. The Wood-claw building had six apartments per floor, and each was fairly spacious. The boys had their own bedrooms now, and although their furniture clearly showed that the family was still living off of a borderline income, it looked like a pretty nice life for them. I thanked them for sparing their clothes, which fit me well.

As the boys led us through their home, I noticed that as per Mrs. Harding's rule concerning non-Wood-claw visitors, every curtain had been closed tightly. I was curious about the quality of the neighborhood, but not enough to risk memory alteration. Outside was dark and mostly quiet.

We were called to the dining room where the table was set for ten. I sat next to Candace, and Alia found her usual place on my other side. It was a pretty tight squeeze putting ten chairs around a table made for four, but Rachael had insisted on keeping an extra spot for Terry just in case she came late. It wasn't a problem for me. I was used to small quarters in our motorhome, and I certainly didn't mind being a little closer to Candace over dinner.

Scott hadn't been kidding when he said that it was going to be a feast. We had plenty of roast chicken and too many side dishes to fit on the table at once. Scott, who had been the best member of my kitchen crew back in Walnut Lane, was the chef of this household. Rachael laughingly explained that Walter and Daniel had permanently banned her from the kitchen.

"I don't think I'm *that* bad a cook, but the boys disagree," said Rachael, "so Scott cooks and I clean."

"And now you two are a finder and hider," James said with a chuckle. "It's like you planned it that way."

"I like this," Alia said quietly in my head. *"It's like we're back in Walnut."*

I agreed. Life on the road these past few months hadn't been all that bad, but I still envied a family that could actually live like one. *Someday soon,* I promised myself.

Before I could tell our story about the cargo plane, Walter asked to hear about our trip to the Historian.

Our official line on our meeting with the Historian was that, since we arrived without gifts, he had refused to give us any information regarding the Angel king, but then took pity on us and teleported us home. Scott and the others had already heard a fair bit about our travels from Terry and James, but they asked us plenty of additional questions about our time in the mountains. We couldn't tell anyone, even our closest friends, what the Historian had revealed about my bloodline, so we focused instead on the Angel pursuit through the mountains and how we survived.

Upset over the loss of Patrick and baby Laila to the Angels, Alia was quieter than usual at the table. Noticing this, our hosts said a whole bunch of things to cheer her up. Scott told her that Dr. Land and Patrick had made a difficult choice, one that might bring them greater happiness than freedom from psionic control. Rachael reminded her that even a psionic king's conversion could be broken by the king's death, and that the Lands would return to us if we won this war. Both assured my sister that she would see

Patrick again soon, and meanwhile she still had plenty of friends and admirers right here in Wood-claw.

Alia knew that they meant well with their words so she did her best to smile, but in truth, she would much rather have been left to eat in peace. My sister had always dealt with her emotions in her own way, and in her own good time. This would be no different.

To spare her from more unwanted cheering-up, I steered the conversation over to the events of the previous night. Everyone insisted on hearing the full story with every little detail. I got Ed Regis to do most of the talking so I could concentrate on eating. Walter and Daniel got a big kick out of our crazy escape, but Scott had known Ms. Decker back in New Haven, and wasn't as amused.

"Jodie Decker was a good friend of my mom's," said Scott. "She had three sons."

"At least the plane didn't kill any innocents on the ground," said Rachael.

"Unfortunately, the good news stops there," I said. "If the Wolves are no longer hunting the Angels, then we just lost our strongest ally."

Candace looked over at the empty seat at the end of the table, saying, "Still, you'd think Terry could have joined us here and told Mrs. Harding tomorrow."

"Terry's just trying to score a bonus point with Harding," I replied with an evil grin. "We're going to need her help, and lots of it."

"Terry is right to be afraid," Ed Regis said gravely. "Psionic factions have always made connections with local government officials to hide their tracks, but to do that on a national level is unprecedented. And I'd bet anything the Angels aren't handing out bribes. They're converting."

"How long do you think we have?" I asked.

"Difficult to say," he replied. "It depends on how much of the government the Angels actually control, and which agencies. But my guess is that if this is happening here, it's probably happening worldwide. The Angels wouldn't want to lock themselves into one country in case they're exposed before they have enough political footholds internationally."

I laughed. "Never ask an adult to give a straight answer to a straight question!"

Ed Regis chuckled, and then said seriously, "Two years, tops."

"What if we just go public?" suggested Daniel. "You know, tell the whole world what's happening? Tell them that if they don't do something, they'll all be living on Planet Randal soon."

Ed Regis gave him a grim smile. "An all-out war? It won't work. People would laugh, and those who believed us would quickly disappear, lose their memories or suddenly have a change of heart. And even if it did lead to open war, it would mostly be a war between common people, between countries, not psionic factions. The Angels could easily create enough confusion to guarantee that no one would know who they were really fighting."

"Besides," added Scott, "you're forgetting the most important thing, Daniel. What if we win? Do you really want to live in a world that knows we exist?"

Daniel frowned at his plate. "I guess not."

"We can't ask the world to pay for our mistakes," I said quietly. "This is a psionics' war. We have to settle it."

I was a little surprised at my own words when I said that. In the past, I had always tried to distance myself from this conflict, insisting that it wasn't really my war and that I was only in it for personal reasons. But perhaps just being psionic is in itself a personal reason. As long as this war continued, one way or another, I would probably be a part of it.

For dessert, Scott passed out slices of cinnamon apple pie which, according to Walter, was a rare treat in this house. It tasted great, but I didn't have room left for all of it.

As we wrapped up our little gathering, I offered to help with the cleanup, but Rachael insisted that we get rested. I didn't offer twice.

Candace saw us back to our apartment door. Ed Regis and James quickly went inside, but Alia stayed by my side, which was annoying.

Candace asked me, "Do you know how long you're staying in Woodclaw?"

"Terry hasn't said anything?" I asked.

"No."

"Well, that's for her to decide," I said with a shrug. "Terry's the leader. I just stumble along in her wake getting shot from time to time."

"I've seen you be a leader, Adrian," said Candace. "A really good one."

I smiled and shook my head. "Blind luck."

"I hope you can stay awhile."

"Me too. Thanks again for everything."

We ignored my sister and took our time saying goodnight. There was no telling how many days I could spend with Candace so I wanted to make them count.

Once she disappeared into the elevator, I rounded on Alia, who was looking up at me disapprovingly.

"What?" I asked brusquely.

"Nothing," said Alia. *"I just thought the Historian told you never to have kids."*

I fixed her with a withering stare. "Kissing doesn't make kids, Alia."

While it was true that I was forbidden offspring, that didn't mean I couldn't have friendly relationships, and I really didn't need my sister to be chaperoning every minute.

Entering the apartment, we found that Terry hadn't returned yet, but we weren't too surprised. Terry had stayed with Mrs. Harding for dinner, which probably meant tea and more chatting afterwards. Mrs. Harding lived with her daughter, son-in-law and three grandchildren, so she wouldn't have been able to discuss much with Terry over their meal.

James had the spare keys to the second guest apartment, so we opened it up and looked inside. It was the same size and shape as our first: a moderately spacious living room, a kitchen, a dining room, and three bedrooms furnished with two beds each. That came to a grand total of six bedrooms between our two apartments, so this time I could stuff my nosy sister in her own room and take one whole bedroom to myself.

Or so I thought until Alia reminded me of a little promise I had made to her back at the Historian's mountain. *"You said we could share a room until I didn't want to anymore, Addy."*

"I suppose I did," I admitted. "You didn't take that seriously, did you?"

"Oh, come on," Alia moaned into my head as she wrapped her arms around my waist. *"Give me a break. Please?"*

I could kill people any day of the week, but I never had the stomach for this kind of battle. Patting her back, I gave her a reassuring smile. "You know it's okay, Alia. Always."

My sister had come a long, long way from the days that she had to snuggle with me under one blanket to keep her nightmares at bay, but it had been only twenty-four hours since she had a gun pressed against her forehead. And when we finally got out of harm's way, Alia had discovered that one of her closest friends had turned Angel. Definitely not one of her best days.

James and Terry were already settled in the first apartment, but there was still one empty bedroom over there. Nevertheless I asked Ed Regis to stay in the second apartment with us. Alia trusted the ex-Wolf just as much as she trusted me, and I knew that it would be better for her to keep him close. Ed Regis took the bedroom next to ours.

Our bedroom here was almost as big as the one we used to share in Cindy's penthouse at the top of New Haven One. The beds were comfortable singles with soft pillows, and there were two dressers and a small table. Two still-life oil paintings hung on the walls. Even with the boarded-up window, it was a fairly homey place.

Sitting down on her bed, Alia looked at me embarrassedly, mumbling, *"Thanks, Addy."*

"It's alright," I assured her. "Are you going to be okay now?"

Alia nodded. *"I guess so. I'm just sad about Patrick."*

"I'm sad about the Lands too," I said. "I was really hoping to see how big that baby got. I'll bet she's talking by now."

Alia smiled and said teasingly, *"At least you have Candace to talk to. But only if you can keep your lips apart."*

I narrowed my eyes. "Are you going to be pestering me about Candace every second of every day here?"

"Of course!" Alia laughed, and then asked seriously, *"But are you going to spend every second with her?"*

"As far as I'm concerned, that's the main reason we came to Woodclaw."

"Because I want to talk to her too, Addy."

I shrugged. "That's okay. I know she's your friend too."

"No, Addy," Alia said emphatically, *"I mean just me and her."*

"Oh?" I said, taken aback. "You make it sound like an interview. What do you want to talk to her about?"

Alia looked away and mumbled, *"Stuff."*

"What stuff?"

"Just... stuff."

"What stuff, Alia?" I pressed.

Alia gave a little shrug. *"Girl stuff."*

"Girl stuff?!" I repeated, staring at her in surprise.

"You know... girl-only stuff."

I raised an eyebrow. "I didn't know you were a girl."

"Addy!" Alia threw her pillow at my face, but I stopped it in midair.

As I levitated the pillow back to her, I said awkwardly, "I'm sorry I asked, Alia. Really sorry. I guess you can't exactly talk to Terry about girl stuff."

Alia replied in her best sarcastic tone, *"I'd just as soon talk to Ed."*

There was a sharp knock on our door, and Ed Regis's voice said, "Hey, I think the bath is full now."

Alia had started running the bathwater as soon as we entered the apartment, and I silently thanked Ed Regis for interrupting this embarrassing conversation not a moment too soon.

Alia jumped up from her bed. *"Finally! Finally! A real bath!"*

I laughed. A real bath for Alia was one that lasted two hours or more.

"Can I please go first, Addy?"

"Go ahead," I said. "I'll take my bath in the other apartment. Try not to fall asleep in the tub. And don't expect me to wait up for you either."

Alia grabbed her duffle bag and headed for the door, but then stopped and looked back at me timidly. *"Um, Addy?"*

I nodded. "I'll make sure you get some time with Candace, okay?"

As she closed the door behind her, I slowly shook my head and muttered to myself, "Girl stuff..."

A minute later, Ed Regis popped his head in to bid me goodnight. It was only a little past 9pm, but I wasn't surprised. Alia and I had managed to get a little sleep in the homeless man's van, but Ed Regis hadn't closed his eyes in two days.

"Goodnight, Ed Regis," I said to him. "Thanks again for keeping us safe."

Ed Regis looked like he wanted to say something, then changed his mind, and then changed his mind again as he stepped into the room and faced me.

"What?" I said hesitantly, remaining seated on my bed.

"Adrian," Ed Regis began equally hesitantly, "about your lack of plan the other day..."

"Oh, come on!" I groaned. "I feel stupid enough about that already. Do you really have to rub my nose in it?"

But Ed Regis insisted on having his say. "Adrian, you are not a child anymore. One of these days, you're the one who's going to underestimate your enemy."

I growled at him, "You know perfectly well that I've already done that, Wolf!"

"Then all the more reason to take me seriously."

"Are you finished?!"

Ed Regis sighed. "Yeah. I'm finished."

After an awkward silence, I stood up from my bed and said to him quietly, "I'm sorry, Ed Regis. It's not that I don't appreciate you looking out for me. It's just that—"

"That I'm a Wolf?" asked Ed Regis.

"You're a soldier," I said, looking away. "I'm not. I don't have your tactical experience. And I think there's a big difference between being overconfident and being desperate."

"Perhaps," said Ed Regis.

"Just out of curiosity, though, what would you have done?"

"I would have waited for the right moment."

"And what if the right moment never came?"

"Then we'd be Angels right now," said Ed Regis, chuckling lightly. "Goodnight."

Ed Regis let himself out.

I grabbed my bag and made my way back to Terry's apartment, where I discovered that Terry had returned from Mrs. Harding's and that the bath was currently occupied by James. Terry informed me that James had only just started his bath, but I had a feeling Alia wouldn't be out from hers until she really was falling asleep, so I decided to wait here.

As we plopped ourselves down on the living-room sofas, Terry asked casually, "Did you finally get your own room this time?"

She was going to find out anyway so I told her.

"Why am I not surprised?" laughed Terry. "For all the complaining you do, Half-head, when it comes to parenting, you have absolutely no spine."

I just shrugged. Terry was probably right anyway.

"How'd it go with Harding?" I asked.

"Well, you're in luck," said Terry, putting her feet up on the coffee table. "She's not going to prosecute. In fact, you're actually a bit of a hero now for giving us a heads-up on the Angels' accelerated progress."

"Good," I yawned. "Now if only we could do something about it."

"Harding still wants to hear the story directly from you and Major Regis to make sure she has every little detail, but she promised to wait until after breakfast tomorrow, so you owe me for that. As for doing something, it depends on how this all plays out. We'll just have to wait and see. But I have some good news. Harding told me that Wood-claw does have occasional contact with the Guardian Resistance in Lumina."

"It really exists?" I asked.

Terry nodded. "It does. Harding sends them money and sometimes lends them Knights. I think Scott shamed her into it."

"And?"

"I don't know yet," Terry said lightly. "Harding wants to share our information with several other breakaways and the Resistance too. Like I said, we'll just have to wait and see."

"Days?" I asked. "Weeks?"

Terry smirked. "Candace asked me the same question yesterday."

I refused to bite, and we sat silently for a while. James was taking his time in the bath.

Suddenly Terry asked, "So how's your sister doing, anyway?"

Her question threw me for a moment. "Fine, I guess," I said, shrugging. "Why wouldn't she be?"

Terry stared at me in disbelief. "Because you chucked her out of an airplane!" she cried in an exasperated tone. "Because her first boyfriend turned Angel on her! Take your pick! Just because I don't treat her like a teddy bear doesn't mean I don't care about her."

I waggled a finger at her angrily. "First of all, Terry, I do not treat Alia like a teddy bear. I'm letting her sleep in my room, not my bed. Second, I didn't throw her out of the plane. That was Ed Regis. And third, Patrick was never..." I shrugged. "Okay, maybe he was, but she'll get over it."

Terry started laughing.

"Anyway, Alia's fine," I repeated. "Or she will be soon. You know how tough she is."

Terry nodded. "Yeah, I know. Alia's really grown."

"No kidding," I said, thinking of the awkward little conversation I just had with my sister.

Between the Angel takeover of the Wolves and Alia's sudden mention of "girl stuff," I had been far less psychologically prepared for the latter. I felt a little guilty about talking behind Alia's back, but I couldn't resist telling Terry how my sister wanted some private time with Candace. To my surprise, however, Terry wasn't nearly as shocked as I had been.

"What did you expect?" was Terry's attitude. "She's almost twelve years old, right?"

"Theoretically," I said evasively.

Alia was officially eleven and a half, but even Cindy had admitted that she was only "pretty sure" about Alia's age.

"Twelve years old, Adrian!" said Terry. "And you're wondering why she has questions about girl stuff?"

"But Ed Regis is right," I said. "She *does* look like a nine-year-old. She doesn't even have... you know..."

"Have what?" Terry asked bluntly. "Tits?"

"Well... yeah," I said uncomfortably. Then I laughed, adding, "Even Decker called her a little girl—right before Alia slapped the gun out of her hand."

"There you go," said Terry, shrugging. "She's not a kid anymore. She hasn't been for a long time."

"I suppose."

Terry threw me a nasty grin and gestured to my clothes. "Anyway, you're hardly one to talk about size, Adrian. That's Daniel's shirt you're wearing, isn't it?"

Before I could think of a retort, a frightening thought popped into my head. "Hey, what if Alia's like the Historian, Terry?" I asked seriously. "You know, never-aging?"

Terry laughed loudly. "She's just a late bloomer, Adrian! It's not so rare with undersized girls, especially if they do sports."

"Are you sure?" I asked uncertainly.

"Trust me. The Historian's power is one of a kind. If Alia had it, the

Historian would have known. Don't worry. She'll grow tits soon enough."

I frowned. "That's kind of what I'm afraid of too, actually. I never really pictured Alia as a teenager."

"Well, ready or not, she's going to be one soon," said Terry. Then she laughed again, adding, "And I bet you haven't even given her the birds-and-bees talk, have you?"

I gaped at her. "Are you nuts?! She's my sister! Do you honestly think I'm going to talk to her about sex?!"

"Well, someone has to," Terry said matter-of-factly. "She doesn't have parents and she's never even been to school. What happens when she gets her first period? What happens if someday she doesn't know how to use a contraceptive? She can't stay a clueless little girl forever."

"Candace will take care of her."

Terry snorted loudly. "You really are spineless, aren't you?"

I nodded. "All my life."

I reminded Terry to keep this conversation private. "Alia doesn't think you're girl enough to talk to about girl stuff."

"She wouldn't be the first," said Terry. "But we're not going to be in Wood-claw forever, and we're definitely not taking Candace with us. You make sure that Alia gets all of her serious girl questions answered before we leave, understand?"

I snapped Terry a salute. "Yes, sir."

It was easy to see why Alia would prefer Candace over Terry in the girl-stuff department, but for my part, Terry's direct manner actually made this kind of conversation slightly less painful. At least Terry wasn't one to giggle.

James finally got out of the bath. "Sorry I took so long, Adrian," he said. "I didn't know you were waiting."

I was about to get up, but then I heard a faint mumbling in my head, which was my sister telepathically talking in her sleep. Unconsciously using powers during the night was not uncommon for child psionics, and until about two years ago, I often woke up hovering. Alia's telepathic murmuring had become a little less frequent these last few months, but she still did it more nights than not.

I looked up at the clock. It had only been about half an hour. Alia must have been pretty sleepy to cut short her long-awaited bath.

Hearing her quiet voice in my head, I suddenly discovered that I was dead tired too. Waking up in the homeless man's van felt like years ago, and the cargo plane ancient history. While sitting around in a public park all day long might sound like a picnic compared to being chased by Angels through a mountain range or being shot at by military gunships, nevertheless today had been a long and nerve-racking (and somewhat disturbing) day in its own right. I was glad it was finally over. I was nearly finished digesting Scott's Welcome to Wood-claw meal so I had little reason to stay awake.

"You want me to refill the tub?" asked James.

"No," I yawned. "Thanks but I think I'll save it for tomorrow."

I got up and, bidding them goodnight, returned to my apartment across the corridor.

Locking the front door, I telekinetically switched off the living-room lights and tiptoed over to my bedroom door. Alia was still mumbling into my head, and I opened the door quietly so as not to wake her. But as my eyes adjusted to the darkness, I discovered that her bed was empty. I first thought that perhaps she had crept into mine, but she wasn't there either.

Turning on the lights, I laughed to myself as I figured it out: Alia really had fallen asleep in the tub!

5. THE HEART OF A KNIGHT

I woke up late for breakfast the next day. I must have slept eleven straight hours. Changing, I groggily stumbled into the dining room where Ed Regis had left me a plate of ham and eggs.

"You should have woken me," I said to him. "I would have done this."

"It's no problem," he replied, clearing the table. By the number of plates, I could tell that Terry and James had eaten here too.

As I sat down in front of my breakfast, I asked, "Where is everyone?"

"Terry and James are back in their apartment."

"And Alia?"

"Picking up where she left off."

I laughed. "Hope she stays awake this time."

Last night had been a bit of a mess. Alia always left the bathroom door unlocked, but remembering Terry's insistence that my sister was no longer a child, I respected her privacy and banged on the door until she woke. But the noise I made woke Ed Regis too, who first thought that we were under attack. It was some time before we could all settle down again.

Ed Regis poured me a glass of orange juice as he said, "I think she's in one of her moods, Adrian. She wouldn't talk during breakfast."

"Did she eat?" I asked.

"A little."

"She'll be fine," I said confidently. "When is Harding coming?"

As if on cue, the doorbell rang, and Ed Regis went to open the door to several voices including those of Mrs. Harding, Terry and James. I couldn't see any of them from the dining room, but I could tell by the sounds that they were being led into the living room.

I heard Terry shout out, "Adrian, you awake yet?!"

"Yeah," I called back. "Just give me a second."

I quickly swallowed two mouthfuls of scrambled egg, washing them down with orange juice. Then, after splashing some water on my face at the kitchen sink, I joined everyone in the living room.

"Your database, Major, as requested," Mrs. Harding was saying to Ed Regis as she handed him the little touch-screen device that contained all of the Wolves' information on psionics. Scott must have passed it on to Mrs. Harding.

"Thank you," said Ed Regis, taking the small black box. "I hope you found some use for it."

"We have been passing along some of its contents to our allies."

"We'll use it here and return it to you before we leave," promised Ed Regis.

Mrs. Harding nodded curtly. "Thank you."

I couldn't help being amused at the tension in Mrs. Harding's tone whenever she talked to Ed Regis. I wondered if she had some personal grudge against the Wolves, something perhaps to rival my own. In stark contrast, Ed Regis seemed completely at ease, always polite and composed in his dealings with Mrs. Harding. It must have annoyed the hell out of her.

There were also two Wood-claw Knights who had accompanied Mrs. Harding to our debriefing. Mrs. Harding introduced one, a middle-aged double-destroyer named Ms. Isabel Ferris, as Wood-claw's Head of Security. Her Knight call sign was Tigress, but I didn't ask why. The other Knight, Mr. Beryl, was a gray-haired man nearly as old as Mrs. Harding herself. Mr. Beryl was Wood-claw's official mind-writer. I don't remember his first name or his call sign, but I'm pretty sure I merely forgot.

We shook hands, and I sat on a sofa next to Terry.

Once we were all settled, Mrs. Harding asked Ed Regis and me to recount our capture and subsequent escape from the military. Alia stayed hidden away in the bathtub, which was fine. This was our third time to tell this story and Alia didn't need to keep reliving that night.

Mrs. Harding was particularly interested in the telephone conversation I had overheard prior to takeoff. She didn't know what RG stood for either, but she promised to look into it. As to Ms. Decker's claim that the government now worked for the Angels, Mrs. Harding wasn't convinced that the situation was as dire as I feared.

"Converts frequently exaggerate the strength of their faction," explained Mrs. Harding. "It is a natural part of their fanatical faith in their master, and a king's conversion would be absolute. Ms. Decker has probably convinced herself that the Angels have much more control over the government than they actually do. As Major Regis has pointed out, if the Wolves and the rest of the government were completely under Angel control, the Angels would not have to keep their king so well hidden."

"But they have more control than we expected so soon," I said.

"Most certainly, dear," agreed Mrs. Harding, "but until we can find out the extent of the Angels' influence, there are few conclusions we can draw nor any reason for immediate action."

I saw Terry's left eye twitch. Though Terry had given me no details last night, I could only imagine that she had already been through a fairly extensive talk with Mrs. Harding over dinner yesterday. I knew Mrs. Harding was anything but an alarmist, and her meticulously cautious personality was sometimes frustrating for me too.

Mrs. Harding had both Ed Regis and me tell our stories two times each, with several questions being thrown in by her Knights. Debriefing was always like this: lots of tedious repetition and confirmation in the hope that some tidbit of loose memory pops back into place. Unfortunately, nothing more came of it.

Ms. Ferris asked if she could interview Alia, but Mrs. Harding insisted that it wasn't necessary, for which I was grateful. Alia had already told her part of the story to Ed Regis and me while we were waiting in the park yesterday. Decker had used the control bands to shock Alia into submission when she broke free of the soldier escorting her to the other helicopter. Aside from that, Alia's story was no different from mine.

We wrapped up the debriefing a little before noon. Before leaving, Mrs. Harding assured us that we could stay for as long as we needed to and that Wood-claw would see to our living expenses. She also promised to provide some financial aid upon our departure, though it was unlikely that she would buy us a new motorhome. We thanked her many times over.

I figured it was only polite that I invite Mrs. Harding to stay for lunch.

"Perhaps not today, dear, but I would love to come to dinner sometime," replied Mrs. Harding, smiling warmly.

As Mrs. Harding and her Knights left, Alia finally ended her bathe-a-thon and came into the living room, fingertips shriveled to the bone.

"Perfect timing, Alia!" laughed Terry. "Were you listening at the door?"

"I wasn't hiding," insisted Alia. "I just wanted some time for myself."

"You okay now?" I asked. "Batteries charged?"

Alia nodded smilingly.

"Then help me make lunch."

After we ate, Terry introduced us to Wood-claw's training gym, which was the apartment across the hall from Scott's place.

Entering the apartment, I found that what would have been the living room had been covered with gym mats to make a small dojo. The other, smaller rooms were stocked with boxing sandbags and weight sets as well as a number of training machines such as treadmills and exercise bikes. According to Terry, Scott was the one who had originally talked Mrs. Harding into funding the gym's creation, and this was where he and Rachael ran their bi-weekly training program for Alia's former students. Though it was empty at the moment, many Wood-claw residents regardless of psionic power or Knight status trained here in the evenings. The door was never locked, and the location was convenient for Alia and Ed Regis who were restricted to this floor.

The gym was too small to have a shooting range, so the Wood-claw Knights practiced at a private range somewhere else. James was vocally disappointed about this but Alia was predictably happy. I too hoped to spend a few consecutive days away from the sound of gunfire.

For much of that afternoon, our team took turns working out on the machines and sparring on the mat.

Even on the road, we had regularly trained and practiced combat, often using the roadside or empty parking lots as our dojo. We were used to training under the stars on warm, clear nights. But since going outside was forbidden at Wood-claw, this gym was the only place that we could get a proper workout. As Terry often said, your skills are only as good as you keep them, and you can't make excuses for laziness if you're dead. Besides, it being a weekday, everyone we knew was either at work or at school. Candace, who had a job at a fast-food restaurant, wouldn't be back until late evening.

Without my telekinesis, I still couldn't last much more than half a minute against Terry or Ed Regis, so I usually paired with James for our training bouts. Although James was bigger than me, I still had the upper hand, rarely if ever losing a match to him. This was something James had been working very hard this summer to change.

James once said to me, "I know I have a long way to go, but if Terry can fight like that with no powers and only one arm, I'm going to get that good too someday."

I delicately suggested he not use Terry as a point of reference.

James had made remarkable progress in combat technique ever since Terry started training him back in Walnut Lane, but he was always wanting more. James's parents were both Guardian Knights, and James had a score to settle with the Angels for what happened that night in New Haven. I understood that part, and though I didn't share his dedication to the Guardian cause, I sympathized with his impatience. James, who was finally nearing the common age range for developing psionic powers, had been itching for his first all summer long. He believed that he would become a pyroid like his father, hopefully before his twentieth birthday, and more hopefully before the next sunset. Unfortunately, psionic powers develop at their own pace with no regard to people's needs or desires. It wasn't all that uncommon for people to come into their powers well into middle age.

With little else to do, we all ended up training longer than we usually did on our days on the road. As evening crept upon us, Rachael popped in to say hello, and later Walter and Daniel joined us for a short workout. Several other Wood-claw residents came too, including Ms. Isabel "Tigress" Ferris. As Head of Security, she was honor-bound to accept Terry's offer for a few non-psionic rounds on the mat. I was impressed with Tigress's moves, but Terry remained undefeated.

Alia and I returned to our apartment a little earlier than the others to wash up and start preparing dinner. I had invited Candace to eat with us that evening, but shortly before she was expected back at Wood-claw, I got a call from Mrs. Harding asking Terry and me to come up to her place for an "update," as she put it. Leaving Alia in charge of the kitchen, I returned to the dojo and told Terry.

"That was quick," remarked Terry. "Let's go see what she has for us."

"You go, Terry," I said. "I want to—"

"—eat with Candace," Terry finished for me nastily. "But Harding invited you, too, didn't she?"

"Yeah," I admitted with a sigh.

"Then you're coming," Terry informed me.

"Don't worry, Adrian," said Ed Regis, who had been listening in. "It's only been one day, so whatever Mrs. Harding has to say to you, I'm sure it'll be quick."

"Not if my luck holds," I muttered.

Dragging my feet a little, I accompanied Terry up the elevator.

Mrs. Harding's apartment made up half of the seventh floor, where she lived with her extended family plus one addition: a Labrador retriever named Puff, as in the magic dragon, I guessed.

Puff was still a puppy, only six months old, but already heavy enough to make me stagger a little when he pounced on me in the living room. I gingerly patted his head as he slobbered onto my shirt, tail a blur. I liked dogs, but I preferred them smaller, and I was relieved when one of Mrs. Harding's grandchildren took Puff into another room.

Then, just as I had feared, Mrs. Harding invited Terry and me to stay for dinner.

I answered for the both of us, saying with a smile, "We'd love to, Mrs. Harding." It wasn't like I could have refused her invitation, anyway.

Mrs. Harding's daughter was still cooking, so while we waited, Terry and I sat with Mrs. Harding at her coffee table.

"I have been in contact with several faction leaders today," Mrs. Harding informed us. "They are grateful for your information, and they will pass it along to the Guardian Council."

Mrs. Harding wasn't referring to the Council that once ruled the Guardians from New Haven—they were either dead or turned into Angels now. The new Guardian Council, formed after the fall of New Haven, commanded what remained of the unified Guardians. But very little remained, so the Guardians allied themselves with independent factions like Wood-claw as much as possible for trading information, gathering resources and occasionally carrying out joint operations.

"You didn't talk to the Council yourself?" I asked.

"I don't often speak with the Council," explained Mrs. Harding. "We usually deal directly with the Resistance, since they are closer."

"Then what of the Resistance?" asked Terry.

"Patience, Teresa dear," said Mrs. Harding. "I have only initiated the contact process with them today. It could take several days to speak with one of their representatives. When it comes to secrecy, they are even more cautious than I am."

Terry frowned. "You do remember my request?"

Mrs. Harding nodded. "I will pass it along at the appropriate time, dear."

Mrs. Harding was called into the kitchen by her daughter, leaving us alone for a moment.

"What request?" I asked Terry.

"For us to join the Resistance in Lumina," she replied. "I figured that it would be the fastest way to meet their leaders."

"What makes you think they'd want us?"

Terry shrugged and said simply, "I'm Terry Henderson."

I chuckled, realizing that Terry had a very good point there. My combat instructor was never one to brag about her skills, but she knew exactly what she was worth.

Terry mused, "The Resistance, like the rest of the Guardians, would have their sights on Randal Divine, not his daughter. If we can use Lumina as our base of operations… who knows where it'll lead us."

"Speaking of requests," I said hesitantly, "have you thought at all about mine?"

Terry refused to look me in the eyes. "I'm still thinking."

The request I was referring to was an awkward one that I had made to her just over a month ago, back when we were still road-bound, and we hadn't talked about it since.

"Well, don't take forever," I said. "I was almost captured the other day. You weren't there."

"Like I said, Adrian, I'm still thinking," Terry said stiffly. "I don't want to talk about it now."

"Ed Regis and James already agreed," I reminded her.

"Well, I'm not them!" Terry shot back. "And you really should tell Alia, you know."

I scoffed at the notion. "Tell her what?"

"Tell her the truth."

"I don't care how old you think she is, Terry. She's not ready for the truth. Not this one, anyway."

"She'll never be ready for it. I'm not even sure I will."

"Get over it," I suggested.

"Quiet!" hissed Terry as Mrs. Harding returned to announce that dinner was served.

Mrs. Harding's son-in-law was out, but the rest of the family ate together. Mrs. Harding didn't like bringing the war to meals, so the table conversation was primarily about the three grandchildren's school day. There was a point at which Mrs. Harding scolded one of the children for something that he said, but I don't remember any details. More about that later.

After dessert, Mrs. Harding served us some tea as her grandchildren excused themselves to finish their homework. Mrs. Harding's daughter made a phone call.

"I am so sorry, dears," Mrs. Harding said to us. "He'll be up in a moment."

"It's no problem," I replied. "But can I ask you a personal question?"

"Certainly, dear."

"What changed your mind, Mrs. Harding?" I asked.

Mrs. Harding looked surprised. "What changed my mind?"

"What put you back into this war?"

Mrs. Harding sipped her tea for a moment before answering slowly, "I suppose you did, Adrian. You and Teresa, and little Alia... I watched her training our young ones, and I saw how you all inspired Arthur, practically a lifelong non-combatant, to risk everything for our freedom."

"We're really sorry about Merlin, Mrs. Harding," said Terry.

"I'm sorry too," said Mrs. Harding. "I'm sorry I took so long to believe what he believed. I had thought for a long time that the Guardians were a lost cause. I thought our only chance of survival was in concealment. I taught my people to think that way. But Scott and the rest of your trainees showed us that the Guardians still have some fight left in them. And at the mountain camp, when we watched Dr. Land leave us, taking Patrick to live in Lumina, we all saw the consequence of our inaction."

I asked hopefully, "Are you thinking of rejoining the Guardians, then?"

"Unfortunately, no," replied Mrs. Harding. "Wood-claw will remain an independent faction. We will support the Resistance and the rest of the Guardians under the new Council to the best of our ability, but we will not take orders from them. As always, I must consider my own people first."

The doorbell rang, and a moment later Mrs. Harding's daughter ushered Mr. Beryl into the living room.

Glancing at Terry and me, Wood-claw's official mind-writer asked in an amused tone, "Trouble already?"

"Some loose lips over dinner," explained Mrs. Harding. "My grandson."

"Very well," said Mr. Beryl.

I felt a little apprehensive as he approached me and placed his hands on my head. The last time someone tampered with my memory, I had spent almost a year in frustrating confusion.

"Please do not try to block me," said Mr. Beryl. "You are still young so we must be careful. Close your eyes and let your mind go blank."

I did, and a minute later, I heard Mr. Beryl say, "Done. Terry next."

And that is why I can't remember what Mrs. Harding's grandson said over dinner, though I'm sure it must have been a street name or something of that nature.

My fears over memory alteration notwithstanding, Mr. Beryl's work left no scars. Mr. Beryl didn't implant false information or erase my memory of him performing the procedure. This ultimately made all the difference in psychologically coping with the memory loss because I knew that I was a willing participant.

Once Mr. Beryl finished with Terry, we bid Mrs. Harding goodnight.

At the door, Terry pressed Mrs. Harding one last time to make sure that the Guardian Resistance knew of our request to join them in Lumina.

"You have my promise," Mrs. Harding said with a touch of exasperation in her tone. "But it takes a long time to communicate anything with them. Assuming that they accept your offer, realistically speaking, you will probably still have to wait several weeks here before transport can be arranged."

"As long as it takes," Terry said in a forced calm. "Meanwhile, we'll do what we can for Wood-claw."

"Thank you, Teresa dear," said Mrs. Harding.

Once Terry and I were alone in the hall, I couldn't help smiling as I said to myself, "Weeks..."

Terry scowled at me. "Happy now?"

"Absolutely."

Terry shook her head, saying, "Are you sure you want to get involved with Candace? It's not like you're going to get very far with her."

"Do you enjoy reminding me of that?" I asked wearily. "Alia said the same damn thing to me yesterday."

"Sorry," mumbled Terry. "I guess it's none of my business."

We got into the elevator.

While we descended, I considered pressing Terry once more for an answer to the request I had made of her, but decided against it. On most issues, Terry was either quick to decide or already decided, so if she needed more time to think, I would have to give it to her.

Back on the second floor, Terry and I parted in the corridor.

Entering my apartment, I found Ed Regis, Alia and Candace in the living room. They had finished the dinner Alia and I had prepared, and now Ed Regis was dazedly watching the news on TV while Alia and Candace were sitting on the floor, faced off over a deck of cards. James wasn't there so I guessed that he had already returned to his apartment.

"How was dinner at Harding's?" asked Candace.

"I don't know," I replied. "They erased my memory of it. But I did find out that we're going to be here for a few weeks."

Candace smiled broadly. "Care to join us? We're playing Concentration."

"Sure," I said, sitting down with them. I suspected that Alia hadn't had a chance to talk girl stuff with Candace yet, but there was no rush anymore.

As Candace dealt the cards facedown on the floor, I asked her, "How was dinner here?"

"Great," said Candace. "You're still the best cook I know."

"I think Alia did most of the work this time," I said.

"Candace brought us presents," Alia informed me, gesturing toward two cardboard boxes set against the wall.

In addition to the deck of cards, Candace had brought us some board games and an assortment of books and magazines to help us pass the time we would spend trapped indoors at Wood-claw. There was also a paper bag filled with more secondhand clothes for Alia, as well as...

"A unicorn?" I asked, spotting the palm-size fluffy white creature lying at Alia's side.

"A pony," Candace corrected apologetically. "I couldn't find a unicorn."

"Ah," I said, noticing the lack of horn.

"It's still really cute," said Alia, giving her new pet a light pat.

Actually, my sister was pretty much done with stuffed animals, unicorns included—she didn't have any on the motorhome—but she still liked the horned beasts and wore her unicorn-shaped bloodstone pendant day and night. Perhaps Alia was just being polite to Candace, but a fluffy white pony wasn't a bad unicorn substitute and Alia looked happy to have it. I thanked Candace for her consideration.

Using my telekinesis to flip the cards, I played two rounds of Concentration with the girls, but I discovered that my body was itching for a little more physical action. Like most cooks, I always enjoyed a meal more when it was prepared by others, and as such I had imprudently accepted seconds at Harding's. Candace had to go home after the second game anyway, so I decided to head to the gym to burn off some of my excess energy.

The matted dojo was empty, but making my way to the weight room, I was surprised to find James practicing his moves on one of the large punching bags.

I chuckled and said, "I guess I'm not the only one who overate tonight."

James didn't reply, keeping his full attention on the punching bag. It was a tower bag—a heavy cylinder mounted on a weighted pedestal—and James should have been wearing gloves to protect his knuckles, but I noticed that he was using just his bare fists.

Standing behind the bag, I steadied it a little for him, asking uncertainly, "You okay, James?"

"I'm fine," replied James, giving the bag one last pounding before stepping away. "Just want to stay in shape. What did Harding have to say to you?"

I passed him Mrs. Harding's update.

When I finished, James threw me a wry smile and said, "So Terry had already asked Harding to set us up with the Resistance?"

I nodded. "I guess it was the first thing she asked of Harding when you two arrived here."

"Terry never told me anything about it."

"Yeah, she didn't tell me either," I said, shrugging. "You know how she is."

"At least you were invited to Harding's today."

I stared at him. "You're not... bothered by that, are you?"

"Of course not," said James, but he refused to meet my eyes.

I grinned. "Because I would've happily swapped with you and stayed home with Candace."

"I'm not jealous or anything," said James, finally looking at me and laughing. "I was just curious what was going on up there."

James took another round against the tower bag, and as I watched him slam his fists into the leather, I decided that he had every right to be bitter.

Back in Walnut Lane, Merlin had refused to accept James into his mind-blocking class, citing the age restriction for safe mind control. And this despite the fact that James was half a year older than me. I had been treated as a special case because of my Honorary Knight status, but James had trained harder than anyone at Walnut, and when our house was attacked, he had unhesitatingly followed me into the tear-gas-engulfed fray. Despite his comparatively few months of training, James proved himself again and again, leading the front-door team when we attacked the Angel outpost to rescue Alia, and even taking a bullet as he helped Terry and Alia through the last leg of their journey to the Historian. Yet for all of that, James wasn't a Guardian Knight, and Mrs. Harding clearly did not see him in the same way that she saw Terry and me.

I remembered how James had apologized for not helping me out against the pair of cops that had tried to arrest Ed Regis. As far as I was concerned, there really was nothing to apologize for, but I knew from a variety of bitter experiences how maddeningly frustrating it was to feel helpless.

"Come on, James," I said brightly. "Enough with the bag. Give me a few rounds now."

"Sure," said James. "It's never fun when your opponent doesn't hit back."

James was certainly in the mood for a few fast and furious bouts against the living, but I wasn't about to let him beat me. We were good friends and that would have been disrespectful even to an enemy.

"I think I preferred the bag," groaned James when I knocked him down for the tenth time.

But I had come dangerously close to losing my winning streak on the last three rounds. Helping James up, I said, "For what it's worth, I'd much rather you fight with me than against me."

James asked hopefully, "You said we're going to be here for a few weeks, right?"

"Probably."

"Do you think Harding might agree to get someone to teach me blocking?"

"Mind blocking?"

"Yeah."

"That's probably a good idea," I said. "Who knows when we'll get another chance, and I wouldn't mind getting some extra practice in as well."

"Would you ask Harding for me?"

"Why don't you call her yourself?" I suggested. "Terry and Ed Regis will probably want in too."

"Sounds good."

We spent an hour working out on the weights and machines, and then went another ten rounds on the mat. James did win once.

Returning to my apartment all sweaty and tired, I found Ed Regis and Alia still in the living room, though Alia had already bathed and changed into her nightclothes. Facing my sister over the coffee table, the ex-Wolf was initiating her into the world of gambling for profit: they were playing poker over a plate of small peanut-butter cookies.

"Try not to smile so much when you have a good hand, Alia," was Ed Regis's expert advice.

Glancing over Alia's shoulder, I discovered that the joke was on Ed Regis. My sister had nothing but a pair of threes.

I showered, changed, and joined them until bedtime.

As we retired to our rooms for the night, I discovered that so much training on my first day in Wood-claw had taken its toll. I was yawning even more than my sister.

I heard Alia let out a little sigh as she propped her stuffed pony onto her nightstand.

"What's the matter?" I asked. "Too small or not enough horns?"

Alia shook her head. *"It's really cute, but Candace thinks I'm a little kid just like everyone else does."*

First James and now Alia!

"I don't know about everyone else, Ali," I said, "but I'm sure Candace doesn't think that. Anyway, most people haven't seen the things you have, so you can't expect them to understand you."

Alia shrugged.

I knew better than to suggest that there was nothing wrong with Alia staying a kid for a while longer. Instead, I telekinetically lifted the pony up from the nightstand, saying teasingly, "Hey, if you're too grown-up for a hornless unicorn..."

"No!" cried Alia, snatching it back.

"That's what I thought," I laughed.

Alia tried to look angry, but she was smiling too.

6. THE RISE OF THE GUARDIAN ANGELS

The next few days passed uneventfully. We trained when we felt like it, rested and played around when we didn't. But we didn't want to take advantage of our welcome at Wood-claw, especially since we still didn't know exactly how long we would be staying.

Thus Alia returned to her position as lead instructor for Scott and Rachael's kiddie-combat classes while Terry agreed to help train the adult Wood-claw Knights, our own former students included. At first, James and I assisted a little too, but I wasn't really at teaching level for real Knights, and James wasn't even close.

Looking for other ways to help, we learned from Scott about Wood-claw's security watch program, of which Scott was the assistant director. Wood-claw volunteers worked in shifts monitoring security cameras from an office upstairs and patrolling the neighborhood for suspicious activity. James and I couldn't do either of these jobs unless we had our memories wiped at the end of each shift, so we proposed to do just that. Citing the age restriction, Mrs. Harding first rejected our offer, but we insisted on doing our part for Wood-claw, and Mrs. Harding eventually gave in. Scott assigned us to the security office where we spent hours staring at monitors displaying scenes in and around Wood-claw. Mr. Beryl was thorough in his work, and I can't even remember what the inside of the security office looked like, to say nothing of what we saw through the cameras.

Ed Regis did his part for Wood-claw too—by quietly staying out of sight.

Despite his formidable combat experience and the fact that he was well within the safe age range for memory modification, he was neither welcome in the training program nor in the security office. Ed Regis spent much of his time looking through the outdated psionic database he had recovered from Mrs. Harding. Though he couldn't find anything useful in our hunt for the Divines, at least it kept him occupied. Ed Regis still trained with us privately, of course, and when Wood-claw residents occasionally found us in the gym, their reactions ranged from an about-face to a polite request for a training match with the Wolf. In non-psionic engagements, Ed Regis, like Terry, never lost.

Candace and I got a little closer but, unfortunately, a real first date was out of the question since I was trapped inside Wood-claw for the duration of my stay here. I tried hard to get some time alone with my girlfriend every day, but that wasn't easy and more often impossible: I didn't want to impose on Candace's foster family, the gym was often crowded, and the time Candace spent with me over at my apartment was usually shared with my sister. Much like how it had been when I was dating Laila Brown, we were more frequently a trio rather than a duo, and our "dates" were often spent lounging around chatting and playing games. Still, my sister's chaperoning didn't keep Candace and me from holding hands or kissing. I knew without being told that I couldn't allow our relationship to go much further than that anyway, but it was still a treat when we got some time to ourselves.

But then the Historian visited me in a dream one night. The little blond-haired boy stood facing me in a cold white room, flashing his baby blue eyes angrily as he said, "Do be careful not to let your primal impulses interfere with your vow, young Adrian."

"I haven't forgotten my vow, Historian!" I snapped at him irritably. "Don't spy on me!"

After I woke, I couldn't be at all sure that the Historian really had been dreamweaving to me or if my dream had been just that: a dream, perhaps triggered by my frustration over a relationship I could never hope to fulfill. It pained me to be so close to Candace and at the same time know that I had to keep her at bay. Perhaps it was for the better that my sister so frequently stuck around us and kept things from escalating.

Though Alia didn't mention it again, I hadn't forgotten the promise I had made to her on our first night in Wood-claw. As per Terry's order, I did have a private and rather embarrassing talk with Candace in which I asked her to make sure that my sister got all of her girl-only issues squared away. Candace probably thought I was a spineless parent too, but she kindly agreed, and during our first week in Wood-claw, Candace invited Alia up to her apartment three times for sleepovers. These visits were blatant violations of Alia's terms of stay, but Candace promised to make sure my sister wouldn't need memory modification and Mrs. Harding didn't make an issue of it. Thus, ironically, Alia ended up getting more one-on-one time with my girlfriend than I did, but at least I slept a little easier at night knowing that I would never have to talk to my sister about the damned birds and the bees.

Meanwhile, James had made his request to Mrs. Harding for a mind-blocking trainer, but this didn't work out as planned.

Scott was our official Wood-claw liaison. For the most part, this just meant that he and Rachael were in charge of our shopping. But when Mrs. Harding turned down James's request, Scott intervened, logically pointing out that since Mrs. Harding had already agreed to let James subject himself to regular memory alteration, there was little reason not to allow him to start his blocking training. Mrs. Harding countered that attempting to block mind control was always more dangerous than willingly accepting it, but Scott persisted, and Mrs. Harding eventually assigned one of her Knights, a delver named Mr. Hamilton, to be James's trainer.

Delving, which was simply reading current thoughts as opposed to altering one's memory or mental state, was considered comparatively safe to block for first-time learners. My own experience with mental blocking so far had been entirely against puppeteers, so despite the possibility that anti-delving would be a lesser challenge, I nevertheless looked forward to joining James's classes and making sure that I could keep prying eyes out of my head.

But then our one-armed leader found out.

"Are you two insane?!" cried Terry. "You can't let a delver teach you blocking! What if you accidentally think something important?"

"What if someday we need to block our thoughts from our enemies and we can't?" countered James.

I nodded in agreement, adding, "We'll just have to be careful during our lessons not to think anything we want to hide."

"That's a lot easier said than done, Half-head," argued Terry. "Let's say this Mr. Hamilton delves you and asks, 'What's your deepest, darkest secret?' Do you honestly think you can keep certain off-limits thoughts from popping into your head?"

Terry was right: It wasn't possible to control what popped into your head. Nor could we ask for a different blocking trainer without arousing suspicion. It was a choice between one risk and another, but James prudently called Mrs. Harding the next day to cancel his request, citing newfound fears about blocking under the age restriction. Mrs. Harding accepted his excuse without question. James still hoped to get his training soon, possibly if and when we joined the Resistance in Lumina.

We had arrived in Wood-claw a few days into October, and after a week and a day spent out of the sunlight, my seventeenth birthday was upon me. Last year, I had been so busy at Walnut Lane that I had actually forgotten about my birthday, and aside from the slight satisfaction of numerically catching up with James, I wasn't all too excited about this one either. I guess that's just the thing about birthdays: they get old after a while.

At least I was happy not having to cook dinner that night. We partied at Scott's place again, and this time everyone came, including Susan and Heather and even a few of Alia's students. Being across from the gym, Scott's apartment was the semi-official gathering place for the New Haven refugees and their friends. Deeming the crowd too large to cook for, Scott ordered out for lots of pizza while Candace, at Alia's request, had baked two large chocolate cakes.

We ate. We talked. We sang, danced and fought. I didn't want to be sung Happy Birthday but Candace and Alia led the chorus anyway—and more than once. Personally, I would have preferred a quieter evening, but it was nice to see everyone having a good time. When it came time to blow out the candles, however, I was in for a big surprise. We all were, actually.

They had lit seventeen long, thin candles on one of the two cakes, and I inhaled deeply to get them all in one breath. But before I could blow on the candles, half of them suddenly flickered out.

"What was that?" I said, as stunned as the crowd watching me.

After a moment of bewildered silence, Terry said in a quiet voice, "I'm not sure, but I think it was me."

"Try it again," suggested Rachael.

Terry looked at the remaining lit candles on the cake, carefully as if studying their weaknesses. Another puff of air blew over the chocolate frosting, and three more candles went dark.

"Congratulations," James said to Terry. "Looks like you're a windmaster."

"The birth of a new psionic!" exclaimed Scott, clapping. "Happy birthday, Terry!"

There were cheers and applause for the newborn psionic, but Terry herself looked more confused than happy. I wondered how she felt about inheriting one of the primary powers of her late grandfather who she had despised so much.

"Be my guest," I said to her, gesturing toward the remaining candles. "Blow them out."

Terry looked again at the cake. But what came next wasn't a mere puff of candle-extinguishing air. It was a gust of hurricane-force wind which tore the top layer off the cake, spattering my shirt and face.

Wiping the chocolate frosting off my cheek, I laughed with the rest of the crowd as I said to Terry, "You're going to need to learn how to control that."

Terry nodded slowly, and then, finally overcoming her shock, smiled.

Though he probably sorely wished it had been himself, James graciously congratulated Terry again. I was happy for her too, as I considered this to be something far more worth celebrating than the seventeenth anniversary of Adrian Howell. Terry didn't really need psionics to complement her already formidable combat skills, but considering the nature of our mission, there was no such thing as too much firepower. I had a feeling that we would need everything we had before we were done.

In the evening of the very next day, Mrs. Harding called for an emergency all-Wood-claw meeting to announce something far less celebratory.

With the exception of Ed Regis, Alia and perhaps a few parents taking care of little kids, everyone in the building had crammed themselves into Mrs. Harding's living room. Poor Puff was nowhere to be seen. Meeting up with Scott, Candace and others, Terry, James and I carefully nudged our way through the crowd to a place by the wall where we could just barely see Mrs.

Harding. The aged leader's frown told us that she was about to say exactly what we had all been afraid of.

Once she had everyone's attention, Mrs. Harding spoke slowly with frequent, deliberate pauses to make sure she wouldn't have to repeat herself. "The official announcement came from Lumina today," she said gravely. "Due to the increasing number of former Guardians, entire breakaway factions, in fact, that have both willingly and unwillingly been absorbed into the Angels, King Divine has now seen fit to rename his faction. They are now officially the Guardian Angels."

One of the men in the crowd asked incredulously, "Is that what we're going to call them?"

"You may call them what you like," replied Mrs. Harding, "but there is no doubt that King Divine has indeed converted and reunified enough of the Guardians to make such a claim. In fact, it seems to be at the request of Mr. Travis Baker himself that King Divine agreed upon the name change. Many of you know this already, but Mr. Baker, once the leader of the New Haven Guardians, is now King Divine's chief political advisor. Many other members of the former New Haven Council also serve in top positions of King Divine's organization, so regardless of what we may choose to call them, they are the de facto Guardian Angels."

There were murmurs of displeasure at this assessment, but nobody contested it.

That Mr. Baker now worked for King Divine wasn't news to me. We had already heard at other Guardian settlements how the old New Haven Council had been folded into King Divine's new government. However, when we discovered that Ms. Jodie Decker, a former top-level Guardian Knight, had been put into a position where she apparently had direct access to the Divine family, it was a troubling new development. Terry had predicted back then that it was only a matter of time before the Angels made this claim of reunification. Randal's announcement would be another severe blow to Guardian morale, and could very likely entice more Guardians as well as independents to surrender and accept conversion.

Always the politician, Mrs. Harding had carefully saved her good news for the end. She cleared her throat to silence the muttering crowd and continued, "As to the rumors of the Guardian Angels being in control of multiple world governments, we believe these stories are, in fact, greatly, greatly exaggerated. There is no evidence what-so-ever that any world leaders have been converted. While it is true that the Guardian Angels seem to have some limited influence over a few of our own government agencies including the police, internal revenue, military intelligence and the Wolves, they do not rule this nation nor any other at the present time. Of course we must remain alert for further developments and be more careful in our dealings with local government and law enforcement, but we must not give up hope or cut our ties with the true Guardians, the Resistance or the Council."

Glancing around the crowd once, Mrs. Harding added, "I strongly feel that it is both irresponsible and counterproductive to act upon hearsay, and I would ask everyone here to be mindful about spreading and believing baseless rumors."

I cringed. Some of those rumors had been started or inflated due to the manner of our arrival in Wood-claw. Following our first dinner at Scott's place, Walter and Daniel had lost no time telling everyone they knew our account of the Wolf plane, and things had snowballed from there.

After taking a few questions, Mrs. Harding announced certain changes in Wood-claw's security measures. This mostly concerned the establishment of a Knight outpost somewhere on the other side of the city, but the specific details of this plan weren't meant for Terry, James and me, so they were later scrubbed from our memories.

"As you all know," Mrs. Harding said at the end, "we have in our company one of the Guardians' greatest Knights, Ms. Teresa Henderson, who is currently volunteering her expertise in our combat training program. I strongly advise all of you to take advantage of this unique opportunity and improve your skills. This war is far from over and, as always, we must do all that we can to protect our future freedom."

With that, Mrs. Harding dismissed the crowd, but she showed no surprise when Terry, James and I remained for a few extra words.

"Still no plan to rejoin the Guardians, Mrs. Harding?" I asked.

"It may come to that," admitted Mrs. Harding, "but not yet."

Terry asked, "What about the Resistance?"

Mrs. Harding nodded. "I have passed on your request, Teresa, and they seemed to regard it favorably. However, it will take some more time to get an official answer and then to organize your passage. The Resistance will be driven deeper underground now that the king's influence is spreading more rapidly."

Terry smirked. "So I guess they weren't all just rumors?"

After an uncomfortable pause, Mrs. Harding replied carefully, "Unfortunately, no, dear. Or rather, they are not entirely *baseless,* but they are still rumors and should be treated as such."

"Which ones?" demanded Terry. "Which ones aren't baseless?"

"All of them."

I realized that one of Mrs. Harding's main reasons for calling this meeting had been fear control. She wanted to keep her people from losing all hope. After all, who was to say how much the self-declared Guardian Angels had infiltrated top-level government or how much faster their progress would become once they got rolling?

This unsettling question, along with Travis Baker and Randal Divine's new name for their faction, kept me awake long after Alia had fallen asleep that night. Alia, perhaps also troubled by Mrs. Harding's announcement (which we had passed to her and Ed Regis over dinner), hadn't let out a single telepathic murmur, and I missed her voice in my head. Unable to keep my eyes closed, I gave up at around midnight and crawled out of my bed, levitating myself to the door so as not to wake Alia with my footsteps.

With only one small nightlight built into the wall, the living room was nearly pitch-black, but I left the lights off as I plopped myself down onto one of the sofas, putting my feet up on the coffee table. Staring blankly into the darkness Alia-fashion, I sorely wished I was back at my favorite window overlooking New Haven where I used to sit with my sister when I couldn't sleep. This place didn't even have windows, and despite being above ground, it suddenly felt more claustrophobic than many of the underground places I had been trapped in. It was strange how something as innocent as a name change could so completely shift my perception of this conflict, but there was no denying that our time was running out. It was like a schoolteacher had just reminded me that a major project he had assigned three weeks ago was due tomorrow morning, and I hadn't even started it.

Sensing motion in the room, I telekinetically flipped on the light switch. Ed Regis jumped a little in surprise.

"I didn't notice you there, Adrian," he said, squinting in the light.

"Can't sleep?" I asked.

Ed Regis nodded.

I got up from my sofa and followed Ed Regis into the kitchen.

"What are you looking for?" I asked as I watched him open several cupboard doors.

"I thought I might pour myself a glass of wine. I know you hide it somewhere around here."

I opened the correct cupboard for him, pulling out a bottle of cheap red that I sometimes used in my cooking. "Grab me a glass too and I'll pour it."

"You?" Ed Regis asked in surprise. "You hardly ever drink."

"It's just one of those nights," I replied.

Ed Regis found the wineglasses, and we returned to the living room.

Ed Regis was right, by the way. After my first monster hangover back in New Haven, I wasn't much more than a very occasional social drinker. Drugs, alcohol and other highs really weren't my thing. As a wild-born psionic destroyer, my life was crazy enough and I had little desire for additional stimulation.

"Guardian Angels..." I mused, sipping slowly. "I guess the storm is finally upon us."

"We were lucky to find a way into the Resistance in time," said Ed Regis.

"Do you really think we're in time?"

Ed Regis shrugged. "We'll find out soon enough."

I said darkly, "Even if we get into Lumina, there's no guarantee that we'll find the next step there."

"One step at a time," said Ed Regis.

I nodded.

We sat silently for a minute. Watching me finish my glass, Ed Regis poured me another and then asked quietly, "What is it, Adrian?"

I stared down at my wine. "Things are getting a lot more dangerous."

"I suppose they are."

"Terry still won't agree to my request."

Ed Regis gave me a wry smile. "I can hardly blame her. To be honest, I'm having some second thoughts as well."

"Well, I'm not letting you off it," I informed him. "You know it's necessary."

"If I had a spare bullet, I'd save it for my enemies."

"If Randal Divine gets me alive, then I will be your enemy."

Ed Regis didn't reply.

I said, "You may think I had no plan on that airplane, Ed Regis, but actually I did. I figured they would kill me or somehow I'd escape, and either way would be a win for us."

Ed Regis shook his head in wonder. "You really are prepared to do anything, aren't you?"

"Not anything," I said, telekinetically lifting the wine bottle and refilling Ed Regis's glass. "But almost."

"In that case, might I return to the topic of next steps for a moment and suggest that the next logical step is already in sight?"

I narrowed my eyes. "What are you talking about?"

"There's only one person in Lumina who could definitely point us to the Divines, Adrian. You know this."

"Never!" I said. "Absolutely not."

Ed Regis cocked an eyebrow. "Are you about to remind me of the rules of war?"

"There are no rules of war with psionics," I replied quietly. "I remember you said that, and maybe it's true. But I still have rules—my own. And one of them is that Cindy is off-limits."

"Cindy Gifford might be our only link to the Divines. Are you really prepared to lose this war over her protection?"

Ed Regis had been with us for a while now, and he should have known better than to try reasoning with me over something like this. I drained my glass and set it down on the coffee table as I said to him icily, "You just don't get it, do you? The only reason I want to win this war *is* for Cindy's protection. I don't care about the rest of the world, Ed Regis. I don't care about justice. I don't care about the future of goddamn strangers. I care for only one future. One specific, personal, selfish future. And that can't become a reality if Cindy isn't in it."

Refusing to back down, Ed Regis finally broke the taboo. "You'd kill your own sister but an adoptive mother is off-limits?"

I glared at him, seething. A crack appeared in my wineglass as I growled through clenched teeth, "I don't have the luxury of principles, Major! I have to save who I can!"

Ed Regis didn't reply, but slowly bowed his head.

I steadied my breathing and forced myself to calm down. Then I said in a low voice, "Just remember, you and Terry may be our leaders, but this is *my* mission, Ed Regis. My mission, my rules."

"Fair enough," said Ed Regis. "But if you feel that strongly about your future, then you had better do your very best to stay alive."

"I always do," I said wryly, standing up. "That's one of my rules too."

I looked down at the hairline crack in my wineglass and sighed. It had been a long time since I had lost control of my power like this. I telekinetically lifted the glass up and tossed it into the trash.

Ed Regis said, "I'm sorry I upset you, Adrian, but I had to try."

"It's alright," I mumbled. "I was already in a pretty foul mood so now was the time to suggest it. Goodnight, Ed Regis."

I returned to my bedroom, quietly shut the door behind me, tiptoed to my bed and slipped under my blanket. After resting my head on my pillow for a minute, I sat back up in my bed and whispered into the darkness, "I can always tell by your breathing when you're awake, Alia."

Alia remained silent, but the dim glow from the nightlight was just enough for me to see her body tense up.

"You were listening at the door, weren't you?" I said.

My sister continued to lie perfectly still, but said quietly into my head, *"You really should, Addy."*

"Should what?"

"Care," she said, sitting up on her bed and looking at me disapprovingly. *"About the world. Cindy isn't the only one we should be trying to save."*

"Why?" I scoffed. "Why should we fight for strangers?"

"Because..." Alia said carefully. *"Because you and me... we were strangers once, a long time ago. And Cindy was a stranger too."*

I smiled, realizing that Alia had a very legitimate point. "Well, in my defense, Alia, if we succeed, it'll help everyone, not just us."

Letting out a little huff, Alia fell back onto her bed and stared up at the ceiling. I wondered if she had been listening to the earlier part of my conversation with Ed Regis as well, but I couldn't exactly ask her.

I didn't have to. Pulling her blanket up around her neck, Alia asked worriedly, *"Did you really have Terry and Ed promise to kill you?"*

There was no way out of it. "There were conditions involved," I explained quietly, "but yes, I did. I asked James too. Only Terry hasn't agreed yet."

My sister didn't reply, and when the silence became unbearable, I added, "I just can't afford to be caught by Randal."

"Cindy was caught," Alia pointed out. *"We can still get her back because she's alive."*

True, but that logic only worked if there was someone left outside of Randal's empire to oppose him. I couldn't take that chance with my own life, especially considering how Randal was planning to use me if he ever managed to get me alive. Even if I failed in my mission to kill the Angel queen, there was no way I could fail my other mission to rid the world of its last master-controller bloodline.

"It's different with Cindy," I said. "Besides, I meant everything else I said too. I don't actually want to die."

"I'm glad," Alia said evenly, *"because if you don't call this off, Adrian, I'm going to talk to them too. I'm going to make them promise me that they won't kill you no matter what happens. Then we'll find out which of us they really listen to."*

This was exactly why I didn't want my sister to know about my request. "Don't fight me on this, Alia," I said weakly. "Please."

Alia turned her head toward me. Even in the darkness I could see the cold fury in her eyes as she whispered, *"You're forgetting, Adrian, that I have a mission too. Someone has to keep you alive."*

"Suit yourself," I said, turning onto my side, away from her.

Sleep still felt like a long way off.

7. POWER AND COMMITMENT

Alia spent much of the next morning in one of her silences, but I could tell that she wasn't as angry at me as she was frustrated with the whole situation. Of course she was angry at me too, and the fact that she had called me Adrian last night showed just how much. But as always, I quietly sat with her until she was ready to talk to me again, and she gave me a weak smile before noon.

That didn't mean I was off the hook, though.

"Last chance to do this yourself, Addy," Alia warned me as the five of us sat down to eat lunch together.

I replied stubbornly, "You have your mission, Alia. I have mine."

So Alia made her case to our team, arguing that I shouldn't have made such an impossible request in the first place. Terry was the quickest to agree, of course. Ed Regis folded next, promising Alia that no situation, however dire, would make him waste a bullet on me.

Only James stood by my side. Despite Alia's best efforts to stare him down, he firmly argued, "The success of this mission is more important than the lives of any one of us, Alia. Adrian knows this, as should we all. If he's willing to sacrifice his life for the greater good, then I think we should respect that."

That wasn't really how I saw it—particularly the part about the "greater good"—but I was grateful for his support.

"You still have the majority," I conceded to Alia over dessert. "Happy now?"

"Not really," Alia replied in a forced calm. "But it's a start."

I had a feeling that James was in for a rough ride.

Later, when I got a moment alone with Ed Regis, I asked him if his new promise to Alia was really going to supersede his agreement with me.

"Let's just say that I promised you both," replied Ed Regis, "and if and when the time comes, I'll decide which promise to break."

"I expected more professionalism from a Wolf," I said reproachfully.

"Ex-Wolf," Ed Regis reminded me. "Besides, I tried being professional last night and you didn't like it."

I scowled at him.

In the evening, I confronted Terry and James in the gym about Ed Regis's unacceptable tactical suggestion regarding the Heart of Lumina. Just as I had suspected, they had both heard the ex-Wolf's idea long ago.

"I told the major that you'd never agree to anything that could end up hurting Cindy," said Terry, shaking her head.

"We both did," put in James.

"How do you really feel about it, though?" I asked, remembering James's assertion over lunch that no one person's life was more important than the success of the mission.

"I'm not all that for it, either," James replied carefully. "But I do think we should keep an open mind to every option."

"This one isn't an option," I said firmly, and we didn't discuss it any further.

Two days later, we learned that the Resistance would indeed allow us into their base of operations within Lumina, but that we would have to wait another three full weeks before transport could be arranged. We wouldn't be leaving Wood-claw until a week into November.

And so the uncomfortable waiting game in Wood-claw continued. Fortunately, we weren't just sitting around. James and I increased our volunteer hours in the security office, allowing other security members more time to their families and thus boosting our standing in the community. Terry and Alia continued teaching their classes. Alia, with the help of Susan, Scott and Rachael, increased her bi-weekly kiddie-combat classes to run every day, and her eager students always showed up. Ed Regis was also to be seen more frequently in the gym, assisting Terry with the adult classes which, after Mrs.

Harding's announcement, had doubled in enrollment.

"I can't thank you enough, Teresa dear," said Mrs. Harding when she visited the gym to observe Terry's lesson once. "The Angels are going to be in for a big surprise if they attack us now."

After Mrs. Harding's initial announcement about the formation of King Divine's Guardian Angels, not even she called them by their new name, so no one else did either. We were all used to calling them the Angels and we had little reason to humor their egos. It was a small defiance, but an important one.

Even in her combat classes, Terry kept her newfound talent as a windmaster so completely out of sight that few people realized she had become psionic at all. After her initial discovery, Terry had been carefully avoiding prying eyes, practicing alone in her room or in the gym during the early mornings. Just occasionally, she let me and Alia watch as she concentrated on moving the air from one side of the room to the other and back again.

The thing about psionic power is that whether you learn to control it or not, it can grow quickly once it gets started. Within a week of my birthday, Terry had pretty much become a full-blown windmaster. She still couldn't control the air very well, but she could create short gusts of wind strong enough to knock down anyone who wasn't bracing for it.

There were two major downsides to becoming psionic: the need for hiding protection out in the open and the ever-present risk of metal draining. Draining was Terry's main concern.

"I don't want to be a windmaster at all if it's going to weaken my real fighting ability," said Terry.

I grinned. "Yeah, well, once you're psionic, you're stuck with it like everyone else so you'd better get used to it."

Despite her concern, Terry didn't develop dire drain-weakness the way that I had. While she claimed that being drained made her tired, it didn't show in her movements as far as I could see. Nevertheless, Terry borrowed my draining ring and used it during her combat training to overcome her new Achilles' heel as completely as possible.

"This air shield is going to come in really handy for crowd control," Terry said happily when she first succeeded in creating a short-lived mini-tornado around her body.

"Just remember what you once said to me about newborn psionics," I warned her.

"I know that, Half-head," Terry replied lightly. "Real power isn't psionics anyway. Real power is just willpower."

In the short term, Terry's psionic training was geared more toward self-control than active use in combat, but I was sure that she would find use for it soon enough. We weren't going to stay in the safety of Wood-claw much longer.

Meanwhile, Alia once again proved that her power was the greatest of all of us when she was called upon to help save the life of a young Wood-claw resident. The child, a four-year-old boy named Samuel, had been born with a congenital heart defect, and his open heart surgery had originally been scheduled for January of the next year. However, jumping on the opportunity to have a psionic healer present at the operation, the boy's family begged Alia's assistance.

"Wood-claw has never had a permanent healer," Samuel's mother said to Alia. "We know it was wrong to let you be taken by the Angels back in Walnut Lane, and we are truly sorry we didn't help."

"That was a long time ago," said Alia, "and your son is innocent."

Mrs. Harding allowed Alia, blindfolded, to accompany the child and his parents to the city hospital. Neither the heart surgeons nor hospital personnel were connected to Wood-claw, so it wasn't easy smuggling an eleven-year-old girl into Samuel's operating room. With the help of other psionics, namely peacemakers and mind-writers, the Wood-claw Knights tightly controlled the scene, thus allowing Alia to assist the non-faction doctors successfully complete Samuel's operation in record time.

Alia, along with Samuel and his parents, returned to Wood-claw all smiles that very night. If Alia hadn't been there, Samuel's recovery might have taken weeks, not hours, to say nothing of the added risks of relying on human medicine. Under the circumstances, the joy that the family felt was only natural, but I was particularly happy for Alia. My sister rarely got the chance to help people outside of the psionic war, and I could see that she was delighted to finally do something other than take care of bloody noses, broken bones and gunshot wounds.

During our stay, we had all done our best to repay the Wood-claw Guardians for their hospitality, but Alia's assistance at the hospital was the icing on the cake. With under a week left till our scheduled departure, Mrs. Harding announced that henceforth, Wood-claw would fully fund our mission against the Angels for however long it took to bring down King Randal Divine.

"Within reasonable bounds, of course," added Mrs. Harding. "We are a small community."

A new motorhome suddenly didn't seem entirely out of the question, but we wouldn't need one in Lumina. In fact, it was hard to know what we would need. This made planning our next step pretty much impossible. All we knew was that the next step, whatever it was, was coming. November was already upon us.

After a full month's vacation, the looming prospect of leaving the sanctuary of Wood-claw and returning to the open world—and the Angel city beyond—was probably what caused it. I woke early one morning with my nose and forehead lightly pressed against the floor as if I had fallen out of my bed, or so it seemed until gravity regained its hold on me and the floor turned out to be the ceiling. It had been so long since this had last happened that I was completely unprepared for it. Alia woke with a start as I made a loud and painful crash-landing.

I gingerly sat up on the cold wooden floor and massaged my throbbing back.

Alia turned on her bedside light, asking, *"Addy? Are you okay? What happened?"*

"Nothing, Ali," I groaned. "I'm fine."

Alia laughed as she realized why I was on the floor. *"I thought only kids did that."*

"I know," I said, cringing. I felt as embarrassed as I would be if I had wet my bed. Seventeen years old and I was sleep-hovering! "Please don't tell anyone," I begged.

"No promises," said Alia as she knelt beside me and lifted my shirt to check for bruises. *"Anyway, it serves you right for trying to act so tough."*

Alia was still upset with me over my position on capture, and she hadn't managed to sway James's opinion either.

"It's not about acting tough," I said patiently as Alia ran her healing hands over my back. "Anything can happen, and I—"

"I know!" Alia cut across me angrily. *"No happily ever after! I remember and I'm okay with that! But if I had asked James and everyone else to kill me, they wouldn't have agreed. And if they did, you would have stopped them. You think you're being noble, Adrian, but you're just being horrible!"*

"I hate it when you call me Adrian," I said miserably, looking away. "You make me feel so small."

After a moment, Alia said in a quieter tone, *"I know this mission is important, Addy, but I can't lose you again. I just can't."*

I closed my eyes and sighed. "Then you had better keep trying to convince James to change his mind."

"I will," said Alia, finishing up the work on my back. *"And you're right, by the way. Anything can happen. Even good things. You'll see. It'll be alright in the end."*

There was never much to be gained by arguing with my sister. If she was proven right, it would be great for me too. If she was wrong, she'd find out soon enough.

As to the possibility of "anything happening," something actually did happen later that very day.

It was a little after 1pm, and I was in the kitchen washing the dishes when the telephone rang. Actually, it didn't ring so much as beep loudly.

"Isn't that the alarm?" called Ed Regis from the living room where he and Alia were playing cards.

All the telephones in the Wood-claw apartments were wired to the building's security office so that this alternate ring of repeating electronic beeps would alert residents to an emergency situation. We had been told about this system upon our arrival, but this was the first time for us to actually hear the alarm go off.

Putting down the plates, I hurried back to the living room. Terry and James joined us in moments. Being a member of Wood-claw's security team, I knew that the main panic alarm was a single, non-stop tone which meant battle stations for everyone, but this current beeping was just a mild caution. James picked up the phone receiver once and put it back down, and the beeping stopped.

"Just stay put," said James who, like me, knew Wood-claw's security protocols inside and out. "That was a low-level alert. No immediate threat. We should be getting a call soon."

The phone rang normally a minute later and James picked it up again to hear what the commotion was about. The security team on duty had to call every apartment in the building so James kept the conversation short, but he still got the basic story.

"There's been an incident at the new outpost," James explained to us. "The Knights caught a pair of Seraphim snooping around their neighborhood. It looks like they were alone, but we have to be ready just in case there're more headed this way."

"Scott's out there," I said, remembering that Scott had gone on a sleepover inspection tour since yesterday morning and wasn't due back until later tonight.

"They said 'caught'?" Terry asked James. "Caught and not killed?"

"Caught," confirmed James. "Alive."

"I'm going out there," said Terry.

"Me too," James and I said together.

"Then I'm going too," said Alia.

I shook my head. "Mrs. Harding won't let you go, Alia. Memory rules."

"I don't care about Mrs. Harding's rules," Alia said defiantly. "I'm going."

I knew why Alia was being so adamant, of course. She was afraid that we—or rather specifically I—was going to hurt or kill the Angel captives. And she was perfectly justified in her assumption.

"You being there isn't going to change anything that happens," I warned her.

"I don't care," Alia said again. "I'm still going."

"Fine," said Terry. "But none of us know the location of the outpost, so we can't go without a guide, and that means we'll need Harding's okay."

I breathed a silent sigh of relief as Terry picked up the phone to call Mrs. Harding. Ed Regis hadn't even joined the conversation, knowing he would never be allowed to visit the outpost. Though for different reasons, Alia would be treated the same as him, which meant that I didn't have to be the one forcing her to stay at home while Terry, James and I questioned the captured Seraphim.

Mrs. Harding's phone line was busy and Terry had to call five times before she got through to one of Mrs. Harding's grandchildren, who informed Terry that Grandma had just left for the outpost.

Slamming down the receiver, Terry said disgustedly, "We should have just gone upstairs!"

"Maybe they're still in the parking lot," said James.

Terry jumped at the idea and sprinted out, returning three minutes later, all smiles.

"Nice call, James," she said. "I got Harding waiting for us in their van. But there are only two seats available." Terry looked at Alia, saying firmly, "You're not coming. Harding's orders."

Alia stared back at her in stony-faced silence.

Only two seats. James and I looked at each other. After a moment of awkward silence, James nodded and said, "You go, Adrian. You and Terry are the ones who need to ask the questions."

"Personally, I would rather it was you," I said honestly. "But you're probably right. We'll try to call you from the outpost."

In addition to Mrs. Harding, Terry and me, the van carried five more, all Knights including Mr. Beryl. We weren't blindfolded this time, but Mr. Beryl later deleted our memories of the roundtrip. In fact, the only part of my visit to the Wood-claw outpost that I remember starts as Terry and I accompany Mrs. Harding down a flight of creaky wooden stairs into a musty basement. The other Knights that came with us in the van stayed upstairs.

We stepped into a makeshift jail cell of concrete and bricks. Scott and two other Wood-claw Knights were there, including Hammer, the grumpy Knight who had originally driven us into Wood-claw. He still looked ill-tempered, but he had good reason this time and he wasn't the only one.

The Seraphim were both dead.

"We're sorry," Hammer said to Mrs. Harding. "They were alive until a short time ago."

The corpses sat slumped down on the floor, their backs resting against the far wall. Their wrists and ankles shackled, the Seraphim had been psionically drained and completely immobilized with heavy iron chains. Their heads were both bloody messes.

"What happened here?" demanded Mrs. Harding.

Hammer explained, "We caught them by surprise and managed to restrain them without too much trouble. But then, down here, we made the mistake of leaving them unattended for a few minutes. No more than five minutes, but it was enough."

I looked at the limp bodies again and realized what had happened. Unable to escape, unable to even move, the Seraphim had bashed their heads against the concrete wall over and over until their skulls cracked open.

"We just didn't expect them to kill themselves," the other Knight said apologetically.

"Why not?" I asked, frustrated.

"Randal Divine's converts don't often commit suicide," explained Scott. "They prefer to fight to the death, and even when they're caught, they never give up trying to fight."

Actually, I did know this. But that signified something even more important which Terry voiced first. "These guys weren't ordinary scouts," she said, frowning at the corpses. "They knew something."

"If they knew anything important, why were they being used as scouts?" asked Scott.

"Maybe they weren't scouts at all," suggested Terry. "Maybe they found this place by accident or something. Whatever the case, they didn't want to risk being delved."

"That's for sure," I muttered, staring at all the blood covering the dead men's faces and stuck to their hair. It wasn't the kind of suicide that just anyone could handle. Not like chugging sleeping pills or jumping off a bridge. You had to be converted to do something this crazy.

Another dead end. We had seen many on the road this year. But this dead end was an especially frustrating one. After all, these Seraphim had killed themselves to avoid interrogation, which practically proved that they had something that could have helped us. Perhaps just a link to another link to yet another, but that still might have taken us all the way to the king himself. And to the queen.

"We need to find out who they were," Terry said quietly. "And more importantly, who they knew."

"We can start with the Wolf database," I suggested. "Did these guys have any ID?"

"No," said Scott. "We found nothing at all on them."

"Then let's wash their faces and take some pictures."

Fortunately, most of the damage to their heads was on the backs and sides, so once we wiped the blood off of their faces, we got fairly decent mug shots of them. We also took fingerprints and hair samples, and Scott informed us that one of the men had been a peacemaker while the other was a light-foot. Evidence in hand, we returned to Wood-claw, arriving just in time for a steak dinner that Alia and Ed Regis had prepared for us. But I had lost most of my appetite.

"Sorry we couldn't call," I said to James. "It didn't go as planned."

"Things rarely do," commented James. "So what did you find out?"

I preferred our dinner conversation to be about something other than people bashing their own skulls apart in desperate suicide, but James and Ed Regis were eager to be filled in, so I let Terry make our report.

"We need to know who these guys are," said Terry, passing the pictures of the Seraphim's faces to Ed Regis.

Ed Regis frowned. "Unfortunately, the portable version of the database doesn't have face or fingerprint matching. I'd need access to the main database at my old office to do a proper search."

"Except that your office belongs to someone else now," James pointed out.

"We'll just have to sift through the mugs on the portable and see if we can match up the faces on our own," said Ed Regis.

"How long is that going to take?"

"There are enough entries in the database to take years, but I'll start with the most likely suspects. I can search by psionic powers and affiliations. Still, it could take several weeks, and that's assuming their faces really are in the database."

"We're gone the day after tomorrow," James reminded him. "You promised to leave the database in Wood-claw."

"That is a problem," admitted Ed Regis.

"I have a better idea," said Terry. "We can just take these photos to the Resistance. They'll have more current data on the Angels and might be able to identify them. These guys were important, after all."

"Agreed," said Ed Regis. "But we should leave copies of these pictures with Scott and let him take a crack at it too. If he gets lucky, he can contact us in Lumina."

Alia had been silent throughout the entire meal, and remained so even after her bath.

"You feel sorry for those men?" I asked as we got ready for the night.

Alia winced. *"Is it that obvious?"*

"To me, yes," I said. "I feel sorry for them, too."

Alia looked up at me in surprise. *"You do?"*

I nodded. "Those men did what they did because they were converted. They were victims of Randal and Catherine just like everyone else. They would have done anything for their master."

"You're really scared of that, aren't you, Addy?"

"I'm not going to end up like them, Alia."

Alia gazed at me silently. I studied her face for a moment, and then cried exasperatedly, "Oh, for the last time, it's just a precaution!"

"A stupid precaution," Alia said resentfully.

"It helps me sleep."

Alia sighed and gave me a sympathetic smile. *"Then you better try to convince Ed and Terry to change their minds."*

I shook my head. "It's okay, Ali. You can keep the majority."

The next day was our last full day in Wood-claw. I spent much of it with Candace, who had taken a day off from work just to be with me. Privacy was still a rare commodity around here, but I asked Alia nicely and she agreed to spend the day out of our way.

I hadn't forgotten my vow or the Historian's warning in my dream, but upon careful consideration, I had come to the conclusion that my vow was specifically about not having children. And I made sure that we didn't. Aside from that detail, exactly how Candace and I spent our last day together is strictly need-to-know, as in you don't.

Finally, the day of our departure was upon us. We were leaving at 6am, but even so, a fair-size crowd had come to see us off. Alia huddled with her combat kids while the rest of us shook hands with the adults. James and I were given a round of applause by our security co-volunteers who assured us that our work had been flawless, though we remembered none of it. Terry also received much thanks for her short but highly intensive combat courses, and even Ed Regis got a few handshakes.

Goodbyes were always tough, but this one was especially hard for me. We had no idea how long we would be in Lumina or where we might head from there, so I couldn't give Candace any assurances at all.

"I really hope I see you again, Adrian," Candace whispered into my good ear as we stood in tight embrace. "But if I don't, it better not be for a lack of trying."

"I promise," I said, and she kissed me in a way that made me levitate.

When we broke apart, Candace said seriously, "Take care of Alia, okay?"

"I always do," I replied, touching my feet back down onto the floor.

"And take care of yourself too."

"I'll try."

I tried to kiss her again, but she stopped me. Taking a step back, Candace giggled and said playfully, "So you have something to come back for."

I smiled.

One last round of goodbyes, thank-yous and well-wishing, and our five-man team was blindfolded and led down into the building's basement parking lot and onto a van. Scott and Rachael accompanied us again along with Wood-claw's Head of Security, Ms. Isabel "Tigress" Ferris. Our blindfolds were removed once our van was sufficiently away from the Wood-claw building.

Although one of the reasons we had originally come to Wood-claw was so that Terry could recruit a few more Knights for a possible attack on an Angel settlement, that plan had been put on indefinite hold, so we weren't actually taking Scott, Rachael or Ms. Ferris into Lumina with us. It was just the five of us again.

I looked over at Alia, who had the window seat next to me. My sister was silently staring outside, unfocused, watching the city go by. We passed into a tunnel. Catching my reflection in the glass, she turned to me and smiled.

"Thanks, Addy," she said quietly.

"For what?" I asked.

"For not telling me to stay behind in Wood-claw."

"I wouldn't have dared," I said with a chuckle. Then I asked, "Are you still mad at me?"

Alia shook her head.

"What we do," I said slowly, "and where we're going now... is dangerous, Alia. I'm going to need you in my corner."

Alia nodded and whispered into my head, *"Always."*

8. RAIDER AND THE PHANTOM TRAIN

Within an hour, we reached an airport at the edge of the city where a small chartered airplane was standing by. There we bid our driver, Scott, goodbye, but Rachael and Ms. Ferris boarded the airplane with us. We were asking the Guardian Resistance to break a few of their security protocols regarding access to their Lumina headquarters, so Ms. Ferris had agreed to come along and vouch for us. Rachael, of course, was our hider, and though she could have simply given us enough individual protection to last up to the handover, after what happened the last time, she didn't want to take any chances.

We landed in the nearest large city to Lumina early that evening. From there, Ms. Ferris drove us in a rented van to our rendezvous with the Resistance representatives who were in charge of smuggling us into the Angel city.

I had been expecting our meeting to take place in some grimy back alley, or perhaps under a bridge, but it turned out to be nothing so secret-agent-ish like that. Instead, Ms. Ferris pulled our van into the parking lot of a large and expensive-looking Chinese restaurant. We parked alongside a dark purple minibus with tinted windows and off-road tires, which I guessed was our next transport. It certainly looked like the kind of vehicle the Guardians would use.

"Hope you're hungry," said Ms. Ferris, cutting the engine.

"I'm sure there are security cameras around the entrances," I said nervously. "We are all wanted fugitives, you know."

"That won't be a problem," said Ms. Ferris. "The Guardians own this place."

Ms. Ferris led us inside, and we were taken to a private dining room on the second floor. One of the Resistance representatives was already there waiting for us. He was a well-built middle-aged man who looked enough like Ed Regis to make me wonder if he too was ex-military.

"I'm Raider," said the man, standing up to greet us but giving us only his Guardian call sign. "You don't have to tell me your names, but I will need your handles or, if you don't have one, a simple alias."

James and Ed Regis didn't have Guardian call signs and I had no intention of going back to Hansel and Gretel. We gave Raider our most recent aliases: Richard, Alyssa, Tiffany, Jack and Edmund. Ms. Ferris gave her call sign, Tigress, and Rachael introduced herself as Rowan, though I didn't know if that really was her official call sign or if she just made it up on the spot.

"I believe one of you is also called Hansel?" asked Raider, looking between James and me.

I reluctantly raised my hand. "That's me."

"You are the leader of this team?"

"That's Tiffany," I replied, gesturing toward Terry. "Also known as Rabbit."

"Yes, of course," said Raider, glancing down at Terry's hook.

Ms. Ferris asked Raider, "Where is your associate?"

"Exercising caution," he replied curtly. "Your troublesome conditions have demanded it."

"Your leaders have agreed to our conditions," countered Ms. Ferris.

"It is nevertheless highly irregular," said Raider. "Five people, all at once, including a young child." He frowned at Alia, and then shared his frown with the rest of us as he added suspiciously, "And no delving allowed. Not even the adult."

Delving for secret motives was one of the standard security measures that the Resistance took with newcomers to their ranks. When arranging for our entry into Lumina, Mrs. Harding, at Terry's request, had specifically asked that our team be exempt from this prescreening. Even Mrs. Harding hadn't known the exact reason for this, but the Resistance leadership still agreed to let us in, probably because they desperately wanted Terry Henderson on their side.

"They are not a threat to the Resistance," said Ms. Ferris. "You have my word, under delving, on that account."

"Then I will ask you now, Tigress," said Raider, who I realized was a delver himself. "Are these people, to the very best of your knowledge, who they claim to be?"

"They are," Ms. Ferris replied calmly.

"Whom do they serve?" asked Raider.

"They serve the cause of freedom."

Raider raised his eyebrows. "Not the cause of the Guardians?"

Ms. Ferris shook her head. "To my understanding, they are, for the most part, independent."

"Whom do they hold as enemies?"

"The forces of King Divine."

"Why do they refuse to be delved?"

"I don't know."

"Do you trust them?"

Ms. Ferris didn't answer aloud, but Raider seemed satisfied with what went through her mind.

Raider nodded slowly, and then turned to Terry. "It's Tiffany, now, is it? As Tigress says, our leadership trusts you enough to spare your team from divulging whatever secrets you are obviously keeping from us. However, I am the one who has to lead you in, and as a favor to me, I ask that you answer me just one question with your mind open."

Terry eyed him for a moment, and then nodded. "Go ahead."

"What brings your team to the Resistance?"

"The freedom to do so," replied Terry.

Raider finally gave us a grudging smile. "Then you are welcome among us." Heading toward the door, he said, "Wait here. I'll go get my partner and then we will eat."

I wasn't sure I liked the sound of that. After delving Ms. Ferris and Terry to make certain that we were enemies of King Divine, Raider had given us no reason to trust him in return. Who was to say there wasn't a bomb planted under the dining table or something?

Catching the uneasiness on my face, Raider said, "Hey, I'm trusting you guys, Hansel, so you'd better trust me in return."

"Richard," I corrected. "Trust is hard to come by these days."

Raider laughed. "Ain't that the truth!"

Raider was gone longer than I felt comfortable with, but at least the room didn't explode. Instead, a pair of young waitresses in red and gold Chinese dresses set our table with the first wave of what would turn out to be an excellent ten-course meal.

Raider returned just as I was about to suggest that we start eating without him. He was followed into the dining room by his partner, an older, gray-haired man who I instantly recognized.

"Mr. Jenson!" I exclaimed, standing up in surprise.

"Call signs only, Richard!" Raider said to me sharply, and then gestured to Mr. Jenson, saying, "This is Sharky. He will be our phantom for the crossing."

"It's good to see you again," said the phantom, shaking my hand.

"It's good to see you, too," I said carefully. The last time I had talked to Mr. Jenson was at the gathering of lesser gods. I had threatened his life and forced him to help me turn invisible so that I could sneak into the Angel camp.

Mr. Jenson showed no resentment at all, shaking Terry's hand next as he said, "It is an honor to meet you again, um..."

"It's Tiffany now," Terry informed him.

"Tiffany, an honor," said Mr. Jenson.

Then he jumped in surprise. "Oh, my goodness!" he cried, looking down at my sister. "You're the little healer from the gathering, aren't you?"

Nodding, Alia gave him a smile.

"I never got the chance to thank you," he said, shaking Alia's hand. "The Guardian Council hadn't yet finalized my re-initiation when New Haven fell. What is your name? I mean, what are you called?"

"Alyssa," Alia told him.

"Thank you, Alyssa," said Mr. Jenson.

I asked Mr. Jenson, "You didn't know it was going to be us?"

"Actually, no," said Mr. Jenson. "Raider had the details and I didn't ask. In our operations, the less you know, the less a liability you can be if you're caught."

"Sharky," said Terry, gesturing to the rest of our group, "these are the other two members of my team, Edmund and Jack, and our friends, Tigress and Rowan."

We were in a private dining room of a Guardian-owned restaurant so I saw little need for all this codename cloak-and-dagger nonsense, but I supposed it was better than taking unnecessary risks. Besides, we would probably be using these aliases during our stay in Lumina, so it would be best to get used to them here and now.

"Let's eat," said Raider as the hand-shaking contest drew to a close. "Our meal's getting cold."

Perhaps partly because we turned out to be acquaintances of his trusted partner, Raider made no further complaints over dinner about our rule-breaking. But nor did he give us many details about the situation in Lumina. He seemed to agree with Mr. Jenson that the less we knew, the safer it was for the cause. If only he knew what we knew!

"Did you find your family among the Guardians, Sharky?" I asked over dessert.

"I did," replied Mr. Jenson. "I was briefly reunited with my son, but now he and his wife serve the Angels while I remain a Guardian."

"Ouch," I commented.

I noticed that like everyone at Wood-claw, Raider and Mr. Jenson both continued to call Randal's faction the "Angels" rather than the "Guardian Angels." I guessed that this was the official position of true Guardians worldwide.

Mr. Jenson continued, "I had to convince our leaders, under delving, that I wouldn't betray the Guardians next and follow my son back to the Angels. And I won't. At least not voluntarily. If I am caught, then that is fate, but I would much rather live to see a future that is free of King Divine's rule, where my son and I can choose our own lives." Mr. Jenson gave me a wry smile and added, "Still, the real reason I haven't been booted from the Resistance is because they have preciously too few phantoms at their disposal. They need me enough to take a small risk."

"One way or another, you'll see your son again soon," Raider said to him darkly. "This war is nearing its tipping point. That's why the Resistance is taking greater risks these days."

"Like with us?" asked James.

Raider didn't reply.

After the meal, we bid Rachael and Ms. Ferris goodbye in the restaurant's parking lot. They would make their way back to Wood-claw by road, hopefully without incident. Raider, in addition to being a delver, was our hider for the rest of our journey.

The dark purple minibus that we had parked alongside turned out to have nothing to do with us. Raider and Mr. Jenson had come in two plain old sedans. Terry and James rode with Raider while Ed Regis, Alia and I rode in Mr. Jenson's car. We were taken to a Guardian safe house on the outskirts of the city.

Inside, Raider had Mr. Jenson run us through the entry procedure that would be used to smuggle us into Lumina the next day.

"Does everyone here know what a phantom train is?" asked Mr. Jenson.

We all nodded, even Alia.

Mr. Jenson next asked, "Has anyone ever been in one?"

Nobody nodded this time. Not even Terry had done this before.

"Five first-timers," muttered Raider, shaking his head in disbelief. "You'd think Proton would have more sense..."

"They'll be fine," Mr. Jenson said to him confidently.

Then Mr. Jenson explained to us, "We usually transport only one or two people at a time. The Angels believe that Raider is one of them, so he is cleared for open operations in Lumina. I am not. I, along with the rest of you, will go in invisible, following Raider."

As a psionic phantom, Mr. Jenson could turn part or all of anything he touched temporarily invisible. How that exactly worked was as beyond me as how any other psionic power worked, but Mr. Jenson could turn his and other people's bodies, clothes and even metallic weapons so transparent that they couldn't be spotted under a noon sun.

There were downsides, however. The most obvious was that if you turned your whole body invisible, you wouldn't be able to see anything because light would pass straight through your eyes. Phantoms usually left just their eyeballs visible, which was creepy but necessary. This time, however, all but Raider would become completely invisible, and holding on to a rope to keep us together, we would be led by Raider into Lumina. This was the "phantom train" that Mr. Jenson was referring to.

But phantom trains, especially long ones, were very risky. In addition to blindness, another major downside to a phantom's invisibility cloak was that any sudden movement, such as falling down or bumping into something, could instantly remove your invisibility right along with the invisibility of anything you were touching. That is, if even one of us tripped on a stone or something, everyone holding the rope could be instantly exposed.

"That's why we practice here," said Raider. "And you're all going to be perfect at this or we're not going anywhere tomorrow."

Raider wanted us visible during our practice in the house, and Mr. Jenson didn't want to turn just our eyeballs invisible because that was truly disgusting. Instead, we wore cloth blindfolds as we lined up behind Raider and had him lead us through the rooms like a group of prisoners on a leash.

Raider taught us his signaling system. "If I cough once, don't stop but expect a low obstruction ahead such as a curb or steps. Two coughs, you stop immediately. We don't want anyone crashing into anything or anyone. I will gently pull the rope when I want you to start walking again."

We carefully weaved our way around the furniture as we listened for Raider's coughs. The going was slow but we gave Raider no reason to scold us. After almost an hour of practice in the house, Raider had us remove our blindfolds, saying grimly, "Time for the real thing."

"I know Richard has experienced cloaking before," said Mr. Jenson, "but have the rest of you ever been cloaked?"

Only Terry raised her hand.

Mr. Jenson then asked, "Completely? Eyes included?"

Terry lowered her hand, saying, "Never. Besides, the last time for me was almost ten years ago."

Mr. Jenson said warningly, "Blindness, even temporary blindness, can freak some first-timers out pretty badly."

"Don't worry, Sharky," replied Terry. "No one on my team freaks out easily."

Mr. Jenson started with James, touching his upper arm, and James instantly disappeared.

"Whoa," said James's disembodied voice. "This is something new."

Next, Ed Regis, and then Alia, then Terry.

"This is so different from a blindfold," remarked Alia, who sounded more awed than afraid. "I can't see anything. It's like I don't even have eyes."

Finally, me. As Mr. Jenson touched my arm, the world around me blinked out of existence. Mr. Jenson made our guide rope invisible too, but we couldn't see it anyway. Groping our way around, we lined up behind Raider: Mr. Jenson first, followed by Ed Regis, James, Terry, Alia, and me at the end.

Then Raider took us on a walk outside, once around the neighborhood. It had been a long time since I had been blind, but it was still a mildly familiar world for me. Constant uncertainty and slow, deliberate steps.

Keeping a tight grip on our guiding rope, we all made it back to the safe house without incident. We turned visible again by stamping our feet on the floor, and as my eyes came back into focus, I saw that Raider finally looked a little impressed with us.

"I had expected at least one or two accidents," said Raider. "We've never had a train this long before."

Terry smiled. "Like I said, we don't freak out easily."

"Alright," Raider said evenly, nodding. "We're going tomorrow."

We spent the night at the safe house on sofas and in sleeping bags on the floor.

The next morning, after breakfast, Mr. Jenson once again turned us and himself invisible for our car ride to the Resistance. Lumina was a five-hour drive from here, which meant that we would arrive a little after lunchtime, but the only person who could be seen outdoors there was Raider. So the real question was how to fit seven people into a single small sports sedan.

The answer: uncomfortably, to put it mildly. Raider of course drove, and Mr. Jenson got the front seat next to him. Meanwhile, I was crammed in the middle of the back seat with Alia on my lap, Ed Regis on my left and Terry on my right. But it was James who really ended up with the short end of the stick: he was put in the trunk with our baggage.

Or maybe James was the lucky one. At least he didn't have to worry about losing his invisibility cloak. Though we weren't barred from talking, we sat silently for most of the ride. Alia felt pretty heavy by the time we finally arrived in the outskirts of Lumina.

Though hungry for lunch, we had no time to eat now. Getting into Lumina wasn't a simple matter of walking with an invisibility cloak. There were thermographic security cameras set in strategic locations all around the Angel city, and through these, the Seraphim could see our body heat. Fortunately,

Resistance hackers had some limited access to these camera systems and could override them at prearranged times and locations.

"The thermographic camera system was originally set up by the Guardians to keep Angel phantoms out of New Haven," Raider had explained to us the day before. "As long as we keep to our course and time schedule, the cameras will always be looking in the wrong direction when we pass them."

We had little choice but to trust him. Keeping us strictly on need-to-know, Raider had told us nothing of our route into Lumina or our final destination.

Getting out of the car, I could tell by the sounds around me that Mr. Jenson was opening the trunk to let James out and re-cloak him. Our duffel bags had to be made invisible too. Mr. Jenson had probably made just his eyes reappear so that he could see what he was doing. In a few minutes, we had shouldered our bags and formed our train, tightly holding the invisible rope that Raider would use to lead us into the Angel city.

Even blind, I could tell that the others were nervous. This was no longer practice. One mistake by any one of us and we would all be discovered. Blindness wasn't a problem for me personally, but I was worried for the others, especially Alia since she would have to walk faster to keep pace with us.

But Raider and Sharky were experienced guides. We would later learn that they had been handpicked by the Resistance leaders to make sure that we arrived safely. Loosely holding the end of the rope, I followed a step behind my sister as we moved carefully and silently toward the center of the Angel city.

As it was midday, and a weekday at that, it wasn't very crowded on the sidewalk and Raider didn't have to rely entirely on coughing signals. As he walked, he would mumble things like "right turn ahead" so that we would be ready when the rope changed direction.

After about thirty minutes, I suddenly recognized the concrete under my feet. I had traveled this road blind many times, and just by the sounds around me and the "feel" of the sidewalk, I knew that we were about to pass right in front of the entrance to New Haven One. This was where the Angels' most prized hider allegedly lived on the topmost floor.

We passed the entrance without stopping.

A little later, we entered the park. Again, my ears and my feet instantly remembered the route I used to jog every day. I remembered the smell of the grassy field where Cindy had taken us to picnic in the summer. This was where I had taught Alia to ride a bike. It was where I had held hands with Laila Brown.

"Addy," Alia whispered into my mind, *"I think we're in the park."*

I smiled. Even Alia, who had never experienced blindness before, knew where we were. So much for Raider's need-to-know route.

As we continued through the park, despite the early-November chill, I heard the voices of a few picnickers, probably senior citizens. I also heard a baby crying in the distance. It made me think about baby Laila, and I had a feeling that Alia was thinking the same thing.

Exiting the park, we crossed a street. Raider coughed a warning. We were led up five steps and into a large room which I guessed was the entrance hall to one of the forty-story high-rises that the Angels had taken from the Guardians. There we stopped once. Raider greeted the lobby security team as if they were friends, but by their conversation, I could tell that these men were Seraphim.

As we started moving again, I felt myself brush up against Alia from behind.

Alia said in a panicked voice, *"Addy! Addy, I lost the rope!"*

This was why Mr. Jenson had asked me to bring up the rear. With my free hand, I grabbed my sister by the back of her jacket and pushed her along in front of me.

We entered an elevator. As it started to climb, I heard Raider let out a sigh of relief, but his relief was nothing compared to mine. I carefully helped Alia find the rope again before the elevator came to a stop.

One short walk down a tiled hallway, through a door, and Raider said, "End of the line. Shake it off."

I stomped my left foot on the floor. My vision returned, and I saw that we were standing in a small living room not unlike the one back in our apartment at Wood-claw.

Alia looked up at me sheepishly. *"Please don't tell anyone."*

I grinned. "No promises."

Raider turned to us, announcing, "This is my place. Yours is below."

"Where are we?" asked Terry.

"New Haven Four?" I guessed.

"Correct," replied Raider, looking surprised, "though now it is known as Lumina Nonus."

"That's Latin for 'ninth,' I believe," said Ed Regis.

"Ah, an educated man," said Raider, nodding appreciatively. "The Angels renumbered the New Haven buildings in Latin with little regard for the Guardians' old system. Only NH-1 retains its place, officially Lumina Primus, though almost everyone calls it Lumina Prime."

"We passed in front of Prime on our way here," I said.

Raider looked stunned. I merely smiled.

"Okay, genius, what floor are we on?" he asked.

"The twenty-first?" I ventured, basing my rough estimate on the length of our elevator ride.

Raider stared at me in utter disbelief. Alia laughed.

We really were on the twenty-first floor, which put us exactly halfway up the building. Raider led us into his bedroom, where he pushed his queen-size bed off of a large rug set in the middle of the room. Then he rolled up the rug to reveal a trapdoor built into the floor.

Raider knocked several times on the trapdoor in a code-like pattern. After waiting for about thirty seconds, he slowly lifted the door up. A short wooden ladder extended down into the space below the floor.

"In you get," said Raider as he tossed our bags down into the hole. "Welcome to the Resistance."

9. NONUS TWENTY POINT FIVE

The ceiling was higher than that of a crawlspace, but only Alia and I could stand up straight. My hair brushed up against the concrete. Everyone else either had to stoop forward or at least bend their necks to the left or right in a comical manner.

Mr. Jenson had come down with us, but Raider remained in his condo to close the trapdoor and hide it again under his rug and bed. There were two men waiting for us: Knights armed with automatic rifles. They greeted us and told us their call signs, and then, along with Mr. Jenson, they led us deep into a maze of corridors littered with supply crates and bulging garbage bags.

"We call this Twenty Point Five," explained Mr. Jenson as we followed the Knights. "It spans the entire floor and serves as our headquarters in Lumina. There are several other entrances from the twentieth floor below and the twenty-first above, and even I probably don't know all of them."

"Where are you taking us, Sharky?" asked Alia.

Mr. Jenson smiled, saying, "To our leaders, of course."

Pipes of all sizes cut across the ceiling, and we had to constantly duck under them as we made our way through the dark and stuffy labyrinth. Most of the corridor walls weren't really walls so much as random sheets of plastic, metal and assorted junk that had been propped up between the thick concrete supports of the building. Through breaks in the various materials and through curtained doorways, we could see little rooms and occasionally a few people inside talking quietly, resting, or studying a computer monitor.

Another turn, and we stepped through a curtain into a largish square room that was dimly lit by two fluorescent lights lashed to the ceiling pipes. In the center of the room was a low coffee table with several mismatched chairs around it. Rectangular wooden boxes were stacked in one corner of the room while a long leather sofa sat against a wall. Against another wall was a dining table cluttered with papers and maps. Two men were hunched over the table, talking in whispers.

As we entered, they turned toward us, and I got an even greater shock than when I first saw Mr. Jenson back at the Chinese restaurant.

One of the men was our long-lost friend, Mark Parnell.

Letting out a cry of joy, Alia rushed forward and jumped into Mark's arms.

The two Knights who had escorted us here reflexively raised their guns, but Mark called to them, "No! It's fine."

Hugging Alia tightly once, he set her back onto the floor and said, "No more sudden movements here, okay? People are very, very jumpy."

Mark looked a little haggard but otherwise just as I remembered him with his shaggy beard, round glasses and his quiet, warm smile.

"What are you doing here?" I asked, shaking his hand. "We thought you were dead."

"I had feared the same of you until we heard from Wood-claw of your visit," replied Mark. "It's good to see you again."

The other man, whom I didn't recognize, said, "Jacob here and I codirect the Resistance movement in Lumina. I'm Proton. Welcome to our headquarters."

We introduced ourselves with our aliases. We were told to keep our real names strictly to ourselves, even between friends. Mark's call sign, Jacob, had been taken from his long-lost twin brother. His partner, Proton, a pyroid and berserker with extensive training in urban warfare, had been a high-ranking Lancer Knight back in the days of New Haven.

"It is an honor to have you with us, Tiffany," said Proton, shaking Terry's hand. "I hear you have become a windmaster like your grandfather."

"Ironic, isn't it?" Terry replied frostily.

Proton turned to my sister. "And Gretel—I mean Alyssa—we are very fortunate to finally have another healer here."

To my surprise, both Terry and Alia already knew Proton fairly well, having accompanied the Lancers during a number of missions against the God-slayers.

"The last time I saw you, Richard," he said to me, cocking an eyebrow, "you were lying in the basement of a Slayer house with a chain around your leg. And you looked pretty dead."

I wasn't sure how to respond to that, so I kept silent.

Proton continued in a friendly tone, "I wasn't at the gathering of lesser gods, but I have heard of your exploits behind enemy lines. Here we need every good Knight we can get, and I'm glad to have you and your friends here."

"Thank you," I said carefully. "We will do all that we can to help."

Proton shook James's hand next, saying, "We've never met, Jack, but I knew your parents well. You look a lot like your father."

James's parents were Lancers like Proton, and Lumina Nonus was former NH-4: the very same building that our refugee children, James included, had escaped during the fall of New Haven. I wondered what floor James used to live on.

"Do you know what happened to my parents, Proton?" asked James.

"Unfortunately, no," Proton replied apologetically. "Many of the Knights are still scattered and unaccounted for. But if we find out anything, we'll let you know."

James nodded his thanks.

Proton didn't know about James's combat experience and he knew nothing of Ed Regis, but Terry assured him that both James and Ed Regis were trustworthy and competent fighters. Though he looked like he had some doubts about James's combat skills simply due to his age, Proton took Terry's word for it on Ed Regis. We openly introduced Ed Regis as a former Wolf and we were happy to see that Proton wasn't as prejudiced as Mrs. Harding.

"If Tiffany vouches for you," Proton said to Ed Regis, "then that is enough for us. At least for now."

I remembered how Mrs. Harding had described the Resistance as being even more security-cautious than she, but between Father Mark Parnell being codirector and Alia and Terry being personal acquaintances of Proton, I could understand why the Resistance had let us in without delving us—even with an ex-Wolf in tow.

Mr. Jenson and the two Knights who had guided us here left the room as Proton, Mark and the rest of us sat on the chairs around the coffee table. The taller people looked happy to finally be able to straighten their spines. A moment later, one of the Knights returned briefly to supply our table with cups of tea. I was as hungry as I was thirsty, but I guessed that Mark and Proton had already eaten.

"So how did you end up here?" I asked Mark.

Mark looked like he was about to explain, but Proton stopped him. "First things first," said Proton, turning to Terry. "Your team came here bearing a secret, Tiffany. Something you couldn't trust our members to delve. We usually do not allow secret-keepers into our ranks. Is this information something that you must keep from Jacob and myself as well?"

Terry nodded, saying, "Unfortunately, yes. I can only promise you that we are on your side. If that isn't good enough for you, then we will leave."

"That won't be necessary," said Proton. "I was merely hoping that your secret, whatever it is, might provide some tactical advantage to us." He let out a quiet sigh. "You see, we're a breath away from losing this war now. The Angels—the *Guardian Angels* as they like to call themselves—have already begun their world conquest. They keep their progress as hidden as possible, but we know that our own government is so saturated with Angels that it is on the verge of being completely taken over. Meanwhile, in some other countries, both democratically elected leaders and military dictators alike are converted Angels."

"The Angels control entire countries?" asked James.

"Not entirely," replied Proton. "Not even King Divine can convert everyone at once. It simply takes too much time and increases the risks of exposure. The Angels have a handful of converts in high positions of almost every world government now, but they are more like spies. They can push their countries' policies in the interests of the Angels, but they can't openly serve Randal Divine because of various checks and balances in their governments. Even converted military dictators need the support of their non-converted government employees to rule their countries."

"But every day more and more people are being converted," put in Mark. "It's a whole new ball game with a psionic king. Conversion never wears off so there's no need to reconvert, which means King Divine's influence has no natural boundaries."

That, of course, wasn't true. Our team knew that Randal Divine wasn't a master controller and that the Angels didn't have the ability to permanently convert anyone. But Catherine Divine was young and powerful, and her conversions wouldn't wear off for many years, even decades. She could keep converting people for now and worry about the maintenance of her empire later.

"People have to be taken to the king to be converted," Ed Regis pointed out. "That means he has to be out there somewhere."

"If we knew where he was," Proton said with a touch of irony in his voice, "we could turn this whole war around in a heartbeat. The Angels know that and they have learned from their mistakes at the gathering of lesser gods. They underestimated the Guardians there. They won't do it again."

The Historian had told me to seek out Randal and Catherine's location from those closer to the conflict. Entirely frustrated, I blurted out, "You don't know anything?"

Proton laughed. "We know some things, Richard."

There was a knock on the doorframe. A Knight stepped through the curtain and announced, "There's a transmission incoming from the Council."

"I'll take it," said Proton, standing up as straight as possible without bashing his head against the concrete ceiling. He said to Mark, "It's probably just a routine update."

Mark nodded. "I'll finish briefing Tiffany's team and then show them around."

Proton left with the Knight.

Not to say that I wasn't interested in the "some things" that Proton claimed the Resistance knew about the Angels, but as he had said, first things first. I asked, "How did you end up becoming the leader of the Guardian Resistance, Mark?"

"Jacob," Mark corrected gently. "Remember, Richard, call signs only in Lumina."

I said exasperatedly, "Can't we at least use our real names when we're alone?"

"No," Terry said flatly. "Jacob is right. We should stay consistent.

Otherwise we might say our names when we shouldn't."

I rolled my eyes. "Fine, Jacob, so how did you become the leader?"

"Co-leader," said Mark, correcting me again. "And there isn't really much to tell. The night that New Haven fell to the Angels, I was being evacuated along with Cindy, Mr. Baker and the rest of the New Haven Council. But when we got to the airport, we discovered that there weren't enough seats on the airplane. Since I was neither psionic nor politically important to the Angels, I was asked to stay behind."

"Lucky you," I commented.

"So it turned out," Mark agreed grimly. "I escaped the city by public transportation. Later, I met Proton and his Lancers at a Guardian outpost. We slowly re-entered this town with the help of a handful of Guardians who had never left. Proton and I have worked here ever since."

Mark was a pacifist like Cindy, and by the brevity of his account, I could sense that he didn't want to talk about some of the things he had seen and done in the service of the Guardians here. I didn't press him for details.

"Now, if it isn't part of your great secret," said Mark, "I would very much like to hear where you people have been all this time."

I was about to start explaining, but just then we all heard a loud whine escape from Alia's stomach.

Trying not to laugh, I said to Mark, "We don't want to be rude, but we missed lunch and we're starving."

Mark immediately called through the makeshift walls for some food to be prepared for us. As we waited, Mark apologetically informed us that Nonus Twenty Point Five didn't have a proper kitchen and that meals were often fairly basic in nature, or "prison grade" as he jokingly put it.

"It's fine," said Terry. "We were spoiled rotten at Wood-claw."

Within minutes, a Knight brought in bowls of instant tomato soup, some dry crackers and very tossed salad.

As we ate, we told Mark most of our story: our escape from New Haven, our training program at Walnut Lane, Alia's abduction and subsequent rescue of her and Ed Regis, our expedition to the Historian and how we ended up at Wood-claw. We of course didn't tell him what the Historian had revealed to us.

When I told him the bit about rescuing Ed Regis from the Angel outpost, Mark was astonished to learn that Ed Regis had been the leader of the Wolf unit that captured and tortured Alia and me so many years ago.

"I was pretty desperate for help, Jacob," was my lame excuse.

"Nevertheless, a forgiving spirit is truly divine," Mark said approvingly.

"Well, who says I've forgiven him?" I chuckled. "But Edmund pulled us through a lot of tough places since then, so I consider us pretty even by now. We wouldn't be here today if it weren't for him."

"Then you have my deepest gratitude, sir," Mark said to Ed Regis.

Ed Regis merely nodded silently.

Mark said to me, "You don't know how happy I was to hear from Woodclaw that you and Alyssa were still alive. I'm so sorry about what happened to Cindy. And of course about your sister Catherine. It must be terrible for you."

Mark's words about Catherine threw me for a moment. Then, understanding what he meant, I replied, "That's why I've come back, Jacob. To save Cat from Randal Divine. If we can somehow kill the Angel king, then my sister's conversion will break and so will Cindy's. We can still save them both."

"I'm hopeful for that, too," said Mark. "I had feared that you and Alyssa had been killed last year, and recovering Cindy would not have saved her in the least if you two were already dead."

We were done with our soup, and Terry decided that it was time to bring the meeting back to its original purpose. "What do you guys know about the Angels and King Divine?" she asked.

Mark replied, "Well, we know that the Divines do not reside in Lumina."

"We suspected that," said James.

We knew from the start that Lumina wouldn't be an ideal spot to keep the world's last psionic master, especially if this master was rumored to be an all-powerful king. Lumina was too obvious a target. If all else failed, our country's government (assuming that it still had the capacity) could just drop a nuclear weapon here to guarantee the king's death.

"But there is a definite connection between this city and the Divines," continued Mark. "Many of the captured members of Guardian breakaways and independent factions are brought to Lumina, some of them from considerably far away. Of these people, the potential converts are held here and evaluated, and then shipped to the king by order of priority. High-ranking Guardians first, of course, followed by Knights and key members of their families. Some low-level Guardians and independents have been held here for months and still haven't been taken for conversion."

"Potential converts..." I repeated. "Does that mean there are people who are brought here but not put on the waiting list for conversion?"

"Certainly," said Mark. "There are simply too many people coming in now for King Divine to convert them all. Nor does he need to. In the case of families that willingly turn themselves in, at most only one member is converted while the rest are screened and then just trusted." He smiled, adding, "Many of our Resistance members come from such families. Raider, who we assigned to bring you here, is one such person. His wife is converted but he and his daughter are not."

"And the Angels don't suspect him at all?" asked James. "Wouldn't his wife turn him in if she found out?"

"I'm quite sure she would turn him in, but the Angels have yet to suspect anything. Raider is a delver himself so he knows a few tricks around delving without directly blocking the mind readers. And if his wife did suspect him, we have our own mind-writers to take care of that, too."

We had gone off topic and I wasn't interested in Raider or his wife. "Tell us what you know of the people who are sent to Randal for conversion," I said.

"They're usually taken in groups of ten to thirty," said Mark. "They disappear from Lumina for a week or more before they return as new converts. We figure the travel time is about two to three days one way. Then there can be extra time depending on how long the conversions take and whether some of the candidates resist or not. All of the candidates are pre-screened and, if necessary, psychologically broken prior to shipment so that they accept their conversions quickly. But some of them probably still resist when they arrive."

I kept my shudder to myself. "Some of them don't come back?" I asked.

Mark nodded. "It's rare, but it happens."

"Three days," mused James. "There are few places in the world that people can't get to in three days."

Ed Regis shook his head. "Not covertly, Jack."

Mark agreed with Ed Regis. "We do believe that the Divines live in this country somewhere."

"I assume you have tried to follow the transports?" asked Ed Regis.

Mark nodded. "We did, back when we still could. They were bussed to a local airport and put on a sightseeing aircraft which did a two-hour loop around the countryside and returned to the same airport. When the planes landed, the candidates were gone. We believe they had been parachuted out at some prearranged location and then shipped on their way."

"What do you mean by 'back when you could'?"

"They stopped bussing people to the airport a few months ago," explained Mark. "Rumor has it a new underground tunnel was completed starting in the gathering place under the Lumina Prime building, and that it stretches to the starting point of the journey to the king's secret palace. The problem is, we can't get into the gathering place, and we can't yet locate where the tunnel comes out."

"It's our own damn gathering place!" James said in a frustrated tone. "You can't get in?"

"Well, no one we sent in came back out," said Mark. Then, after a moment's pause, he corrected himself, saying, "Actually, two did come back out. But they had been converted."

"So what is the Resistance actually accomplishing here?" asked James.

"Not as much as we would like," admitted Mark. "Our presence here has grown greatly these last few months. At any given time, we have between fifty to eighty operatives working in Lumina. But our operation remains primarily observation, occasionally punctuated by kidnapping and general mischief. Recently, we managed to capture one of the Seraphim's top commanders. We were hoping that he would know the whereabouts of King Divine. Unfortunately, he managed to kill himself before we could extract any information."

"That seems to be going around," Terry said wryly.

Better safe than sorry, I thought to myself as Terry told Mark the story about the two Angels who cracked their heads open at the Wood-claw outpost three days ago.

When Terry finished, Mark nodded and said, "I agree that it sounds like they knew something important."

"We've brought photos and fingerprints of them if you're interested," said Terry.

"We're always interested in any possible leads."

"They're in my bag, which I think we left at the trapdoor," said Terry. "I'll get them to you later."

"Thank you," said Mark. "We need everything we can get our hands on right now. As Proton said, the only thing we really need to do is kill the king, but that is proving most difficult. Even high-level Seraphim who are part of the shipping process know only their own small segments of the path that the prisoners are taken on. And, of course, the returning converts have their memories of the journey completely erased."

I could sense Ed Regis itching to ask about Cindy, so I saved him the trouble by bringing it up myself. "Does Cindy really live at the top of Lumina Prime?"

"We believe she does, Richard," replied Mark, "but we have never seen her out of the building."

I explained stiffly, "Some of us think that Cindy might know where Randal Divine is hiding."

"And we agree that it's possible," Mark said carefully. "But capturing Cindy Gifford alive may prove nearly as difficult as capturing Randal Divine himself. Also, as she is a converted Angel, it's doubtful that we could extract the information we need without causing severe damage to her mind."

I could tell that Mark was as against going after Cindy as I was, but it annoyed me that he didn't straight-out say so. At first, Mark had looked like the same nice man I had known when I was a boy. Now I could see how much this war had changed everyone.

Mark continued in a businesslike tone, "At the present, in addition to searching for the exit point of the secret tunnel, we are constantly on the lookout for other potential targets who might supply us with a lead on the Divines."

"You really talk like a military commander, Jacob," I remarked, shaking my head.

Mark shrugged. "I am, in a manner of speaking."

"You used to be a priest."

"And I hope to be one again someday," Mark said with a grim smile. Then, leaning forward in his chair, he said, "But since you mention Cindy, Richard, there is something I have been meaning to ask you about her. That is, of course, assuming you were still alive to ask."

"And here I am," I said evenly. "So what about Cindy?"

"A long time ago now, Cindy's husband, Eric Laude, killed the last

Guardian queen, Diana Granados," said Mark.

"So I heard," I replied, remembering the story Cindy had told me in her car one wintry night.

"Then I assume you also heard that Eric was killed by Ralph Henderson and that Cindy went into hiding shortly thereafter."

I nodded.

"When she fled the Guardians, Richard, Cindy stole a number of top-secret files which she planned to use as insurance against Guardian pursuit."

"I didn't know that," I said, surprised. I looked over at Alia. "Did you?"

My sister shook her head.

Mark continued, "Shortly after her escape from the Guardians, Cindy entrusted these documents to me. I was asked to hang on to them in case something happened to her. But after a few years, Cindy felt safe enough to ask me to return them to her, which I did."

"Then obviously you must have read them," said James.

"Yeah," I agreed. "Why are you asking me about them?"

"I never read them," said Mark. "The documents were sealed in a large envelope which Cindy had asked me not to open, partly for my own safety."

"And you were never tempted to peek inside?" asked Terry.

"Of course I was tempted!" laughed Mark. "I am only human, after all. But Cindy trusted me because I was a priest and I wasn't going to abuse that trust."

"Then you have no idea what's in these files," I said, still not understanding why Mark had brought this topic up.

"Actually, I do know," said Mark. "As I said, Cindy didn't want me to have the specific details, but she was kind enough to tell me that the envelope contained lists of Guardian spies in the Angels at the time, and, much more importantly for us now, it detailed the locations of several Guardian safe houses. Some of these places were so secret that only the very top members of Diana Granados's government ever visited them."

"And you think that Randal Divine might be hiding in a former Guardian safe house?" I asked incredulously.

But Mark was dead serious. "The only Guardians who would have known the most secret of these locations are people like Cindy, Travis Baker or Ralph Henderson. In other words, either converted or dead. Therefore, we consider it a distinct possibility that Randal believes these old Guardian hideouts to be safer than those belonging to the Angels, which, after all, are well known among the personal guards of the late Larissa Divine."

"I guess that makes some sense," I agreed.

"We think that Cindy might have kept the documents hidden in her house after I returned them to her," said Mark. "You lived there with her for a time before your capture by the Wolves, Richard. One of the reasons I pressured Proton into letting you come here was to ask you about this directly. Please take a moment and try to remember."

I closed my eyes, thinking back upon those days when I lived with Cindy and Alia in that suburban house. Back then, I was mainly concerned about my own survival, about finding Cat, and teaching Alia to speak with her mouth. The things I remembered most clearly were Cindy's cooking lessons and power-balance meditations, our outings to the countryside lake and the rest of the time we spent at home as we slowly became a family.

I shook my head. "I'm sorry, Jacob, but I never saw any files like you're describing."

Perhaps in mild desperation, Mark turned to my sister. "Alyssa?"

Alia shook her head too, saying, "I don't know either. Besides, I didn't know how to read back then anyway."

"There was a room," I said, remembering, "on the second floor, filled with boxes and old furniture and stuff. Cindy's envelope might be in there somewhere."

"It's not," Ed Regis suddenly said.

We all looked at him.

"I was there in person," explained Ed Regis, giving me an uncomfortable look. "After you gave me her address."

"Go on," I said.

"Well, we cleaned out the entire house," said Ed Regis. "We even pulled up the floorboards and opened up the walls. But we found nothing. There were many boxes in the second-floor storage room, but they contained mostly clothes, books and a few photo albums. There was hardly anything related to the Guardians or psionics. Everything in that house was moved to one of our secure facilities."

"Those belong to the Angels now," said Mark. "There was nothing else?"

"Actually, there was something," said Ed Regis. "Dust patterns on the floor suggested that the storage room had been recently searched. The other rooms had also been searched prior to our arrival."

"That's because we left Ralph Henderson tied to a chair there when we left," I explained. "Ralph must have recovered the files for the Guardians when he managed to get free."

"No," said Terry. "He certainly would have if the files had been left there, but Cindy wouldn't have left them at her house. Why would she? She wasn't planning on coming back."

"Tiffy has a point," I said, realizing the flaw in my logic. "Cindy had probably hid them in the baggage that we took to Mark's—I mean Jacob's house."

"We were there too," Ed Regis said with an apologetic look in Mark's direction. "There was nothing at Father Parnell's house or at his church."

Mark's lips didn't even show a hint of a frown. "When Cindy and I discovered that the Wolves were after us, we dropped everything and ran," he said. "I'm certain that Cindy didn't have the files on her."

"So these documents just went poof?" asked James.

I looked at Alia for help, but she just stared blankly back.

Terry pointed out, "If these documents were to act as insurance against the Guardians, Cindy wouldn't have kept them on her. She would have passed them to someone else just like she passed them to Jacob once."

"That's exactly what she did!" I exclaimed, almost jumping out of my seat when it hit me. "Jacob, you remember how Cindy left your house for a day and a night?"

"I do," Mark said slowly.

"She must have passed the files on to someone then. Someone she could trust."

"Cindy trusted nobody back then, Richard."

"She trusted you, didn't she?" I argued.

"Because I wasn't a faction member," said Mark.

"Well, then she passed the files to another non-faction member," I said. "And I think I know who."

"Who?" everyone demanded at once.

"A friend. A cop. I think his name was Bird or something."

"Bird?!"

"No!" I jumped again as I remembered. "Brian! Cindy said he owed her a favor."

"Brian what?" asked Mark.

"I don't know. But he worked at the police station across the street from Cindy's old hospital."

"Cindy wasn't gone long enough to make a roundtrip back to her hometown," said Mark.

I nodded. "I know, and I don't think she would've risked it. When she left, she told me that she might have found a new home for Alyssa and me. But she was lying because she didn't want me to know about the files either. No, she drove to another town near yours to hide her trail, called Brian and mailed the files directly to him."

"It's possible," said Mark, "but there's no guarantee."

"Well, you said she hardly trusted anyone, Jacob. Edmund claims the files weren't at her house or yours. So Brian's worth a check, don't you think?"

Mark nodded. "We will pass this information on to the Council. Their Knights can seek him out. Thank you, Richard."

"Glad I could help," I replied, though I had a feeling that Bullet-in-the-Butt Brian was in for a very bad day.

Terry said teasingly to Mark, "Bet you wish you peeked in that envelope when you could."

Mark shook his head. "I never regret my civility, Tiffany."

There was a knock on the doorframe. Proton pulled himself through the curtain and said wryly to Mark, "If only the Council could fight as much as they can talk."

"Are they still waiting for the Meridian to officially join the Guardians?" Mark asked pleasantly.

"If they are, they're in for a long wait," replied Proton. "The Meridian has just submitted its surrender to King Divine. The leaders will be brought to Lumina within a week to be processed for conversion."

After the Guardians, the Meridian had been one of the largest psionic factions in the country. Another big step forward for the Angels.

"Anyway," said Proton, looking around at us, "has Jacob already briefed you all on your responsibilities here?"

"Not yet," said Mark. "But I think we'll just put them all on the camera crew for now so that we can relieve some of our other operatives for tourist duty. Jack and Edmund might qualify as tourists later, but I fear the rest are too famous for outdoor work in Lumina."

"I agree with Richard and Tiffany remaining on the camera crew," said Proton, "but I want Alyssa with the blood runners as soon as possible."

"I'll see what I can set up for her," said Mark.

I didn't understand the jargon at all, but I already didn't like what they were saying about my sister. For the moment, however, I kept my mouth shut.

Checking his watch, Proton said to Mark, "We have about an hour now to the S&D at Quintus. Let's get them armed and settled. Then they can watch a show and learn their first job at the same time."

"I'll show them around," said Mark.

Leaving Proton there, the six of us exited the meeting room.

"First, the armory," said Mark as he led us through the low-ceilinged maze. "As you may have guessed by now, though Proton and I are officially codirectors of the Resistance, Proton is the leader and I am more his assistant than his equal. But that is for the best. It is important that we have a single, strong leader to follow in these difficult times."

"What was all that about camera crews, tourists and blood runners?" I asked.

Mark explained, "The camera crew watches Lumina day and night from the surveillance room here on Twenty Point Five. We've hacked into almost every security camera that the Angels have. Tourists are people like Raider who are cleared for outdoor duty, pretending to be Angels or ordinary non-faction people living in this area. They hide in plain sight and have the advantage of being able to follow our targets around and cause mischief when necessary. Blood runners are medics, also an outdoor job. We call them blood runners because the most common injuries here are those that require an immediate response. We have six doctors and nurses, and now, with Alyssa here, three healers."

Mark stopped at a doorframe and pulled the curtain aside. "Here we are. This is the armory."

We entered a long rectangular room lined with wooden crates filled with grenades and an assortment of guns of all sizes. Terry and James had brought their own pistols from Wood-claw, but Ed Regis and I had been weaponless ever since our run-in with the Wolves.

"Take whatever you feel comfortable with," offered Mark.

"That would be nothing," I informed him.

Mark smiled. "Cindy would be happy to hear that."

My ever-increasing dislike of firearms notwithstanding, I dutifully picked out a pistol and two spare clips, and Ed Regis chose an automatic rifle.

"I'm just used to the weight," said Ed Regis, who also took a sidearm for good measure.

Alia, predictably, refused to touch any part of the arsenal.

Terry gave her a disgusted look. "You insist on coming with us, Alyssa. You agree to fight with us. And yet you still cling to your pacifist nonsense. You're even worse than your brother."

"There's more than one way to fight a war, Tiffany," Alia replied defiantly.

Mark cleared his throat once and said, "I'll show you your sleeping quarters now."

We exited the armory, and as we walked on, Mark continued, "Many of our operatives sleep in the barracks on the west side, but I insisted on you guys getting a private room. That way, it'll be easier for you to keep your secret, whatever it is, to yourselves."

"Thank you," said Terry.

"The walls are very thin, however, so if you're talking about anything private, speak in whispers," warned Mark. "Also, I'm afraid we can only give you one room."

I wasn't about to complain about room assignments in a place like this. "We're motorhome people," I reassured him. "We're used to living small."

James bumped his forehead against a pipe running along the ceiling. "Ow! I don't know if I'll ever get used to this ceiling."

We entered the tiny square room that Mark had appropriated for our private use. It was about the size of a walk-in closet. Like the rest of Twenty Point Five, the walls here were made of random pieces of junk: a cracked plastic sheet, a wide wooden table turned on end, a thick blanket hanging down from a pipe, and several stacks of large cardboard boxes.

"This was a storage space until yesterday," said Mark, "so don't be too surprised if someone tries to dump some boxes in here. Just have them talk to me."

"Nice and cozy," James remarked unenthusiastically.

But our tiny room had been properly prepared. Lined up along the cardboard-box wall were five tightly rolled sleeping bags and foam mats. In one corner was a wooden crate full of water bottles. Our duffle bags containing our clothes and other belongings, which we had left under Raider's trapdoor, had also been brought in. "Cozy" was an understatement: there was hardly any visible floor.

"You'll be working in shifts," said Mark, "so it's unlikely you'll ever have to all sleep in here at once."

Alia asked Mark about the plumbing.

"Nonexistent, Alyssa," Mark informed her. "There are no baths or showers on Twenty Point Five. We don't have any running water here, and the toilets are just buckets with lids on them, sort of like indoor outhouses. Hold your nose as you use them and try not to fall in."

"That's disgusting," said Alia.

"Not as disgusting as the job of emptying the buckets," said Mark, and laughed as Alia moaned loudly.

"Bet you wish you stayed in Wood-claw now," I whispered to Alia teasingly.

Alia stuck her tongue out at me.

"As for keeping clean," said Mark, "we take turns sneaking into the showers of our allied condos on floors twenty and twenty-one, but not very often. Fortunately for you, Alyssa, being a blood runner requires you to stay presentable."

"Don't you mean 'invisible'?" I asked.

Mark shook his head. "Setting up phantom trains takes preparation and timing to avoid the thermographic cameras, so we only use them to move people that the Angels would recognize, such as Tiffany and yourself. A blood runner has to be ready to move at a moment's notice."

"Alyssa is pretty well known among the Angels, too," I argued.

"I know," said Mark. "That's why I hesitated at first to make her a blood runner. But Proton is right. There's little point in having a healer here if she can't move about. We'll set her up with a proper disguise. I think Raider's daughter might be about her size."

That didn't sound very reassuring.

Rummaging through her duffle bag, Terry pulled out an envelope containing all the information we had on the suicide Angels and passed it to Mark.

"I'll have our intelligence people look this over," promised Mark.

Suddenly we heard a distant voice say, "Jacob, please report to Proton in the conference room."

What happened next was really strange: the message was repeated by several other voices from near and far.

"Jacob coming," Mark called through the wall. Again, several voices echoed his reply.

"What was that?" I asked, trying not to laugh.

"Our intercom system," said Mark, grinning. "We don't have a proper one of those either, so if you hear an order or request, call it out so that the message gets passed around the floor."

"Just like on a sailing ship," remarked Ed Regis.

Terry rolled her eyes at the lack of technology. "You've got to be kidding!"

"It works," said Mark. "Besides, the floor and ceiling here are built like a bunker so you don't have to worry about being heard on the other floors. Just don't shout too loudly near any of the pipes marked with red paint and it'll be okay."

James grinned. "Nice."

"I'll be back in a few minutes to show you to the surveillance room," said Mark. "For the moment, make yourselves comfortable here—if that's at all physically possible."

We laughed, and Mark ducked out through the curtain.

Unrolling the foam mats, we sat down on our sleeping bags.

Terry let out a dejected huff and said, "Well, that was thoroughly disappointing. The Guardians really have no leads at all. Not even here in Lumina."

"They do now," I reminded her. "Cindy's secret envelope."

"That just goes to show how desperate they are," countered Terry.

"What are the chances that this Brian has Cindy's old files, even assuming he was the one who got them from Cindy in the first place? More likely, wherever Cindy sent those documents, the New Haven Council would have recovered them after Cindy agreed to join, years ago."

"It's still a chance," I insisted.

Terry shook her head. "It'll just end up being another wild-goose chase."

Refusing to give up, I asked, "Well, what about those Angels that killed themselves at the outpost?"

"I suppose there's a bit of hope in that," said Terry, still frowning, "but only if the Guardians can identify them and link them to a viable target."

"So, what now?" asked James.

"We don't have anywhere better to be at the moment," said Terry, "so we might as well stick around for a while and see what turns up."

"True," agreed James. "At least this is where the action is."

Sitting across from my sister, I noticed a contented smile on her face, and I found it decidedly suspicious considering Mark's announcement about the lack of proper toilets and the complete absence of bathing facilities on Twenty Point Five. "What are you grinning about?" I asked her.

"What Mark—I mean Jacob—said earlier," explained Alia, "about how not everyone is converted, especially if they come here willingly. I bet Patrick was never converted. Laila too."

"I agree," I said, and then added warningly, "But that doesn't mean you call them up and invite them over for tea. Understand?"

"Of course," Alia said in a hurt tone. "But who knows? Maybe Patrick could help us."

"Out of the question, Alyssa," Terry said sternly. "We're not here to make friends with traitors."

"Okay," said Alia, shrugging. But she kept her smile.

"Richard," Ed Regis said hesitantly, "you bringing Cindy Gifford up at the meeting..."

"Means nothing," I assured him icily. "I was just curious. Like I said before, Major, my rules."

This time Ed Regis backed down immediately. "As you wish."

"Besides," I added, "as Jacob made perfectly clear back there, Cindy isn't a viable target."

My initial shock at finding Mark at the head of the Resistance had quickly turned into utter relief. Mark would never lead the Guardians on a mission that could hurt Cindy. I even wondered if perhaps he had come here specifically to guarantee Cindy's safety. There was something else I suspected of Mark now too, but I wanted to be more certain before I said anything about it.

Someone called out, "Raider, report to the conference room."

Again, the human intercom system rapidly relayed the message throughout Twenty Point Five, followed by Raider's reply.

"That's going to take a little getting used to," remarked James as "Raider on the way" was parroted around the floor.

"Well, if we're going to work here, we might as well join the chorus from the next one," said Ed Regis.

James wondered, "How did Raider get in here, anyway? He couldn't follow us down his trapdoor because he had to move his bed back over it."

"Probably from another entrance," I said, remembering how Mr. Jenson had said that there were several ways in and out of Twenty Point Five.

A few minutes later, Raider himself appeared at our curtain.

"Well, well, a private room on your first day in," he remarked with more than a touch of distain in his voice. "It looks like you really do have Proton's favor."

"Apparently so," Terry replied evenly.

"Jacob is busy now," said Raider. "I was told to take you to the surveillance room and explain to you your first duties. Right this way, new people."

Clearly irked by Raider's condescending tone, James threw me a wry smile, shaking his head, but I just shrugged. I knew that Raider wasn't really mean or anything. He just had a bit of an attitude, which was fine.

The surveillance room was just down the hall from our sleeping quarters. It was a fairly large rectangular space lined with desks and tables, each with an office chair facing three large computer monitors set side by side. There were a total of eight work stations, and each of the twenty-four computer monitors displayed multiple security camera images from all over Lumina. I suspected that Wood-claw's security office was similar to this on a smaller scale, but as my memory of working there had been completely wiped by Mr. Beryl, the

Resistance surveillance room was a real eye-opener for me.

"This is one of our two main surveillance stations," explained Raider. "The other is in a different building." Then he added wryly, "Thanks to a certain famous hider that lives at the top of Lumina Prime, our finders are completely useless in tracking Angel psionics in Lumina. That's why we need this crazy setup."

The eight Knights manning the work stations swiveled their chairs around to look at us. People didn't stand up here if they could help it. We briefly exchanged introductions and handshakes before letting them get back to their jobs of quietly staring at their screens and occasionally typing memos into their computers.

"Keep your voices tolerably down in this room," warned Raider, gently tapping one of several pipes running along the ceiling. I noticed that it had been sprayed with red paint.

"We've heard about the pipes," said James.

Peering over the shoulders of the Knights, I could see in the monitors that the sun was just beginning to set over Lumina. I saw people strolling along the sidewalks, children running and playing in the park, and Angels chatting in the Lumina building lobbies. Some of the cameras were fixed in place while others slowly panned from side to side. I could see the hospital ward in New Haven Three as well as the insides of various stores and restaurants in the Lumina area.

There were even a few cameras hidden in people's homes, which I guessed belonged to prominent Angels. We were spying on their dining rooms, living rooms and even bedrooms. I saw a man lying half-naked on his bed, flipping through a sports magazine. It made me think of the PRC, and how Alia and I were under constant surveillance there by the Central Control Room that watched our every move from upstairs.

"So," said Raider, gesturing toward the monitoring stations, "this is your first job. Each of these stations is handled by two Knights working in twelve-hour shifts. You track the movements of all Angels that pass in front of your cameras, but especially the Seraphim and high-level Angel officials. You keep a log detailing when and where each Angel goes, how long they stay and when they return. You watch for signs of any unusual activity and report it. You can learn the specifics on the job from your coworkers."

"Great," James said with forced enthusiasm. "When do we start?"

"At the turn of the next shift, which is 8pm," said Raider, and pointed to one of the desks. "Tiffany and Richard can take Station B here, relieving Axel and his partner who are both already cleared for tourist work. And until Jack and Edmund become tourists, they can work at C, which belongs to me and Dizzy at the moment."

The Knight called Dizzy turned to Raider and said, "I think the S&D is starting early."

"Good," replied Raider. "I was just running out of things to explain."

Raider motioned for us to crowd around Station C. The monitors displayed several images of the area around what used to be called New Haven Six. A few of the other Knights also got up from their chairs and joined us at Dizzy's station.

"That's Lumina Quintus," said Dizzy, pointing to the building. "You can see the Seraphim gathering."

"What's an S&D?" I asked.

"Search and detain," explained Dizzy. "It's a flash raid acting on an anonymous tip about Guardian spies hiding in one of the Quintus condos."

The nonchalant way Dizzy said that struck me as odd. Terry thought it strange too, and asked, "So what's the big joke?"

"It's our tip," said Dizzy, smiling. "Quintus is the only building in Lumina that doesn't have any Guardian presence at all, but the Angels are dead certain that our command center is in there somewhere. They've been trying to find it for months now."

We watched through an outdoor camera as a team of about fifteen Seraphim dressed in dark suits gathered in front of the building. As they entered, we followed them through another camera that was set in the lobby. The team divided into two groups, one remaining in the lobby as the other entered the elevator. We watched the men inside the elevator from a ceiling-mounted security camera.

"Thirty-third floor," said Dizzy, punching a few buttons on her keyboard. "Too easy."

One of the monitors now displayed a hallway, and we watched the Seraphim knock on a door and quickly arrest a family of four. I saw a blond-haired girl about Alia's size and her younger brother clinging to their parents in the hallway. The mother was crying and shouting something. The father looked terrified as the dark-suited men marched the whole family into the elevator.

"What will happen to them?" asked Alia.

"They'll be taken to the Department of Allegiance for questioning," said Dizzy. "They'll be delved and, hopefully, let go at that."

"And if they're not?" I asked.

"Depends on which way the wind is blowing," Raider said lightly. "Torture, execution, reconversion... anything can happen."

Alia shook her head. *"This is wrong, Addy."*

"I know," I replied quietly as I watched the family being escorted out of the building.

Outside, the sky was getting darker.

"So that's our show for the day," said Raider. "You can decide amongst yourselves who gets the night shift, but make sure these seats aren't empty at 8:01 tonight. Meanwhile, you are free to explore the rest of Twenty Point Five and get to know the other Knights working here, but don't go opening up any trapdoors on the floors or ceilings. There are usually guards at the gates, but sometimes they get a little lax. We also have a mess hall somewhere around here. Find it when you get hungry, but don't expect any service."

"Thank you," I said.

"I'm the one to thank you," replied Raider. "At least now I can go outside a little more. This place is like a dungeon."

I couldn't say that I disagreed, but I guessed it was still better to be here than headed to the Department of Allegiance.

10. THE BLOOD RUNNER

Twelve hours is a very long time to be staring at a bunch of computer monitors and typing notes into a log book. Ed Regis and I got the night shifts: Ed Regis because he offered and I because Terry ordered me. Not that the shifts made that much difference here. Like at Wood-claw, day and night were essentially what the clock said.

In leaving Wood-claw's windowless apartments behind, we had merely traded one sun-deprived residence for another, but Nonus Twenty Point Five was truly the pits. Being far above ground didn't change the fact that it felt like a deep dungeon. By the second day, I missed Candace horribly, but at least there was a little comfort to be had in the knowledge that I was back inside Cindy's famously large hiding bubble. Of course I couldn't feel its effects in any tangible way, but it was nevertheless a pleasant thought.

Mark was furious (in his own gentle manner) at Raider for implying to us that we were bound to ever-recurring twelve-hour shifts.

"You can ask for a break whenever you need one," Mark assured us. "The gate guards are often willing to take on a shift, or at least half a shift, just to get a break from the monotony and be able to look outside."

We also learned quickly on the job that we weren't expected to be glued to the monitors every minute. Unless something exceptionally interesting was happening outside, most Knights took short breaks every few hours, and often a full hour for lunch. It wasn't uncommon to find a few seats empty at any given time.

And though I missed Wood-claw, I was glad for Mark's company whenever he could spare some time to join me in the surveillance room. I also got to know the other camera-crew Knights fairly well. Though we still called each other only by our aliases, with my disparately colored eyes and missing right ear, however well hidden by my long hair, my true identity was no mystery to anyone here.

"It's good of Proton to keep you and Tiffany off the streets," one camera-crew Knight called Willow said to me on my third night. "There're some pretty big prices on your heads, I hear."

"It's so great to be wanted," I joked.

"I am also wanted," said Willow, lighting up a cigarette, "ever since my cover was blown two months ago. That's why I'm stuck in here."

"You were a spy?" asked Ed Regis, who had been listening to our conversation from the side.

"A tourist, a scout, a spy, whatever you want to call it," Willow replied casually. She puffed on her cigarette for a moment. "Now I'm forever on the camera crew, which I'm sure you know by now is one of the least-sought-after positions inside the Resistance."

We laughed.

"Still, it was worth it," said Willow, giving her mildly bulging belly a light pat. "At least I got the bastard who killed my husband."

"Are you really supposed to be smoking?" I asked. "Doesn't it hurt the baby?"

"I'm trying very hard to cut down," replied Willow, eyeing her cigarette distastefully. She gave it one more long drag and then snubbed it out. "I've managed to limit myself to three or four a day."

Willow was almost four months pregnant with the child of her late husband. I wondered if she was really going to have her baby right here in Twenty Point Five. More likely, she would be escorted out on a phantom train before much longer.

"I suppose a little smoke wouldn't make a big difference in a place like this," I said, still not used to the musty air and various unpleasant fragrances. "But at least they could have given you the day shift."

"Actually, I requested the night shift," said Willow. "The day shift is much busier."

I learned from Willow that the majority of Resistance operatives, including the camera-crew Knights, were cleared for active tourist duty. This was because Proton carefully recruited people unknown to the Angels, usually from distant Guardian settlements and small independent factions like Woodclaw. (The exceptions to this policy included necessary VIPs such as intelligence officers, former New Haven security technicians, and the occasional celebrity Knight like Terry Henderson or Adrian Howell.) Most of the tourists hid in plain sight in and around the Lumina area, doing everything from running local coffee shops to working in the maintenance crews of the Angel-owned buildings.

"That's how we regained control of many of the cameras," said Willow. "Supposedly, we even have a few tourists inside Lumina Prime and in the Department of Allegiance."

"Supposedly?" I repeated.

"Well, only Proton and Jacob know who and where everyone is, of course," said Willow. "The rest of us are better off not knowing. After all, captured tourists can endanger everyone connected to them."

"What about Angel spies in our ranks?" asked Ed Regis.

"Uncommon," said Willow. "There're so few of us in Lumina that our organization is much harder to penetrate than theirs. But that doesn't mean they don't try. The worst case we had was back in July when the Seraphim managed to infiltrate one of our safe houses in Septimus. We lost nine of our men there, including two of our best blood runners." Willow looked longingly at her pack of cigarettes on her desk, but didn't reach for it. "Still, it could have been worse. They didn't even find the other safe house in the same building."

"And you still use that building?" said Ed Regis, who had camera access to the lobby of Septimus.

"We're more careful about it now, but yes," Willow said lightly. "Proton says to always assume that there are at least two spies somewhere in the Resistance. But I can guarantee that the Seraphim have never gotten into Twenty Point Five."

"How can you be so sure of that?" I asked skeptically.

Willow smiled. "Because we're all still here."

"That's reassuring." I couldn't help my sarcasm.

Willow laughed, and I asked her hesitantly, "What happens if the Seraphim do attack us?"

"It depends on how they attack," she replied with a shrug, "but we have a few ways to get out."

Ed Regis gave me a smirk. "Thinking of doing another nosedive into a dumpster?"

"Saved your life, didn't it?" I reminded him.

Willow said, "Don't worry too much. We've been around for a while now. These days, we're usually pretty good at spotting Angel spies well before they know it. That's how we managed to feed the Seraphim the idea that our command center is in Quintus rather than Nonus."

I remembered the family that was arrested on my first day here. "So you use their own spies against them?"

Willow nodded. "Whenever possible. The thing with Lumina now is that the Angel population is expanding so quickly that there's a lot of chaos. And where there's chaos, there're openings. That means opportunities for us."

Opportunities like the ones Willow was referring to always came with risks. While camera crew might be one of the least-sought-after positions here, it was undoubtedly one of the safest. At greater risk were the tourists, and at even greater risk were the blood runners.

Despite Proton's original plan, neither James nor Ed Regis was assigned to tourist duty. The Guardian intelligence team had deemed both unfit for outdoor work in Lumina. James was the son of two Guardian Knights and Ed Regis had been a senior member of the Wolves, meaning there was a good chance the Seraphim would recognize them both. Disguises were considered, but since having them work in the surveillance room allowed more qualified tourists to work outside, Mark told them that they would remain on the camera crew for the foreseeable future.

But for Alia, blood runner it was.

There were only two psionic healers in the Resistance aside from my sister, so I could understand Proton's demand and even Mark's agreement with making her a blood runner. But I wasn't at all happy.

"You wanted to come," I reminded Alia when she insisted on getting my permission. "It's your risk to accept, Alyssa."

"I want to help the people here, Richard," said Alia. "But I know you don't want me going out there."

Just because she could see right through me didn't mean I was going to admit it. "You're a Guardian Knight," I said, patting her back. "Do what you have to."

The deal was finalized near the end of our first week in Twenty Point Five. Being of school age, Alia's blood running would have to be restricted to weekends and weekday evenings, but even that, according to Proton, was a great help. The other two blood-runner healers were stationed at other safe houses, and they too could only work within specific timeframes.

"This expands our coverage of the city considerably," said Proton. "We've already lost too many operatives to the Seraphim simply because we couldn't reach them in time."

Alia's disguise was exactly as Mark had originally suggested: She would walk through Lumina as Raider's only child, Marion. Alia had to dye her hair a little lighter and lengthen it with a wig. I was skeptical about the wig at first, but outside was cold enough to merit a knit cap that hid the evidence well. Marion was on the tall side for a second grader, and aside from their shoe sizes, their clothes were a spot-on match. Once Alia was properly dressed, the only real difference between her and Marion was that Alia was psionic. But being inside Cindy's hiding bubble, as long as she didn't walk right next to any finders, healers or telepaths, she would be okay.

But the clothes were just one part of it. After all, the real Marion couldn't be seen outside at the same time as her double. Fortunately, Raider's converted Angel wife was a hardcore businesswoman who often spent days, sometimes as long as a week, out of Lumina. Raider's tourist cover was that of a handyman. This allowed him plenty of freedom to move about the Angel city whenever he needed to, and he had a special understanding with his daughter about "Mommy's problem." Put simply, Marion was a Guardian Resistance tourist too.

Still on the night shift, 4pm was early morning for me, but I was wide awake for Alia's first training mission. It was just one lap around Lumina with Raider to hold her hand. I trusted Raider a lot more than I liked him, but even so, I had plenty of doubts.

Terry and I followed Alia up to Raider's living room, where Marion quietly sat with a Guardian-appointed babysitter.

"Wish me luck, Addy," Alia whispered into my mind as she hugged me one last time.

"You don't need luck," I told her. "You've got Cindy watching out for you. You'll be fine."

Raider gave me a reassuring look and said, "The Seraphim won't bother checking a child her size too closely, especially since she's with me. Don't worry. I will guarantee Alyssa's safety."

"On your life," I informed him.

Raider grinned. "What did I tell you about trust, kid?"

As I watched them leave, I muttered under my breath, "I am really getting tired of people calling me kid."

"Come on," said Terry, pulling on my hand. "Let's go watch the monitors."

We did. I watched Raider take my sister through the park and out to the local supermarket. I watched them return with bags of groceries. I held my breath every time they passed someone on the sidewalk. As I watched them, I told myself over and over that this wasn't so different from the time we sent Alia out to help Samuel's heart surgery. I told myself that Alia was a soldier, and that I had allowed her to accept this risk, which she had every right to accept even without my consent.

"You do realize that this is just a training mission, don't you?" said Terry, watching me with amusement.

"Huh?" was my unfocused response.

"Come on, Richard! This is nothing compared to what she's already done."

That was as true as it was irrelevant. Sure, Alia had been through plenty of tighter spots than a milk run to a nearby store, but the thing about taking risks is that the law of averages eventually catches up with you. How much you have survived in the past is no indicator of what could happen in the next five seconds.

As I watched Alia and Raider chatting their way back to Nonus, I couldn't help but think of how Cindy had so loathed the idea of me joining Guardian missions with Terry. Now I finally understood what Cindy had felt as she watched me leave for the Holy Land. My sister was walking amongst Angel Seraphim right now, and all I could do was watch her through a camera. It was a truly humbling experience to discover how much worse that felt than being out there myself.

Alia returned safely to Nonus Twenty Point Five with a carton of fresh milk and a bag of chocolate chip cookies.

"See?" I said as we shared the cookies in the surveillance room. "I knew you'd be fine out there."

Alia laughed. *"Liar!"*

Now that she was officially a blood runner, Alia, who had often been staying up with me during the night shift, readjusted her sleep schedule to ensure that she was awake and ready for a real blood run with Raider.

The first one came near the end of November. A pair of tourists had been discovered by the Seraphim. One of them had managed to escape alive, but he had suffered severe burns on his upper body as well as taken a focused telekinetic blast to his right arm. Raider quietly escorted Alia out to a Resistance safe house located in the basement of a coffee shop where the injured tourist had taken refuge.

Again, I breathlessly watched their progress from the surveillance room. Alia returned all smiles, as she did from two more blood runs during the first half of December. I began to get a little used to it. I was mildly amused to discover that on her blood runs, Alia always carried around the little pony doll that Candace had given her. If I was keeping my fears to myself, Alia was putting on her bravest face too.

In addition to the actual blood runs, Raider periodically took Alia out on training missions, walking her around Lumina and visiting safe houses in every building that had them. One of the reasons for this was to familiarize Alia with the Resistance network in case she got separated from Raider. Alia, despite having no mental blocking training, wasn't considered a security risk simply because no one in their right mind would delve a child. According to Alia, some of the locations she visited were new even to Raider.

Since Alia's second mission, James had kindly swapped his day shift with me so that I could be up during my sister's blood-running hours. Willow had warned me, but the day shift was considerably busier than the night. There were many more people outside that we had to watch and log, not to mention the frequent parroting of announcements on the human intercom system.

Alia often sat with Terry and me during our day shifts. She didn't have many other places to be, anyway, so she worked as part-time camera crew. The first snow fell in early December, and we sometimes saw Patrick Land and a few of his school friends having snowball fights in the park. I could tell that Alia longed to be out there, but she watched the monitors and said nothing.

In the after-school hours, we would also catch glimpses of the real Marion outside playing with her friends or walking with her father. Many of our cameras were shared by Angel security elsewhere, so I made my sister study Marion's manner carefully. Marion liked to skip and let her long hair dance about as she walked. Alia did her best to imitate this. Even from a fair distance, I could always tell the difference between Marion and Alia, but I was relieved to see that, at least in their heavy winter jackets, the girls looked convincingly identical on the video.

Over the weeks, Alia had become very close to Raider and to her body double. Raider even jokingly called Alia his "other daughter," which greatly eased my mind since I knew he would look after her with his life, and I had asked for nothing less. Marion, who looked up to Alia like a big sister, sometimes came down into Twenty Point Five to play. In turn, Alia and I occasionally spent time with Marion up in Raider's condo, secretly cooking up proper meals when we could no longer stand the prison-grade food in Twenty Point Five's mess hall. Whenever I could get someone to cover the day shift for me in the surveillance room, we spent the whole day up there, which allowed me to enjoy the sunlight through the windows in Raider's living room. Even a winter sun was much better than none at all.

Just about any lifestyle can become routine. Even one in a place like Nonus Twenty Point Five. But things were still moving along outside and everywhere. Before the end of the year, Mark had dinner (breakfast for James and Ed Regis) with us in the mess hall where he gave us a report on the information we had provided upon our arrival.

"The Guardian Council identified Cindy's policeman friend as one Sergeant Brian Desmond," said Mark, "and it appears that Richard was right about Cindy sending Brian the Guardians' secret files."

By the word "appears," I could already guess what we were about to be told next. I raised my eyebrows and braced myself.

"Unfortunately, Sergeant Desmond is dead," reported Mark. "He shot himself several years ago. It was deemed a suicide."

"How typical," I said sarcastically.

Of course I felt sorry for Bullet-in-the-Butt Brian, yet another outside casualty of our psionic war, but more than that, I was just plain frustrated. Terry had warned me that this would end up being another wild-goose chase, but I had still hoped for something small to come of it. Every time we hit one of these dead ends, I felt as if we were trapped in a room full of locked doors where successfully picking one of the locks would only reveal a brick wall behind it.

"What about those two dead Angels from Wood-claw?" asked Terry.

"Our intelligence team is still working on that one," said Mark. When Terry gave him an incredulous stare, he explained, "Neither of them matches any of the Seraphim or even common Angels in Lumina or at other major Angel settlements. We're currently exploring the possibility that they may have been members of a separate Seraph division."

"What separate division?" asked James.

Mark replied evasively, "It's just a theory. We've heard rumors of the existence of a small, very select group of Angels that run top-secret operations for the king."

"Such as?"

"We don't honestly know," said Mark. "But King Divine knows that we have plenty of eyes and ears in his new capital city, as of course we do. He knows this city once belonged to the Guardians and that destroying the Resistance is nearly impossible because we're usually a step ahead of the Lumina government. Meanwhile, the Guardian Council has its spies in many of the other Angel settlements all over this country and abroad. That's why it's taking King Divine so long to destroy us."

Ed Regis asked, "So this supposed secret Seraph team works outside of the usual chain of command?"

Mark nodded. "We believe there are a handful of well-trusted people who only take orders directly from and report directly to Randal Divine himself. But we don't know who they are, where they are, or what, exactly, they're planning here or elsewhere. And that's assuming they even exist."

James said in a frustrated tone, "Then if Wood-claw could have kept those guys from killing themselves, they really might have taken us to the king."

Mark shrugged. "Again, it's just a theory."

"So we're another two leads down and nothing new in Lumina," I said dejectedly. "If we don't get something soon, this war could be over for us before the end of next year."

"As Cindy was so fond of saying, Richard, we just have to be patient."

"Tell that to our allies!" I snapped back.

Over the last few weeks, a host of small independent psionic settlements had followed the example set by the Meridian and openly declared their allegiance to the Angels. We knew that a few of them had only done so in order to avoid direct conflict while they continued to secretly assist the Guardian Council, but most of the factions were serious in their commitment. Their leaders and family heads were turning themselves in for conversion. Our hourglass was emptying at an increasingly alarming pace, and every time I heard of yet another surrender, I was reminded of Raider's words at the Chinese restaurant about the approaching tipping point of this war. How much longer did we really have?

Terry, who no doubt felt the same impatience, suddenly asked, "Just out of curiosity, Jacob, what about the Dog's Gate?"

"What about it?" asked Mark.

"Do the Guardians still use it?"

"Yes, but not often," said Mark. "Under the circumstances, there's very little left to negotiate."

Looking around, I could tell that Alia and I were the only ones who didn't know what the Dog's Gate was. Even our ex-Wolf seemed to be following the conversation. I was hoping my sister might ask in my stead so that I would be spared another embarrassing admission of how little I knew about the psionic world, but no such luck: Alia kept her mouth shut.

Putting my hand up, I asked, "What's the Dog's Gate?"

Predictably, Terry gave me a "you've got to be joking" look.

Ed Regis explained, "It's a bar and restaurant out east. It's run by an independent faction with ties to the Historian, and it serves as neutral ground for all of the psionic factions. Even the Wolves used to occasionally drop in to speak with faction representatives and negotiate temporary truces or request the extradition of psionic criminals."

I shrugged. "Never heard of it."

"Why do you ask?" Mark said to Terry. "The Dog's Gate and fifty miles around it is neutral ground. You know this. You can't capture or interrogate Angels there, and they won't simply tell you their deepest secrets because you buy them a drink."

Terry silently stared back at Mark.

Mark asked uncomfortably, "You're not planning on breaking neutral ground, are you?"

Terry still didn't reply, looking equally uncomfortable with the idea, so I answered in her stead, "Never ask us what we're prepared to break to win this war."

Mark said warningly, "You would risk the anger of the Historian, Richard."

"I'm not afraid of that brat," I replied evenly.

"Never mind, Jacob," said Terry, finding her voice again. "It was just a thought. A possible last resort."

Mark gave her a worried frown. "I would hate to be the one that tells Cindy that her children were killed over a neutral-ground violation."

"I'm not Cindy's child," said Terry. "Anyway, forget about it for now."

We finished our dinner and, parting with Mark, headed back down the narrow, cluttered corridors, carefully ducking the ceiling pipes.

As we walked, Alia, who had been silent all through dinner, griped, "I wish we didn't have to talk about dead people when we're eating."

I agreed, but I doubted the food here would have tasted that much better one way or the other.

Ignoring Alia's complaint, Terry whispered, "Assuming those Angels really were members of some super top-secret task force that reports straight to Randal Divine, what the hell were they doing snooping around the Wood-claw outpost?"

It was a rhetorical question but I answered it anyway. "They were looking for me."

Terry nodded. "They knew that you were on the Wolf plane and that you bailed over the city. They probably didn't know exactly where Wood-claw itself was hidden, but they'd assume that's where you were hiding."

I smiled. "So I guess we dodged another bullet, huh?"

"Dodging bullets doesn't help, Half-head," said Terry, her voice rising in frustration. "Damn the Wood-claw Knights! Those Angels could have changed everything."

The corridor was empty but I still put a finger to my lips to quiet her down. "Let's just work with what we have, Tiffy," I said calmingly.

Terry didn't reply, but James said darkly, "That'd be easier if we actually had something, Richard. Maybe we're wasting our time here."

"Where do you think we should be?" I asked him.

"Somewhere where we could hunt the Angels on our own terms," said James. "This is just sitting around and watching the world turn. It's not getting us anywhere."

I nodded in agreement. Back during our months traveling around the country in a motorhome, the Guardian Resistance in Lumina had seemed like the best place for us to be, but now I wasn't so sure. With the exception of keeping an additional blood runner in Lumina, our presence here wasn't making any great difference in the war effort. Nor in the course of almost two months helping to catalog the movements of Lumina's Angels had we come across anything that could lead us a step closer to the secret location of Randal Divine and his adopted daughter.

"How much longer are we going to stay here?" James asked Terry.

"As long as it takes," she replied automatically.

James let out a frustrated little huff.

I knew that James's discontent wasn't only caused by our collective lack of progress, but also his own. During the first week of our stay, Proton had made it absolutely clear that under no circumstance would James be given psionic blocking training at Nonus Twenty Point Five. Being a powerful berserker himself, Proton was keenly aware of the dangers associated with mind control. Though the official minimum age was eighteen, Proton believed in twenty-plus, and since James was restricted to the camera crew anyway, there was no reason to risk damaging his brain.

"We're rotting away in front of computers when we could be out there fighting this war," said James.

"Believe me, Jack," said Terry, "I'm just as frustrated as you, but we really have nothing to go on right now. At least here we still have a chance. Like Jacob said, be patient."

This from our fearless leader, who not many months ago had been considering attacking a random Angel outpost on the slim chance that someone there might have information. But Terry had given up on that plan entirely. Our time in the surveillance room had taught us that Randal Divine had hidden himself far too well for hit and miss tactics to work.

Making our way through the now familiar maze, we found Raider at the door to our sleeping quarters.

"I was looking for you," he said to Alia.

"Another run?" I asked apprehensively.

"No," replied Raider. "My wife had to leave on one last emergency business trip before the holidays and Marion wanted to invite her stunt double up for a sleepover tonight."

Alia jumped at the offer. "Can I go?" she asked me excitedly. "Please?"

"Sure," I said. It wasn't Alia's first sleepover with Marion, and the conversation there would probably be more to her liking anyway.

Alia grabbed her duffle bag and left with Raider.

Watching them go, James said, "When I first met that guy, I really didn't like him very much."

"Raider's a good man," I said. "He just takes some getting used to."

There was still almost an hour left to the end of the day shift, and Terry and I were supposed to head directly back to the surveillance room after dinner, but James and Ed Regis offered to start their shift early.

"Night is easier anyway," said James, who had experienced both and knew how much busier the daytime was.

Terry and I thanked them, watched them leave, and then stretched out as best we could in our cramped quarters.

It was still much too early for sleep.

The low ceiling in Twenty Point Five precluded any real combat training, but there was a weight room where we often spent an hour or so before bed. I thought about heading over there, but first I wanted to ask Terry a little more about the Dog's Gate.

"It was just an idea, Richard," insisted Terry. "Probably not a very good one."

I laughed. "Prudence was never one of your virtues, Tiffy. I think Jack has a point. We could stay here till the world ended and not be any closer to Randal than we are right now."

"Actually, I'm not too worried about breaking neutral ground," said Terry. "Considering our mission, I have a feeling the Historian would be willing to overlook it for us. But Jacob had it right during dinner. How are we supposed to find the right target? So few Angels seem to have any direct connection with Randal Divine."

I agreed that we had no answer to that problem. If we were going to grab a random Angel at the Dog's Gate, we might as well just grab one right here in Lumina. Either way, our chances of getting anywhere were equally minuscule.

But with Terry's mention of Mark, I had a different question. "Do you ever get the feeling that Jacob is keeping something from us?"

"Jacob is the codirector of the Resistance," Terry pointed out. "I'm sure there are many things he can't tell us."

I shook my head. "Not that kind of secret. Something more personal."

"Why do you say that?"

"Gut feeling," I admitted, my confidence rapidly fading.

Terry shrugged. "We're keeping a secret too. Anyway, I don't know him as well as you. He's your friend. Why don't you just talk to him?"

"Yeah," I said. "Maybe I will."

11. MATTERS OF TRUST

I didn't confront Mark that day or the day after, partly because I still had plenty of doubts about my gut feeling, and partly because I was distracted by a special New Year's mission that the Resistance had started up.

The Guardians were getting ready to pay the Angels back in kind for a prank that they had once played on us in New Haven. And our payment was going to be made with a considerable amount of interest. During the last week of December, our tourists carefully planted small explosives in strategic locations in and around the Lumina buildings. When detonated at the stroke of midnight on New Year's Eve, these bombs would sound like fireworks but kill or maim a fair number of Seraphim and common Angels. As our tourists worked outside, the camera crew carefully monitored their progress while all blood runners were kept on high alert, ready to move out at a moment's notice.

After days of watching over our tourists as they sprinkled Lumina with their deadly packages, I couldn't help feeling some disgust with the Guardians' idea of fun and games. It wasn't like I hadn't killed people too, but I felt that our moral standards here had reached a new low.

"Wasn't there something in the Bible about not killing people?" I asked Mark sarcastically.

"It's one of the Ten Commandments," confirmed Mark, "though we break it fairly frequently here. It's been a long time since I was a priest."

"Even I've heard of the Ten Commandments," I told him.

"In a perfect world, Richard, we wouldn't need them."

The mission was, for the most part, a success, even though one of our tourists was killed on the day before New Year's Eve while she was planting a bomb. Once the Seraphim discovered what we were up to, they doubled their guard and canceled several of their planned New Year's parties. A few of our bombs were found and defused before midnight but the Seraphim couldn't locate them all. As for the tourist who died, I had never even met her, and I found myself secretly relieved that she had been killed rather than wounded. It spared Alia from an extremely high-risk blood run through teams of Seraphim that were openly patrolling the streets and park.

There was, of course, no real New Year's party at Twenty Point Five. Instead, everyone crowded into the surveillance room at midnight to watch our fireworks wreak havoc on the Angels. Proton led the New Year's toast shortly after the mission ended with nineteen confirmed kills and three dozen more severely wounded. I didn't feel like celebrating a terrorist attack on our former capital, but I downed my wine and quietly cheered.

Miraculously, Alia had no blood runs during the first half of January, but Raider still took her out on short training runs every two or three days. Alia insisted, and I agreed, that Raider was as trustworthy a protector as Ed Regis and myself, but I knew that the Seraphim were seriously riled after our New Year's prank. Despite Raider's assurances that every precaution was being taken, I watched my sister through the cameras like a hawk with asthma.

In the overlap hours between the day shifts and night shifts, Alia and I still met Willow from time to time. In a small personal victory, the pregnant Guardian had finally managed to quit smoking. And her baby had started to kick. Alia couldn't get enough of that.

"When are you leaving Lumina?" I asked as Willow let Alia touch her belly and feel the baby moving around.

"I'm not sure yet," replied Willow. "But I might just have the baby right here."

"You're kidding, right?" I said.

Willow's stomach had grown so much by now that she was having lots of trouble navigating the cluttered, low-ceilinged corridors of Twenty Point Five.

"It won't be easy," admitted Willow, "but I want to keep making a difference. Even a little one."

Because she had lost her tourist status, Willow couldn't even visit a maternity hospital without getting a phantom train to take her out of the Lumina area. Proton and Mark were more than willing to accommodate her, but Willow insisted on receiving no special treatment. "We're all Resistance fighters," she often said. "Even the baby."

"But what if something happens?" I asked. "What if you get sick?"

"Birth is a natural process, Richard," Willow replied confidently. "Women have been having babies since prehistoric times. Besides, we have doctors here and even a brave little healer." She patted Alia's head. "I'm sure the baby and I will be just fine."

Alia asked, "Have you decided on a name yet?"

"Still working on that," said Willow. "I'm pretty sure it's a boy, and if it is, I'll probably name him Dominic after my husband."

"What if it's a girl?" asked Alia.

Willow smiled. "Then I might just name her after you."

"You mean Alyssa?"

"That's not a bad name, but I like your real one better."

Alia jumped a little in excitement. "It's kicking again! I think it's happy."

Willow laughed. "A little too happy."

Willow offered to let me feel her baby kicking, but I declined. Maybe putting her hands on a woman's big belly was okay for Alia, but I felt much too awkward about it. Still, it was nice to see that Willow and her baby were doing well. There was just so little good news these days.

Three weeks into the new year, my sister was finally ordered on a real blood run, but this one didn't go as smoothly as her last three.

It was a snowy Saturday afternoon. Raider escorted Alia to a safe house in Lumina Octavus where a large team of tourists had taken refuge after they came under heavy fire from Angel forces. They had managed to escape without any deaths mainly because two members of the Seraphim hunting them were actually Guardian spies. Nevertheless, reported injuries included gunshot wounds, cuts, burns, bruises and broken bones. Alia certainly had her work cut out for her, but she was joined in Octavus by four other blood runners, including one of the other two healers.

But when Raider returned to Nonus later that evening, Alia wasn't with him.

"Alyssa got blood on her jacket and pants so I couldn't bring her back," Raider informed me. "I had to make it look like a sleepover with friends. I'll go collect her tomorrow."

But that night I was woken at 1am by Ed Regis who told me that Octavus had just been targeted by an S&D.

"Casualties?" I asked, instantly wide awake and trying to keep myself from shaking.

"None," said Ed Regis, putting a calming hand on my shoulder. "The Seraphim didn't find our safe house there. But they were pretty close. They know we have people in that building and they're keeping a sharp eye on it."

Unable to go back to sleep, I joined Ed Regis and James in the surveillance room, but nothing else happened, and eventually I fell asleep in my chair.

When I woke in the late morning, Raider gave me a small update. "As a precaution, Alyssa and several others have been relocated to another hideout," he told me. "Proton says it's too dangerous to move anyone back here at the moment, so your sister will have to stay holed up there for a few days."

"Better her than Marion, huh?" I said savagely.

"I'm certain Alyssa is alright," said Raider. "I'll get her back safely." Then, with a wink and a smile, he added, "On my life."

I didn't smile back. "If anything happens to her, Raider, I swear you'll be the first to know whether I was joking when I said that."

Raider wiped the smile from his face and quietly left the room.

I knew that Raider was worried about his "other daughter" too, and that Alia had chosen to accept the risks involved in blood running for the Resistance. It was just easier to be angry at Raider right now.

Mark echo-called me to a meeting room for a private chat later that day.

"Raider is one of our most trusted, most reliable operatives, Richard," he began. "You threatened his life today."

"He told you?" I asked, surprised at Raider's lack of backbone.

"No, of course not," said Mark. "I actually heard you. Through the walls."

"Oh," I said, feeling stupid. "Well, I didn't say I'd kill him."

"Nor did I say I was disappointed in you," Mark said evenly. "Though I am."

I huffed. "You want me to go and apologize to him?"

"Later," said Mark, "if you feel like it. I didn't call you here to lecture you, but to answer any concerns you may have over Alyssa's situation."

"Tomorrow is Monday," I said. "Marion goes to school. Except Marion is supposed to be out on a sleepover."

"Marion will be snuck out of this building tomorrow and go to school as if directly from her sleepover," said Mark. Before I could argue, he added, "And if this ends up dragging out, we will deal carefully with all of the ensuing discrepancies. We've been in Lumina quite awhile and we're pretty good at these things."

"Not good enough to keep your people from getting shot, burned and killed," I reminded him. "Or else we wouldn't need healers here."

Mark said patiently, "For security reasons, I can't give you specific details, but I can assure you that our blood runners are given the highest priority for protection. I wouldn't have allowed Alyssa to become one otherwise. She is protected in more ways than you can possibly know, not only by Raider, but throughout our entire network in Lumina. We value her very much." After a short pause, Mark corrected himself, saying quietly, "I value her very much."

"I'll apologize to Raider when I see him," I promised.

Mark smiled. "Thank you."

I laughed embarrassedly. "You actually heard me through the walls this morning?"

"Well, you weren't exactly keeping your voice down," said Mark, laughing also. "Privacy is hard to get in Twenty Point Five. That's why we have meeting rooms like this one."

"Soundproof?" I asked doubtfully, looking around at the shabby walls.

"Surprisingly soundproof," confirmed Mark. "But only if you keep your voice down. Why? Are you considering telling me whatever secret it is that you brought here from Wood-claw?"

"No," I said, dropping my volume down considerably. "But as long as we're here, I'd like to ask you a question. Something I've been wondering about since I came to Lumina."

"Be my guest," said Mark, bringing his voice down a notch as well.

"And so long as we're whispering here," I began, "is it alright if I call you Mark?"

Mark smiled warmly. "Sure, Adrian. But that wasn't your question, was it?"

I shook my head. "I remember sitting in that little confession room at your church. It was a long time ago, but I think you said that you were bound by some seal or something that made you keep people's secrets."

Mark looked at me quizzically.

"I sort of wish we were back there now," I said.

"The confessional is just a symbol, Adrian," said Mark. "If you discuss something with me that has to stay between us, I promise that it will."

I nodded slowly. Then, taking a deep breath, I looked him in the eyes and asked, "You already know my secret, don't you, Mark?"

Mark didn't immediately reply. He looked down at his hands folded in his lap, breathing quietly.

Then he nodded.

"Does anyone else know?" I asked.

Mark shook his head. "Not from me."

"How did you find out?"

"From Cindy. Shortly after the gathering of lesser gods."

I nodded, understanding. "Ralph Henderson had written a letter to Cindy that was to be delivered if he died. He wanted Cindy to know the truth so that she could keep me safe until I had kids of my own."

"Yes," said Mark. "But back then, Cindy was afraid that the Angels might try to kill her in retaliation for the assassination of their queen."

"So she passed Ralph's envelope to you."

"It wasn't sealed."

I smiled grimly. "So you know exactly why I have come to Lumina, Mark. You know what I'm trying to do."

"Yes, Adrian," breathed Mark. "I know why you're here."

We sat silently for a minute. I gazed down at the amethyst pendant resting on my chest.

"Someone here needs to know who the real target is," I whispered. "It's better this way. It's better that you know. Cindy trusted you. I will trust her and you. If I fail, and I probably will, then I need you to pick this up and finish it for me. The Havels cannot be allowed to rule this world any more than the Divines, or anyone. Nothing else matters."

"Nothing?" asked Mark.

I knew then that Mark really had come to Lumina to protect Cindy.

I asked slowly, "Do you still believe in God, Mark?"

Mark nodded, saying quietly, "I won't deny that I've had my moments of doubt, Adrian, but yes, I do."

"You believe he watches over us?"

Mark nodded again.

"And judges us?" I asked.

"And judges us," confirmed Mark.

I shook my head. "How will he judge me, Mark? How will he judge what I'm trying to do?"

"As he judges all things, Adrian," Mark said gently. "With grace."

After that conversation, apologizing to Raider for my death threat seemed pretty trivial, and I did later that evening.

"I'm sorry for how I spoke to you," I said to him as humbly as I could. "I know what happened isn't your fault. I was upset. I'm sorry."

Raider seemed quite taken off guard by my sudden apology. "Believe me, Richard, you have nothing to be sorry about," he replied understandingly. "If our positions had been reversed, I probably would have said the same things to you."

"I really am happy that you're the one assigned to my sister's protection," I said, and I meant it.

That night, Terry, who had been in the surveillance room with me when I was summoned by Mark, asked me what we had discussed. I told her. Terry agreed that it was probably a good thing that Mark knew our secret.

"Though if this leaks out," she warned, "you'll never be able to live with the Guardians again. Half of them will be trying to catch you and the other half will be trying to kill you."

"That's assuming there're Guardians left when this is over," I replied lightly. With my sister still stuck in some ditch across town, I had little capacity for such trivial concerns.

During that night and the following day, the Seraphim conducted five

S&Ds in and around Lumina Octavus. The Seraphim, convinced that at least one of our healers had gone to the aid of the injured tourists, were hell-bent on finding them.

On Proton's orders, Raider and Mr. "Sharky" Jenson organized a number of phantom trains to move our people farther away from the search area and distribute them into several separate hideouts.

"We're going on the safe-house grand tour," Raider said wryly when he returned.

Due to some technicality involving the thermographic cameras, Alia still couldn't be returned to Twenty Point Five. Again I was painfully reminded of what I must have put Cindy through when I was caught by the God-slayers.

"How is she doing?" I asked Raider.

"She looked a little tired and was complaining about her hair being itchy, but otherwise she was in good spirits," said Raider. "Just hang in there, Richard. Trust me, and trust the Guardians to keep her from harm."

Finally, three days later, another phantom train was set up, this time one that could avoid the body-heat cameras. Raider and Mr. Jenson returned Alia to Nonus in the late evening. My sister looked pretty worn out, but uninjured.

"It must have been quite a battle, Alyssa," I said as she hugged me in the surveillance room. "You've got dried blood all over your clothes."

"It's not my blood," said Alia. *"But I'm really hungry."*

Over dinner, she told me about how she had spent much of the last two days curled up in a suitcase-size space under some floorboards in a small restaurant.

"I couldn't come out at all during the daytime," said Alia. *"I was so thirsty. The Angels came in and searched the place twice but they couldn't find me."*

Though shaken by her ordeal, Alia was determined to continue blood running with Raider. I didn't try to talk her out of it.

"I'm actually kind of impressed with you," Terry said teasingly to me. "You used to be such a watchdog."

"There's nothing to be gained from arguing with a stubborn healer," I replied resignedly.

But that didn't make it any easier for me to bear when, only two days later, my sister was asked to go on another blood run. Adding additional fuel to my fear was the fact that the target safe house was once again in Lumina Octavus.

"This one's just in and out," Raider assured me as Alia quickly pulled her little pony out of her duffle bag. "Only one guy hurt. No drama, I promise. We'll be back for dinner."

"Go," I said to Alia. "Be safe, don't slip on the snow."

True to Raider's word, my sister returned safely from Octavus this time, as she did from three more blood runs during the first half of February. These were to other, comparatively safe locations, and though I still kept a watchful eye through the cameras, I was no longer changing color in my seat.

When Catherine Divine's fifteenth birthday arrived in mid-February, aside from briefly wondering how old she would have to be before Randal trusted her to openly rule her empire, I really wanted to let the day pass unmarked. I had decided that since Catherine was no longer my sister, I would no more celebrate her birthday than I would Randal's. Apart from my mission to end it, Queen Divine's life was none of my business.

But Catherine Divine's fifteenth turned into a day that I would never forget.

That afternoon, Raider came into the surveillance room to fetch Alia, quietly announcing that they had been called out to Lumina Octavus again. I was a little apprehensive about the location, but after all, this would be my sister's third trip to Octavus and her sixth blood run of the year. I sent her off with a confident smile.

It was a particularly cold winter and there was still a fair amount of snow on the ground. From the comparative comfort of the surveillance room, I watched Raider take his "daughter" out, across the street and into the park. Both wore heavy winter jackets and warm knit caps. Holding her little pony in one hand, Alia skipped along the asphalt path much like Marion would.

Soon I lost sight of Raider and Alia among the snow-covered trees. With a few keystrokes, I switched my main monitor to a camera that would show the pair coming out of the park on the other side.

When they did, Alia had lost the skip. She and Raider were still walking at a normal pace and my camera view was too distant to make out my sister's expression, but something about her movements made me uncomfortable. I rapidly flipped through the nearby cameras to check for Angel activity, but found nothing.

Terry, sitting next to me, noticed my tension. "What is it, Richard?"

"I'm not sure," I said uneasily. "Maybe it's nothing."

Terry laughed. "Still a watchdog!"

I figured she was probably right. I was just nervous because it was another Octavus run.

I continued to closely monitor Raider and Alia's progress to Lumina Octavus and then, breathing a sigh of relief when they re-emerged from the lobby, I watched them return by the same road.

But when I saw them up close through Nonus's lobby security camera, it was clear to me that Alia really was troubled by something. I noticed something else about her too: she wasn't holding her pony.

I met my sister at the bottom of the ladder under Raider's trapdoor. Because he had to move his bed back into place, Raider didn't follow Alia down into Twenty Point Five. Alia had changed out of her Marion disguise and back into her regular clothes, and I pretended not to notice the missing pony doll as she silently wrapped her arms around me and started to cry into my shoulder.

The trapdoor guard was looking curiously at us, so I said to him, "It's alright. She gets like this sometimes."

But it wasn't alright. Something was deathly wrong. Alia still said nothing, so I took her hand and slowly led her back to the surveillance room.

"Alyssa!" Terry quietly exclaimed when we arrived. "Are you okay?"

Alia nodded dully.

"What happened?" asked Terry.

"I lost my unicorn," Alia whispered hoarsely. "I left it at Octavus."

"That's it?!" Terry looked incredulous. "You're all teary-eyed over a stuffed animal?"

"Listen," I said to Terry, "can you cover for me for a while? I want to take her back to our quarters."

"Sure," said Terry. Glancing over at my monitors, she asked, "Hey, isn't that Raider?"

Through the main monitor of my station, which was still set to the Nonus lobby, I saw Raider leading the real Marion outside. It seemed a little strange since the lobby security had just seen him return here with Marion, but no doubt Raider had some good excuse. Right now, I was much more concerned for my sister.

"I'll be back later, Tiffy," I said, leading Alia out of the surveillance room.

Our tiny little room was empty. It was a little past 6pm, and James and Ed Regis had already woken and presumably gone to the mess hall for their breakfast. I knelt in front of Alia so that I was eye level with her and asked quietly, "So how did you lose your little pet?"

"I left it at Octavus," repeated Alia, her eyes still red with tears.

"But you wouldn't have done that if you weren't really bothered by something else," I said. "Tell me. Something happened in the park on your way out there, didn't it?"

Alia stared down at her feet for a moment, and then nodded.

"What happened?" I asked.

More tears welling in her eyes, Alia stammered into my head, *"I... I can't, Addy..."*

"What happened?!" I pressed. "Tell me!"

"It was an accident," whispered Alia. *"I didn't mean to..."*

"What did you do?" I asked slowly, but then I understood. "You met Patrick, didn't you?"

Alia started to sob. *"I saw him on the path. I wasn't trying to talk to him, Addy. It—it just popped out."*

I grabbed her shoulders. "What did you say to him?!"

"I called his name."

"In his head?"

Alia nodded miserably. *"I didn't mean to."*

"Then what happened?"

"He looked at me. He looked at my eyes. He knew it was me. He smiled, and then he waved. Then he ran off. He didn't even say anything."

"Still, Raider must have noticed."

"He didn't know Patrick, Addy. I told him that Patrick was the brother of one of Marion's friends."

"You have to tell him, Alia!" I said, forgetting to call her Alyssa. "Raider will probably find out soon enough anyway. We need to tell Proton about this as soon as possible."

Shaking her head, Alia cried into my head, *"You can't, Addy! They'll do something horrible to him. They might even kill him!"*

"I'm worried about Patrick too," I said, "but I'm more worried about what he might do to us."

"No, Addy, Patrick won't tell. I know he won't! He's not converted!"

"But his mother is," I pointed out.

"So is Marion's!"

"This is dangerous, Alia!"

"Please, Addy!" Alia begged hysterically, tears streaming down her cheeks. *"Please don't say anything to Proton! They'll kill Patrick! They'll kill him! I know it!"*

I roughly grabbed her by the front of her shirt and shouted, "The only reason the Guardians let you out of this building is to serve their cause! Don't you dare forget which side you're on!"

Alia stopped crying. She looked at me like I had slapped her.

Suddenly the curtain opened and Terry stepped inside, saying, "Hey, Richard, your voice is carrying."

"I'm sure it wasn't carrying all the way to the surveillance room!" I snapped. "What are you doing here?"

"I got curious," said Terry. "What's going on?"

I explained in a whisper.

"You've got to be kidding me," breathed Terry. "We have to alert the intelligence crew before this gets out of hand."

But just then we heard a call echo through the floor: "Alert status. S&D on Nonus."

I looked at Terry grimly. "I think it just did."

Terry glared at Alia. "This better not be your boyfriend's doing!"

Alia opened and closed her mouth a few times, but no words came out. Not even telepathically.

12. DEUS EX MACHINA

It wasn't the first S&D in Nonus since our arrival. In fact, we had watched three of these from the surveillance room already. Thanks to our counter-intelligence team, each time the Seraphim came, they searched floors that were either much higher or lower than Twenty Point Five. And only one of their raids had caught us by surprise. We had known about the other two well before they happened.

But this was different. A flash raid right after Alia had been identified by a child of an Angel family. Though I was still desperately clinging to the hope that it was a coincidence, I wasn't about to keep Alia's secret.

"Proton and Jacob," I called out, "please report to the surveillance room." The request was picked up by several others and passed on.

"Let's go," said Terry. "Edmund and Jack will probably head there too."

Terry was right. We found Ed Regis and James in the surveillance room, and Mark arrived moments later, followed by several Knights.

"Where's Proton?" I asked Mark.

"He's out," said Mark. "I'm in command. We're on an S&D alert, Richard, so this had better be an emergency."

I poked Alia in the back. "You tell him or I will."

Alia spoke to Mark telepathically, staring down at her feet ashen-faced. Meanwhile, through the monitors, I counted eleven dark-suited Seraphim gather in the Nonus lobby.

"It's alright, Alyssa," said Mark, putting a comforting hand on her shoulder. "Let's just watch and see what happens."

"What's going on?" asked James, who, like everyone else in the surveillance room, hadn't heard Alia's telepathic confession to Mark.

"It seems as though the Seraphim may have found one of our entrances," announced Mark. "Raider's place. We need to get Raider and his child out of there now."

"They're already out," reported Terry. "I think Raider took Marion grocery shopping or something."

"Good," said Mark. He turned to one of the Knights who had followed him into the surveillance room and commanded, "Go to the communications room and send a message out to have our tourists intercept Proton and Raider and anyone else scheduled to return here today. Make sure everyone stays clear of Nonus until we're sure it's safe."

As the Knight hurriedly left, Mark turned to us and said, "Don't worry. Even if they do find the trapdoor, they'll still have to break through it, and we have plenty of other exits to evacuate from."

Alia looked up at Mark again, probably speaking telepathically.

"It's alright, Alyssa," Mark said gently. "We've been ready for this for quite a while now."

By now, most of the Knights in Twenty Point Five had gathered in the surveillance room. The nearly thirty Guardians here were members of the intelligence team, the camera crew, door guards and off-duty tourists. About half of them were either psionic destroyers or had other powers that could assist in combat. But regardless of psionic powers, everyone was armed with pistols or automatic rifles, including Terry, James, Ed Regis, and even Mark. The only exceptions were Alia and me. I had left my pistol in our sleeping quarters since my first day here. I thought about running back to retrieve it, but then a camera-crew Knight said, "They're coming up."

The Knight's monitor displayed the inside of the elevator carrying the Seraph S&D team.

"They hit the button for the twenty-first," announced the Knight. Then he muttered, "Looks like they finally got us."

Others murmured in agreement.

Through the corner of my mouth, I asked Ed Regis, "Have you decided which promise you're going to keep?"

"Ask me again in five minutes," replied Ed Regis, checking his automatic rifle.

I looked at him grimly. "We may not be here in five minutes."

One of the day-shift camera-crew Knights vacated his seat in order to allow Willow, whose pregnancy was approaching its bursting point, to sit down. I wondered how Willow was going to keep up with the evacuation in her heavy condition, but I said nothing.

We didn't have a hallway camera on the twenty-first, but we did have a hidden camera in Raider's living room, put there by Raider himself of course. We watched the Seraphim enter Raider's condo and start poking around.

The Knight that Mark had sent to the communications room returned and reported, "Proton is clear, but I'm afraid Raider may have been arrested."

"Understood," said Mark.

"This is my fault," Alia said shakily into my head.

"It's not," I whispered back. "Hush and stay sharp."

"Jacob?" said one of the senior Knights. "Which evac plan are we going with?"

"Not sure yet," replied Mark. "Probably shaft to basement. Get your team to Raider's gate and hold position. Everyone else stand fast."

The Knight and six others left the room.

Mark explained, "The Seraphim don't seem to know that they've stumbled across our command center. They think it's just another small hideout so we still outnumber them. We'll lure them down here and then fall back into the elevator shaft. The Seraphim control the lobby, but we can drop down to the basement parking lot and, with the help of our phantoms, get out before the Angels know what's going on."

We all knew this, of course. The elevator shaft had a service ladder built into the wall, but it was a very long climb down. Once invisible, we would just have to take our chances with the thermographic cameras outside.

An alternative plan involved parachuting everyone out from the twentieth-floor windows. But if we did that, the Seraphim would probably spot us in the air and then we could end up being used for target practice. Phantoms couldn't help us jump invisibly because the jolt of a parachute snapping open would shake the cloak off.

"Jacob," called Willow, "the S&D team is moving out of Raider's place. I think they may have missed the trapdoor."

"That's hard to believe," said Mark.

Ed Regis nodded. "Perhaps they do know what they've stumbled across."

As if to confirm this assessment, we were suddenly plunged into darkness as Nonus Twenty Point Five lost all electrical power.

"Stand fast!" commanded Mark.

Several Knights switched on their gun-mounted flashlights while the pyroids produced little balls of flame on their palms, restoring just enough light to make out the many tense faces in the room.

"It looks like they shut down the whole building, sir," said one of the Knights.

"They're probably gathering their forces outside," said Mark. "We may not be able to go through the basement after all."

"Jump?" suggested Willow.

"Yes," replied Mark. "Before it's too late. We'll drop into the twentieth floor on the southern side and jump from the back of the building."

I knew that we only had about twenty parachutes stocked. Several of the Knights would have to jump tandem, though Willow would certainly get a parachute to herself. Once again, I would do without a pack, but I hoped at least Terry, James and Ed Regis would each get one so that I wouldn't have to worry about carrying any of them down this time. Alia could either hover-jump with me or go tandem with Ed Regis again.

Using the flashlights and pyroid flames to find our way in the otherwise pitch-black corridors, we started filing toward the storage room where the parachutes were kept. Mark called out to the team of Knights that he had sent to guard Raider's trapdoor, ordering them to come back and join us at the storage room.

Before we reached the parachutes, however, the Seraphim made their move.

First there was a massive explosion in the direction of Raider's entrance, and the whole building trembled as the trapdoor blew apart. Then the shooting started.

"Get down!" shouted several voices at once.

I grabbed Alia and pulled her to the concrete floor. In the darkness, I couldn't see anyone else from my team except Ed Regis, who had also hit the deck when the first shots rang out through Twenty Point Five.

Our Knights immediately opened fire in the direction of the Seraphim, shooting their guns right through our thin, makeshift walls. Pulling Alia along, I followed Ed Regis to a space behind one of the concrete columns which provided the only real cover aside from the darkness.

"We've got to get to the parachutes!" shouted Ed Regis as he fired his automatic rifle at the Seraphim from around our cover.

"There's no way through this!" I shouted back, pushing Alia into a safer position behind the column. "Where's Terry?!"

Ed Regis didn't answer. From there, everything was screaming, gunfire, psionic flames, blasts, lightning bolts, wind and chaos. The walls fell apart around us as bullets and telekinetic blasts pounded the thin wood, plastic and glass into little fragments, which were then whipped up in violent gusts of wind that tore through the darkness. There were at least three Guardian windmasters here including Terry, and though the wind was probably meant to help cover our escape, we could hardly keep our eyes open. The Seraphim had a few windmasters on their side as well. Pyroid fireballs flew erratically in the psionic storm, impacting on the pipes and concrete columns, or sometimes just exploding in midair, sending little sparks in every direction.

Ed Regis continued to fire his rifle in very short bursts at the Angel invaders. I doubted the ex-Wolf would have to save a bullet for me after all. The Seraphim were giving us everything they had, with no intention of taking prisoners. I looked around for Terry and James, but they were nowhere in sight. The few other Knights I could see were pinned down like we were, returning fire with their guns and psionics. There was nowhere to escape to. I wondered if perhaps Terry and James were already dead.

I pulled Ed Regis's pistol from its holster and, flipping off the safety, fired a few random shots at the Seraphim too. If we were all going to die here, then at least I wanted to die fighting.

Suddenly I found myself face to face with James, who hollered, "We gotta get down to twenty! There's a trapdoor over there!"

"Ed Regis doesn't have his chute yet!" I shouted back over the wind and explosions.

"Doesn't matter!" screamed James. "Stay here and we're all dead!"

I heard Alia call into my head, *"Addy!"*

"Alia!" I shouted as I realized that I was no longer holding her hand. "Where are you?!"

"I've got her," called Ed Regis from my left. "Come on! Let's go!"

James was holding his own pistol in his right hand and what looked like Terry's in his left, and he simultaneously fired a few covering rounds from both at the Seraphim coming down Raider's trapdoor.

"Heads down!" he shouted. "Crawl forward!"

I saw Ed Regis discard his rifle and push Alia ahead of him as James led us through the firefight. Bringing up the rear, I followed closely behind Ed Regis's feet.

But the Seraphim weren't only coming in from Raider's bedroom. Other explosions had opened up several entry points, and the Seraphim were dropping down into Twenty Point Five from all around us now. Using the concrete columns for cover, the remaining Guardians were doing all they could to hold the Angel forces back, but we were being swarmed. As I crawled behind Ed Regis toward wherever it was that James was leading us, I saw three Guardians die. One of them was screaming horribly as she was engulfed in pyroid flames. It was Willow.

"Down the hole!" shouted James, nodding toward a small square opening in the floor. "Go! Go!"

He rolled over and sat up on the concrete. Aiming his pistols in separate directions, he fired them both empty as Alia and then Ed Regis dove headfirst into the trapdoor.

"Go!" James shouted again as I scrambled forward. "Get down there!"

I was about to dive in, but the next instant I saw James's body shudder violently as a dozen rounds of gunfire ripped into his chest. I felt his warm blood spatter onto my face. Even over the screaming wind and incessant gunshots, I clearly heard the sick hissing sound of the air leaving his lungs. James opened his mouth to scream, but nothing came out, and I knew that this wasn't the kind of thing my sister could heal.

James fell heavily onto his back. His eyes followed mine as I crouched next to him.

"Go, Adrian..." he slowly mouthed, blood pouring from his lips. "Finish this."

I nodded once, and then pulled myself into the trapdoor.

I fell down onto a springy mattress. It was a bedroom with the lights dimmed so that the Seraphim above wouldn't easily spot the trapdoor. Hands grabbed me and pulled me off the bed. A small but painfully bright light was shined into my face.

"Richard!" said Terry, pulling me toward the only door. "Where's Jack?! He went back up to find you! Where is he?!"

I shook my head, still dazed from what I had just seen. James's eyes were still looking at me.

"Where is he?" Terry asked frantically. "Didn't you see him?!"

I shook my head again and mumbled, "He's gone, Terry. He's gone."

In the next room, I found a handful of Guardians including Ed Regis, Alia, Mark and Mr. Jenson. Alia was helping heal the badly burned right arm of one of the Knights.

"How many more of ours up there, Richard?" Mark asked me.

"I don't know," I breathed. Using my sleeve, I wiped most of James's blood from my face, which cleared my head a little. "I think they're mostly dead."

"Alright, let's close it up," said Mark. "We've got to move quickly."

The Knights sealed the trapdoor, but we weren't out of danger yet. Not by a mile. Aside from what was left of my team, there was Mark and Mr. Jenson and eight other Knights here. That totaled only fourteen people.

"We couldn't get to our parachutes, so we're going by the shaft," announced Mark.

Lumina Nonus was still without power, which was to our advantage at the moment because this meant the security cameras couldn't spot us as we left the condo and headed toward the elevator. The Seraphim had all attacked from the twenty-first floor, and none were on the twentieth yet.

The Knights pried open the elevator's double doors, and in we went, single file down the iron service ladder. The inside of the elevator shaft was too dark to see far in either direction. Under more normal circumstances, this would have been a harrowing experience in its own right, but after what we had just escaped, no one complained or hesitated in the least.

Instead of telekinetically hovering my way down, I used the ladder like everyone else. I had wiped my face as well as I could but I was still being slightly drained by James's blood. Besides, I wanted to save my psionic power in case I needed it later.

The last Knight in had closed the elevator doors so that we wouldn't be tracked. We got to the bottom of the shaft in good time and without Angel contact.

Gesturing to the double doors that led to the basement parking lot, Mark whispered, "They could be right outside."

"Only one way to find out," said Terry. "Open it."

The Knights who still had guns trained them on the doors. I had lost Ed Regis's pistol somewhere, but I prepared a focused blast in my right index finger as Mark and Mr. Jenson carefully pried the doors open.

There was nothing waiting for us.

We climbed out of the shaft and into the basement parking lot. The fluorescent tubes lining the ceiling were all dead, and by now the outside was so dark that very little light shined down the exit ramp into the parking lot.

"It's too damn quiet," said Ed Regis. "They didn't even close the shutter on the exit ramp."

"That's the only way out," said Mark. "It could be a trap but we can't stay here."

Mark turned to Mr. Jenson, saying, "Sharky, set us up."

"Alright," said Mr. Jenson. "Three trains, five, five and four. Once outside, we'll split up and head to our designated safe houses."

Mr. Jenson quickly divided up the Knights so that he and Mark would each lead a group of five, leaving Terry, Alia, Ed Regis and me in the last group. As train leaders, Mr. Jenson and Mark would have to keep their eyes visible in order to see where they were going, but that meant attentive Seraphim around Nonus could spot them. I wasn't going to take that chance.

"I'll lead my team, Sharky," I told Mr. Jenson. "No eyes."

"Are you sure, Richard?" asked Mr. Jenson.

"You know me," I said. "I don't get lost in the dark."

"But do you know where you're going?"

"Not really," I admitted.

Mark said to me, "Do you remember that store across from the pool you used to swim at during the summers?"

I nodded.

"Don't lose your cloak until you're inside the store. If the front door is locked, move around to the back from the left side. There's a back door that will be open."

"Got it. Will we see you there?"

"Not for a few days. I'll be at a different safe house until this blows over." Mark looked around at us. "Good luck, all of you. I'm sorry about your friend."

We didn't have a rope this time so we had to hold hands. Terry hooked the back of my shirt collar and put Alia behind her, followed by Ed Regis who brought up the rear.

Then Mr. Jenson turned all of us invisible from head to toe. As my world flickered into oblivion, I realized my mistake: I didn't even have a stick to guide me.

But it was too late to do anything about it. The other two teams were already on the move. I remembered the general direction of the exit ramp and started walking, choking a little as Terry's hook pulled on the back of my collar.

"Keep pace," I croaked.

Walking blind, my own pace was probably much slower than Mark's and Mr. Jenson's, but after counting roughly fifty paces, my left hand found what I believed to be the concrete wall that would lead us up the exit ramp. I soon found the incline with my feet and, running my left hand fingertips along the wall, I slowly led my team upwards.

I guessed the other two trains were already well out of Nonus, and I still didn't hear any sounds of fighting. I knew that this ramp led up onto a fairly large street with plenty of non-faction people. The Seraphim would be unable to attack us once we were outside.

We reached the top of the ramp and stepped out onto the sidewalk.

Suddenly Terry's hook yanked on my shirt collar, pulling me down as I heard several surprised yelps and my vision instantly returned.

Looking around, I discovered that a suited businessman had walked right into our invisible train, tripping over Alia and falling facedown onto the sidewalk. Our train had lost its cloak upon impact. So much for the no-eyes plan.

Painfully picking himself up and looking utterly bewildered, the man said to Alia, "I'm sorry. I didn't see you there. I was running and—"

"It's okay," said Ed Regis, shoving the man away and frantically looking around for more serious threats.

Terry, Alia and I looked around too, but there were no Seraphim in sight.

We were no longer carrying any guns, having lost them during the firefight in Twenty Point Five, but our group still stood out on the street: Despite the February chill, we didn't have winter jackets. Our clothes were dirty and bloodstained, and Terry was wearing her hook.

"Let's go," said Terry.

We quickly made our way down the sidewalk between small piles of shoveled snow. My heart was still racing and I hardly noticed the cold.

When we tried to turn a corner, we were met by a team of six dark-suited Seraphim. They recognized us instantly, but they didn't attack. There were still plenty of pedestrians on the sidewalk and cars running up and down the street.

The Seraph team leader stepped forward and looked around at us. His eyes stopped on Terry's hook for a second, and then he said to me, "Adrian Howell, I presume?"

I nodded as Alia gripped my left hand. I instinctively prepared a blast in my right.

The leader smiled like a peacemaker. "If you will quietly come with us, the rest of your team may go free."

"I've heard lies like that before," I replied evenly.

"We control the law in this town," said the leader. "If you refuse, we can simply have you arrested by the police."

Ed Regis took a step forward and growled, "You'll have to call them first."

"Come on," said Terry, pulling on my arm and leading us in the opposite direction. "Don't even look back. They can't touch us if we stay in the open."

"But we can't go to the safe house like this," I argued. "They'll follow us there."

The Seraphim were trailing us at a distance of only about ten yards.

"I'll think of something," said Terry.

We continued walking. The Seraphim kept pace. The park was just ahead of us now, and I suspected that Terry wanted to lead the Angels inside and deal with them there.

That was when we noticed the flashing red and blues of a police car coming up the road from behind us.

I heard the Seraph team leader call out, "I beg of you not to resist."

"Run?" I whispered.

"Now!" shouted Terry.

We sprinted down the sidewalk, Ed Regis in the lead pushing people out of our way. The police siren began to blare. Over it, I heard the Seraph leader shout at his team, "No! Don't shoot! You'll hit him!"

Drivers slammed on their brakes as we cut across an intersection and into the park.

"Get off the path," said Ed Regis as he picked Alia up in his arms without breaking pace. "Straight line to the other side!"

We ran through a snow-covered field, through a line of trees, across a jogging path and into another field.

"Angels on our nine!" warned Terry.

"I see them," said Ed Regis.

I saw them too. Another small band of Seraphim had broken through a line of trees to our left and were headed our way.

As Ed Regis led us diagonally away from them, I heard one of the Seraphim shout, "Hold your fire! It's Adrian Howell! Hold your fire!"

"They sure are hell-bent on keeping you alive!" said Terry as we followed Ed Regis through a clump of bushes.

"Lucky me," I panted, using my telekinesis to help me keep pace.

"Fly, Addy," said Alia. *"They're not after us."*

I shook my head. "Yes they are and you know it."

There were no witnesses here and the only reason that the Seraphim weren't attacking was because they didn't want to risk killing me. If I flew away now, Terry, Alia and Ed Regis would either be shot to death or captured.

Crossing another small clearing and pushing through a few more bushes, we found ourselves on the sidewalk at the other end of the park. A few pedestrians stopped to stare at us as we brushed the twigs and snow off of our wet, tattered clothes.

"Now what?" I asked.

"Keep going," said Ed Regis, setting Alia back down onto the sidewalk.

We jogged forward, but I had a feeling that even Ed Regis didn't really know where we were going. Maybe the Seraphim couldn't attack us in the open, but there was no doubt that police backup was on the way. Soon they would be joined by the Wolves, who also worked for the Angels now. I strained my ears for the sound of helicopters, but none had found us yet.

A distant voice from behind us shouted, "Adrian Howell! Stop!"

It was the Seraph team that had intercepted us in the park. They were still more than a hundred yards away but catching up fast. We picked up our pace too.

A deep telepathic voice growled into my head, *"Stop this nonsense right now, Adrian Howell, or we will be forced to open fire."*

Go ahead, I thought savagely. *Save me the trouble.*

"Hey! Stop!" another voice called. "Richard! Tiffany!"

At the sound of our aliases, we immediately stopped running and spun around.

A large black van screeched to a halt beside us, bumping its tires up onto the curb as the driver shouted, "Need a lift?"

"Raider!" I cried.

"Get in!"

Ed Regis opened the side door and we all jumped inside as the Seraphim closed in on us.

A fireball impacted on the back of the van, cracking the rear window.

"Go!" shouted Terry. "Go! Go! Go!"

As the van lurched forward, I heard the Seraph leader shout, "No! Goddamn it! Hold your fire!"

I telekinetically slid the side door closed as the van picked up speed.

"Marion!" exclaimed Alia.

Marion was sitting in the back seat, eyes closed and seemingly unconscious.

"Everyone, hang on!" shouted Raider.

Ignoring the lanes, Raider weaved his van through the traffic until we were clear of the Lumina area. I kept a tense lookout for police cars and military helicopters, but saw none, and soon Raider slowed down and joined the flock of cars headed toward the river at the city's edge.

"Thanks, Raider," I said, breathing easier. "We thought the Seraphim had arrested you."

Raider grinned in the rearview mirror. "So did the Seraphim. But there were only two of them and they thought I would come peacefully. Lucky for you guys too, huh, Richard?"

"Adrian," I said quietly. "My name's Adrian."

"I know that, Adrian," said Raider. "But don't expect me to tell you my name in return. You probably already know it from my daughter anyway."

I did, but if he wanted to continue being called Raider, that was fine by me.

"What's wrong with Marion?" I asked, incredulous that the kid could have slept through our escape. "Is she alright?"

"She's fine," Raider said reassuringly. "I had to drug her a little to keep her safe and quiet. She'll wake in a few hours."

"We were told to go to a safe house, Raider," said Terry. "It's—"

Raider cut her off, saying, "Forget the safe house! My cover's been blown. I'm going to get us out of the city once."

Raider's black van had tinted windows. Terry and I sat in the middle seat while Alia sat between Marion and Ed Regis in the back. I looked at the empty seat next to Raider. If James had been with us, that's where he would have been sitting.

There were still no police cars or helicopters in sight, but I couldn't be sure that we weren't being followed by the Seraphim in ordinary vehicles. Still, I remembered that Raider was a psionic hider in addition to a delver, and that he would have put a hiding field around his van as we left the protection of Cindy's giant bubble over Lumina.

"So, what happened to the command center?" asked Raider, keeping his eyes on the road. "I heard it was attacked."

"Twenty Point Five is lost," Terry reported bitterly. "They completely cleared us out."

I heard my sister let out a quiet sob from behind me.

Raider asked, "How the hell did they find us?"

Not wanting to bring up Alia's mistake, Terry said simply, "They just did, Raider."

"I suppose it was only a matter of time," said Raider. "Our casualties?"

"About half of us got out," said Terry. "Proton was already outside, and Jacob made it out too. But we split up at the exit so I don't know if the others reached their hideouts."

"What about your buddy? Jack, was it?"

Terry didn't reply.

"James," I told Raider. "He's dead."

Raider nodded solemnly. "I'm sorry."

"No," Alia whimpered from the back, "I'm sorry."

"What?" said Ed Regis, who hadn't heard the full story. "What are you sorry for, Alia?"

"I... I..." Alia broke down, sobbing into her hands.

Turning around in my seat, I told Ed Regis, "Alia thinks she's responsible for what happened back there."

"Why?" asked Raider.

Alia couldn't speak, but I could tell that she wanted them to know. I retold her story as simply as possible. Ed Regis put an arm around my sister's quivering shoulders as she continued to drip tears onto her shirt.

"I should have been more attentive," said Raider. "If I had known about this Patrick boy, I could have called Jacob from Octavus and we might have been able to keep any of this from happening."

"I trusted him," cried Alia, finally finding her voice again. "I'm so sorry. I trusted Patrick and now James and Willow and her baby and everyone else is dead because of me."

"That's not true, Alia," said Ed Regis.

But my sister was inconsolable. "It is true!" she wailed, pulling herself free of Ed Regis's arm. "You know it's true! Don't say it's not true! They're dead and I killed them!"

"You didn't kill anyone, Alia," Ed Regis said forcefully, hugging her from the side again. "You might have made a mistake, but you didn't kill them! Twenty Point Five was always a security risk. Every time someone went outside, there was the chance of discovery. It just so happened to be you. It could have been anybody."

"But it wasn't anybody!" cried Alia. "It was me! They died because of me! Just like Max and Felicity!"

"They died because this is a war," Ed Regis said patiently. "They died because they're soldiers, and sometimes dying comes with the job. There was no way for you to know that Patrick would tell his parents about you."

Alia shook her head, her voice completely cracked as she said, "I should've known, Ed. Addy told me. Terry told me. I didn't believe them. And James… James came back for us in there, didn't he? He didn't have to, and he did. That's why he died when it should have been me. It should've been me!"

"James died saving my life, Alia," I said firmly. "And yours, and Ed Regis's. He died fighting. Like Terry would. Like a Knight would. That's all he ever wanted. He wanted to be a Knight like his parents, and like us. Max and Felicity were no different. They wanted to fight. I will never understand that, but that's what James wanted."

"Don't blame yourself for his sacrifice, Alia," agreed Terry. "James insisted on going back into the command center alone, and I trusted him to get you out safely, which he did. He saved your life so that you can save others'. Don't waste your time blaming yourself. Honor him, Alia. Honor his choice."

"This is so wrong," sobbed Alia. "Everything about this is wrong! Everyone is killing each other and Patrick was waving and smiling and…"

It was a nightmare inside a nightmare. Alia had lost her voice, but she continued weeping into Ed Regis's shoulder. Trapped in the middle seat, I couldn't comfort her, but Ed Regis was doing a good enough job. And as much as I felt sorry for my sister even while I was haunted by the image of James's last moments, now burned into my memory for eternity, there was yet another horrible thought eating at me.

I looked past Alia at the damaged rear window and the dark road beyond. We had already crossed over the river and into the countryside. On one side of the road was a thick forest; on the other, a grassy field. For a few quiet minutes, I watched the empty road fading into the night.

Then I turned back around and said weakly to Raider, "Stop the car, please. I think I'm going to throw up."

Raider immediately hit the brakes and pulled over to the side of the road. "Do it from the door, Adrian," he said. "I have a hiding field around the van but it's not big."

Ignoring his request, I slid open the side door and stumbled out into the night chill.

"Come on!" said Raider, getting out of the van himself. "We have to stay hidden!"

I spun around and, throwing my arms forward, blasted Raider hard in the chest. He was knocked back against the van, and as he slid down the side, I telekinetically pulled his pistol out from its holster and flew it into my right hand. Flipping off the safety, I leveled the pistol on Raider's head.

Terry jumped out of the van, crying, "What the hell are you doing, Adrian?!"

I ignored her, keeping my attention on Raider, who was coughing feebly as he looked up at the pistol in my hand.

"You're really something, aren't you, Raider?" I breathed, taking a step forward. "Willow warned me to always assume that there were at least two spies in the Resistance. You, my friend, are worth twenty."

Terry let out a quiet gasp as Raider smiled up at me and asked, "How did you know?"

"I'm Adrian Howell," I reminded him savagely. "So where's the pursuit? There's a whole city full of Angels out there looking for me, and you just conveniently show up and drive away with us in a car like this that anyone could follow? Where are the Seraphim? Where are the police?! Where are the goddamn Wolves?!"

Terry said in an awestruck tone, "This guy is one of Divine's, isn't he? Like the pair at Wood-claw."

I nodded. "He isn't a part of the Lumina Angels. It's just like Mark said. Raider is working directly for Randal Divine. Even the Seraphim don't know who he is. That's why the Guardians never caught him."

I looked down at Raider. "You knew about Patrick, didn't you?" I asked, my voice shaking in cold fury. "You knew Alia had lied to you. You're a delver."

"I would never delve a child," said Raider, sounding genuinely insulted. "But I did suspect that something was amiss."

"You suspected that there was going to be an attack!" I spat back. "That's why you brought Alia back and then left the building again with Marion."

"Well, I had to choose one of them," Raider said mildly.

I pulled the pistol's hammer back.

"You should thank me," said Raider. "If I hadn't called King Divine and told him where you were, the Seraphim would have finished all of you off before you could leave Nonus."

So that was why they hadn't pursued us down the elevator shaft. When Randal Divine learned that I was in Twenty Point Five, he had sent an order to halt the attack on the command center and let all the survivors escape, hoping that I was still among them. Once Raider picked us up at the side of the park, the pursuit was ended there so that there would be no more risks to us as Raider quietly handed us in.

"But you could have had me anytime," I said. "You knew King Divine wanted me alive. Why did you wait so long?"

"Because you were never my mission," said Raider. "Every time the Seraphim clear out one of the Resistance hideouts, the Knights just slither into another. My mission was to map out all of the safe houses for one, final, clean sweep of Lumina."

"Then you weren't after me at all?"

Raider shook his head. "You just fell into my life by chance, Adrian. I've no idea why King Divine insists on getting you alive, but when Alia made her little slip today, I figured I couldn't stand by and let the Seraphim accidentally kill you. My mapping mission has failed, but so long as I can't go back to the Resistance anymore, I wanted to deliver you to King Divine in person."

"I'm afraid that's not going to happen now."

"So go ahead and kill me," said Raider. "Do it before Marion wakes up."

I lowered the pistol and returned the hammer. "You say that I fell into your life by chance, Raider, but you're the one who fell into mine. Get back in the car and drive. Safely. Remember that yours isn't the only life at stake here."

Raider silently stood up and got back into the driver's seat, and Terry and I sat behind him.

Ed Regis had stayed in the back seat keeping a comforting arm around Alia, but he had heard everything. I wasn't as sure about my sister, whose red, puffy eyes were open but unfocused, still slowly dripping tears as they stared off into space. Marion remained blissfully unconscious.

I passed Raider's pistol to Ed Regis and he holstered it. Then I closed the side door and put on my seatbelt.

No one spoke.

Ever so gently, Raider pulled his van back onto the dark country road.

13. FOR THE LOVE OF A KING

It was still only about 10pm when Terry spotted a lonely two-story summer house that we could use for the night. The largish cabin was a little off the main road and unoccupied at this frozen time of year, with the added bonus of being alarm-free.

"You can hide a house this size, yes?" Terry asked Raider as he pulled the van around to the back of the house.

"Of course," said Raider.

"Then do it," snapped Terry. "And remember that if anyone bothers us here, Marion will be the first to die."

"Have you no conscience?" asked Raider.

"No," she informed him. "Now get to work."

Remaining in the driver's seat, Raider closed his eyes in concentration.

The invisible, intangible nature of hiding fields would, in theory, allow Raider the perfect opportunity to betray our location to the Angels, but I wasn't worried. Raider might be King Divine's loyal subject, but he was also a father.

After a few minutes, Raider opened his eyes and frowned at us in the mirror, saying, "The house and thirty yards around in every direction. Happy?"

"Congratulations," I said to him, opening the side door and getting out. "You've just dug the first corner of your own grave."

My sister was wide awake, and as she followed Terry and Ed Regis out of the van, she looked at me in a way that made me instantly regret my words.

A few hours of silence had brought Alia back to a comparatively normal condition. I suspected that she had been listening to my earlier confrontation with Raider after all, and that she understood what was happening now.

Marion stirred a little in her seat. I telekinetically undid her seatbelt and levitated her out of the van. Raider put his arms around her, holding her tightly. Perhaps because of the sudden exposure to the freezing night air, Marion stirred again, and then opened her eyes.

"Where are we, Daddy?" she asked groggily.

"Safe," whispered Raider. "Go back to sleep."

Marion rested her head on Raider's shoulder and closed her eyes again.

I moved around to the side of the house and telekinetically unlocked a window so that we could enter without breaking anything. Once inside, Ed Regis kept an eye on Raider and Marion in the living room while the rest of us spent a few minutes restoring electricity to and exploring our temporary home.

The living room and dining room were spacious, the kitchen outdated but clean. There were three bedrooms on the second floor, and a narrow flight of stairs led down into a two-room basement. Though there was no second-floor balcony, this house reminded me a little of the Angel outpost we had attacked last year. I took a moment in the bathroom to finish wiping James's dried blood off of my face.

Most of the furniture in the house was covered with dusty sheets. As we returned to the living room, I pulled off one of the covers, revealing a plush velvet armchair with a tall back.

"I wish we could stay here forever," I said sadly, running my fingertips over the soft armrest.

Terry looked at me grimly. "Let's get this over with."

I looked at Raider and his daughter. Marion had woken up completely. She was standing close to her father, holding his hand and looking around at us anxiously. She knew intuitively that something was very wrong. Kids can always sense evil in the air.

"Alia," I said, "I want you to take Marion upstairs and watch over her."

Alia didn't need to sense it. She understood exactly what I was asking of her.

"Please don't argue," I said, staring down at my feet.

"Your brother's right, Alia," said Ed Regis. "You don't have to be a part of this, and you don't want this girl to see it either."

I heard my sister say hoarsely, "Look at me, Adrian."

Slowly, I did. It hurt worse than being kicked in the gut, but I forced myself to raise my head and look into Alia's eyes. Alia stared back at me for a silent, excruciating eternity. Then she went up to Marion and took her free hand. "Come on, Marion," she said gently. "Let's go upstairs."

But Marion refused to let go of her father's hand.

"Go on," Raider said to her, pulling his hand free. "Go upstairs with Alia. It'll be okay."

Alia looked like she said something telepathically to Marion, and finally Marion nodded and let my sister lead her away from her father.

I hollowly watched them exit the room, and then followed Ed Regis and Terry as they escorted Raider down into the basement. Terry brought a wooden straight-back chair down from the dining room. Ed Regis found some thin rope, which he used to tie Raider down onto the chair. Ed Regis wrapped the rope several times around Raider's upper body, and then tightly secured his wrists to the armrests and his ankles to the chair's front legs.

Once that was done, we just stood there for a moment as if taking in the atmosphere. Raider looked up at each of our faces in turn. He looked at me longest. I remembered the times he had invited me into his home. Despite his sometimes blunt manner, Raider had been my friend, and more importantly, Alia's protector. We had known each other well. But not as well as I had thought.

Ed Regis asked, "You want me to talk to him, Terry?"

Terry didn't answer.

"I'll talk to him," I said quietly.

Ed Regis looked at me in surprise. "Adrian, you don't need to be here, either," he said, shaking his head. "Someone really should keep watch on the first floor."

"Then you go, Ed Regis," I replied. "I don't want to do this with you watching, anyway."

I knew that Ed Regis was just trying to do Alia and me a favor, and I knew that he was the certified expert in this particular field. But this was something I had to do myself. Here, finally, we had found someone who could lead us to Randal Divine, and to Catherine. No matter how wrong Alia felt this was, it nevertheless had to be done. And if, someday soon, I was going to kill my own first sister, then I couldn't be afraid to get my hands dirty.

"Terry?" Ed Regis asked hesitantly.

"Take the first watch, Major," said Terry. "We'll call if we need you."

"And make sure my sister doesn't come down here," I added.

Ed Regis asked, "Do you mind if I keep an ear to the floor?"

"As you wish," I said.

Ed Regis climbed up the stairs and out of the basement, but he left the door open so he could hear us.

Raider hadn't spoken a word since parting with his daughter.

"We have questions," I said to him quietly.

Raider raised his eyebrows, perhaps surprised by such an obvious statement.

I had learned long ago that a standard psionic interrogation involved asking questions to the subject while a delver looked into his thoughts, as people usually think the truth before they lie. But delving could be blocked with a strong mental focus. Hence, torture. In this case, however, the only delver in the room was the interrogation subject himself, and I doubted he was going to make this easy for us just to avoid a little pain.

I glanced at Terry, who gave me a little shrug. To the best of my knowledge, my combat instructor was no more experienced in interrogation tactics than I was. Perhaps we did need Ed Regis after all, but I wasn't going to call him back down just yet.

"I once worked for a man who enjoyed burning people alive," I said to Raider. "Today we can either start with a polite conversation or a pair of pliers. It's your choice. But I watched my best friend die today, so even assuming that I have any mercy left, don't expect me to waste any on you."

"What do you want?" asked Raider.

Terry brought the tip of her hook to Raider's neck. "Divine."

Raider looked like he wanted to laugh at the absurdity of our demand. "And you think I'm going to help you find and kill my master? Do you honestly think I'm capable of that?"

"I think you're capable of being persuaded," I told him.

I had seen the madness that conversion could cause. I remembered the insane pyroid at the PRC. I remembered the manic eyes and fanatical tone of

Mr. Simms and Ms. Decker, and how the Angels at the Wood-claw outpost had bashed their own heads open out of loyalty to their master. Converts—especially new converts—frequently sacrificed themselves for their master.

But conversion affected people in different ways. And as Cindy had once said, converts could still think and feel and choose their own lives, which meant that they could have other priorities too. Earlier, Raider had freely given me details of his secret mission in the Resistance, which proved that he wasn't so completely soaked in conversion that he was beyond reasoning with. Raider clearly cared for his daughter and for his own future raising her.

"Would you like me to find you some pliers, Adrian?" asked Terry. "Or do you want to get straight into something more persuasive?"

"Your hook will do just fine," I replied. "But not yet. I haven't finished asking him nicely."

Raider said matter-of-factly, "Asking won't help. I have sworn my life to the service of King Divine. Do not question my loyalty. I will never give up my king."

I shook my head. If Raider's conversion had turned him into an Angel fanatic with absolute submission to his king, he would never have been able to keep his identity hidden among the Guardians. Still, as a converted Angel, there would be a limit to how much he could assist us before the guilt of his betrayal became too much to bear. Fortunately, I had a workaround for this.

"Relax, Raider," I told him. "We're not asking you to give up your king at all."

Raider looked at me questioningly.

I asked him, "Do you remember delving Tigress from Wood-claw? Remember how she told you that we were independent of the Guardians?"

Raider nodded slightly.

"We're kind of like you, Raider," said Terry, still keeping the tip of her hook pressed lightly against Raider's neck. "We don't answer to the Guardian Council. And like Adrian said, we're not interested in your king."

"Then who are you interested in?" asked Raider.

"His daughter," I told him.

"Daughter?" repeated Raider. "You mean Cathy Divine?"

"The same."

"You're lying."

"Delve me and find out," I said evenly.

"Adrian?" said Terry. "Are you sure?"

"It's okay," I said, carefully pulling Terry's hook away so that Raider wouldn't be drained.

"Do it," I said to him. "Ask me."

The only time I had ever been delved before was by the Historian in his mountain home, and the Historian could do it so subtly that I could never tell when he was looking into my consciousness. But with Raider, I instantly recognized his psionic presence in the back of my mind, carefully watching my every thought. I had a feeling I could block him if I wanted to, but I kept my head calm and clear.

"Admit it!" Raider said in a commanding tone. "You are trying to kill my king!"

I shook my head, and Raider's eyes widened as he realized that I was telling the truth.

"Enough," said Terry, touching Raider's neck with her hook again.

"Why are you after his daughter?" asked Raider.

"That's our business," said Terry.

Raider didn't know my relationship to Catherine Divine any more than he knew who his real master was, but I wasn't surprised. Aside from Cindy and Mr. Baker, who now both held high positions in Randal Divine's government, how many other people actually knew that Catherine Divine was my sister? There was Mark, and then the late Laila Brown, Mr. Simms and Mr. Barnum, and perhaps a few others, but that was it. I wasn't the only Guardian with a price on my head, and devout Angels knew better than to question their king's motives.

"Cathy isn't even King Divine's real daughter," said Raider. "You didn't know that, did you?"

I didn't reply, and Raider continued in a smug tone, "Cathy isn't really a Divine by blood, Adrian. The king adopted that child back during the rule of Larissa Divine. It was just a publicity stunt to better the image of the Divine family. You'll gain nothing from her."

"Then you have no reason not to tell us," I pointed out.

I found it mildly amusing that Raider thought we were after Catherine because of her bloodline, which of course we were, and yet he still believed that Randal Divine, not Catherine, was the master. But it was also true that my workaround wasn't working as well as I had hoped.

"Cathy Divine is worth nothing to you," insisted Raider. "She's just a girl, plain and simple!"

Terry pressed her hook harder against Raider's neck, drawing blood as she said, "Then you are going to give us this plain and simple girl."

"Your loyalty is to King Divine," I reminded Raider. "Give us the child and everybody wins."

"I can't do that," panted Raider as blood trickled down his neck and soaked into his shirt. "Cathy is an adopted daughter, that's true, but I've seen King Divine with her. He dotes on her like she's his own flesh and blood. He spends every second of his waking day with her. Even if I could somehow lead you to Cathy without giving away my king, to betray Cathy Divine would be no different from betraying King Divine! I simply can't do it!"

Terry said to me, "I think asking nicely isn't working, Adrian."

"No," I admitted, "it's not."

"Then it's my turn to persuade him."

Without further warning, Terry grabbed Raider's left ring finger and yanked it back until it snapped. Raider, caught off guard, howled in pain.

"Don't tell us there are things you can't do, Raider!" Terry barked over his screams. "Because you have no idea what we can!"

Raider struggled against the ropes binding him to his chair, and I grabbed the back of it so he wouldn't fall over. Terry broke Raider's left middle finger next.

The door at the top of the stairs was still open, so I telekinetically pulled it shut. I suspected that Raider's screams would still carry straight up to the second floor, but at least they would be quieter.

"I've got a healer waiting upstairs," said Terry as Raider clenched his teeth in agony. "We can do this over and over, as many times as it takes until you're ready to tell us where we can find Catherine Divine."

Raider shook his head frantically.

"You want to go for a third?!" cried Terry, making a credible show of hysteria.

Raider cursed at her loudly in reply. Terry punched him twice in the face, bloodying his mouth and nose, and then added several more blows to his chest and stomach.

"The king is my lord, my father, my protector," wheezed Raider, eyes closed and coughing blood. "The king is—"

Raider screamed again as Terry brought the finger total to three.

Having been on the receiving end of this sort of attention myself, I knew that the problem with the common approach was that it relied too much on physical pain. Not that pain wasn't serious persuasion, especially in the hands of a dedicated interrogator, but it wasn't pain that broke me years ago in the little metal room where Ed Regis and I first met.

I stopped Terry before she hit Raider again. "Let's try to keep him conscious," I suggested.

Then I turned to Raider. "You'll have to forgive my hot-tempered partner," I said to him mildly. "Terry has been itching for a lead like you for months."

"You'll get nothing from me!" spat Raider, breathing heavily. "I am the loyal servant of King Divine."

"You're a fool and a father," I countered. "I remember what you said to me about trust, Raider. I trusted you with my sister's life. Now you'll trust me with Marion's. Her life for Catherine's location. I hope for Marion's sake that you'll agree to a fair trade."

"You bastard," breathed Raider, horrified. "Marion is innocent. How could you bring a child into this?"

"Don't lecture me about using children," I replied callously. "You used Alia to get yourself off the camera crew and then marched her all around Lumina so you could continue your mapping mission. You can think of King Divine as your father as much as you like, but you had better not forget who your real family is."

Raider silently glared at me. I could feel the hatred burning in his eyes.

"My sister likes Marion a lot," I continued, "but don't imagine for a second that I won't kill her if you love her less than the adopted daughter of your King Divine. A king, I might add, who thinks nothing of putting you and Marion in harm's way."

Raider still remained silent.

"Fine," I said, turning to Terry. "Bring Marion down, please." Then I looked into Raider's eyes again, saying, "I want you to watch her die."

Terry started for the stairs. She made five and a half steps before Raider frantically cried out, "Wait!"

Terry stopped.

"Wait, please," begged Raider. "You can't! You can't do this!"

"No, you're the one who can't, Raider," Terry reminded him. "We can. And we will."

Terry started to turn toward the stairs again, but Raider shouted, "No! Wait, goddamn it! Do you really think it's just a simple matter of knocking on King Divine's door?"

"You know where his door is," I said. "You're going to tell us."

"Nobody has a direct line to the king, Adrian," said Raider. "The shippers only know their small parts of the road."

"You are not a shipper!" said Terry. Returning to Raider's side, she grabbed his broken fingers and played with them in a way that made him groan loudly. "You're inner circle, Raider. You called your king up on a phone!"

"Is that what you want?" gasped Raider. "A phone call?! Yes, I can call him up in an emergency. That doesn't mean I know where he lives!"

Terry kept her hand resting lightly on Raider's broken fingers. "You were delivering Adrian to him."

"You're insane!" cried Raider. "You think I know his home address? All I know is the Royal Gate. That's where my ticket stops."

"What's the Royal Gate?" I asked.

Raider looked at me, wide-eyed.

Terry jerked Raider's hand again. "Answer him!"

Wincing in pain, Raider mumbled through clenched teeth, "It's the guard post where the High Seraphim check and finalize transport for those who seek an audience with the king. I was delivering you there so that we could be escorted in. The king is invisible, Tiffany or Terry or whatever the hell your name is! The king is untouchable!"

Terry released her grip on Raider's fingers.

"What do you think?" I asked her.

"I think he could be telling the truth," Terry said thoughtfully. "King Divine probably wouldn't send out spies that could lead assassins directly back to him."

"You're damn right he wouldn't!" snapped Raider. "The only way anyone meets the king is through the High Seraphim at the Royal Gate. You think a phantom train is going to get you through King Divine's personal guard?"

"No," I replied. "But I think we'll settle for the location of the Royal Gate and the names of your contacts in the High Seraphim."

Raider shook his head. "You will never get that from me."

"Why not?" I scoffed. "According to you, we'd never get past them anyway."

"Because I serve my king," he said. Then he looked me in the eyes and repeated with more resolve than I thought he had left, "I will never betray my king."

"Too bad for Marion," I said pitilessly. "But I guess you had to choose one of them, right?"

Raider glared at me with bloodshot eyes. "I love my daughter, Adrian. I love her like the sun and the moon but King Divine is my lord. King Divine is my god! Do you really think I would turn on my own god?"

I shook my head. "I don't care about your pitiful excuse for a god, Raider. But I want Catherine. Give me Randal's child and yours will be spared. That isn't an unreasonable exchange."

Raider shook his head.

Terry looked like she was about to do something painful to him again, but this time I beat her to it, slamming my fist down onto Raider's damaged hand.

Grabbing Raider by the front of his shirt, I hissed into his ear, "Do you honestly think I'm just going to kill Marion? Think again! I'll make her death last a week! You'll watch, Raider, as I cut pieces from her! I'll shove the parts down your throat! I'll bathe you in her blood!"

"Goddamn it, Adrian! I can't tell you!" hollered Raider, tears streaming down his cheeks. "I can't betray my king any more than I already have! I can't! I can't!"

I released his shirt and took a step back, breathing heavily. Raider stared off into space as he continued whimpering about his king. He looked as lost as Alia did on her worst days.

I turned to Terry, feeling sick to my stomach. "I think we need a short timeout."

Terry looked at me questioningly.

"I want to talk to you and Ed Regis upstairs," I said.

Terry shook her head. "We can't just leave him down here alone, Adrian."

I understood Terry's concern but I doubted Raider's conversion was strong enough for him to pull off a suicide like the ones at Wood-claw. Besides, we would hear it if his chair fell over.

Just in case, however, I said to Raider, "If we find you dead in here when we return, Marion will join you. And if there's an afterlife, you can ask her how long it took for her to die."

Terry and I went back up to the living room, where we found Ed Regis standing at the window.

Turning around to face us, he said, "I'm afraid Marion came running down when she first heard her father screaming. Fortunately Alia caught her and hauled her back."

I would deal with the fallout of that later. I asked Ed Regis, "Have you been listening in?"

Ed Regis shook his head. "I couldn't make out most of your conversation after you closed the door. How is it going?"

Terry briefly explained.

"The RG," said Ed Regis, nodding. "So that was the Royal Gate that the Angel Wolves were talking about. We need to find out where it is."

"That's the problem," I said. "I don't think we're going to get anything more out of Raider. I mean, if he won't tell us to save his own kid, then he's insane. And if he's insane, we can't trust anything he says."

"That's assuming he believed your threat, Adrian," Ed Regis pointed out.

"True," I admitted, and then asked Terry, "Do you think he believed me?"

"You did sound pretty convincing," said Terry. "But I still don't think he's insane. He's just converted."

"Conversion is a type of insanity as far as I'm concerned," I said.

"Fine," said Terry, shrugging, "then he's insane. But that doesn't change the fact that he has information we need."

"Many converted people put their master above or at least equal to their families," said Ed Regis, probably speaking from direct experience.

"Forcing Raider to reveal the location of this Royal Gate could break his mind."

"I don't care about Raider's mind," said Terry. "If he's really not going to tell us, then he's not worth anything more to us anyway. We might as well kill him and be done with."

"I don't care about him either, Terry," I said. "But do you really want to take Marion down there and bleed her in front of Raider?"

"I thought *you* were going to do that."

I gave her a disbelieving stare. "You're joking, right?"

Terry stared right back.

"Ed Regis?" I said, hoping that he might restore some sanity to our conversation.

"This is your mission, Adrian," Ed Regis reminded me. "You said you'd do anything to get Cindy back."

"Almost anything!" I countered. "That doesn't include torturing second graders. Raider is right. Marion is innocent."

"Well, I don't know where that puts us," said Ed Regis, shaking his head. "Unless you're asking me to—"

"No!" I said. "Of course not, Ed Regis." Thinking for a moment, I suggested, "How about we take Raider to the nearest Guardian settlement and have the Knights there work on him with a proper delver?"

This time it was Terry's turn to stare at me in disbelief. Realizing that I had missed yet another obvious fact about psionics, I braced myself.

"Delvers are impossible to accurately delve," Terry explained to me in an exasperated tone. "They have too much control over their own thoughts. If we took Raider to the Knights, they'd do exactly what we're doing now."

I doubted that it would be *exactly* the same. They would use Marion for sure.

"Besides," added Terry, "if at all possible, I don't want to risk traveling long-distance with Raider in tow."

Ed Regis said carefully, "Well, if you're dead set against using the child, then your only other option is to continue trying to beat the information out of him. But I doubt you'll succeed against a convert and experienced spy like Raider."

"I've got a better idea," I said as the thought popped into my mind. "What if we can unhinge his conversion just a little? Then maybe he'll be willing to tell us where the Royal Gate is in return for Marion."

"What do you mean?" asked Terry. "How do you unhinge conversion?"

I smiled grimly as I told her.

"It might work, Adrian," Terry agreed slowly. "At least it has the virtue of never having been tried before."

Ed Regis nodded. "I'm sure it'll unhinge him. I just hope he doesn't snap completely."

14. THE POWER OF TRUTH

I asked Ed Regis to remain on lookout and took Terry back down into the basement. Hearing us enter, Raider turned his head and looked at us apprehensively, but then seemed to calm down a little when he saw that we hadn't brought Marion.

"What now?" Raider asked defiantly. "More fingers?"

"No," I said quietly as I walked up to him. "Just truth."

"Truth?"

"The truth, Raider," I repeated as Terry silently watched me. "For starters, the truth is that you are going to die in this room tonight. You've probably figured that out for yourself by now, but we're not going to let you leave this place alive whether you help us or not. You already know that we're after Catherine. This is something we can't let you leave here with."

"And Marion?"

"I told you to trust me," I said. "Marion will live, but only if you help us."

"Which I can't," said Raider. He stared straight into my eyes as he said resolutely, "I won't."

"For your king?" I asked.

"That's right," said Raider. "For my king."

I had always imagined the long-term connection between master and convert to be like the thin, silky strands of a spider web spread out in a massive, worldwide pattern. Like all Angels, Raider's memory had been altered post-conversion to make him see Randal Divine as his master. The

Historian had said that this was a viable temporary solution, but I doubted such a facade would hold up against truth. After all, if you wanted to know where a line really led, all you had to do was pull on it. Nothing could ever have prepared me for what the Historian told me about Catherine. No lie, no fiction could be as powerful as the truth. It was time to give Raider the full treatment.

"I will do anything for my king," said Raider.

"For your queen," I corrected gently. "For your queen, Raider."

Raider looked up at me, blinking, unable to comprehend.

"Randal Divine isn't your master," I said. "Your master is, and has always been, Catherine."

Raider shook his head. "That's absurd. It's impossible."

"But it's true," I told him. "And deep down, you know it's true. Deep down, Raider, you've always known."

Just like I had known. A man could live his entire life in denial and be all the happier for it. Truth has no mercy. Truth has no compassion, no honor, and no redemption.

"You're lying," said Raider, but I could already see the uncertainty in his eyes. "Cathy isn't a Divine. The old queen forced the adoption."

"Larissa knew what Catherine's blood contained," I said. "She knew Catherine would become a master someday."

"No!" Raider shouted furiously. "No! It's not true! Randal Divine is my king! He is my god!"

"Search your heart," I said. "Randal is no god. He's no king. He's nothing but a cheap lying thug who put himself at the top of the Angels by using a child master as his shield. You owe him nothing."

Raider was hyperventilating, his whole body shaking as he stared at me in horror.

"Tell us where the Royal Gate is," I said soothingly. "Be free of him. Be free of your false god once and for all."

Raider closed his eyes tightly as tears streamed down his cheeks. He looked like he was in far more pain than Terry could ever have put him through.

"Do it for your real family, Raider," I whispered. "For Marion. You can still save her."

Raider stopped shaking, and his breathing slowly returned to normal. He opened his eyes.

Then he smiled. I took an involuntary step back.

"It's so clear to me now," Raider said in a quiet, awestruck tone. "I had always felt that I was a part of something truly special. Randal Divine... not the king, but what true genius! What sacrifices he must have made to protect our queen, and to bring us all together, to reunite the Guardian Angels..."

I shook my head. Terry was staring at Raider, openmouthed.

"Thank you, Adrian Howell," continued Raider. "Everything makes sense. Everything is right. Now I can die knowing that my life has not been in vain... that my daughter's life, however you choose to end it, is truly worth the sacrifice. Thank you."

As Terry had said, it was a plan that had never been tried before. I hadn't expected it to backfire so completely. The truth about his master hadn't unhinged Raider's conversion at all. It had solidified it.

Truth was indeed a double-edged sword.

So this was the future of the Guardian Angels once Randal Divine renounced his throne. Instead of rebelling against the deception, the converts would be purged of all doubt, giving Queen Divine complete control over her faction and, soon thereafter, the entire world.

"Damn," breathed Terry. "I didn't think it would turn out this way. I mean, in retrospect, I guess this was a probable outcome, but still..."

"He's not going to talk, is he?" I said to Terry, unable to pull my eyes away from Raider's sick little smile. It was the same smile Mr. Simms had given me just before I blasted a hole in his head. "It looks like he's gone full-blown."

"I agree," said Terry. "Even if he did give us a place and name, most likely it would just be a trap."

I cursed. Another brick wall. I was used to things not working out the way I wanted, but this had been our greatest lead in a year full of disappointments. Now the location of the High Seraphim who guarded the gate to Catherine Divine was locked away in the mind of a delver who would see his own daughter tortured to death before he gave up his psionic master. Had Randal known? Had he perhaps already tested this scenario out on someone? Trying to use the truth to unhinge Raider's conversion was arguably my worst plan ever. My only consolation was in the fact that I hadn't been the only one who believed it would work.

"At least we know about the Royal Gate," said Terry. "The name alone might get us somewhere."

I nodded and asked, "Are we done here?"

"Yeah," said Terry. "We're done."

I pointed my right index finger at Raider's forehead, preparing a focused telekinetic blast. "Don't worry, Raider," I said to him. "Marion will live. I'll make sure she gets back to her mother."

"Thank you," Raider said contentedly, and then closed his eyes. "Goodbye."

My blast was ready.

I wasn't.

Feeling my power reabsorb into my body, I lowered my arm and said to Terry, "You do it."

"I don't have a gun," said Terry.

"Then go get Raider's from Ed Regis."

Terry didn't understand. "Just kill him, Adrian," she said. "Save us a bullet."

I looked at Raider again. "I... I can't."

"What do you mean, you can't?!" snapped Terry. "Don't start talking like Raider."

I pointed my finger at Raider again. I lowered it again.

"We can't let him live," said Terry. "Think of what he knows."

I knew that Raider had to die. There was too much at stake to let him walk free. I remembered James's last words to me in the command center.

Finish this.

Why was it so difficult? I had killed plenty of people before, and not only in the heat of combat. So why couldn't I execute this man? Sure, I had known him as a friend once, but even then he had been a spy for the Angels, using my sister as his cover. Now that I knew what he was, I didn't care about Raider any more than I cared about Mr. Simms or Ms. Decker or any Angel that had gotten in my way.

Aside from my bluff about hurting Marion, I had been entirely truthful with Raider. I had known when we brought him down here that we were going to kill him. I knew this well and I accepted it. This wasn't about anger or revenge or anything. I would take no more pleasure in killing Raider than I would in emptying the toilet buckets in Twenty Point Five, but that didn't change the fact that it had to be done. And as Terry had said, why waste a bullet when I could simply use a finger blast?

Raider kept his eyes closed. He couldn't have made it any easier for me.

"Come on," Terry said impatiently. "It's enough that we're sparing his kid."

I still didn't move. My blast simply wouldn't focus.

Why couldn't I kill Raider? Was it because of his daughter? But Marion would hardly be the first child to lose a parent in this war. No doubt many of the people I had killed had left behind family and friends. That was just the nature of conflict.

Was it because of my sister? Was it the way Alia had looked at me before escorting Marion upstairs? That might have been a part of it, but there was something else.

"Adrian!" shouted Terry.

"I can't," I whimpered.

Terry let out a frustrated huff. Then she stepped forward, grabbed Raider's hair with her right hand, and slashed her hook across his throat.

"You picked a hell of a time to develop a conscience, Adrian!" snapped Terry as I watched Raider's body convulse violently, blood pouring down his front. "I hope you're happy," Terry said disgustedly. "Now I've got his blood all over me and I don't even have a change of clothes. What a mess."

I turned and ran. Up the stairs and out the front door, I collapsed onto the porch, panting heavily. I was as confused as I was disgusted. And my disgust was not with Raider's death, but with myself. All I had to do was blast a hole in his head. It would have been an easier death for him.

Picking myself up, I slowly walked down the porch steps and stopped a few paces from the house. I looked up at the night sky. It was almost entirely covered in dark clouds that were sprinkling a few small snowflakes here and there.

"He needed to die, Adrian," said Terry's voice from behind me.

"I know that, Terry," I said, turning toward her.

Her shirt spattered with blood, Terry was standing on the porch and looking down at me like an irate mother.

"You're all talk and no action!" she spat. "You can kill in a fight but you still can't kill when you need to!"

"I know how to kill, Terry!" I countered heatedly. "I've done it before and I can do it again!"

"Then why couldn't you do it in there?!" demanded Terry. "Why?!"

"I don't know."

"You killed Mr. Simms for who he was and what he did. Why not Raider? Because of Marion?"

"No."

"Then why?!"

"I don't know!" I cried.

We gazed at each other for a moment. Terry looked more disappointed than angry.

"I just don't know," I said again.

"I think I do," Terry said in a softer tone, looking me in the eyes. "Adrian, can you honestly say that you're prepared to kill your own sister?"

I took a step back. I opened my mouth. Nothing came out. I stood there feeling the snowflakes fall around me until, with incredible effort, I finally managed to whisper, "No."

"That's what I thought," Terry said quietly.

"I can't do this, Terry," I said, shaking my head. "I thought I could, but I can't do this anymore."

"You promised the Historian."

"I promised myself," I said wretchedly. "But I can't, Terry. I just can't."

"You promised him that you would kill Catherine Divine. There's no breaking a promise with the Historian."

"There's nothing he can do to me that could be worse than what he's asking me to do."

By refusing to have Ed Regis do my dirty work for me, I had tried to prove to myself once and for all that I could do anything, even the unspeakable. Instead, I ended up proving the opposite. How was I ever going to kill the Angel queen if I couldn't even execute an Angel spy?

"Come inside," Terry said gently. "It's cold out here."

Back in the living room, I couldn't face Terry or Ed Regis. I wondered if James really had died for nothing.

"What do you want to do now, Adrian?" asked Terry. "Is the mission over?"

I shook my head. "I don't know."

Terry gave me a pitying look. "The major and I will take the watch tonight. Go on upstairs and make sure that your sister's okay. Marion too. Then get some rest."

I dragged my feet up the stairs, one heavy step at a time.

Alia was waiting for me in the hallway at the top. She looked at me, not with anger or resentment, not with hurt or disappointment, but sadness. Pure, simple, quiet sadness.

"You're right, Alia," I said hoarsely. "Everything is wrong tonight."

Unable to remain standing, I sat down in the hallway, resting my back against the wall.

"I'm sorry about James, Addy," said Alia, sitting on the floor next to me and gently holding my hand.

"I'm sorry about Raider," I mumbled, staring at the opposite wall.

"Is he dead?"

I nodded dully.

"Marion's asleep now." Alia gestured toward the nearest door. *"I tried my best to comfort her, but there wasn't much I could say. I wish this was all just a bad dream."*

"Then we could still wake from it."

"But you didn't kill Raider, did you, Addy?" said Alia. *"I heard you and Terry talking outside. You didn't kill him."*

"I couldn't kill him, Alia," I said, staring down at my knees in shame. "I should have. I wanted to. But I couldn't. Terry had to do it for me."

"I'm glad you couldn't kill him, Addy. And I'm glad you can't kill your sister."

I looked at her miserably. "Then what have we been doing all these months, Alia?"

"Finding that out." Alia's eyes seemed to smile as she squeezed my hand. *"We were finding that out, Addy."*

"I'm sorry," I said, wiping my eyes with the back of my free hand. "I promised you that we'd get Cindy back from the Angels. I told you that we could save everyone, even strangers. But I'm still a coward. I can't do this anymore. I'm so sorry."

"Remember what you told me once," said Alia, putting an arm around my side. *"Don't ever be sorry for how you feel."*

Lacking the willpower to stand up, I fell asleep sitting next to Alia in the hallway.

When I opened my eyes again, the lights were off and Alia was no longer there.

But someone else was.

I slowly stood up and faced the small figure in the darkness. "You tricked me," I said accusingly.

"You tricked yourself, young Adrian," said the Historian, taking a step closer. "I tried to warn you. I told you that this would test your resolve. I gave you the chance to back out."

I glared at him, furious at the truth in his words.

"James died today," I told him. "Many people died today."

"People die all the time," the Historian said dismissively.

"But not you. You just watch."

"That's right," said the Historian. "I watch. Just as I've been watching you, young Adrian."

"Go watch someone else," I said frostily.

"You are truly bold in the presence of a living god," said the Historian. "I like that about you. It's one of your very few redeeming qualities."

I huffed loudly.

"You gave me your story, remember?" said the Historian. "I knew then what I could expect of you, and I knew how little you understood yourself when you so lightly agreed to become a kin slayer."

"You're wrong," I told him.

The Historian looked amused. "Wrong, am I? You would risk your life to gain the trust of a wild-born you had never met, and then claim to have no interest in the fortunes of strangers. You would leave a man to die in a tunnel for a crime you never witnessed, all the while turning a blind eye to the atrocities committed under your own nose. You kill people one day and cry for them the next, and yet you think you know something about fairness. You are as weak in your heart as you are inconsistent in your justice. Ever you insist on playing the hero, unable to fully embrace what you know you will have to become if you are to do what needs to be done."

I wasn't about to stand here and be psychoanalyzed by this child hermit. "What are you doing out of your mountain?" I asked him. "Why have you come here?"

"I have come to remind you of your vow."

"I haven't forgotten," I said. "You wanted to know how my story ends. It ends here, Historian. I'm through and done."

The Historian seemed to grow taller in the darkness, almost reaching Alia's full height as he said viciously, "I sincerely doubt that, young Adrian. For if you break your oath to me, you will condemn your friends to the most gruesome fates imaginable. What did you say to that man about his daughter? 'You will watch as I cut pieces from her'? 'I will bathe you in her blood'? Merely words from your mouth, Adrian. Well spoken, but merely words. I, on the other hand, am quite capable of demonstrating them to you."

I stared at him, horrorstruck.

"Did you really think that there would be no consequences to others?" the Historian said with a cruel little smirk. "As with so many mortals before you, your only true strength has always been your greatest weakness. You've sworn an oath to take your own blood, and yet you're still trying to live your life according to some self-serving set of rules that you think will save your soul."

"They're all I have left!" I replied furiously.

"Then you have nothing," said the Historian.

"Get out of my head!" I bellowed.

The Historian laughed loudly. "What makes you think I'm even here?"

I woke with a start. Reflexively putting my right palm on my chest, I felt my pendant over my racing heart. I was lying on a soft bed in a semi-dark room. I wasn't sure how I got here. Probably Ed Regis.

"Addy? Are you okay?" said Alia, crouching next to me on my mattress and peering into my eyes. *"You were having a nightmare."*

"Were you sleeping in my bed again?" I asked, wondering if she had heard me cry out in my sleep.

"No," she replied, nodding toward a bed on the other side of the room where a small shape stirred quietly. *"With Marion."*

"What time is it?"

"Almost morning, I think."

Resting my head back on my pillow, I closed my eyes again for a moment. I heard the Historian's voice in my head echoing slightly as he said, *"Your oath is to continue hunting Catherine Divine until either you or she is dead. I never said that you have to personally end her life, but you will not stray from your path until the deed is done one way or another. That is the only way you will protect everyone else who is dear to you. You have my word, young Adrian."*

"I must be going insane," I muttered to myself, opening my eyes and getting out of bed. "I need some air."

Alia followed me out of the bedroom and down the stairs. The light from the living room was pouring into the hallway through the open door, and Ed Regis called my name as we passed, but I ignored him. Alia followed me out onto the front porch, shivering in the chill.

The clouds had cleared but the stars were growing dimmer in the pale violet sky. I faintly saw my breath as I exhaled. Alia was hugging herself to keep warm. I hardly felt the cold. My whole existence seemed numbed out, almost like being drained.

It had been much clearer than his short message to me at Wood-claw, but had the Historian really been dreamweaving to me? How far was his range? Could it have all just been in my head? But even if it had, what would the Historian really do if I broke my promise?

And more importantly, did I even want to?

As a master controller, the existence of Catherine Divine stood against everything I believed in. Everything except what I had to do to stop her.

Why had the Historian asked for my vow? He knew I was weak. He knew I was unbalanced. Was it despite who I was, or because of it, that he had set me on this path? He knew then, as I had finally discovered, that this was the one road I could neither take nor avoid.

"I'm not quitting," I whispered.

Alia looked up at me in surprise. *"But you said—"*

"I know what I said, Alia! And I can't kill Catherine Divine. But I can't quit, either."

"Why?"

"I just can't."

"Then you're not going to stop?"

"No, Alia, I'm not," I said resolutely. But then my voice faltered as I added, "I just don't know how I'm going to go on."

Gazing into my eyes, Alia suggested gently, *"How about with the truth?"*

"Truth?" I asked, bewildered.

Alia nodded solemnly. *"You hate calling Cat your sister, Addy, but inside, you know that she is."*

Of course I knew. That was the problem. "Please don't call her that," I said, shaking my head. "I can't do this if I see her that way."

"It doesn't matter how you see her," argued Alia. *"She's still your sister. You can't escape that."*

"She's Queen Divine, Alia!" I said forcefully. "She's not my sister!"

"Yes she is, Adrian!" Alia shot back furiously. *"You know she is!"*

I didn't know what to say.

Alia took my hand as she said soothingly, *"Just admit to yourself what you're doing, Addy. She's not Queen Divine to you. She's not Catherine Divine. She's not even Catherine Howell. She's Cat. She's your sister. You love her as much as I love you. You can try all you want, but you can't escape the truth. Stop trying to fool yourself. It never works anyway."*

"You really have grown, haven't you?" I said in wonder as I once again saw Cindy Gifford standing before me.

Alia smiled. *"Just try it, Addy."*

"I am trying to kill my sister," I whispered, looking up at the last stars in the dawn sky. And then, more loudly, "I am trying to find and kill Cat."

"Say it again, Addy."

I did. "I am trying to kill Cat."

"Again."

I said it again and again, over and over, louder and louder. And as I did, I felt as if the poison I had been force-feeding myself ever since I left the Historian's mountain was finally beginning to leave my blood. There was no release from the guilt of my vow. But Alia was right: I did breathe just a little easier. It was the most horrible truth that I could ever say. But at least it was the truth.

I heard Terry ask from behind me, "Does that mean this mission isn't over yet?"

I turned around and saw her standing at the door with Ed Regis.

"It's not over," I confirmed. "We're still going after Div... I mean, we're still going after Cat. I promised the Historian and I promised myself that I would never stop hunting my sister. And I won't. As long as we're both alive, this doesn't end."

"And can you kill her?" asked Ed Regis. "Or at least stand by and let one of us do it?"

I glanced at Alia. She gave me a little nod and whispered into my head, *"Truth, Addy."*

"No, Ed Regis," I replied. "I can't kill her. And I can't let you or Terry or anyone else do it either."

Ed Regis frowned. "Then you're hoping that our mission will fail."

"No," I said again, "I am not. I will do anything and everything I can to find and kill Cat."

"That sounds very much like a paradox."

I gave him a wry smile. "Try living it."

If Ed Regis found my position paradoxical, I could only agree. But just because I didn't have it in me to do something didn't excuse me from doing it. My first sister still had to die, and I owed it to her to end her life myself. Cat was once my master, but she was always my family, and you never turn your back on family. Failure would be just as much a betrayal as success, and I couldn't allow either.

Terry gave me a grim look, asking, "Then what happens if, by some unhappy miracle, we actually do find her?"

"How are we supposed to kill her, Adrian?" added Ed Regis. "Over your dead body?"

"If it comes to that," I said evenly. "But one thing at a time. We still have to find her."

15. THE TIPPING POINT

Alia went upstairs to check on Marion. She wanted to be there when the poor kid woke.

Back in the comparative warmth of the living room, I asked Terry and Ed Regis, "So, what do we do now?"

"We might as well just leave Raider where he is," said Terry. "Someone will find the body sooner or later anyway, and I'd rather get back on the road before the hiding bubble around the van fades completely. Who knows how many days we'll get before Randal Divine discovers that we're not being taken to the Royal Gate."

"But where are we going to go?" I asked.

"We could try returning to Lumina," said Terry.

"That would be dangerous," warned Ed Regis. "Even if we could somehow get to our assigned safe house, the Seraphim will double their patrols and S&Ds after yesterday's attack. There's also a good chance that the information from Raider's mapping mission, however incomplete, will be used against the Resistance before long."

"That's assuming Raider had been giving periodic updates to Randal Divine," said Terry, "which, admittedly, is possible."

"We should consider the worst-case scenario and warn the Resistance quickly," said Ed Regis, "but from outside of Lumina. We can't risk capture ourselves."

"To the Council, then?" suggested Terry. "If we could get to the nearest

Guardian settlement, we could probably contact the Council from there."

"That might be best," agreed Ed Regis.

Personally, I didn't fancy the idea of taking Marion with us to a Guardian settlement. Her mother was still a converted Angel, and I couldn't imagine the Guardians not using Marion against her if they found out. Still, I kept my opinion to myself. As always, the mission specifics were best left to the experts.

"Adrian," Terry said suddenly, "what do you think we should do?"

I looked at her in surprise. "What are you asking me for? You've always steered this boat."

"True," said Terry. "Just not in the right direction."

"Tiffy—I mean Terry," I said uncomfortably, "you're the leader."

"Then as the leader," Terry said with a touch of exasperation in her voice, "I'm asking you for your opinion, Adrian."

"I don't know," I said stupidly. "Personally, I'd rather return to Wood-claw than go to some random Guardian settlement. At least at Wood-claw they'd trust us and we can trust them too."

"You may have a point," said Ed Regis. "If we just show up unannounced at a Guardian settlement, it could take some time to earn their trust. Besides, Wood-claw isn't that much farther than the nearest outpost that we know of."

"I suppose there's some sense to that," agreed Terry. "That way Harding could contact the Resistance directly. And she might even remember her promise to fund our mission."

Nobody would say it out loud, but I think we all just wanted a break, a chance to regain a little sanity.

"Let's get going," said Ed Regis. "We need to warn the Resistance before Randal Divine realizes that Raider has been compromised."

As Terry and Ed Regis quickly searched the house for things we might be able to use on the road, I went upstairs to find Alia and have her wake Marion.

When I entered the room, Alia was sitting on the edge of Marion's bed, blankly staring off into space. I wasn't sure if she was focused enough to hear my words, so I said nothing for a while. Eventually, Alia turned her head and looked at me. *"Willow's baby,"* she said in a monotone. *"Do you think it was a girl or a boy?"*

"I don't know," I whispered. "Willow thought it was a boy. She's probably right."

Alia looked out the window. *"All those people died so quickly."*

"Don't do this to yourself, Alia," I said, putting a hand on her shoulder. "This is a war. It's nobody's fault."

Alia didn't reply, her eyes fixed on the dawn sky.

"Come on," I said gently. "Give yourself a break. Just this once."

Alia took a minute more to breathe. Then she looked up at me again, saying quietly, *"I just wish people would stop hurting each other."*

"One way or another, it'll be over soon," I assured her. "Wake Marion up and put her in the van."

"What should I tell her happened to her father?"

"What have you told her so far?"

"Just that he was having an argument with you and Terry," said Alia. *"And that everything was going to be okay in the end."*

"Good," I said, nodding. "Then tell her that Raider returned to Lumina by himself."

"I don't like lying."

I shrugged. "Tell her the truth if you want. Just wake her up and get her ready. We've got a long road ahead."

Ed Regis and Terry came up with next to nothing in their search: no money, no weapons and no spare gasoline.

Not surprisingly, the refrigerator was empty, but there were some cans and pickle jars in the pantry, and we took those to the van. In the bedrooms, we found some spare clothes. It was mostly summer stuff, but at least it was clean. Terry didn't want to show Marion the blood on her shirt.

We filed quietly into Raider's van. Ed Regis took the driver's seat while the rest of us hid in the back behind the tinted windows. Marion, looking a bit dazed, remained silent, sticking close to Alia in the back seat as Ed Regis pulled the van back onto the empty country road.

For most of that day, we rode in silence.

Alia said nothing more about the fall of the command center, so no one else brought it up either. I was sure that she still felt responsible for the deaths of those Resistance Knights, including Willow's unborn child, but there was nothing more I could say to comfort her. If we were still alive when the war ended, we would have plenty of time to mourn.

Marion also talked very little. When she did, she spoke in whispers, and mostly to Alia. To keep his cover intact, Raider had lied as convincingly to Marion as he had to the Guardians. Marion never suspected that her father had been an Angel Seraph. Outwardly, she seemed to accept our claim that Raider had returned to the Resistance alone, leaving her in our care until things cooled down. Marion had heard her father screaming in the basement, so no doubt she suspected foul play, but either afraid or simply unwilling, she didn't question our story.

We had come from Wood-claw by air, but we were returning by road, which would take considerably longer. Once in Wood-claw's city, we would have to wait for pickup by Scott and company. I wondered how long we really had before Randal Divine discovered that Raider had failed to deliver us. How much time did we have before the hunt for Adrian Howell resumed?

Ed Regis figured that we had just enough cash, taken from Raider's wallet, to get us back to Wood-claw. He kept Raider's pistol, which had a full clip and was our only weapon aside from Terry's and my psionics.

But Raider's van, with its cracked rear windshield, was a dead giveaway. At the first small town we came to, with Terry's help, Ed Regis acquired something less conspicuous: a dusty four-door dark brown SUV that, though I won't bother with the details, was guaranteed not to be reported stolen for at least a week.

No longer concealed by Raider's hiding bubble, Terry, Alia and I went back to using metal draining to hide our psionic presence as best we could.

"This draining really is a pain in the neck," admitted Terry when she realized that she had to stay in the car as Ed Regis did our food shopping for us.

Terry and I took turns driving when we were in the countryside, and Ed Regis took the wheel whenever we passed through anywhere populated. But whether by luck or by the order of Randal Divine, we met no obstacles on the road.

It was a race against the clock and we didn't stop for the night. By midnight, we were already on the last, long stretch to Wood-claw's city. Terry was at the wheel, and I was sitting next to her and keeping her company as Ed Regis, Alia and Marion slept in the back.

"We're making good time," said Terry, using her hook to steer the SUV around a gentle curve in the road. "We might even be in Wood-claw for breakfast tomorrow."

Sitting beside her, I had been lost in my dismal thoughts as I watched the dark gray countryside drifting by. I turned to her and smiled. "It'd be nice to have a normal breakfast for a change."

"Agreed, but you know we can't stay in Wood-claw for very long. We need to find that Royal Gate somehow."

Terry had said that more than once on the road so far. But "somehow" wasn't a proven method for finding something.

"I sure hope Mrs. Harding can help," I said. It wasn't the first time I had said this either, but it was the only response I could give.

Terry wasn't just making conversation, though.

"If the Council really had heard of the Royal Gate," she continued, "and if they knew where it was, then they would have hit it by now. They probably don't even know of its existence. We can ask, but don't expect a miracle."

"I never ask for miracles," I informed her.

"We may need one before long, Adrian," said Terry. "Ever since the Meridian folded, our allies are disappearing fast and quiet. Even if the Resistance and the Council don't surrender, it won't matter soon."

I knew that. "What's your point?"

Terry kept her eyes on the road as she said quietly, "Maybe it's time to try something crazy."

"Such as?"

"Not everyone fighting the Angels is allied with the Guardians. If our friends can't help, then maybe our enemies can."

I was usually the one to come up with the wild ideas, but it still took a moment before I fully understood what Terry was suggesting.

"No," I said flatly.

"They may not be psionic, Adrian, but they're the biggest faction left," argued Terry. "They have a fairly extensive information network. Maybe not as complete as the Guardians', but that's precisely the point. They could have stumbled across something that they themselves don't fully understand."

"You really want to ask the God-slayers for help?" I asked incredulously. "You're insane."

Terry seemed to smile. "Then I'm in good company."

"I'm not going to beg the Slayers for anything, Terry. Not ever."

“Why not?” scoffed Terry. “You made nice with the Wolves, didn’t you?”

“The Wolves are soldiers!” I countered vehemently. “The Slayers are just psychopaths.”

“Well-funded and dedicated psychopaths,” said Terry. “And their cause is not that different from ours anymore. If we offered them the chance to kill the world’s last master controller, I’ll bet they’d help us.”

“No.”

“A master controller, Adrian! You think they wouldn’t side with us for that? Come on, it’s not like you have any real principles left to break anyway.”

I glared at her. “Have you forgotten what they did to me?”

“Have you forgotten what we did to them?” Terry replied evenly.

I looked away. My slightly sunken, mismatching eyes reflected in the window stared back at me.

“Let’s at least try our luck with the Council first,” I said wearily.

“Of course,” Terry replied with an air of victory. “I was just considering options.”

“You mean you were testing my resolve,” I said dryly, finally realizing that she had set me up. “You really think I want this mission to fail, don’t you?”

“I didn’t say that,” said Terry. “I’m just worried about you.”

“Well, don’t worry,” I said. “I still know how to kill people.”

“I hope that’s true.”

Ever since returning from the Historian’s mountain, my mission rules had been pretty straightforward: One, kill the Angel master. Two, don’t get converted. Three, save Cindy. Four, return Alia. And five, if at all possible, get through this alive. But my inability to kill Raider, the Historian’s dream and Alia’s insistence on truth had forced me to acknowledge that I had one more rule: Don’t kill Cat. This one had also been there from the start.

No, I didn’t want our mission to fail, but nor could I allow it to succeed. And I still had no idea what would really happen if I came face to face with my first sister like this. So, in short, yes, Terry was right to be concerned.

Even so, I felt incredibly stupid for stepping into her little trap. But if Terry thought that it was okay to challenge my commitment by bringing up something as painful to me as the God-slayers, then I was going to have my say too.

"Now you tell me something, Terry," I breathed. "What really happened back in the command center?"

"What do you mean?" asked Terry. She tried to make it sound innocent, but I could tell that she was bracing herself.

"You've been itching for a battle all last year," I said. "I know you wished you were on that Wolf plane with us. And I've never seen you miss an opportunity to kill some Angels."

"What happened in Nonus wasn't an opportunity," Terry said stiffly. "It was a deathtrap. If we hadn't retreated, we would have all died in there. Every last one of us."

"Still, that was a pretty quick retreat."

Terry shook her head. "When Mark led us to the trapdoor, I thought you were right behind us. I was so sure you had heard James and me calling. We were both yelling like crazy. But when we got down to the twentieth, you weren't there."

"So why didn't you come back? Why did you send James?"

"Are you questioning my honor?!" snapped Terry.

"I'm just curious, Terry," I said in a monotone. "You gave your gun to James and sent him back in."

"Because he insisted! Because he wanted to prove something, and..."

"Terry?"

Suddenly Terry pulled the SUV to the side of the road. "You want to know what really happened?" she asked, her voice quivering. "The truth? The truth is that I froze up. I was scared, alright?! It was just a second, but James saw it. He told me to give him my gun, and I did."

I nodded silently.

Terry looked away as she mumbled, "I tried to justify it by thinking it was a firefight, not a brawl, and since James had two hands to use two guns, he had a better chance. But that's just stupid. You're right, Adrian. I should have gone back in with him."

"I didn't say that," I insisted. "I was just curious why you didn't."

"I never thought I'd hesitate," Terry said with a sigh, and then let out a hollow little laugh. "Maybe I'm just getting old."

I smiled sympathetically. "I think you're only human, Terry."

"It won't happen again. I swear it won't."

"Hey," Ed Regis called sleepily from the back. "What's going on? Why are we stopped?"

"Nothing," I replied. "We're just making sure that we're both still cold-blooded murderers. Go back to sleep."

As Terry pulled our vehicle back onto the road, I looked down at my hands and sighed heavily. I wondered if I could ever look at my hands again without remembering the people I had killed with them. I wondered how many more lives I had yet to take.

By daybreak, we had arrived back on the outskirts of Wood-claw's city. It was much too early to check in at a hotel and we weren't sure we would need one anyway. Terry parked the SUV on the roadside and swapped places with Ed Regis so that she could sleep a little as we waited for our Wood-claw escorts. I didn't feel particularly sleepy myself until I heard Terry snoring in the back.

When I woke, it was past noon and we were still parked.

"They haven't come yet, Adrian," said Ed Regis, still sitting next to me in the driver's seat.

Terry, Alia and I had stopped draining ourselves as soon as we entered the city, so Scott should have found us by now.

"Well, that's Harding for you," I muttered as I stretched my arms and legs a little. Then I let out a loud, deliberate and annoyed yawn. We had driven all night so that we could deliver our warning to the Resistance as soon as possible, but now we were at the mercy of Mrs. Harding's excruciatingly unhurried security protocols.

We ate lunch in the car, and then Ed Regis drove us to a nearby hotel.

The layout was basically the same as the last time: Ed Regis got us two twin rooms, and like before, they were side by side on the second floor with balconies that looked down onto the parking lot.

"We're out of cash," announced Ed Regis as we inspected our rooms. "We won't be able to stay two nights here."

"Don't worry," Terry said confidently. "They'll come today. Who knows? We might even be in Wood-claw in time for dinner tonight."

Terry had said something similar last night about breakfast. "What makes you such an optimist?" I asked her.

Terry smirked. "Because Scott and the others won't leave us out here no matter what Harding says."

The hotel staff had provided a cot for Marion in the girls' room, but even if we ended up staying the night, I knew it wouldn't be used. Marion and Alia would share a bed again, which was probably a good thing for Alia too, since she so liked being needed.

Once we were settled, we passed the time with a deck of cards and a few bags of chips. Even Marion joined us, and though she still spoke mostly in whispers, just occasionally, she smiled a little.

Though I would never mourn her father's passing, I still felt horrible every time I looked at Marion. Terry was far better at guilt management than me. If Terry felt at all sorry for leaving Marion fatherless, she didn't show it. She could talk to Marion and treat her like a friend. I still couldn't meet Marion's eyes. And though I knew that I still had a much harder (and more likely impossible) mission ahead of me, my current primary objective was to see Marion safely delivered back to her Angel mother. That much I felt I owed to her, and to her father. I hoped that Mrs. Harding would agree.

"They're here," announced Alia, who had been peeking down from the balcony every time she heard a car pull into the parking lot.

It was still early evening, so it looked like we really would make it back to Wood-claw in time for dinner. That is, assuming we were all going to be taken in together this time. However, my hopes for that were dampened the moment I saw who had arrived to guide us in. Neither Scott nor Rachael, nor any of our former combat students were part of the welcoming party. Instead, Wood-claw had sent four serious-looking men, and to top it all off, they were once again led by the ill-tempered Knight, Hammer.

"Back without warning, I see," said Hammer as he and his buddies entered our room.

"You haven't heard anything about the Resistance?" I asked.

"Nothing recent," replied Hammer.

I wasn't too surprised about that considering how long it usually took for Wood-claw to communicate with the Resistance. Besides, with the command center down, most of the Resistance fighters were probably still hiding in their safe houses.

Hammer added brusquely, "Whatever your news is, it can wait till we get you back to Wood-claw and you can tell Mrs. Harding yourself."

"Well, let's get going, then," said Terry.

"You two first," said Hammer, pointing at Terry and me. "The others can wait."

I shook my head. "If only two are going, I want Marion to go first. She can go with Terry."

"Don't you contradict me, young man," said Hammer, bristling. "I said you and Terry first, and that's the way it's going to be."

I wasn't worried about leaving Alia behind, but the sooner we got Marion to safety, the sooner I would feel comfortable about this whole nasty mess. Besides, I didn't like Hammer's tone any more than he liked mine.

"Might I remind you that we are guests of Mrs. Harding," I said coldly. "We are not under her command. Nor yours, Hammer."

Hammer's scowl deepened for a moment. Then he let out a dismissive little grunt. "Suit yourself, kid. Terry and... who the hell is Marion?"

I pointed her out, saying, "It's a long story."

Hammer turned to one of his teammates, a hider I knew by the call sign Jerky. "You'll stay here with me, Jerk," said Hammer. Then he said to his two other Knights, "You guys get these girls to Wood-claw and come right back. I don't want to stay here all night if we can help it."

Marion was hesitant to leave Alia's side, but Alia said something into her head and then Terry took her hand and escorted her from the hotel room. I followed them out to the parking lot. Marion refused to get into the Wood-claw van, anxiously looking up at Alia, who was waving to her from the balcony.

"Don't worry, Marion," I said as Terry pushed her into the car. "Alia will be right behind you."

"Thank you, Richard," whispered Marion, giving me a faint smile. "I mean Addy."

I nodded and said dully, "We'll see you soon."

Then I turned to Terry, but before I could say anything, she said, "Trust me. I'll talk to Harding as soon as I get there. We'll get the message out to the Resistance if I have to deliver it myself."

"See you later tonight," I said, and watched them go.

"Come on," I heard Hammer call from the balcony. "Get back up here."

Back in our room, I asked Hammer, "How long do you think it'll take?"

"As long as it takes," he replied gruffly.

"Probably not before midnight," added Jerky.

I didn't want to judge Hammer too harshly. I could only guess that Wood-claw, like all the other independent factions out there that were still free of Angel control, was having to take increasingly serious measures to ensure its security.

We didn't even have any cash left for dinner, but Hammer sent Jerky off to get some takeout, and the five of us resumed our card game after burgers and fries.

I figured that, by now, the advance team would have reached the Wood-claw building. Marion was probably already in Candace's capable hands while Terry spoke to Mrs. Harding about the possible threat to the Resistance from Raider's mapping mission.

But once that issue was dealt with, what next? Though I still couldn't be entirely sure that Terry wasn't joking about asking the God-slayers for help, I had to agree that the Guardian Council probably couldn't help us find the Royal Gate. Nor, for that matter, was there any guarantee that the Slayers could help. Were we back to square one, doomed to randomly travel around the country looking for lost clues and hoping for lucky breaks?

Raider had been driving us straight to the Royal Gate, which was exactly where I would have ended up had I remained on the Wolf plane. Twice now I had narrowly avoided the reunion that could have brought this mission to a close. The easiest way—and perhaps the only way—to meet my first sister was to simply get caught by the Angels. But that negated the possibility of killing her and getting away with it.

But what if I didn't need to get away with it?

I immediately shook the thought from my mind. No, that wasn't an option I was prepared to entertain. Assuming that I could somehow resolve my conflicting mission rules about killing and not killing Cat, I also had to come back alive. Despite the awful request that I had once made of my team, surviving this mission was one of my rules too. For Cindy and for Alia, and of course for myself, I had to restore the only real family I had left.

"Adrian?" said Ed Regis. "You in or out?"

"Huh?" I said. I looked down at the cards in my hand and mumbled,

"Out, I think."

"You okay? You look a little dazed."

"Oh, I guess I'm just sleepy."

I had stayed up with Terry all through the previous night, and though I had slept in the car seat during the morning, I still felt worn out. It was only about 8pm but I bid the crowd goodnight and headed to the room next door.

Alia followed me. My sister probably wasn't that sleepy, but she looked like she was tired of the card game and wanted a little quiet time.

We didn't bother changing. As we slipped into our beds, Alia said nervously into my head, *"I hope Terry doesn't tell Mrs. Harding that Marion is Raider's daughter."*

"You don't trust Harding?" I yawned.

Alia shook her head. *"I don't trust anybody when it comes to how we treat our enemies."*

I bit my lip. "Well, like Raider once said, she trusts us so we should trust her in return."

"I suppose."

"At least she's not a Guardian," I added as I telekinetically flipped off the lights. "I'm sure she'll do what's right for Marion."

And with that last, comforting thought, I closed my eyes.

When I woke, the room was still dark, and I heard Alia's quiet snores over her telepathic murmuring. The bedside clock read a little past 1am.

I stretched my arms and legs a little, and then rested my head back onto my pillow, wondering if Ed Regis and the Wood-claw Knights were still playing cards next door. Perhaps I would join them.

Turning my head, I looked over at Alia's bed and listened to her quiet telepathic gibberish. I had become so accustomed to my sister's nighttime telepathy that I knew I would miss it horribly when she someday outgrew it.

"Danger..."

I wondered for a moment if I had just imagined it. Alia didn't usually say anything coherent in her sleep.

"Danger... Out..."

"Alia," I said quietly. "Wake up."

"Out!"

I telekinetically shook her body a little. "Wake up, Ali! You're having a nightmare."

Alia sat up on her bed and looked over at me. *"Addy?"*

"It's okay," I said soothingly. "You were just having a nightmare."

Alia blinked twice. *"No I wasn't."*

I stared at her, listening to the silence for a minute more.

"Come with me," I said to her as I got out of my bed and put my shoes on. "Something's wrong."

I made my way back toward the other room with Alia on my heels. I knocked loudly on the door, and it was opened by Ed Regis. The lights were still on inside, as was, by the look of the table, the card game.

"They're not here yet," Jerky informed me from the table.

"How much longer?" I asked, stepping into the room.

"Like I said before," growled Hammer, "they'll get here when they do."

"What's the matter?" asked Ed Regis.

"I'm not sure," I replied honestly, still listening to the ever-so-faint sounds in my head, "but I think we're in some kind of trouble."

"What kind of trouble?" Hammer asked sharply, standing up from the table.

"Like I said, I don't know." I walked over to one of the beds where Hammer had carelessly left his pistol. "I think you might need this," I said, picking it up and checking the safety.

"Danger... Claw... Out... Coming..."

"Well, hand it here, then," said Hammer, reaching out to take the gun from my hand.

I was about to give it to him, but just then the message finally became clear in my head.

"Hey!" said Hammer, entirely unamused as he watched me level the pistol on him. "Never point a gun at someone unless you—"

I shot him twice in the chest.

Jerky drew his gun from his side holster. But before he could even flip off the safety, Ed Regis slammed his fist into Jerky's face, knocking him down onto the floor and sending the gun flying.

Ed Regis had acted on instinct, but he was just as surprised as Hammer had been at my treachery. "What the hell is going on?!" he yelled at me.

"Danger, Adrian!" said Candace's frantic voice in my head. *"Get out*

now! Wood-claw has fallen! They're coming for you!"

I didn't need to relay the message. We heard tires screeching outside.

Ed Regis checked the balcony as I fired a single round into each of Jerky's legs. Alia was screaming a protest into my head but I wasn't listening.

"We can't use the car," reported Ed Regis. "They've blocked off the exits."

I tucked Hammer's pistol under my belt. Ed Regis led Alia and me out of our room and down the corridor. As we got to the stairs, we heard shouts and many rushing footsteps from below.

"Back! Back!" yelled Ed Regis, pulling us in the opposite direction. "Adrian, make an exit!"

He meant the window at the end of the corridor, and I telekinetically blasted it out without stretching my arms forward.

"Go!" shouted Ed Regis as we got to the shattered window.

He turned around and, pointing his pistol down the corridor, fired several times at the Wood-claw Knights that had just reached the top of the stairs.

I grabbed Alia's hand and we jumped from the window together. It was only one floor down and I didn't bother using my telekinesis to soften our landing.

"Come on!" I shouted up at Ed Regis.

After releasing a few more covering rounds, Ed Regis jumped down too, landing heavily but without injury.

We were on the left side of the hotel, opposite the parking lot, and we sprinted toward the road as two fireballs from the pyroid Knights at the window smacked into the concrete. Another fireball grazed my left arm, setting my sleeve alight, but I quickly slapped it out with my right palm and kept running.

There were only a few cars on the road, which was good because otherwise there might have been a major accident when Ed Regis boldly stepped in front of the first one that came our way. It was a junky beige pickup truck.

As the pickup came to a screeching halt just inches from Ed Regis, the driver stuck his head out his door window and bellowed, "What the hell do you think you're doing?!"

"Get out," commanded Ed Regis, pointing his pistol at the driver. "Leave the keys."

"Over my dead body!" the man yelled back.

Before Ed Regis could call the man's bluff, I telekinetically unlocked the pickup's passenger-side door, opened it, undid the driver's seatbelt, and yanked the very surprised man out onto the side of the road.

"Give me your gun," Ed Regis said to me. "You drive."

I pulled Hammer's pistol from my belt and tossed it to Ed Regis, who caught it in his left hand. Ed Regis climbed onto the pickup's cargo bed, which was empty. Alia followed me into the front and pulled the door closed as I floored the accelerator.

I had been expecting the Knights to jump out the window and chase us on foot, but they had doubled back to their vehicles. In the rearview mirror, I saw a dark green van and a hefty black SUV pull out of the hotel's parking lot and join the pursuit. Our pickup truck wouldn't be able to outrun them.

We were on a wide, open road that ran around the edge of the city, and there wasn't enough traffic at this time of night to dissuade the Knights from coming at us full force.

"Seatbelts, Alia!" I shouted, keeping my hands firmly on the wheel. "Mine first!"

As Alia reached around my body to pull my seatbelt, I caught sight of something metallic in her hand. "Where'd you get the gun?!"

"It's Jerky's," Alia replied aloud, drained by the pistol she was holding.

I snatched it from her.

"You drive!" I said, opening the rear window and crawling out onto the cargo bed.

Ed Regis gave me a disbelieving look as I sat down next to him, but now wasn't the time to argue tactics. Alia knew how to drive, and she could probably even reach the accelerator.

Ed Regis and I watched from the cargo bed as the SUV and van closed their distance. I couldn't tell in the darkness how many people were on board, but they weren't firing at us. They wanted me alive, which meant they were probably trying to drive us off the road.

"I'll take the van," said Ed Regis.

I pointed my pistol at the driver of the SUV, who was now close enough to identify. It was Wood-claw's Head of Security, Isabel "Tigress" Ferris.

"Addy!"

My pistol was knocked from my hands as we were engulfed in the deafening sound of shattering glass and twisting metal. Alia had run a red light, and a small sedan had slammed into us from the left side. Our pickup's rear swung wildly from side to side as Alia fought to regain control.

I felt my power drain slightly and discovered that I had a little cut on my left hand. Ed Regis was also injured. He had hit his head against something, and blood was trickling down the side of his face.

Ed Regis had lost his guns too, but I found one of them lying next to me and passed it back to him. Alia had managed to steady our pickup and was regaining speed.

The sedan that had broadsided us was out of sight, but the two Wood-claw vehicles were close upon us now. Ed Regis fired at the van's windshield until his gun was empty, and a second later the van veered sharply to the right and tipped over onto its side, grinding to a stop.

There was no time to celebrate. Tigress's SUV slammed into the rear of our pickup, jolting us violently. I tried to telekinetically grab the SUV's steering wheel, but Tigress kept a firm grip on it. I couldn't focus my power well because of the cut on my hand. Tigress hit us again, this time from the rear right, and Alia finally lost control of the pickup.

As we spun out on the road, the SUV came to a halt beside us, and four men, armed with pistols, jumped out from the rear. Three survivors from the overturned van had also come running. Two of them carried automatic rifles.

"That's enough!" shouted Tigress, getting out of the SUV and walking up to us, pistol drawn. "No more running! It's over!"

She quickly opened the driver-side door and pulled Alia out, firmly holding her upper right arm. Alia didn't struggle.

"It's over," Tigress said again, breathing heavily. "The war is over. It's time to stop running."

I saw another one of our pistols lying at my feet. I was too drained for a focused blast, but I wasn't going to be taken alive like this.

I was about to grab the pistol, but before I could, a small black dot appeared between Tigress's eyes. Releasing her grip on Alia, Tigress crumpled backwards down onto the road. Two more shots rang out, and two more

Knights fell. Both were headshots.

"On your left!" Candace shouted into my head as the remaining Wood-claw Knights scrambled for cover behind their SUV.

Ed Regis and I jumped down from the cargo bed. Ed Regis grabbed Alia's hand and pulled her along as we sprinted toward Scott's white van that had materialized at the corner of the street. The side door was open, and Candace and Scott were providing covering fire from inside as the Wood-claw Knights shot back at us, no longer trying to take us alive. Little holes appeared all over the side of the van as its windows exploded, and even more bullets ricocheted around us, but we didn't stop.

"Go! Go! Go!" shouted Scott as we piled into his van.

The van lurched forward. Scott slid up front beside Rachael, who was driving, and Ed Regis pulled Alia into the back with him. Candace closed the side door and sat with me in the middle.

Still high on adrenaline, I couldn't help laughing as I turned to Candace and said, "I didn't know you turned telepathic!"

"Bet you didn't think I could shoot either," said Candace, giving me a quick peck on the cheek.

"Everyone alright back there?" called Rachael.

"We're good," I reported automatically.

"Stay sharp," said Rachael. "We're not out of this yet."

Rachael was right: Though there was no immediate pursuit, our windows were shot out and the side of the van was riddled with bullet holes. We weren't going to get far before someone called the police on us. But I was more worried about Terry and Marion right now. What had happened to them? Were they still alive?

I was about to ask Candace when Ed Regis said from behind me, "Adrian, we have a problem."

I turned around in my seat. Ed Regis had a fair amount of blood on his face and neck, but I suspected that it looked a lot worse than it really was. I was about to tell Alia to heal him, but then I saw Alia, whose face looked paler in the moonlight.

I saw the blood trickling from her lips.

16. ON THE FAR SIDE OF DARKNESS

Entering her lower back dangerously close to her spine, the bullet had gone straight through her, opening a hole on both sides of her body. Panting heavily, she opened her mouth to say something, but then her body went limp. She was bleeding out.

"Give me something to cut her shirt with!" said Ed Regis, keeping his hands pressed hard over the entry and exit points.

Scott handed me a small knife, which I passed to Ed Regis. My hands felt sluggish and everything was in slow motion as my whole world was plunged into icy waters. Ed Regis quickly cut up Alia's blood-soaked shirt to make bandages like he had for me when I got blasted in the mountains. As he worked, all I could see was my sister's deathly white face, her eyes open but hardly moving. Alia had managed to heal herself just a little before losing her power completely, but even so, there was a lot of blood. By the smell, I knew that it wasn't just torn flesh.

"It should have been me," I mumbled dazedly. "She could have healed me."

I couldn't shake the irony of how, in the middle of all that gunfire, the only one of us that got hit was the smallest. And the most irreplaceable.

"There!" shouted Candace. "Look! It says 'clinic' right there!"

"But that's not a—" began Rachael.

"Any clinic is fine!" said Ed Regis, not looking up from his work. "Just get us there."

I hadn't seen the roadside sign either, but it could have been a maternity hospital for all I cared. We needed a doctor. Any doctor.

Rachael pulled off of the main road and, a few minutes later, parked the van in the shadow of a square, single-story building that looked more like a house than a hospital. The lights were all off, but Scott and Rachael got out anyway, ran up to the front door and started pounding on it. I followed them.

There was a large white sign on the wall next to the front door, and seeing it, I understood Rachael's initial reaction. It was a veterinary clinic.

"Hey," called a voice from behind us. "Hey! We're closed at night."

Turning around, we saw an elderly man walking toward us from the house adjacent to the clinic.

I asked frantically, "Are you the doctor here?"

"Yes," he replied tartly. "Alfred Hanson, DVM, at your very sleepy service. Do you kids have any idea what time it is?"

"It's an emergency, Dr. Hanson," said Rachael. "You have to help us!"

"Well, I'm already up," sighed the man, stepping up to the front door and unlocking it for us. "What do you have?"

"Gunshot wound," I told him.

"A dog?"

"Not exactly."

Scott and I escorted the veterinarian over to the side of our van where Ed Regis had already pulled Alia outside, holding her carefully in his arms.

"But I'm a vet!" protested Dr. Hanson. "That's a person!"

"She's a mammal, isn't she?!" snapped Ed Regis. "You're going to treat her."

"She needs an emergency room! I'm not qualified."

I pulled on his arm. "We have no time to explain but we can't take her to a human hospital. Please, Doctor. Please!"

"I could lose my license over this," he said, shaking his head.

"You'll lose a lot more than a license," warned Candace, waving her gun at him.

Ed Regis took a step forward and snarled, "You save this child's life or I swear to God I'll personally take you on a tour through realms of pain you never dreamed existed!"

"I'll be sixty-three years old in a month," the doctor replied evenly.

"What exactly did you have in mind?"

"Please," I said to him, unable to hold my tears back. "She's dying. She's my sister. I'm begging you, Doctor. Please don't let her die here."

The animal doctor's eyes moved from Ed Regis's furious, bloody glare to Candace's gun, and finally to my sister's lifeless form.

"Alright, bring her in," he said, heading for the door. "Quickly!"

We followed Ed Regis as he carried Alia into the small clinic and placed her gently down onto a rectangular operating table.

As we watched breathlessly, the old veterinarian inspected the wounds on Alia's stomach and back. He frowned at Ed Regis's first aid. His eyes stopped briefly on the many crisscrossing scars across Alia's back and my old blast mark on her left side, but he didn't comment.

"She's gone into shock," he said. "We need to get her to a real hospital. Otherwise she'll die for certain."

"Out of the question," said Ed Regis. "Do what you can here."

"You asked me to save her life, sir!" the vet said heatedly. "I can stitch up the wounds but she's lost too much blood. She needs a transfusion."

"Then we'll do it here," I said.

"For Christ's sake, kid, I don't keep human blood at an animal clinic!"

"You've got needles, don't you?!" I shot back. "I'll take care of the blood. You get to the stitching."

"You know how to draw blood, kid?" the vet asked skeptically.

I nodded. "I'm actually pretty good with a hypodermic."

The old man shook his head and muttered something ugly about drug addicts.

Improvising with the vet's tools which, after all, weren't meant for people, I handled the transfusions myself.

Normal blood transfusions aren't just about type matching. They're complex processes, with screening for special conditions, allergies, infections and the like, but we didn't have the time or the expertise for it. I knew Alia's blood type from our time at the PRC, and I wasn't a viable donor. But I knew that Ed Regis was a match. Asking the others, I found that Scott and Candace also shared Alia's blood type. Three people was a lucky start, and if that wasn't enough, I was prepared to do a little blood running of my own, breaking into the neighboring houses and bringing back donors at gunpoint.

As the vet worked on my sister's injuries, I started out with Ed Regis, drawing a little more than a pint of his blood and transferring it straight to Alia, who was still losing blood through her open wounds.

"More," said the vet when the transfusion was complete.

"My turn," said Candace, sitting down with me.

Candace winced a little as I inserted the hypodermic needle into her arm.

"Sorry," I said. My hands were shaking a little. "I haven't done this in years."

"Where did you learn?" Ed Regis asked from my side.

"You don't want to know," I replied.

"The PRC?"

I nodded, and then, if only to help suppress my anxiety by keeping my mouth moving, I explained, "When Alia was little, she couldn't even stay in the same room with a stranger. She used to spit her guts up whenever someone touched her. So I asked the doctors to teach me how to take her blood samples. I gave her other shots too, when the experiments required it."

Ed Regis put a hand on my shoulder. "She's going to be okay, Adrian."

I shook my head. "Who are you trying to convince?"

The minutes ticked by like a slow-moving storm.

Scott and Rachael spent some time cleaning and patching up the gash on Ed Regis's head. Meanwhile, Candace looked at the cut on my left hand, but it was small and already closed up. I didn't really need a bandage, but Candace insisted and I didn't protest. My head cleared just a little when she washed the dried blood off with disinfectant.

"I'm taking a little extra, Scott," I said as I drew his blood last. "Lie down if you feel faint."

"Take all you need," he replied resolutely.

I kept my eyes on my work, unable to look at Alia and the vet. My sister had lost consciousness in the van, and she hadn't woken or made any sounds since we brought her here. All I knew was that she was still alive. But only just. The vet had already resuscitated her twice. If her heart stopped again, it could easily be for the last time.

"That's enough blood, Adrian," said Dr. Hanson. "Don't kill your friends."

By the time Dr. Hanson finished operating, I felt pretty faint myself.

"She's going to be alright, isn't she?" I pleaded.

"She's a strong child," Dr. Hanson replied quietly. "We'll just have to see."

"Thank you."

Dr. Hanson nodded. "I wish I could move her to a more comfortable bed, but I don't have anything for human beings here."

"How about in your house?" suggested Ed Regis. "It'll probably take a while for her to recover and we don't want anyone finding her in your clinic anyway."

"Are you still threatening me, sir?" asked Dr. Hanson.

"No," said Ed Regis. "I apologize for my words earlier, Doctor. Now I'm begging you for just a little more help."

"You people don't look like criminals," said Dr. Hanson. "Are you sure you won't tell me why you brought this girl to me instead of taking her to a hospital?"

"You're safer not knowing," warned Ed Regis.

Dr. Hanson shook his head. "I'll take the chance."

"Fine," I said. "I want to move Alia before the sun comes up, anyway."

The veterinarian's eyes widened as I telekinetically lifted my sister up off the operating table.

Then he laughed out loud.

"I always believed you guys were real," he said, smiling broadly. "I just never thought I'd meet any in my lifetime."

"We're real, alright," said Scott, smiling also. "We're psionic."

"Come," said Dr. Hanson, his tone noticeably lighter. "You may stay in my home as long as you need."

The old veterinarian led us over to his house: a quiet blue two-story with a neatly cut lawn. It had a shuttered garage large enough for two vehicles, and Scott was allowed to hide his van inside.

As I walked with Dr. Hanson, levitating Alia in front of me, I was surprised at how light my sister felt in my mind. Perhaps I was just dazed by what was happening. Here was a man who was actually happy to discover that psionics really existed.

Dr. Hanson lived alone. His wife had passed away several years ago and his children lived far away. It was hard to know how he really felt about suddenly having six fugitive houseguests, but he seemed okay. Of course, there was no way to be sure that Dr. Hanson wouldn't betray us. Who was to say he wouldn't call up the police or something the first chance he got? But we had to trust him. The only alternative would have been to hold him prisoner inside his house, and if this doctor suddenly went missing so soon after what had happened at the hotel and on the road, the police would come to this house and either way we would be caught.

We moved Alia into one of Dr. Hanson's two guestrooms. I set my sister down onto the bed and then carefully tucked her in. Alia's face still looked pale and lifeless, and her breathing was barely noticeable. But she was alive.

"She'll need to be watched constantly for the next few hours," said Dr. Hanson.

"I'll watch her," I said.

"Me too," said Candace.

Everyone else quietly exited the room. Before leaving us, Ed Regis told me that he would speak to Scott about somehow getting an emergency message out to the Resistance. Honestly, I had forgotten about Raider's mapping mission, but I was glad that Ed Regis would take care of it.

Standing next to me as I gazed down at Alia's face, Candace took my hand and gave my fingers a squeeze. "Good thing Rachael's a hider," she said. "This place is way too close to Wood-claw, but at least we'll be safe here until..." Her voice faltered a little as she said quietly, "I hope she wakes up."

I forced a smile. "Don't worry. She'll wake up. Give it a day or two and she'll be fine. She'll be just fine."

I was saying it as much to myself as to Candace, but I meant every word. I knew that my sister was going to be okay. Because that was the only way it could be.

"You sure picked the clinic, Candace," I said, wiping my eyes. "Wait till Alia hears she was saved by a puppy doctor."

"I was so scared."

"Alia's strong. You've no idea how strong she is. She'll be fine. I promise."

During the surgery, Dr. Hanson had removed Alia's bloodstone pendant, and I discovered that I still had it in my pocket. I carefully hung the little unicorn from one of the bedposts so that Alia would see it when she woke.

"She'll be fine," I said again. "We just need to give her some time."

"Come on, Adrian," said Candace, gently pulling me toward a long sofa set diagonally across from the bed. "Let's at least sit down. I'm feeling a little light right now."

"Sorry," I said, remembering how much blood I had taken from her. Sitting beside her, I said, "Thanks for saving our lives back there. You really have turned into a Knight."

"I just turned psionic a month ago," said Candace, and then added into my head, *"I didn't think you'd hear me in time."*

"What happened out there?" I asked. "Why Wood-claw? How did the Angels get in?"

Candace took a moment before she answered slowly, "We weren't discovered, Adrian. Mrs. Harding just announced that it was 'time to make the transition.' Those were her words. Some of us disagreed, but there was a vote and..."

I gave her a disbelieving look. "You mean Wood-claw voted to accept the rule of a tyrant?"

Candace nodded.

After all her talk about not going down without a fight, Mrs. Harding and the majority of her followers had elected to accept Angel conversion and join the flock. Perhaps Tigress was right. Perhaps the war really was over and we just didn't know it yet.

Candace explained, "We were all on lockdown for the transition when Terry showed up with that girl. No one was allowed in or out without Mrs. Harding's permission. That's why we couldn't warn you."

"And Terry?" I asked, dreading the answer.

"I can't be sure," said Candace. "When she found out what was going on, Terry went berserk. You should have seen her. She tore the whole place apart. She killed Mrs. Harding with her hook, and her dog too. And how many more Knights, I don't know."

"Where is she now?"

Candace sighed. "It was our fault. Scott and Rachael and me... we tried to help her. Terry held the Knights off so we could escape. But she didn't make it out." Candace's voice cracked as she said, "They shot her twice, Adrian. At least twice."

"Dead?"

"Maybe," said Candace, shaking her head miserably. "I don't know."

I did. If she couldn't escape, then Terry would have fought to the death. I regretted my words to her back in the car. It was wrong of me to question her courage. Terry Henderson was the greatest warrior I had ever known. It burned me up to think that after everything she had done for us, for me personally, for Alia, for the Guardians, and for Wood-claw, that she would die at the hands of gutless turncoats. It wasn't the ending she deserved. It was a cruel fate brought about by an unforgivable betrayal. And yet, if not for her sacrifice, Scott and the others would never have been able to rescue us from the Wood-claw Knights.

"I'm really sorry, Adrian," said Candace.

"Don't be," I said resolutely. "She knew what she was doing."

I didn't cry for Terry. I was too spent to cry anyway, but more than that, I took just a little comfort in the knowledge that Terry had died fighting for us, which was the way she would have wanted it. Just like James. Just like a Knight. As Ed Regis had said to Alia, we were all soldiers, and sometimes dying came with the job. And we all meet our end someday.

"What about the other girl?" I asked. "The little one. What happened to her?"

"I think she's okay. Terry left her in Scott's place before the fighting started."

"Good," I said quietly.

"Who is she?"

"Someone who belongs with the Angels," I replied. "So I guess she'll be going home soon. Alia will be happy when I tell her."

I looked over at the bed. My sister's breathing was still pretty shallow, but otherwise she seemed comfortable. Closing my eyes for a moment, I decided that I would tell her about Marion first, and wait till she recovered her full strength before telling her about Terry.

As we sat together waiting for the dawn, Candace asked me about my time in the Resistance, and I told her what little I could. But I would have preferred to sit in silence, and Candace eventually got the message. We sat quietly for several more hours, and once we started yawning a little too frequently, I closed my eyes and asked Candace if she could telepathically call Ed Regis up to relieve us.

I woke on the sofa with Candace's head on my shoulder. Candace had fallen asleep too, but Ed Regis was sitting in another chair, watching over my sister. By the light streaming in through the curtains, I guessed it was around noon.

Ed Regis turned to me and said pleasantly, "Good morning, Adrian."

"Is it?" I asked quietly so as not to wake Candace.

"Well, Alia's still alive," said Ed Regis. "And Scott said he could get a message out to the Guardian Council. We might still be in time to warn the Resistance about what Raider was up to."

"Then I guess it is a good morning."

Ed Regis frowned, saying, "Scott and Rachael told me about Terry. They said she was killed."

I nodded with my eyes. "I heard too."

"So I guess it's just you and me now, huh?"

"And Alia," I reminded him.

"Yeah," he breathed. "About Alia... Dr. Hanson says he's going to call a friend that he's sure he can trust. The guy's a physician, and he'll be able to set up the feeding tubes and everything."

"Feeding tubes..." I repeated quietly.

"Well, we don't know how long she'll be out, after all," said Ed Regis. "I figured that as long as we're trusting Dr. Hanson, we might as well trust him all the way. The vet has done all he can. We need a human doctor now."

"She hasn't woken yet?" I asked. "Not even for a few seconds?"

"Not yet."

"I guess it's still too early," I said, moving my head and accidentally waking Candace.

"Rise and shine," I said to her. "It's a new day."

Borrowing Dr. Hanson's motorcycle, Scott had left early in the morning to send out our warning message to the Guardian Council. Though I didn't have the details, I knew that this wasn't as simple as making a phone call or mailing a letter. Even if all went smoothly, Scott wouldn't be back until late night, maybe even early tomorrow morning.

Before sending Scott out, Ed Regis had also asked him to pass on our request for any information they had related to the Angels' Royal Gate. Ed Regis had carefully debriefed our new teammates without giving away our true target. The official line was that we were still hunting King Divine and that the Royal Gate was our ticket to his hideout. We weren't very hopeful that the Council could provide us with useable intelligence, but it was a start.

Rachael had given Scott all the hiding protection she could: enough to last him two full days. I knew how worried she was and sympathized with her, but my primary concern was still my sister. I sat by Alia's bed all day and called her name over and over. She didn't open her eyes, and I heard nothing in my head.

The physician, Dr. Greene, arrived in the late afternoon. He was the same age as Dr. Hanson, and they had been friends since high school. As much as he trusted his friend, Dr. Greene was skeptical about the existence of psionics. Candace, who we discovered had become a graviton in addition to a telepath, made him a believer.

"I'll be goddamned," said Dr. Greene when he found that his feet had become too heavy to lift, anchoring him to the floor.

"You will be if you tell anyone," Ed Regis warned him. "I guarantee it."

Before leading him up to Alia's room, we briefly explained to the doctor about the psionic world, the war and what we were trying to do. Just like with Dr. Hanson, we didn't give him too many details, but enough to satisfy his curiosity and feed his fears about what could happen if he loosened his lips. I also gave him a little of Alia's personal history so that he wouldn't be too shocked by all the other scars on her body.

Dr. Greene gave my sister as complete an examination as was possible with just the contents of his medical bag. He looked at Alia's eyes and in her mouth, listened to her heart and breathing with a stethoscope, checked her motor reflexes and measured her blood pressure. In other words, nothing more than the basics that anyone would get at a common health examination, but I was immensely grateful nonetheless. Dr. Greene also looked over Dr. Hanson's handiwork on Alia's bullet holes, and then jokingly concluded that if ever he was shot, he wanted a vet to handle the operation. I wasn't amused, but I was relieved to hear Dr. Greene's praise of Dr. Hanson's skill.

Then he gave us the bad news.

"To the best of my diagnostic capabilities, I suspect that Alia is in a coma," said Dr. Greene, "probably caused by temporary lack of oxygen to the brain during her injury."

"Please speak plainly, Doctor," I said. "How long do you think she'll be asleep?"

"To be honest, I don't know," said Dr. Greene. "A coma can last hours, days, weeks..."

"Months?" asked Ed Regis. "Years?"

"It's impossible to say," said Dr. Greene. "But if she has major brain damage, then it's quite possible that she will never wake."

"You just said you didn't know!" I countered angrily.

"Without taking her to a hospital, yes," Dr. Greene replied calmly. "I am no expert in this field myself, but I do know that people who recover from trauma cases like this usually start to show improvement within hours, or a few days at the very most. So we'll just have to wait and see."

Patience, Adrian.

"She just needs time to recover her strength," I said. "She'll wake up in a day or two."

"She could very well do just that," the doctor agreed in a cautious voice. "What's important is that you're there when she does, Adrian. Do you understand me?"

I nodded.

"I'll check in on her every two days," promised Dr. Greene. "But if anything changes, you call me immediately, alright?"

"Thank you, Doctor," I said, breathing slightly easier.

Dr. Greene then taught us how to insert and use Alia's feeding tube, which went into her nose and down her throat. I had some direct experience with these tubes myself, but I still didn't like using them on my sister. There was just something disturbing about how people looked with plastic tubes sticking into their bodies, and I didn't like seeing my sister that way. But Alia had to eat somehow if she was to recover.

Dr. Greene further explained that the feeding tube had to be regularly removed and replaced to avoid various medical complications, and that, if Alia didn't wake in a few weeks, she would eventually need a more permanent kind of tube that went directly into the front of her stomach, sort of like an umbilical cord. I assured the doctor that this wouldn't be necessary.

But taking care of an unconscious person wasn't just about feeding her through her nose.

"Adrian," Candace said awkwardly, "I know you're her brother and you're sort of her mother and father too, but Alia's almost a teenager now. I don't think she'd want you to... you know... so I'll handle all of her washing and her diaper-changing and all that, okay?"

"Be my guest," I said, grateful for Candace's offer.

Dr. Greene stayed for dinner. Our host, apparently overjoyed to have so many houseguests at once, prepared a gorgeous feast for us. But I didn't have much of an appetite. It wasn't just the feeding tube stuck into Alia's nose, but Dr. Greene's words about comas and brain damage. Of course I knew he was wrong. I knew that my sister would recover. But I still couldn't eat.

Scott returned safely just before midnight.

"Mission complete, message delivered," reported Scott. "I just hope we're in time."

"Did you learn anything from your contact?" asked Ed Regis. "Any news?"

"Yeah, they told me that Wood-claw joined the Angels," Scott replied wryly, adding, "They almost shot me before I could convince them that I wasn't converted."

"What about the Royal Gate?" asked Ed Regis.

"They said they'd look into it," said Scott. "I'll have to check back in a week."

"That's fine," I said. "It'll give my sister time to recover and I could use a week's rest too."

I figured that once Alia regained consciousness, she could use her healing power to accelerate her recovery. As long as she woke up in the next few days, then if the Council really could point us toward the Royal Gate, we would already be prepared to move out. The loss of Wood-claw had made me realize again just how little time was left to us.

"Come on, Ali," I whispered to her before I turned in for the night. "Snap out of this so we can go finish this war together."

When I woke the next morning, my sister was still asleep. She looked as physically stable as Dr. Greene had claimed, but also just as brain-dead. Her eyes remained shut, her body completely limp. I reminded myself that I had been unconscious for longer periods of time, such as when I had drowned in the sinking towboat.

Candace shooed me out of the room so she could change Alia's diaper and give her a sponge bath, and later we sat together on the sofa again, waiting.

That evening, on a hunch, I pulled Alia's blanket down and lifted her shirt to examine the large square bandage on her abdomen. I carefully peeled it off, and smiled. The wound had already healed.

"Alia, wake up," I said happily. "Wake up!"

My sister didn't move, so finally I even shook her shoulders a little, but she remained oblivious to my calls.

Dr. Greene stopped by the next day to check up on us.

"A miracle!" he exclaimed, examining the light scarring over the otherwise completely healed entry and exit points on Alia's body. "Truly marvelous power."

"I told you she was special," I said, adding confidently, "She'll be up any day now."

But despite his amazement at Alia's psionic healing, the doctor wasn't as convinced. "I'm afraid she is still showing no changes in her bodily reflexes," he said after the examination. "She is still comatose."

"Trust me, Doctor," I said to him. "She'll be up by tomorrow."

But Alia didn't wake up the next day, nor the next.

Nor the next.

I took to quietly meditating in Dr. Hanson's guestroom, sitting on the floor cross-legged like I used to do with Cindy, trying to find an inner peace that just wasn't there to be found. At nights, I slept fitfully on the sofa or on the floor next to Alia's bed. Whenever I thought I heard the slightest whisper in my head, I immediately pulled my sister's eyelids up and looked anxiously into her dark pupils, desperately searching for any sign of recognition or consciousness. But nothing changed.

Scott returned safely from his second meeting with his Council contact, but he bore grave news. The Council had passed our warning to the Resistance, but not soon enough for them to prepare countermeasures. The Seraphim had attacked the very next day, and even though Raider's mapping mission had ended prematurely, Guardian safe houses all across Lumina had been decimated. The full casualty count wasn't in yet, but the Council believed that more than two thirds of the Resistance was lost. Mark and Proton were both unaccounted for, which meant that they were either dead or captured. And if they had been captured, once they were converted, the Angels would know the exact locations of the remaining safe houses.

"It's over," concluded Scott. "We lost."

"The Council isn't giving up, is it?" asked Rachael.

"No," said Scott, "but in a few more months, it'll hardly make a difference."

"We can still make a difference," said Ed Regis. "We just need to find the Royal Gate."

Scott shook his head. "The Council reps claim that they haven't even heard of the Royal Gate. They could be lying, of course. That kind of intelligence would be top secret, and they wouldn't easily share it with independents like us."

"You'll need to ask them again," said Ed Regis. "Convince them to help us. We gave them a heads-up on Raider's mission. Even if it didn't work, they owe us their trust."

"I'll try again in a few days."

He did, but once again returned with nothing to report regarding the Royal Gate. I didn't care. I wasn't leaving here without my sister.

March was upon us, and as each day and night passed in silence, I felt like I was thirteen years old again, back at the PRC, drained and helpless. I started to hate Dr. Greene's visits. Every time he checked Alia over, his answer was unchanging except to note how many days Alia had gone without any sign of improvement.

Dr. Greene wasn't a coma specialist, but he had done a fair amount of reading on the subject since first seeing Alia. Personally, I didn't want to hear the ugly details, but Ed Regis asked Dr. Greene for them, so I was required to listen too.

"Perhaps you've seen a movie or television show where a person who has been in a coma for years suddenly wakes up," said Dr. Greene. "Unfortunately, that hardly ever happens in real life. The only reason we sometimes hear about such miracles in the news is because they are so very rare. Far more commonly, a comatose patient progresses into PVS, or 'persistent vegetative state.' And neither coma nor PVS are stable, non-progressive conditions. Various medical complications arise from long-term immobility."

"Such as?" asked Ed Regis.

"Muscles waste away while limbs become contracted. Lungs can become scarred and collapse over time. Then there are various infections, ulcers—"

"I get it," interrupted Ed Regis, who also seemed to regret asking for specifics.

Dr. Greene nodded understandingly. "The point is, Mr. Regis, if she doesn't show any sign of improvement in the very near future, you will have to start considering more long-term care. I know you can't simply put a psionic up in a major hospital, but comatose patients can do well on home care."

I wanted to plug my ears. Dr. Greene even had the nerve to warn us that if Alia woke at all, not only would she need extensive rehabilitation, but there was a good chance she would be severely mentally handicapped for the rest of her life. And that was *if* she woke, which, now that more than two weeks had passed without her so much as twitching, he claimed was highly unlikely. The stupid physician never had anything good to say, so why couldn't he just leave us alone?

Even when I wasn't meditating, I often wasn't in the mood for talking with anyone. Not even with Candace, who meant well but didn't share my faith in Alia's resilience as much as I wanted her to. She suggested that if Alia didn't show any change by her upcoming twelfth birthday, we should take Dr. Greene's advice and start looking for long-term care options.

We had a very loud argument, and after that, Candace spent more time out of the room. Though she still came in to wash and change Alia, sometimes she refused to meet my eyes. I knew that she and the others were talking behind my back. I was furious that they suspected Alia was lost.

I don't know how everyone else was spending their time in Dr. Hanson's house. I hardly ever left my sister's side. Candace brought my meals up for me so that we could eat with Alia, but I usually left more than half of my plate untouched. It wasn't just the lack of physical activity that was killing my appetite. Though I still couldn't bear to face it, I too had begun to fear that there just might be a grain of truth to Dr. Greene's prognosis, and that my sister was now well beyond the possibility of any meaningful recovery.

More days passed. I desperately wanted to stop counting, but I couldn't.

"Why are you so eager to bury her?" I asked brusquely when Ed Regis suggested to me that we start planning our next move.

"I'm not," insisted Ed Regis. "But we can't stay here much longer, Adrian. James and Terry are dead. The Resistance is gone. Scott still hasn't gotten anything from the Council. If we're going to find the Royal Gate, then we need to get moving again. Candace has already agreed to take care of Alia for as long as it takes until she recovers."

"You had no right to ask her that!" I said crossly. "Alia doesn't need long-term care. She'll wake up and she'll come with us when we leave!"

"We can't hide her here forever."

"You handle the preparations, Ed Regis," I said, turning away from him and looking down at my sister's sleeping face. "Alia will be up by her birthday."

March was halfway over already, and there was only a week left now till Alia's finding day. She had to wake up before that.

I heard Candace's footsteps enter the room, but I didn't turn around.

"I know what you're going to say, Candace," I said hoarsely, "so please don't say it."

Candace gently touched my right arm. "I'm worried about her too, Adrian."

"She can be like this sometimes," I said, blinking back my tears. "She just needs a little time, that's all. She just needs some time."

"It's been four weeks," Candace reminded me. "She hasn't gotten any better."

"She healed herself, didn't she?!" I snapped, wiping my eyes. "She'll wake by her birthday. I promise she will. One more week. She'll wake up."

"Alright, Adrian," Ed Regis said with a resigned sigh. "I'll handle the preparations for our departure. One more week."

"And make sure you pack for three!"

"I will."

They left me alone, and I continued to sit, watch, listen and meditate. As the days crawled by, I heard the sounds of the coming spring from the window, but not one telepathic murmur in my mind. And with each passing stroke of midnight, as the 24th of March approached, I felt as if I was counting the days to my own execution, or worse, to Alia's.

When the day came, I sat by her bed from dawn to dusk, still waiting, still unable to stop believing.

"You are my family, Alia," I whispered to her as the sunlight faded. "You are my sister, my daughter, my protector and my friend. Please come back. Please don't leave me like this."

After dinner, Candace insisted on feeding Alia's tube with the liquid equivalent of a slice of birthday cake.

"You should have some too," she said, offering me a real slice from the chocolate cake that she and Scott had baked.

"I'm not hungry."

"You never eat enough, Adrian," said Candace. "You're going to make yourself sick."

"I said I'm not hungry."

The lights seemed dimmer in the room. The whole world felt colder. I felt like I was surrounded by shadows flickering about me. And Candace's cake was the one, horrible, inescapable reminder that my sister had now been unconscious for more than a month, and that Dr. Greene and everyone else was right. Alia wasn't recovering at all. She was slipping deeper into her coma.

Candace put the cake down and said carefully, "Mr. Regis said he wanted to get out of here in a few more days if possible."

I remained silent, still watching Alia's face for signs of movement. There were still a few hours left to our arbitrary deadline. She could still wake up.

Candace continued, "Scott says we can relocate to one of the Guardian outposts far from Lumina. Alia will be safe there. I promise we'll take good care of her."

"She's alive," I said. "She's alive and I'm taking her with me."

"She's alive," Candace agreed quietly.

"Don't, Candace."

"Adrian... You know she's not coming back."

"No!" I hollered, jumping up from my chair. "You don't say that!"

I lost control of my power, putting a long crack in the ceiling above Alia's bed. Candace tried to take my hand but I snatched it away.

She gave me an injured look and said, "Please, Adrian. I know it hurts."

"Get out!" I bellowed, turning away from her. "Just get out!"

"It's alright, Candace," I heard Ed Regis say quietly behind me. "Just let him be."

Soon I was alone in the room. But the shadows around me were larger now, dancing in front of the light, growing ever heavier in the pit of my soul. As I continued to look down at Alia's peaceful expression, I realized that the shadows, the darkness... all of it was my own doing.

The time for self-deception was finally over.

Candace was right: I did know that Alia wasn't coming back. I had known for weeks now. All these years, I had tried so hard to be Alia's unicorn, to be her real-life guardian angel, just as she had always been mine, but now it was over.

Ever since the gathering of lesser gods, I had slowly learned to accept my sister as a soldier, not all that different from Terry or James. Alia was the youngest-ever Honorary Guardian Knight. I had complete confidence in her courage and strength.

But that was never who she was to me, and I wasn't at all prepared to deal with the reality of losing her like this.

For all the risks I had watched her take, from our raid on the towboat to her blood running in Lumina, I could never once bring myself to imagine how I would feel if she really were to be killed in combat. From the day I met her and even now, my mind just couldn't cope with the idea of her death, and so I had managed to trick myself into believing that it couldn't happen, that somehow the rules of this war didn't apply to my sister. That she would always be there, even long after I died.

But Alia had gone first.

And in a way, what happened to my sister was even worse than being killed in combat. At least James and Terry had ended their lives with dignity. Alia was bound to a bed, a plastic tube shoved into her slowly decaying body, unable to wake, unable to die. As if it wasn't enough that she had lived so much of her life in terrible pain, now her end would be the same. It would have been much more merciful if she had been killed instantly.

But nobody is destined to live or die. That was the one lesson I had learned over and over in my years as a psionic. It was the one lesson I knew best.

Friend or foe hardly made a difference anymore.

This war had claimed so many lives.

Guardian Knights and Angel Seraphim...

Innocent bystanders...

My mother and my father.

Dr. Kellogg...

Dr. Otis and Dr. Denman.

Riles... Gabriel...

Mr. Watson. Mr. Barnum...

Grace. Charles. Growler. Mr. Simms.

Laila Brown.

Ralph P. Henderson. Queen Larissa Divine...

Peter. Max. Felicity. Steven. Merlin...

Ms. Decker. James. Willow and her baby. Raider. Terry...

Alia.

The lights were still on, but the room was pitch-black. I could see nothing but the endless shadows of all the people I had killed and all the people I had watched die.

And here, at last, on the far side of darkness, my paradox was solved.

Here, on the far side of darkness, I had found the one road that I could still take.

Because the girl that lay on the bed that I could no longer see, lost from this world, wasn't just my sister. She was all that was left of my pathetic excuse for a heart. Now I was free to finish this in my own way.

Adrian Howell.

Cat.

I nodded slowly and smiled to myself. A grim but satisfied smile. Anyone seeing me smile under these circumstances would probably conclude without doubt that I had gone insane, but nevertheless I couldn't help smiling. Just this once, I would choose my own fate.

I heard the door open behind me.

"Adrian?" whispered Ed Regis.

"Yeah?"

"It's past midnight."

"I know," I replied emptily. "Everything is dark."

"I think you should get some sleep."

Stepping up to the bed, Ed Regis looked down at Alia's motionless form.

"She's dead," I told him. "She died in the car."

"I know that," Ed Regis said softly. After a moment of silence, he asked hesitantly, "Were you crying, Adrian?"

I slowly shook my head. Then I looked up at him. "Major Regis?"

"Yes?"

"No more rules."

17. OPENING THE GATE

As the colorless, nearly full moon disappeared behind a veil of thin clouds, Ed Regis eased our rented jet-black two-door sedan into a dirty alleyway between two old redbrick apartment buildings. He put the gear into park, but kept the engine running.

I looked down at the silver chains around my wrists and breathed slowly.

Ed Regis looked down at his chains too. "This is it," he said quietly. "They should be here soon."

I didn't reply. As I sat silently in my seat, I found my right hand fingering the pendant around my neck, gently stroking the tiny horn protruding from the little horse's head.

"Last chance, Adrian," said Ed Regis. "There's no turning back after this."

I let go of my sister's unicorn pendant and scoffed. "What makes you think I want to turn back?"

"We should probably wait outside," said Ed Regis, "where they can see us."

But still he didn't cut the engine.

We sat in the car, waiting.

It had been just over two weeks since Ed Regis and I left Dr. Hanson's house, and I was glad that the journey was finally over.

On the morning after Alia's finding day, when I had explained to Ed Regis my plan, he listened with a cautious frown, and when I was done, he asked, "Are you sure that's how you want your life to end, Adrian?"

"It's not about what I want," I replied quietly, "but yes. Everybody ends someday, and this still might be a better end than others."

Ed Regis said cautiously, "If we do this, we're going to need help from someone outside of the psionic factions."

I agreed. There were too many Angel spies in the Guardian network, and too much at risk. But I had an answer for that too: Terry's answer. After all, no one can keep secrets like the faithful.

"The God-slayers will help us," I said confidently. "There's no one else left, anyway."

Ed Regis wasn't as certain, but he didn't argue. He told me that we could leave at any time.

"Today, then," I said. "I'm tired of being patient."

Leaving me in Alia's room, Ed Regis went to speak with Scott and Dr. Hanson. Candace came up to deliver my breakfast and tube-feed Alia.

"I'm sorry I was so horrible to you, Candace," I said.

Candace just shook her head sadly.

"I'm leaving with Ed Regis today," I told her. "We still need to find the Royal Gate and stop King Divine."

"I'll take good care of Alia," promised Candace. "We'll find a quiet place."

"I know you will," I said.

"I love you, Adrian," she said. Putting her arms around me, she whispered into my ear, "But I know you're keeping something from me. Are you sure you don't want to share it?"

"I love you too, Candace," I said. "But this is something I have to keep."

"You sound like you're not coming back."

I didn't want to lie, so I said nothing.

As we held each other, Candace let out a quiet sob and said, "You should at least leave her a letter. In case she wakes up."

I shook my head. "I'm sorry, but I don't believe in miracles."

We broke apart, and I looked down at Alia's bed. My eyes moved slowly from my sister's peaceful face to her unicorn pendant still hanging from the bedpost.

After an awkward silence, I took a deep breath and said, "There's something else I need to ask of you, Candace." I closed my eyes for a moment, and then added, "Something horrible."

Candace didn't reply, but she probably already suspected what I was about to ask her to do. I figured that I should just go ahead and say it.

"Half a year," I said. "Give her half a year, and then let her die."

"Adrian, no."

"And when she's dead," I said, speaking quickly to get it all out, "destroy the body. Burn it. Leave nothing behind, not even the bones. If I succeed in killing the Angel king, the balance of power will eventually return, and so will the Wolves. Alia is the greatest healer who ever lived. I don't want anyone finding her again."

Candace looked at me, but I couldn't meet her eyes.

Taking another deep breath to steady my trembling voice, I said, "Promise me, Candace. Please. She's been through enough already."

Candace slowly took my hand and held it tightly as she said into my head, *"I promise."*

"Thank you," I whispered.

"But write her a letter, Adrian," insisted Candace, forcing a smile through her tears. "Do it for me."

I nodded slowly. "I will." Then I smiled too, adding, "But you don't get to read it."

Later, Candace found me some paper and an envelope. As she and the others prepared lunch in the kitchen, I sat alone at the writing desk in Alia's room, trying to think of what I could write. After what I had committed myself to last night, I felt there was nothing I could say that would do my sister justice, and I was tempted to simply seal the envelope with some blank paper. After all, what were the chances of Alia ever opening it? But that just didn't seem right after the terrible responsibility I had forced upon Candace.

I looked over at Alia's calm, sleeping face, and decided that the truth wasn't such a bad thing after all. Slowly, I let the words, along with the last of my tears, fall onto the paper. As to what, specifically, I said to her, that is between me and Alia.

On the front of the envelope, I wrote simply, "To my sister." Then, neatly folding my letter, I slid it into the envelope. I was about to seal it, but I stopped.

Looking over at Alia again, I carefully removed my amethyst pendant from around my neck. I held it in my hand for a minute, and then placed the stone into the envelope with my letter. I wasn't exactly sure why I did that. Perhaps I just didn't need it anymore. Or maybe I was asking for a miracle after all.

It was a Sunday and Dr. Hanson's clinic was closed. I ate lunch with Dr. Hanson and everyone in the dining room that day. Ed Regis and I were leaving right after the meal. Scott, Rachael and Candace would remain here for two more days before loading Alia into a car and heading out to a semi-independent Guardian settlement where they hoped to find work and shelter.

As we wrapped up our farewell lunch, Ed Regis said to Dr. Hanson, "We're sorry if we overstayed our welcome."

"Not at all," said Dr. Hanson. "It was nice having people in my house again."

"We were really lucky to find someone like you," said Rachael. "It's not often that we meet someone so understanding of our kind."

Dr. Hanson turned to me and said, "I'm sorry I couldn't be of greater help, Adrian. I did my best."

"I know," I said, shaking his hand. "Thank you, Doctor."

Having quietly disposed of Scott's bullet-ridden van, Ed Regis had acquired two new vehicles for us. In addition to another van for Scott's team, he had found a small black sedan for himself and me. Our bags were already on board.

"Don't you want to see her one more time?" Candace asked me at the front door.

I shook my head. "I'd rather not."

"Where's your letter?"

"I left it on her bed," I said. "The envelope is bulging a bit because I put my pendant in there too. Make sure she gets it if she wakes up."

"I will," said Candace, and then added with a wink, "Don't worry, Adrian. I won't open it."

"Thanks."

"Where's your jacket?" she asked. "It's still cold out there."

I swore under my breath. "I left it upstairs in Alia's room."

I really didn't want to go back up there and have to say goodbye all over again.

Candace nodded understandingly. "I'll go get it for you."

She did, and once we were outside, we spent a few last minutes saying goodbye to each other. But it wasn't like the first two times when I had left her to head for the Historian and to the Resistance. Though I had given Candace no details, she knew that I wasn't coming back. She knew that this was our last time together.

"Take care of yourself, Adrian," she said bravely as we embraced on the porch, "and I'll take care of Alia."

"You take care of yourself too, Candace," I said. "I love you."

"I love you, too," said Candace, holding me tighter. Her voice cracked a little as she said, "It's just not fair."

"I know," I said to her softly. "I'm really sorry that it has to be this way. You know I never wanted any of us to be a part of this war."

"I know you didn't," said Candace. Barely fighting back her tears, Candace said into my head, *"I don't want you to go, Adrian. I don't want you to die."*

"Listen to me, Candace," I said firmly. "This war is going to end soon. The world is going to change. It's going to be a better place."

"But you won't be there."

"I'll be there," I told her as I wiped a teardrop from her cheek. "One way or another, I'll always be there."

"It won't be the same."

"No," I agreed quietly, "it won't."

As Candace cried into my shoulder, I was a little surprised at my own detached calm over this. Didn't I care that we would never see each other again? It was like I had left the bulk of my emotions up in Alia's room, sealed inside that envelope along with my pendant. Of course I would miss Candace, and I would miss everyone, and I would miss life. But I had made my decision. And I was no longer the unbalanced child who believed that life should be in any way fair.

I let Candace cry herself out, and when her eyes finally dried up, she gave me a sad little smile and one last, long, beautiful kiss goodbye.

Later, as Ed Regis drove our sedan into the night, I found two things in my jacket pocket that I hadn't expected. One was Alia's unicorn pendant. The other was a little note in Candace's handwriting that read, "Don't forget to believe in miracles, Addy."

I put the unicorn around my neck. I kept the note in my pocket.

From there, it took fifteen days, some luck, and a little help from the Guardians, but Ed Regis and I finally managed to locate a God-slayer sect that would hear our proposal.

Our meeting came with conditions: We would approach them unarmed, openly wearing metal chains to prove that we were drained. We would speak to them at gunpoint. And if they didn't like what we said, they would execute us then and there. All this I agreed to. Honestly, it felt pretty trivial.

"Adrian?" said Ed Regis. "Adrian!"

I looked up from the chains around my wrists. "Are they here?"

"They're here," confirmed Ed Regis, finally cutting the engine. "Step out slowly."

We carefully opened the doors and got out of our car.

I saw five men standing side by side at the end of the alleyway. Ed Regis and I spread our arms out wide and slowly walked toward them.

When we were twenty paces apart, the man in the center called out, "That's far enough, demons. Get down on your knees."

We did, keeping our arms spread wide and our chains in plain sight. Ed Regis, being non-psionic, had no reason to wear the chains, but the Slayers didn't know that.

The men cautiously walked toward us, pistols drawn and aimed at our heads. I kept my eyes straight forward. The man who had spoken walked around us once in a wide circle. Then he said quietly, "You two have an appointment with Father Stanton, and later with God."

Adjusting the position of our chains, the men painfully handcuffed our wrists behind our backs, blindfolded us and loaded us onto a vehicle. Nobody spoke a single word as we rode for what felt like an hour, and then we were led into a building. They took us down two flights of stairs.

By our echoing footsteps on the concrete and the familiar dank air, I knew that we were right where I wanted to be right now.

"Kneel," commanded a voice.

I did. My blindfold was removed from behind and I found that I was no longer with Ed Regis. An elderly man was standing before me, dressed in a simple black suit. He had a gangly form and curly blond hair that reminded me just a little of Ralph.

"I'm Adrian Howell," I said, looking up at him.

"I am Father Stanton," he replied, a predator's smile on his lips.

"Where is my friend?"

"He is safe in another room," said the Slayer priest. "Please forgive my caution, Adrian. I have never welcomed any lesser gods into my home. Not like this, anyway. What brings you to us?"

"The will of your greater god," I informed him. "Probably."

"And what do you seek?"

I looked him in the eye. "Death."

"Then speak your piece, and let the Lord judge your words."

As he listened to my carefully abridged story and why I had come to him, the elderly priest's bright blue eyes shifted from disgust to astonishment, and finally to jubilant excitement.

"Let me see if I fully understand what you're proposing, young demon," said Father Stanton, unable to keep the sick little grin off of his face. "You want us to surgically implant a voice-activated bomb inside your body so that you can kill the Angels' last master controller and end the unholy tyranny that is threatening our world?"

I nodded, adding, "And, as an extra bonus, I die too. That means you have nothing to lose by letting me go."

"Your demon blood disgusts me," said the priest, "but perhaps this is the Lord's way of absolving you of your sins."

"Nothing will absolve me of my sins," I replied evenly. "Not after this. So, do we have a deal?"

"If we can make this work, then we have a deal," he said. "You will remain in our custody until we are ready."

"Then I expect acceptable living conditions here," I said. "Drained in the basement is fine, but you will at least provide some bedding and proper meals."

Since I had no hiding protection, remaining drained and two stories underground was necessary to keep me out of sight from the psionic world. But Father Stanton was exceptionally accommodating in all other regards. The Slayers furnished one of their concrete cells with a carpet and proper furniture, including a desk, a table and two beds so that Ed Regis and I could share the room.

Ed Regis was still uneasy about putting our fates in the hands of religious fanatics, but I told him to get over it. "Relax, Ed Regis," I said to him. "The worst they can do is kill us."

Father Stanton had even given us permission to leave our cell with an escort and visit other parts of the basement. The underground area wasn't just for storage or keeping psionics. It was almost as extensive as the gathering place under the former New Haven One building, with a shooting range, training gym, and living quarters for many of the Slayers. This was a fairly large Slayer sect, and the above-ground living areas were strictly for the high-ranking members.

Ed Regis and I lived in Father Stanton's basement for over a week as the Slayers prepared the device. Despite my continued hatred of this sick religious cult bent on exterminating psionics worldwide, and despite their equally vehement hatred of us, over the sunless days and moonless nights, slowly, we got to know each other just a little.

We eventually managed to convince Father Stanton that Ed Regis wasn't a psionic, the logic of our argument being that if we really didn't want to be found, which we obviously didn't, then Ed Regis wouldn't agree to remove his draining chains. And just like that, Father Stanton stopped calling Ed Regis a demon and apologized for his mistake.

I discovered that the Slayers, at least among themselves, were pretty civil people. They rarely shouted, never swore, said grace before meals and prayed before bed. They ate simple, primarily vegetarian food and lived a frugal life. At first glance, they looked like hardworking model citizens.

But that didn't change the fact that they despised psionics with every fiber of their being. Father Stanton often sat me down after lunch or dinner and made me read selected passages from his Bible, after which he would explain to me how these words clearly justified the cold-blooded murder of all psionics. This was the same holy book that Mark had always used to preach tolerance and love. I found it amazing how easily Father Stanton could twist around its words. Still, I hadn't come here for a debate on theology, so I nodded and smiled at him, which probably annoyed him even more than if I had argued.

"You are truly strange, young demon," he said to me, clearly frustrated at my refusal to give him more reason to hate me. "I can't imagine what you are thinking."

"I get that a lot," I told him.

The next day, Father Stanton visited our cell just after breakfast. He was carrying a round metal object the size of a small apple. It was finally complete.

"Here it is," said Father Stanton, handing the ball to Ed Regis. Ed Regis looked at it for a moment and then passed it to me.

"It's a little high-tech compared to what we usually work with," explained Father Stanton as I studied the thin lines on the casing and tried to figure out how it opened. "As per your request, it comes with a voice-activated detonator."

"The yield?" asked Ed Regis.

"Comparable to a hand grenade," said Father Stanton. "And I'm told that once implanted, the microphone power will last at least ten days, maybe twenty."

"I'm not about to wait around," I said.

"Go ahead and test the voice activation," said Father Stanton. "It won't explode."

"What do I say to it?"

Father Stanton smiled. "You say to it, 'Let there be light.'"

I heard a little click inside the ball which I assumed was the detonator switch. I frowned. "It answers to any voice?"

"Yes," confirmed Father Stanton, "and the voice recognition may not be entirely accurate. We've found that it responds equally well to, 'Get bears to fight,' and other similarities. But the good part is that since it will be implanted under your flesh, the command will have to be given in a fairly loud voice for the detonator to hear it. It's unlikely to be set off accidentally by background chatter."

"Can it distinguish sounds from under flesh?" asked Ed Regis.

"We have, of course, tested that to make sure it works," said Father Stanton, and then added hastily, "With a pile of steak meat."

"Then let's get this over with," I said, tossing the bomb back to Father Stanton.

They operated on me that very afternoon.

The Slayer doctor gave me a towel to bite on, but nothing else for the pain as he cut open my lower left side. I clenched my fists and kept myself from letting out even the slightest whimper, knowing that the Slayers would enjoy seeing me in pain. Besides, I knew that I deserved this pain. The Slayer doctor did a fairly good job stitching me up, and in three more days, though the cut still throbbed when I moved, I was fit enough to travel.

So now I'm a human bomb, I thought to myself. *A suicide bomber just like the crazies in the news sometimes. But this time it's me.* And strangely, or perhaps predictably, I felt perfectly normal with that now.

I even found it funny (in a sick sort of way) to think that I was most likely the world's first agnostic suicide bomber. Just about anyone crazy enough to do something like this had to also be crazy enough to believe that they were following the will of some angry god. But not me. I was just following my own will. I wasn't looking for any heavenly rewards. Far from it. If there was a heaven and hell, I was certain that I would end up in the latter. My only consolation was in the poetic justice that I would die first, if only a microsecond before my sister.

In the middle of the night, Ed Regis and I were once again blindfolded and taken out of the Slayer house. Again we rode in silence as we were taken across town to a parking lot where the Slayers had brought our sedan. When our blindfolds were removed, I discovered that Father Stanton himself had come with us to bid us farewell.

"Don't expect me to thank you, Father," I said to him. "You wanted this as much as I did."

Father Stanton nodded.

Ed Regis opened the car door for me, helped me in, closed my door and then walked around to the driver's side.

Once Ed Regis started the engine, I rolled down my window and looked up at Father Stanton, forcing a smile. "But thank you anyway, Father."

Father Stanton shook his head and sighed. Then he said hesitantly, "If you don't mind my asking, young demon, how do you really feel about what you are doing?"

"I feel nothing," I told him.

"I see," he said, shaking his head again. "Well then, may the Lord and the Devil be with you, son."

I gave Father Stanton a wry smile. "I'm sure at least one of them will."

Ed Regis put the car in gear and slowly backed out of the parking space. I looked at Father Stanton one last time through the windshield, catching the triumphant look on his face. Perhaps we had far more in common than either of us was willing to admit. I didn't like that idea very much, but at least I got what I had come for.

The last step of my journey was pretty straightforward. I needed an audience with Queen Cat, and I had to make it look like I was caught as opposed to simply turning myself in. I had given up on the Royal Gate. While waiting in Father Stanton's basement, Ed Regis and I had weighed several other options. We could return to Lumina and get caught trying to kidnap Cindy. We could return to Wood-claw to take revenge for Terry. We could even attack a random Angel settlement. Ed Regis ruled them all out as being too risky. Even though the Angels were still trying to take me alive at all costs, all of these plans could wind up getting me shot and killed by accident.

Thus it was that after two uncomfortably long days on the road, Ed Regis pulled our sedan up onto the curb of a narrow, slummy road at the edge of a small coastal city. The dashboard clock showed that it was still only 7pm, but the dark, graffiti-covered walls and flickering neon lights made it feel much later.

"This is where I leave you, Adrian," said Ed Regis. "Go down to the end of this block, turn left, two blocks, turn right, two blocks. You'll see the sign at the corner. You can't miss it."

"Thanks for being there," I said, shaking his hand.

"It was my pleasure," he replied solemnly.

I was glad Ed Regis had stopped trying to talk me out of doing this. I didn't want to imagine the pain of having my bomb removed.

"Keep an eye on Candace for me," I said quietly. "Make sure she keeps her promise. Help her if she needs it."

"I will," said Ed Regis.

I opened the door and stepped out of the car.

"Be careful you don't start any fights you can't finish in there," was Ed Regis's last warning.

Then he drove away.

I stood on the street for a moment, steeling myself for what I had to do.

Out of sheer habit, I gave Alia's pendant a light tap, and remembered the little note from Candace still folded neatly in my jacket pocket: "Don't forget to believe in miracles, Addy."

It'll be a miracle if I can pull this off, I thought to myself.

The cut on my left side was still a little red and swollen, but I could walk without too much pain. Soon I saw the double doors on the street corner, and the red and blue neon sign above them: The Dog's Gate.

Self-conscious about my height and the fact that nothing about my appearance properly fit into a bar setting, I warily approached the entrance, expecting at any moment to be stopped by someone. Two tall men in black leather jackets eyed me curiously, but let me pass unhindered.

Inside was surprisingly clean and orderly. It looked more like a restaurant than a bar, though there was a long counter at the far end. Only about half of the tables were occupied, but it would probably get more crowded later. I saw two pool tables to my right, and for a second I pictured myself there with Terry, just having fun together like we used to in our old penthouse. Though she was horrible at it, Alia had liked playing pool too.

"Hey, kid!" called one of three men standing around the pool tables. "Where's your mommy?"

The other two laughed, but I ignored them and headed toward the counter.

The whole bar was under a psionic hiding field, but as I passed by the tables, I could sense a few destroyer powers of the people drinking and chatting away. Some of them looked up at me, but I wasn't sure if they recognized me or if they were simply wondering how old I was.

The barman was a burly redhead with eyes that looked like they had seen it all. He took little notice of me as I sat on a stool at the counter.

I telekinetically tugged a little on his right sleeve.

"What do you want, kid?" he asked gruffly.

"A beer," I replied as casually as I could. "And I was hoping you could point me toward someone I could talk to about the Royal Gate."

"Listen," he said in an annoyed tone, "I don't point people here. They come in and they talk. As for this Royal Gate, whatever it is, I can only tell you that you're at the wrong gate." He filled up a beer mug with tap water and smacked it down in front of me. "This one's on the house. Drink it and get the hell out."

"I thought I ordered a beer," I said evenly, telekinetically sliding the mug of water back toward him.

The barman grabbed it before it slid off the counter. "Don't do that in here, kid," he said warningly under his breath. "Normal folk sometimes come in for a drink too."

"If you're not going to point anyone out for me, then maybe you can help," I said.

"I told you already," said the barman, "I don't know nothing about no Royal Gate."

"Okay. Then how about you tell me where I can find Randal Divine?"

"Excuse me?"

"I said I want to find Randal Divine," I repeated loudly. "You've heard of him, haven't you?"

A hush fell over the bar. I didn't turn around, but I could almost count the number of eyes that were on my back. Even the pool players had stopped their game.

The barman chuckled. "I'm afraid I haven't, kid. Randal Divine? Sorry. Never heard of him."

Standing up from my stool, I gave the barman a smile and a nod. Then I telekinetically grabbed him by his hair and slammed his face down onto the counter. I released him, and he staggered back upright, holding his bleeding face.

"You broke my nose!" he yelled through the blood.

"Another cute word and I'll break your neck!" I snapped.

I rounded on the crowd behind me and said furiously, "Has anybody else here not heard of Randal Divine?!"

Nobody moved. They just stared at me. If anything, they looked like they were amused by my performance.

Ed Regis had warned me not to start a large fight, and I wasn't planning to. The basic rule of neutral ground at the Dog's Gate was this: Anyone who struck anyone first would risk the wrath of the one and only true god among psionics. No one here was going to cross the Historian over me. Only the barman had the right to strike back, and if he did, I was prepared to lose.

But he didn't strike back. When I turned to him again, he was carefully wiping his face with a wet paper towel. His nose was still bleeding but clearly not broken.

He said irately, "You're heading into a world of trouble, you know that?"

I shrugged. "Believe me, sir, I'm already there."

The barman narrowed his eyes. "Who the hell are you, kid?"

I looked at him in surprise. Did he honestly not know? I had assumed that a man like him would recognize me on sight.

"I'm Adrian Howell," I told him.

"Yeah, and I'm Teresa Henderson," the barman sneered.

I couldn't help laughing at that. "You are nowhere near man enough to be Terry."

Finally the barman seemed to notice my disparately colored eyes. "You're really him?!"

I nodded. "Unfortunately, yes."

"There's a bounty on your head, Adrian Howell."

"So claim it," I challenged icily. "Claim it or help me. Take your pick."

The barman finished wiping the blood off of his face.

"Okay," he said, stepping closer to the counter, "I'll claim it."

I felt his power instantly grab hold of my limbs, immobilizing me.

"No! Don't do this!" I shouted desperately. "Please! You have to help me kill Randal Divine! You can't let him have the world!"

The barman, I discovered, was a fairly powerful puppeteer, but I could have blocked him if I wanted to. I did make a decent show of struggling, but I let him march my body through a rear door as many of the patrons laughed, cheered and applauded.

The barman led me down a narrow corridor and into a rectangular meeting room where he forced me to remove my jacket and then sat me down into an armchair.

"Thought you could just come in here and do whatever you wanted, did you?" he said mockingly. "Now the joke's on you, Adrian Howell, and I will be well rewarded for my service. You're a stupid kid."

I shot him a furious look, but inside, I was elated at my success. This stupid man would hand me over to the Seraphim, and they would take me straight on to the Royal Gate and finally to the secret home of Randal Divine and my first sister. I hoped that they would use another Wolf plane. Then perhaps this could all be finished by tomorrow.

The barman opened a desk drawer and produced a pair of thin gloves.

"You'll understand, of course," he said as he pulled them on, "that I don't give a rat's ass why King Divine wants you or what he plans to do with the world. The Dog's Gate is under the protection of the Historian. You and King Divine are not."

The barman reached into the drawer again and brought out two pairs of steel handcuffs and a black cloth bag. He locked my wrists behind my back with one pair of handcuffs, and then put the other on my ankles.

"Whatever your game was, kid," he said as he pulled the cloth bag over my head, "it's over now."

About an hour later, I heard several pairs of footsteps enter the room.

Someone lifted up my left shirtsleeve to expose my P-47 tattoo.

"It's him," said a female voice. "Let's go."

I felt a prick on my arm as a hypodermic needle injected something that instantly made me feel extremely dizzy.

I had suspected that the Seraphim would render me unconscious for the trip. That was why I had to be caught instead of surrendering. If I had surrendered, they would have suspected a trap. They still might suspect a trap, but my chances were far better this way.

As my consciousness faded away, I did hope for a miracle. Just one small miracle.

18. THE QUEEN'S REASON

I woke on a soft bed, but that was the only comfortable part of it. My muscles ached all over. My eyes were taking their time focusing, and my head was throbbing like a particularly nasty hangover. I felt terribly drained.

Slowly bringing my right hand to my forehead, I found that I wasn't being physically restrained. But I was wearing a pair of psionic control bands on my wrists. Their metal rods were extended, touching my skin and keeping me from regaining my full strength.

Once my vision had cleared enough, I looked over at the empty bed across from mine. I recognized the bed, and I gasped as my eyes fell upon the giant fluffy white unicorn doll standing next to it.

I was in my old bedroom in Cindy's penthouse!

Why was I here? I looked around in panic. I saw my white cane propped up against the side of my wooden desk. I saw the chairs beside the window where Alia and I used to sit when we couldn't sleep. Everything was just the way we had left it when we fled New Haven. But why had I been brought here, and not to Randal and Cat's home? This was all wrong!

I was alone in the room so I quickly checked myself over. Someone had removed my old clothes as I slept and dressed me in a dark green sweatshirt and matching sweatpants, but I discovered that I was still wearing Alia's unicorn pendant around my neck. Giving it a little pat, I tucked it under my sweatshirt.

Next, I examined the cut across my lower left side. The swelling was gone, as were the stitches, and I realized with a touch of horror that I had received the attentions of a psionic healer, possibly en route. Holding my breath, I gingerly pressed my fingertips into my lower abdomen, searching for the all-important package. I let out a long sigh of relief as I felt the little metal bomb still inside my body. The healer, whoever he was, had simply finished healing the wound for me.

But I still couldn't understand what I was doing in my room. My bedside clock had stopped, but by the light outside the window, I guessed that it was early afternoon.

I got up from the bed and made my way to the door. Opening it, I cautiously stepped into the hallway.

A man was standing there.

He was dressed in a black suit typical of the Angel Seraphim I had watched from Nonus's surveillance room. I looked at him questioningly. He just smiled and gestured toward the living room down the hall.

Giving him a little nod, I made my way toward the living room, keeping a steadying hand on one wall as I walked. I still felt a little queasy, and being drained by the control bands wasn't helping at all. The Seraph remained standing guard by my bedroom door.

I heard voices from the living room, quiet but cheerful. Entering, I found Cindy and another suited Seraph sitting across from each other, sipping coffee. They both immediately stood up and looked at me.

"Hi," I said quietly.

Cindy smiled. "Adrian! You're up."

She briskly walked up to me and stretched out her arms to hug me, but I took a step back.

Her long silvery hair was draped over her shoulders. There might have been a few more wrinkles around her calm, peaceful eyes, but otherwise she was, for the most part, just as I remembered her. But something was different. Was it her smile? The way she walked? The way her hands moved? I couldn't put my finger on it. It might have been all in my head, but something about her was just a little... less Cindy.

"Adrian," she said gently. "Adrian, it's me."

I shook my head. "No, it's not."

Cindy turned to the Seraph and said, "Could you please give us a moment alone?"

"Certainly," the man replied politely.

He gave me a curt nod before disappearing into the dining room, and Cindy turned back to me.

"What's with the Seraphim, Cindy?" I asked her. "You never allowed live-in security here before."

"Times have changed," said Cindy. "There are so many more people depending on me now."

I lifted my wrists a little and showed her my control bands.

"I'm sorry, but those stay on," said Cindy. "Just for a little longer. Until you're safe."

I nodded sadly.

Cindy knelt in front of me and grasped my arms. "Adrian! It really is me. I know you're worried about conversion, but it's not as terrible as you think. I'm still the same person you knew two years ago."

"Then why haven't you asked me about Alia?" I asked coldly. "Why haven't you asked me where she is, or if she's alright?"

"I heard that she was injured in an accident," said Cindy. "I thought maybe you didn't want to talk about it."

"Injured in an accident?" I repeated savagely. "She was shot in the back! She's not injured, Cindy. She's dead."

Still kneeling, Cindy stared into my eyes. She blinked, and a single teardrop fell to the floor.

"You were supposed to look after her," she whispered.

"As were you!" I hissed back.

Cindy looked away. "I have... other... responsibilities as well now."

I pulled my arms free of her and walked across the room.

Turning around, I said furiously, "For two years I dreamed of coming back here, Cindy! I dreamed of bringing Alia back so that we could be a family again. And all this time you were here playing hider for Randal and Cat!"

"I searched for you," said Cindy, standing up. "I searched for Alia. There was nothing I wanted more than to find you again!"

"Except to serve your master," I said, my voice shaking horribly. "Betraying the Guardians wasn't enough, was it? You had to cheat the Angels too!"

"That's not true."

"I heard from Mark what Ralph told you about my bloodline, Cindy! Randal couldn't have erased a memory that old. You know what Cat is! You've always known that the Angels are deceived."

"I am a loyal servant of my queen, Adrian," Cindy said unapologetically. "It was her wish that her father remained king for a while longer."

I scoffed at her words. "And you think you're still the same person who rescued me from that rooftop? You used to know the difference between freedom and slavery, Cindy."

"And you used to know the difference between right and wrong!" Cindy shot back. "Don't pretend like I'm the only one who changed! I've heard of the things you've been up to since you left Lumina."

"Since I left New Haven," I corrected.

"The risks you took... the risks you made Alia take!"

"What I did was for our family, Cindy! Not some... Angel queen!"

"That Angel queen is your sister!" Cindy said heatedly. "She's no different from Alia. And yet you were out there trying to kill her! Your own sister! How could you, Adrian?!"

I let out a quiet huff and looked away. I didn't want to argue that point with Cindy, especially since her allegiance to Cat rendered her just as blind to reason as I was.

Cindy took a few steps toward me as she said, "Queen Catherine Divine was originally of the Angels, and you are of the Guardians. You could help your sister bring order to the Guardian Angels. You could help bridge the gap between us and the rest of the Guardians who haven't joined us yet. We need unity, Adrian. The Guardian Angels have always been there for humanity in times of great need. Now is such a time, more than ever."

"You're crazy."

"The world is crazy!" countered Cindy. "Millions of people are starving every day. People are dying needlessly because those who have refuse to share. Human greed is eating up our planet, and wars over water and other resources will destroy us all. With psionics in charge, all of that could be fixed. Your sister could lead humanity to peace and equality. Don't you see? This is what the Guardian Angels were meant to do. We guide and protect. Just because there's a master makes no difference in the final outcome."

"It makes all the difference in the world, Cindy," I said, looking her in the eyes. "Who wants to live like a drone?"

"Adrian, you make it sound much worse than it really is. I told you before that conversion doesn't rob you of your free will. You can still have your opinions and likes and dislikes. You can still choose your own life."

"So then it's your own will and your own choice that you help the Seraphim hunt down Guardian children to force their parents to surrender?"

"I am not in complete agreement with all of King Divine's tactics."

"But you still support him. Because you've been converted and your queen tells you what to think."

"No, Adrian! Because this really is the only way to end this horrible war before even more people are hurt and killed."

"You're wrong, Cindy," I told her quietly. "You're wrong."

Cindy smiled. "You'll see things differently very soon. You see, the Seraphim brought you straight to Lumina because your sister and her father are currently visiting for a special celebration. In fact, they're in the gathering place right now, and you'll be converted as soon as I get you down there."

"What are they celebrating?" I asked apprehensively.

"The official surrender of the Guardian Council," said Cindy, confirming my fears. "There are still many breakaways and independent factions out there, but with the dissolution of the Council, the war is officially over now. The Guardian Angels have won."

"Congratulations," I said coolly. "But I'm not going to be converted, Cindy. Not today. Not ever."

"I know you're scared, Adrian. I was the one who taught you to hate and fear master controllers. To hate peace and order." Cindy sighed heavily once and then forced a smile. "But you will be converted. And once you see the truth in our ways, if you want, we can live here again as a family."

I showed her my control bands again. "Do you really think draining is going to stop me? Do you think I couldn't kill you with my bare hands?"

"It doesn't matter whether you could," said Cindy. "You won't. I know you better than that."

"Do you?" I said evenly.

Cindy calmly walked up to me.

For a moment, I really did think of attacking her. I wanted to reach out and break her neck. Even though I knew she was converted, her betrayal had hurt so much. To think she had but one tear to shed for Alia! Did she know that Terry was dead too? Did she even care?

But I still had the bomb in me, and I knew that this was my last chance to reverse the course of this war.

Cindy reached out to hug me. I looked at her peaceful, unafraid smile, and I decided that so long as I was going to die today, even this broken, twisted Cindy was better than none at all.

I held her tightly, and she whispered into my ear, “Welcome home, Adrian.”

Then Cindy made a quick phone call.

Five minutes later, a team of four “Seraph Knights,” as Cindy called them, came up to the penthouse and escorted me into the elevator. Cindy didn’t come with us, but said to me at the door, “Please don’t resist, Adrian. It could really hurt you if you do. I’ve seen it.”

“I won’t,” I said. I wanted to say goodbye, but that would have been suspicious.

My escorts took me down the elevator and into the concrete entrance hall of the underground gathering place. They led me through a side door and down a narrow corridor which brought us into a small square interrogation chamber. The room was furnished with just a single straight-back chair set in the middle. The chair was equipped with leather restraints on its armrests and front legs.

“Have a seat,” said one of the Seraphim, gesturing toward the chair.

“I prefer to stand,” I told him.

“Your preferences will receive due consideration once you are one of us,” he replied, forcing me into the chair and tightening the restraints around my forearms and ankles.

Two of the guards remained in the room with me as the other two disappeared, presumably to go fetch their master.

But when the door opened again, it wasn’t the queen of the Angels that entered.

“Leave us,” Randal Divine commanded the Seraphim, and they quietly bowed themselves out.

Alone, Randal slowly approached my chair.

I glared up at him. He smiled back.

"The prodigal son returns," he whispered.

Let there be light, I thought to myself. *But not yet.*

"You once told me to pray that I would never see you again, Adrian Howell," said Randal, bringing his face up close to mine. "But I have prayed. For Cathy, I have prayed for your return. And finally, now, here you are."

I stared stonily back at him.

Randal took a step back and shook his head in wonder, saying, "To think I almost killed you at the gathering of lesser gods. But of course I didn't know how special you were, Adrian. Not just to Cathy, but to the future of our world. You see, in order to keep Cathy from harm, my aunt, the late Queen Divine, may God rest her soul, kept your lineage secret even from me. I only learned the truth when, as fate would have it, only three days after my aunt was killed, Cathy came into her full power as a master controller. Since then, I too have done everything in my power to protect her secret... and yours."

Still I said nothing. There was nothing to say to this man. As soon as he brought Cat in here, he would die too.

"You hate me," Randal said quietly. "I know, and I don't blame you. But try to understand that when my aunt asked me to raise Cathy as my daughter, I did not take her in out of greed or duty. I love her. She is a part of my family, and we both want you to be a part of it too."

I slowly shook my head.

Randal sighed heavily. "She still loves you, Adrian. And she knows that you have been on a mission to kill her. She has known for a long time, and it has hurt her more than you can imagine. I have watched her suffer. I have watched her cry for you."

"You wanted me back," I said in a low voice. "I'm here. Get this over with."

Randal studied my face for a moment, and then said, "My daughter wishes to speak with you privately. I trust you will hear her words better than you hear mine."

He turned around and left the room.

Less than a minute later, the door opened again, and in stepped Queen Catherine "Cat" Howell-Divine.

She had cut her once-long hair really short, a bit like Terry's. It made her look very grown-up. She was wearing a simple but elegant violet dress and matching silk gloves. Cat was smiling, but everything else about her looked sad.

Let there be light, I thought to myself again. But I didn't say it. I couldn't detonate the bomb just yet. Not because Randal wasn't in the room. He was just a bonus extra, anyway. But I had to be sure of what I was doing. I had come this far and I was certainly prepared to take the final step, but first I had to be absolutely sure that there was no other way.

"Hello, Catherine," I said stiffly.

"I had a feeling I would see you again," said Cat, shaking her head a little. "Just not like this."

"Are you really going to convert me?" I asked.

"I wish I didn't have to," Cat said unhappily. "But it's probably for the best. Father thinks you can't be trusted."

"What do you think?"

"I want to trust you, Adrian. But you were trying to kill me."

"I was trying to kill the last psionic master," I informed her. "I was trying to keep the Angels from taking over the world. I was trying to keep my sister from becoming a tyrant."

Cat gave me an injured look. "Won't you at least hear my side of it?"

"I've heard plenty from Cindy already, thank you," I said savagely. "I heard about all the wonderful things the Guardian Angels are going to do for the world."

"It's all true, Adrian," said Cat. "I never wanted anything for myself. And I know that humans would be better off in our care."

"I was human once, Cat," I said evenly. "As were you. It is not our place to rule them."

"And why not?" she asked, taking a step closer to my chair. "It would be a far better world for everyone than if we continued to let humans rule themselves. We could put an end to all of their ridiculous wars. We could unite the entire human race under one flag. Think about it, Adrian. A world without borders. We could end conflict for good."

"You're fifteen years old," I scoffed. "What do you know about running a planet?"

"Not much," admitted Cat. "But I do know what the biggest problems are. After I came into my power, Father took me on a trip around the world. I traveled with him for half a year. I saw babies starving to death in tiny dirt huts, and I dined under crystal chandeliers in the palaces of kings. Father showed me how unbalanced this world really is, and how close we all are to destruction."

"It's not for us to change that, Cat. You know it isn't. You can't force the world to change."

"You're wrong, Adrian. This is exactly what the Guardian Angels are all about."

"Controlling the minds of billions of people?" I asked disgustedly.

"Of course not!" Cat said in a scandalized tone. "I couldn't do that if I tried. Just the leaders, Adrian. The leaders of politics and the economy. We need to make them think of the masses first and their own personal gain second. If only they worked together, all of our problems would be solved. That is what we're about. That is what the original Guardian Angels were created to do. To protect humanity from its own mistakes. It's the only reason psionics exist."

"What makes you think you're so superior to them?"

"We *are* superior, Adrian," argued Cat. "Look at the things we can do. The people need us. Even if they don't want us, they still need us."

"That is the excuse of every dictator the world has ever seen."

Cat shook her head. "You're blinded by your hate."

"I have reason to hate!" I shot back. "So should you. Our parents—"

"Our parents were casualties of war!" cried Cat. "Of a pointless, stupid war that Father and I have just ended once and for all! And now we can end all the other stupid wars. We can save billions of lives!"

"You honestly think that you're doing this planet a favor? You think injustice and inequality justify what you've been doing?"

"And what have you been doing, Adrian?! Look at you! You're nothing but a killer! I'm offering a chance for peace! I'm trying to make a world where people can stop butchering each other over their petty differences! Why can't you see that?!"

"All I see is the difference between freedom and slavery. That is not a petty difference, Cat!"

Cat looked away, saying quietly, "What's so great about freedom, Adrian? What about the freedom to live without fear of being attacked in the middle of the night? What about the freedom to live with the people you love? Our parents were murdered by the Guardians because they wanted me so badly that they didn't care what happened to anyone else. They wanted a master controller. They wanted to do exactly the same thing I'm doing."

I sighed. It was useless to try to convince her that our parents had been killed by a member of the Seraphim. It didn't matter who had killed them anymore. Cat and I were just talking in circles.

Cat knelt in front of my chair and grasped my hands. "You and me, Adrian, we both wanted the same thing. We still do."

"I doubt that, Catherine Divine," I replied coldly, "because I wanted you dead. I still want you dead."

"Why do you say such horrible things?" Cat asked in a hurt tone. "We both want peace."

"There will be no peace as long as the world is run by a master controller. There will be no equality. No justice. No end of suffering."

"I know it won't be perfect," whispered Cat, "but it will be better."

"I'm sorry that you think so."

"I think Father is right," Cat said sadly, standing up. "This really is the only way I can save you." Cat carefully placed her right hand on the top of my head. "Please don't fight me. It could damage your mind if you do."

I smiled grimly. "I'm glad that we got to talk before you converted me, Cat," I told her. "I wanted to make sure that I hadn't just imagined what you are. Now I really have no regrets."

And with one last deep breath, I said as loudly and as clearly as I could, "Let there be light!"

19. THE LOSS OF SILENCE

Cat took a step back and stared at me. I stared back.

Nothing happened.

"Let there be light!" I shouted again. "Let there be light! Let there be light!"

I looked down at my stomach. I knew the bomb was still inside me. Why didn't it work? It had to work!

"Let there be light!" I hollered furiously.

But Cat and I were both still alive, engulfed in a deafening silence.

"Adrian..." said Cat.

I looked up at her. Tears were welling in her eyes.

Suddenly Cat reached forward and slapped me across the face. Then again, and again.

"I trusted you, Adrian!" she wailed. "I promised Father you'd never do it! But he was right! You really are nothing but a murderer!"

Randal entered the room and, with a frown in my direction, strode up to Cat.

Cat turned and buried her face in his chest, her whole body shaking as she cried loudly, "He said the words, Father! He tried to kill me! Oh, Father, he tried to kill me!"

I finally understood. The Seraphim had removed the bomb in my sleep, disarmed it, and put it back into my body so that I wouldn't know. Randal had been putting me to a sick little test, and in Cat's eyes, I had failed her.

And far more importantly, I had failed myself. The war really was over now.

"I'm so sorry, Cathy," said Randal, putting his arms around my sister. "I tried to warn you, dear. This is what the Guardians do to their followers. They don't even need a master to do it. They will sacrifice anything, even their own families, to bring anarchy to this world. But it is not your brother's fault. He has been brainwashed to believe that we are evil."

I glared furiously at Randal Divine. He gave me a wry smile and said, "I so wanted my daughter to be right this time."

Then, still holding Cat, he whispered to her, "You can still save him. You can turn him around. You can release him from the evil that the Guardians have poisoned him with."

"I can't," Cat said hoarsely. "He'll resist. He won't accept conversion like this. I know it."

"Then let us give him some time to come to his senses," suggested Randal. "That usually works."

"Please, Father!" cried Cat. "Please don't send him to the Department of Allegiance!"

"Of course not, dear," Randal said soothingly. "We will let him live with Ms. Gifford right here in Lumina Primus. Give him time, dear Cathy. As long as it takes. He'll come around."

"I love you, Father," said Cat, hugging him tightly.

"I love you too, dear," said Randal. "Come now."

Randal escorted Cat out of the room.

Then he came back alone.

His eyes cold and fierce, he slowly walked up to me, drawing a small white remote control from his pocket as he did.

"This is for breaking my daughter's heart," he said, pushing a few buttons.

The powerful electric surge from my control bands jolted my body, but I refused to scream.

Randal shocked me again as he said, "When you are ready to accept your inevitable fate, Adrian Howell, you may ask Cathy for her forgiveness, and then you may ask her again for conversion."

He cuffed me across the face once, and then left.

I sat alone, lost in the shame of my failure.

The guards didn't return for a long time. When they finally did, they were accompanied by a surgeon and a healer.

They escorted me to a nearby room that had a bed, and there they removed my bomb. Unlike the Slayers, the Angels were kind enough to give me a localized anesthetic before cutting me open, and the healer closed up the wound before any pain returned. The whole operation took just fifteen minutes.

But the guards didn't take me back up to the penthouse just yet. They returned me to the interrogation room, strapped me back into the chair and left me there. They didn't tell me why.

After a while, the door opened, and Cat came in by herself. Her eyes were still red from crying.

"Father and I are leaving Lumina tonight," she informed me.

"So go," I said, shrugging.

"When the time comes, we'll be a family again," said Cat, her voice trembling. "I'm going to fix you, just like I'm going to fix the rest of the world."

I shrugged again. "Keep telling yourself that, Catherine."

"But first I want to know why," said Cat. "You were going to die too. You were going to die in this room with me. How could you do something like this?"

"Our parents died because of people like you," I replied. Looking away, I added quietly, "And because of people like me."

"That's no excuse."

"I have nothing more to say to you about this," I said, shaking my head. "You won, Cat. That should be enough."

"You have something of mine," Cat said evenly, walking up to me. "I want it back now."

My pendant was still tucked under my sweatshirt, but Cat pulled it up by its leather cord.

She looked at the bloodstone unicorn in surprise. "What happened to my lucky pendant, Adrian?" she asked.

"I lost it," I told her.

"And what's this?" she asked innocently. "A replacement?"

"It belonged to my sister."

"Your sister?" repeated Cat, staring at me.

I nodded. "My sister. The one I was trying to save."

Suddenly Cat's eyes burned with rage. She yanked hard on the pendant until the leather cord snapped. "Now it belongs to your real sister!" she shouted, holding the stone tightly in her fist. "Or maybe in the garbage!"

Tears streaming down her cheeks, she turned and ran out.

Another hour or so passed. I started wondering if I had been forgotten. Perhaps I would be left here to rot, which, under the circumstances, wasn't such a terrible prospect. But then the door opened again and a suited Seraph Knight entered.

"Escorting prisoners isn't a part of my regular duties," the Seraph said with a smile, "but I wanted an excuse to see you."

"You are supposed to be dead," I said, trying hard to hide my surprise.

"I was dead," said Terry. "For a while, anyway. They shot me four times, and Wood-claw doesn't have a healer, you know."

"I heard that you killed Harding for turning Angel," I said with a grin. "Nice."

"I've done many things I regret," replied Terry. "Even so, my new master has given me the opportunity to repent and make amends."

"If you want to make amends, perhaps you could kindly break my neck right here?" I suggested. "Save someone the trouble of stopping another attempt on your master's life."

"I heard about the bomb, Adrian."

I raised my eyebrows. "And?"

"I think it was a very good plan," said Terry. "An ingenious device."

"Compliments of the God-slayers," I informed her.

Terry smiled. "So you've finally learned to do all that you have to. I was very impressed with you. Horrified, of course, but very impressed."

"You taught me well, Terry," I said. "But Alia taught me last."

Terry nodded solemnly. "I always knew that Alia had more guts than me. I never thought you did too."

Terry reached down and undid my restraints. I carefully stood up. Even if the control bands weren't still draining me, there was no point in trying to fight her. She knew she wasn't supposed to kill me.

"They allowed me into the High Seraphim," Terry told me with a touch of pride in her voice. "It's the first time any former Guardian Knight made the High Seraphim. I'm now a member of your sister's personal guard." She gave me a wink, adding, "And King Divine's."

"You must be very pleased," I said evenly.

"I am, Adrian," replied Terry. "I'm currently assigned to the Royal Gate. It's a great honor for someone as unworthy as me."

I gave her a wry smile. "I'm sure you'll make an excellent security guard, Teresa."

Terry sighed and said in an understanding tone, "I know where you're coming from, Adrian. You really have to experience this to fully appreciate it."

"Conversion?"

"It's really something," she said with a dreamy expression that made me want to scream. "You can't know until you actually feel it. Conversion isn't mind control at all. It's mind release. It's complete freedom from all the silly, trivial things we cling to."

"Like the memory of your brother?" I asked. "The one they sent back to you in installments?"

"Gabriel was a casualty of war," said Terry. "A war that is finally coming to an end after seven hundred years. He would be happy if he was alive today."

"Alia's dead too," I told her.

"Oh," said Terry, looking away. "I didn't know. I'm sorry, Adrian."

"I'm sure you are," I said disgustedly. "Cindy was sorry too. But I guess Alia's just another casualty of war, right? Just like James. And Laila."

"They were important to me too," said Terry. "I really am sorry."

"Conversion must be something real special, Terry. I can't wait."

Terry ignored my sarcasm. "Once you're on our side, I'll try to get you into the High Seraphim. We can be a team again."

Terry escorted me out of the room, back to the elevator and up to the penthouse.

Cindy had already known that Terry was alive and working for the High Seraphim. They said their goodbyes in the living room.

"Keep an eye on our true master for me, Terry," said Cindy. "I'm so proud of you."

"Make sure Adrian stays out of trouble," said Terry.

Cindy laughed. "I've been trying to do that for years. But maybe this time I'll succeed." After giving Terry a quick hug, she added, "I know work comes first, Terry, but come and visit whenever you can. You are always welcome here."

Before she left, Terry said to me, "I'll be waiting for you at the Royal Gate, Half-head."

I didn't reply.

Once Terry was gone, Cindy gave me a sympathetic look, saying gently, "I'm sorry it didn't work out the way you wanted, Adrian. But I promise you'll find a new life here."

I started my new life in silence. I refused to say a word to Cindy, or eat or drink in her presence. For the most part, I stayed in my room, away from my converted adoptive mother and her live-in security. Cindy had four bodyguards who lived out of Terry's old room, working in pairs through two shifts. I didn't bother learning their names. I had nothing to say to them either.

My control bands had been replaced with a solid steel ring that was locked around my right ankle. It couldn't electrocute me, but it kept me drained all day and all night. This wasn't just a security measure. The idea was that prolonged draining weakened the spirit.

Mark Parnell visited me on my third day back. He had also been converted, and I refused to speak with him. He didn't visit again.

I was told that I would remain under house arrest until I agreed to freely accept conversion or until Cindy deemed me ready. I wasn't about to be broken that easily, but at the same time, I wasn't entirely sure why I was resisting anymore.

Everything we had done since returning from the Historian's mountain had failed. We never found the Royal Gate. James and Alia were gone. Terry was as good as a loss. Candace, Ed Regis and the others, even if they were still free, would soon be caught or killed. And my final, desperate attempt to end this war, and all the pain that I had gone through to finally accept Alia's death and my own... all of it had been for nothing. I felt like my entire existence had been completely emptied. Hollowed out. Lost.

I sat in my room all day, silently meditating. I hardly ever opened my eyes.

I remembered asking Cindy, years ago, what conversion really felt like.

She had told me that it was like being in love, and that conversion gave meaning to life. But I had always thought of conversion as something far less wholesome. More like a drug addiction.

Cat had described our parents as being "casualties of war," and Terry had said the exact same thing about her brother. That was the horrible thing about conversion: It diminished your capacity for caring about anyone other than your beloved master. That was why converts could sacrifice themselves and their loved ones so easily, writing them off as casualties of war. Conversion lessened the pain of their losses.

So I certainly believed Cindy when she told me that I would see things differently once I was converted. But that was the whole point: I didn't want to see things differently. I didn't want a release from my pain. I needed my pain. It was all that I had left. I couldn't let the Angels take that too.

Cindy let me live in peace, either because she didn't care or because she understood my need for silence. Either way, I was grateful.

But then one day, nearly a week into my stay, when Cindy delivered my lunch to my room as she always did, I broke my silence for a very brief moment.

"This was Alia's," I said, fingering the bloodstone unicorn that Cindy had placed on the corner of my tray.

"I know," said Cindy. "I found it lying on the floor in the gathering place a few days ago. I thought you'd like to have it back."

Cat must have thrown it away before she left Lumina. I could hardly blame her. She had every right to be furious with me.

But then I wondered why Cindy had taken so long to return Alia's pendant.

I handed the little unicorn back to her. "Keep it," I said quietly. "I think she would've wanted you to have it."

And with that, I returned to my silence.

Late the following night, when I stepped out of my room to get a glass of water, I found Cindy in the dining room, sitting at the table and quietly weeping into her hands. Alia's unicorn was lying in front of her. Without a word, I passed her, got my water, and returned to my room.

The next evening, I saw her crying again, and I suspected that she was doing it a lot more when I wasn't there. Perhaps when I first told Cindy that

Alia was dead, the weight of my message hadn't fully registered in Cindy's mind. It had taken me more than a month to come to terms with it, after all. As the days passed, I still stuck mostly to my room, but I began to notice that Cindy's eyes were always red when she delivered my meals.

I welcomed it. I wanted her to suffer. It made her a little more real in my mind. Even converted, the Cindy I had known was incapable of not caring. The Cindy I had known wouldn't have just cried for Alia. Like me, she would have died for her.

I even considered talking to Cindy again, but I had a feeling that if I did that, she would deem me ready for conversion.

But then again, why not? How many others had already given in and joined the flock? Why was I being so stubborn when I had nothing left to lose?

Except my pain.

"Addy, wake up."

"I don't want to wake up, Alia," I told her. "I never want to wake up again."

"But if you don't open your eyes, how will you know what happens next?"

I shook my head. "I don't want to know what happens next. I've seen enough."

"I know," Alia said sadly. *"But it's still time to wake up."*

"No, Alia," I told her firmly. "I'm tired of the shadows."

"Don't be afraid of the darkness, Addy." Alia touched my hand. *"See? I'm right here."*

I woke on my bed.

The room was dark, but I wasn't alone.

I saw Cindy's wide, frantic eyes looking down at me. "Get up," she said hoarsely.

Cautiously, I pulled off my blanket and got to my feet.

"The guards are asleep," said Cindy.

"What's going on?" I asked, eyeing her suspiciously.

Panting slightly, she said, "It's time for you to leave, Adrian."

She pulled out a key and unlocked my anklet.

As soon as I felt my power return in full force, I telekinetically grabbed Cindy by the throat and growled, "What is this?! What are you doing?!"

"Betraying my master," she croaked, beads of sweat trickling down her face.

"Why?!"

"For... for everything..."

I released her. Breathing heavily, Cindy passed me an envelope stuffed with money, and then we made our way out of my bedroom.

In the living room, I saw two dark figures lying on the floor, fast asleep. I suspected that Cindy, who used to be a nurse, had given them something non-lethal but nevertheless completely incapacitating.

Cindy stopped me before I could open the front door. Reaching around my body, she pressed her palms onto my chest and back to give me personal hiding protection. But then she quickly pulled her hands back again.

"No," she breathed, shaking her head. "I can't. This is wrong."

"It's right," I told her. "Please, Cindy. You know it's right."

Cindy gulped hard, and then put her hands on me again. She looked like she was in considerable pain, and she probably was. I noticed Alia's unicorn pendant, leather cord restored, around Cindy's neck.

"No more," said Cindy. "I can't do this."

"It's enough," I said. I suspected that my hiding bubble would last at least a day or two.

"The cameras outside..." said Cindy, whimpering pitifully. "The security room will know as soon as you open the door. Get up onto the roof and fly, Adrian. Fly straight up into the clouds before going anywhere else."

"You have the key to the roof."

Cindy shut her eyes tightly and nodded.

"Give it to me," I said.

Cindy reached into her pocket, pulling out a silver key, but she didn't hand it to me. She couldn't. I snatched it out of her trembling hand and pocketed it.

I wanted to tell her to come with me, to tell her that we could jump over the side together and escape on foot. But I knew she couldn't leave. What she was doing now was already more than she could bear.

"There's something else," said Cindy, shaking her head furiously. "But I can't. I just can't!"

She couldn't tell me, but I already knew. I prepared a focused blast in my right index finger. Then, in one fluid move, I telekinetically opened the front door, stepped through and blasted a hole between the eyes of the Seraph standing guard outside.

As the guard crumpled to the floor, the panic alarm went off inside our penthouse and the elevator immediately shut down. The security cameras had seen me.

I rushed toward the stairs. All I had to do was climb one flight, unlock one door, and I would be free.

"Stop!" shouted Cindy.

I turned around and faced her. Cindy had taken the pistol from the Seraph I had killed. She was pointing it at me. Her hands were shaking so badly that I feared the gun could go off at any moment, but the bullet would probably miss by a mile.

"You're not going to kill me, Cindy," I said, and turned my back to her again.

Cindy followed me as I climbed the stairs, unlocked the rooftop door, and stepped out.

"Don't, Adrian!" Cindy shouted hysterically, hands still shaking but nevertheless leveling the pistol more carefully on my chest. "If you fly, I swear I'll shoot you!"

At this point I really didn't care.

But as we faced each other on the roof of Lumina Primus, Cindy holding me at gunpoint as the Seraphim rushed up the building toward us, I realized that I couldn't just fly away.

"Tell me where they are!" I shouted over the wind.

"No!" cried Cindy. "I can't."

"You've come this far, Cindy! You can tell me!"

She lowered the gun slightly. "Go, Adrian! Go now! Please!"

"No! Tell me where they are! Tell me!"

"I can't!" she wailed.

"You can't have it both ways, Cindy!" I touched the tip of my index finger to the bottom of my chin. "Tell me or watch me die! Choose now! Your master or me!"

Cindy screamed. The pistol went off in her hands. The bullet ricocheted off the roof. Dropping the gun, Cindy fell to her knees, clutching her head in both hands. She screamed louder, her expression as tortured as if she was being roasted alive in an open flame.

"Your master or me!" I shouted again.

"I can't, Adrian! Oh, God, I can't!"

"Tell me!" I hollered at the top of my lungs. "Your master or me! Tell me now!"

Cindy stopped screaming, but her mouth remained wide open.

She looked at me with bloodshot eyes. And slowly, silently, she mouthed, "Where would you be, Adrian? Where would you be if you had the choice?"

I stared back at her.

And I knew.

And Cindy knew that I knew.

Slowly, her hands found the pistol lying beside her. She picked it up and touched the barrel to her head.

As she pulled the trigger, I telekinetically yanked the pistol from her hand.

The bullet grazed the side of her head. She was bleeding, but alive. I tossed the pistol over the edge of the roof.

"No, Cindy," I said quietly, shaking my head. "Too many good people have died already."

Cindy looked up at me. Still kneeling, her eyes wide in horror, she started wailing again. She couldn't stop. It got louder and louder as she screamed at the top of her lungs. She just kept on screaming.

Focusing my telekinesis around my body, I jumped into the air. I flew straight up, higher and higher into the night sky. But still I could hear Cindy's tortured screams.

In a way, I never stopped hearing them.

20. EQUILIBRIUM

Even today, the tombstone of Queen Catherine "Cat" Howell-Divine stands next to her adoptive father's, in the very same graveyard as her birth parents', and mine. But I've never been out there. Not since I put her there.

The Historian had once told me that I would find Cat's whereabouts in the hands of those closer to this war. Though he claimed to be no oracle, his words had nevertheless turned out to be truly prophetic. For who was closer to this war than I?

Leaving Cindy behind on the rooftop of Lumina Primus, I immediately returned to my hometown, to the familiar two-story house that I had grown up in with my parents and my sister before any of this had ever happened.

And there they were: Catherine and Randal Divine, living quietly together with just two dedicated bodyguards, confident in their clever concealment. I watched them from afar, through binoculars as they visited my parents' graves.

Later that night, I dropped quietly down out of the sky, made a few telekinetic adjustments from outside of their kitchen window, and flew away.

When I heard the massive explosion in the distance behind me, I felt almost nothing. No remorse. No shame. Not even relief. It was like the very first time I had killed, when I shot Riles in the towboat. These were people that I had to end, and so I ended them. Call me a coward for doing it from a distance, but I did it myself, the way I knew from the start that it had to be. But there was no satisfaction to be had in what I did. It was no victory. There was no one left for me to save.

Being assigned to the High Seraphim at the Royal Gate might have been honor enough for Terry, but it turned out that, during the weeks I spent in Cindy's penthouse, my combat instructor had been promoted to an even higher station. Randal Divine had handpicked her to be one of his two personal live-in bodyguards, so Terry also died in the blast. To this day, I feel very little guilt in this matter. Terry was a casualty of war, just like everyone else. But I do miss her dearly. Sometimes I spend hours upon hours just missing her. As Terry had once said about Laila Brown, I miss her fire.

Randal Divine, though horribly burned and mutilated, survived the explosion. But when the Angels' conversions began to fade shortly thereafter and they discovered the truth about him, King Divine was put on a show trial for his deceit and then executed by his own High Seraphim. He never stopped mourning Cat's death, and welcomed his own. It was his dying wish to be buried next to his adopted daughter. Or so I heard.

In the chaos that followed, the Guardian Angels splintered into seven large factions and hundreds of smaller ones, and even as they fought over their petty differences, most of them insisted on calling themselves the "true Guardian Angels." But as time went by, some of these factions combined while others broke further apart, and they eventually adopted their own, more appropriate names. The Guardians and the Angels were reborn, as were the Meridian and other psionic factions both large and small. A number of the lesser factions continued to call themselves the Guardian Angels, but no one took them seriously. Over the course of the next ten years, the balance of power, as envisioned by the Historian, was slowly restored.

Soon after Cat's death, the Guardians regained control of their city and officially changed its name back to New Haven. This was perhaps inevitable since the majority of the psionic population there was comprised of former Guardians anyway. Many of the Angels fled the city, but those who wished to stay were allowed to join the Guardians. Even some of the Seraphim remained and swore allegiance to the restored Guardian Council, and the term "Seraph Knights" is still sometimes used to describe New Haven's combined forces.

Meanwhile, the Angels re-established themselves across many small to medium-size settlements, as was more common for psionics. With the loss of their last master, they too were forced to quickly form a new governing body, a council of sorts made up of their two ruling families, the Divines and the Harrows, as well as members of their High Seraphim. But just like the Guardians back when they lost their last queen, there was plenty of dissention in the Angels' ranks as their top members fought each other for control. Thus, even though the Angels would remain the largest single psionic faction for many years to come, they had little real power.

Though the psionic war was far from over, inter-faction conflicts subsided considerably for a time as each group focused on dealing with the consequences of living in a brave, new, and comparatively free world. For many of us, it was a small touch of peace.

But I never returned to the Guardians.

Instead, I first took refuge in a psionic settlement loosely associated with the restored Meridian. I lived alone, quietly watching the world change. I rarely met anyone from the Guardians or from Wood-claw.

But I kept in touch.

Scott and Rachael had returned to Wood-claw, and from them I learned that Marion had been reunited with her mother in New Haven. Though Marion's mother had come to New Haven as a converted Angel, she had originally been a Guardian who had unwittingly married the Seraph spy, Raider. Now, free of her conversion and of her deceased husband, she kept her condominium in NH-4. But she was still a frequently traveling hardcore businesswoman with little interest in taking care of a young, traumatized daughter. Marion was passed around several homes belonging to increasingly distant relatives, spending very little time in New Haven. Later, when one of her temporary families joined the Angels, Marion went away with them.

I tried to locate James's parents to tell them how their son died, but I learned that both had been killed during the Angel takeover of New Haven. James Turner was posthumously awarded the title of Honorary Guardian Knight for his services in Nonus Twenty Point Five. His name, along with his parents' and Willow's and the many others' who had died in the defense of New Haven, is carved into a stone memorial that stands in the entrance hall of the gathering place under NH-1.

Mr. Travis Baker, who had served Randal Divine as his personal healer and chief political advisor, never returned to the Guardian Council. Fearing that he too would be executed by the High Seraphim, Mr. Baker fled back to the Guardians, where he was granted asylum in New Haven. But the new Council wouldn't allow him back into politics. When he pushed his case too far, he was banished from the psionic city. Mr. Baker was later found dead in the river that runs along the edge of New Haven. It was deemed a suicide.

Mark Parnell returned to his church in New Haven. There he preached about peace and understanding for several more years until he died of heart failure at the age of fifty-four. Far too young, I know, but I have no reason to suspect that he was murdered. Mark never found, nor ever found out what happened to, his twin brother. Mark was a good man. I wish I had known him better.

Meanwhile, Cynthia Gifford was committed to the psychiatric ward of the psionic hospital in New Haven Three. Betraying her master had broken Cindy's mind, and she spent much of her days pacing aimlessly around the hospital ward or sitting in her room and drooling onto her bib. At night, the doctors often had to sedate her to keep her from screaming herself hoarse in the darkness.

I visited Cindy in New Haven every few months. I sat with her, calling her name, telling her mine. Just occasionally, her vacant eyes would flicker with a hint of recognition, but soon she would tilt her head to one side and mumble something incomprehensible, her expression blank and uncaring.

But I knew that Cindy was still in there somewhere. She always wore Alia's unicorn pendant. Her hiding bubble still covered the city. So I continued to pray for her recovery with all the faith an agnostic could muster, but Cindy died twenty-two years later, having never spoken another coherent word in her life. Not a day goes by that I don't mourn her loss or remember the heartless act that destroyed her.

But not even the psionic war could claim everyone.

Soon after the Guardians retook New Haven, Mr. Koontz, the dreamweaver Alia and I had first met at the PRC, turned up alive and well in a neighboring psionic settlement. Mr. Koontz had been one of the few who had escaped New Haven in time to avoid being forced to join the Angels. Having no family in the Guardian city to compel him to return, he remained at his new home. He is still very much a night owl.

Ed Regis found permanent work with the Guardians in New Haven, running an advanced training program for Knights selected by the Council for special operations. The former Wolf also commanded the primary security team for Council members and other VIPs, but even this job was considerably less hazardous than his previous assignments. At least he was never shot again.

Heather, Walter, Daniel and Susan all returned to New Haven safely, where they were reunited with their families after almost two years apart. Not everyone found both of their parents still alive, but it was the start of a new and hopefully happier life for them. Later, all but Daniel joined the Lancer Knights. Daniel turned out to have more brains than we gave him credit for, and after attending medical school abroad, he worked as a surgeon at the Guardian hospital in New Haven Three.

Scott and Rachael were married two years after the dissolution of the Guardian Angels. Mark, who had known Scott's family back in New Haven, handled the ceremony, and I attended it too, serving as Scott's best man. After the wedding, though they both had found their families alive in New Haven, Scott and Rachael continued to live in Wood-claw which, under new leadership, now had much stronger ties to the New Haven Guardians. A year and a half later, Rachael had her first baby: a healthy, beautiful girl who carried both her mother's hider bloodline and her father's finder bloodline. They named her Cynthia.

But my single greatest piece of news came from Candace long before Scott and Rachael's marriage. Near the end of the very first summer, after more than six months in a coma, Alia Gifford had briefly opened her eyes.

Candace called it a miracle, but just as Dr. Greene had predicted, Alia's recovery was a long and very painful climb. She still needed her feeding tube. It took months before she could start to move, and even then she could speak only with her telepathy, and only in very short sentences. Eventually, she learned to make sounds with her mouth and to walk with a cane.

Candace sent me periodic updates. I was, of course, happy to hear of Alia's progress, and I did make brief visits from time to time. But for the most part, I kept my distance. I had killed Alia once in my mind, and haunted by the memory of what I had done in the aftermath, I just couldn't go back to being her Addy.

Early the next year, when Alia was deemed fit to travel, Candace brought her to my house. Alia had lost a fair bit of her memory, some of which she would never regain, but she still remembered me. I insisted that she start calling me Adrian, and we talked quietly for many hours. I made no excuses as I gave her the full story. She nodded sadly and said that she understood, and that she forgave me. But I couldn't forgive myself. When Alia asked if she could live with me again, I told her no.

Instead, with Mark's help, I enrolled Alia in a church-run all-girls boarding school where the teachers could attend to her special needs and rather unique personality. At first, I feared that a religious school might in some way be monitored by the God-slayers, but the good nuns knew how to keep a secret.

Having never attended school before in her life, Alia was understandably apprehensive about her new environment, but she adapted quickly. From the cheerful messages she often sent me, I could only conclude that those were the best years of Alia's childhood—what very little remained of it.

Since she was no longer taking care of Alia, Candace suggested that she and I get back together and see if we could patch up our lives. Candace had also lost both of her parents and most of her relatives, and she had nowhere to go except perhaps back to Wood-claw. I pitied her, but I had no intention of patching up our lives.

I couldn't stay with Candace.

It was mostly for the same reasons that I couldn't stay with Alia. I had set out to die, and in a way, I really had died. Occasional reunions were tolerable, but I couldn't live my day-to-day in the company of people who had been a part of those tumultuous years of my life. Not when I so desperately wanted to put them behind me.

I begged Candace to understand that, but she didn't. She insisted that us being together would heal my pain. Our final parting was very bitter, and I'm sorry for having hurt her so much.

Shortly after I broke up with Candace, I joined a Meridian-funded expedition to the Historian's mountain. There were a few bumps on the road, but we arrived intact.

In his bizarrely decorated home office, the eccentric 3000-year-old child thanked me for my work, easily forgave me for breaking neutral ground at the Dog's Gate, and outright refused to confirm or deny ever sending me dreamweaves.

Laughing, he said enigmatically, "People never believe you when you say you're innocent, so why are they so certain that you're telling the truth if you say you're guilty?"

In retribution, I refused his request to read my past a second time, but he wasn't very upset. I had completed my mission to restore chaos to the world of psionics, and that was enough for him.

The Meridian expedition remained at the Historian's mountain home for six days. As I waited, I considered a lifetime stay. Here I would be safe from anyone who might recognize me as the last living descendant of a lost master-controller bloodline. The servant Havel assured me that my skills as a cook would be most welcome in the Historian's home.

But in the end, I decided to risk the open world. No matter what the dangers, I wasn't going to spend the rest of my life under a rock.

Back when I had set Cat's house to explode, it had crossed my mind to just stay there and let myself die in the same blast. But I didn't do that for two reasons. The first was that, in case Cat somehow survived the explosion, I had to make sure that I could finish the job. The second reason was that it felt like cheating. Cindy had wanted me to live.

And so I returned to civilization and started planning out a new life.

I had to be careful. With Ed Regis's help, I changed every aspect of my identity. I had a new name, a new birth certificate, high school diploma, driver's license, passport, everything. I also found a plastic surgeon who could make my bullet-torn right ear more presentable, no questions asked. Whenever necessary, I wore color contact lenses to balance out my eyes. I even had my P-47 tattoo removed.

What I really wanted was to get out of the psionic world completely, and perhaps find a restaurant job somewhere far from any of the factions, but that just wasn't going to happen. I never gained a second psionic power, and I was no hider. Alone, I constantly risked capture by factions that were looking to add new members to their fighting ranks.

After some cautious searching, I finally found a small, independent psionic settlement where the members were willing to trust me without delving my mind. I freely admitted to them that I carried secrets, and they welcomed me because they needed to boost their defenses as the faction war rekindled.

But I spent more time cooking than being a soldier. This settlement was much like Mrs. Harding's in that it relied primarily on concealment. I was told by the leader not to unnecessarily rock the boat, and I certainly had no intention to. I knew that this was the place for me.

But even there, I never fully lost touch with my former life.

I occasionally met with Scott's family in Wood-claw, and continued to visit Cindy in New Haven. Alia still sent me stories about her life at her boarding school and told me how much she missed being my little sister.

The years passed.

I started dating a woman who, for once, wasn't taller than me, and we got along so well that we almost started a family together. However, a few months into our engagement, we hit a brick wall. She wanted children; I had sworn not to. Personally, I would have been happy just to adopt, but she desperately wanted her own, so we went our separate ways. I felt guilty about being unable to tell her why I couldn't have children. She never knew what I was, and since I had no intention of telling her, perhaps such a union based on lies would never have worked anyway.

Meanwhile, Alia, having graduated high school, returned to New Haven to work at the Guardian hospital in NH-3. It was the perfect place for a powerful healer, especially because there Alia could see Cindy again. When I had first talked to Alia after her coma, she had told me that she couldn't remember anything about her adoptive mother, which was really sad. I suspected that Alia's memory had recovered a bit more since then. She wanted to be near Cindy again, and to take care of her. That I understood.

But Alia didn't stay in the hospital forever.

She started dating a young doctor there named Daniel (yes, the same one) who she married the year after Mark's death. The wedding was held in Mark's old church. Scott was the best man this time, and though I would have preferred to just sit and watch, Alia insisted that I walk her down the aisle. I knew better than to argue.

Daniel and Alia settled down together in a condo several floors above the hospital in New Haven Three. Though Alia's past injuries prevented her from ever having children, she seemed happy with her married life.

But that ended the following year when Daniel was killed in a flash raid by the Angels. The Guardian Council, overconfident in New Haven's unified strength, hadn't been as prepared for the Angels as they thought they were. In addition to Alia's husband, seven other Guardians were killed, including two small children.

From then on, though Alia continued to work as a healer in NH-3, she turned more and more to politics, hoping to save lives by influencing Council policy. Through hard work and some celebrity status being New Haven's youngest-ever Honorary Guardian Knight, Alia soon earned herself a position on the New Haven Council. She was just twenty-seven years old when she took office: yet another youngest-ever record broken.

A few years later, when a scandal involving the Guardians and the Meridian left the head of the Council permanently banished from New Haven, Alia Gifford was sworn in as the new leader of the Guardians.

I guess some people's lives are just meant to be extraordinary. Some people really are meant for greatness, not because it's their destiny, but rather simply by the nature of their character and the principles they live by.

For myself, I wanted none of that, and I was glad to be living a simple life. With the exception of very occasional, unavoidable destroyer work, I lived my life peacefully, hoping that someday I really would find peace. I enjoyed the smaller things in life: neighborly friendship, clean air, a hot meal, a soothing bath and a soft bed. I did a fair bit of gardening too.

I still woke up breathless from time to time, but it wasn't as bad as before.

So I told myself that someday my world really would be still and silent, and that I would stop hearing the screams. And I believed it, too. Especially in the summertime, as I watched the sun slowly rise and felt its comforting warmth on my face, I believed it with all my heart.

But if you think that this is the end of my story, then you are dead wrong. Stories don't actually end in real life. They just linger, or smolder on, until the next chapter. But as for how much of my story I'm going to share, well, I'll write one more chapter and then I'm done. Read it and perhaps you'll understand why.

21. THE BOY WHO CAME HOME

The well-waxed silver sports sedan glinted in the sunlight as it came to a smooth stop in front of my vegetable garden where I had been plucking a few wayward weeds. Wiping the sweat from my brow, I looked up from my work as two women stepped out of the car's rear doors.

The driver who had escorted the women into our settlement was a trusted member of my security team. I stood up and frowned at him through the windshield. It was part of my job here to know when psionics visited from other factions. No one had told me about this visit.

But I wasn't too alarmed: I recognized one of the women. She was a high-ranking Guardian Knight, and my faction was on very good terms with the Guardians.

"Andy Kellogg, it's been way too long," said the Knight, coming up to me and extending her arm out.

"Hello, Susan," I said, wiping my dirty fingers on my shirt before shaking her hand.

"Rabbit," she corrected, reminding me of her Guardian call sign.

"Where?" I teased, looking around my garden.

Susan chuckled. Then she gestured to her partner, a muscular, blond-haired woman who appeared to be in her early twenties. "This is my associate, Vixen."

"Good afternoon, Vixen," I said as I shook the young Knight's hand.

Vixen was a double-destroyer, combining formidable telekinetic and pyroid powers. "It's a pleasure to meet you, Mr. Kellogg," she said politely. "May we come in?"

"Certainly," I replied, escorting them into my air-conditioned living room. At least we could do away with the fake identities once we were indoors.

As I served them iced lemonade, the women exchanged a mysterious, knowing glance.

Then Susan grinned as she asked me, "You don't recognize her at all, do you, Adrian?"

"I've been away for a while," I reminded her.

Susan's grin widened as she gestured to Vixen and explained, "This is Ms. Laila Land, who recently transferred into my Lancer unit."

"Oh," I said, feeling a little awkward. "I'm sorry, Ms. Land, you were... uh... smaller when I last saw you."

Laila Land laughed and then gave me a little bow. "I've heard so much about you, Mr. Howell."

"Whatever it is, I'll deny it," I assured her.

Then I turned to Susan again, saying, "I'm sorry you were sent all the way out here, but my answer is still no."

It had been "no" all summer. After two decades of dedicated service, Ed Regis was finally retiring as Head of Council Security, and Alia had been begging me to take his place at her side. It was absurd. I hadn't seen combat in more than four years.

"Adrian, please," said Susan. "We are not here to—"

"I am not returning to New Haven," I told her firmly. "You'd think that after all these years, they would have figured that out by now."

Susan shook her head. "Ms. Gifford requests an audience with you on an entirely different matter."

"Oh, yeah?" I said. "What?"

"We can't tell you," said Susan. Catching the look in my eyes, she added hastily, "Because we don't know."

"Our orders are simply to deliver you to New Haven, sir," said Laila Land.

"First of all, please don't call me 'sir,' Ms. Land," I said. "Second, I don't jump on the Guardians' say-so."

"We've already made our request to your settlement leader," said

Susan. "It is his order that you accompany us."

"You talked to him directly?" I asked, annoyed. "I'm Head of Security here, Susan. Those kinds of requests have to be passed through me."

"I know!" laughed Susan. "But you would have refused."

I scowled at her. "When do we leave?"

"Now," she said crisply. "You have fifteen minutes to pack. We have a flight to catch."

"At least finish your drinks," I said.

They took me to a small private airfield at the edge of town. I sat in the chartered helicopter feeling irate and uncomfortable. I didn't like surprises and I hated mysteries, and being snatched away by a pair of Guardian Knights in broad daylight for reasons they themselves didn't know stank of both.

We arrived in New Haven in the early evening of the next day.

I wasn't actually under arrest or anything, but Susan and Laila insisted on escorting me through the NH-1 lobby security. They even wanted to come up the elevator to the penthouse with me, but I stopped them.

"No, Susan," I said dryly. "You've already dragged me halfway across the country without knowing what for, so you might as well stay on need-to-know."

"You're probably right," agreed Susan. "The way things are these days, the less you know, the longer you live."

I shook hands with her and Laila once more before stepping into the elevator alone.

On the fortieth floor, two security guards stood sandwiching the front door to Alia Gifford's penthouse. The guards recognized me and opened the door.

"Welcome back, Mr. Kellogg," said one of the guards. "We're under orders not to accompany you."

Giving them a curt nod, I stepped into the penthouse living room.

The Guardian leader looked pretty much the same as I remembered her from our last meeting: a short, slender woman in her mid-thirties with long walnut-brown hair that almost reached the small of her back.

"Adrian Howell reporting in as ordered, Ms. Gifford," I said as she rushed up to me and hugged me tightly.

"It's so good to see you again, Adrian," Alia said happily into my head.

"I can tell," I laughed, hugging her back a little before pulling myself free. I noticed the unicorn pendant around her neck and gave it a light telekinetic tug. "Are you still wearing that every day?"

"I like it," she said simply. Then she frowned. *"You haven't been back here since Cindy's funeral. That's almost a year now."*

"I'm sorry," I said. "I've been busy."

Alia led me into the kitchen, dragging her left leg a little as she always did. She hadn't needed a cane since graduating high school, but she would probably never lose the limp.

Opening the refrigerator, Alia pulled out a carton of orange juice and poured two tall glasses for us. Neither of us drank coffee regularly. I carried the glasses as I followed Alia into the dining room. We sat together around the corner of her large oak table.

"My faction is getting bigger, Alia," I insisted as I sipped my juice. "There's just more work these days."

"I'm not stupid, you know," Alia said in a sullen tone.

I grinned. "I would never dream of accusing the leader of a major psionic faction of being stupid."

Alia didn't smile. *"You used to come to New Haven four or five times a year back when Cindy was alive. And on our birthdays, too."*

"I'm sorry I haven't been around more," I said quietly.

"Is it really that painful for you to come see me?"

I looked away. "It's not like that."

"Yes it is," she contradicted. *"It's always been that way with you. I knew exactly how you felt when you stuck me in that boarding school."*

I shook my head. "I thought you liked it there."

"I did like it there! I had fun and I made friends and I learned so many things I needed to learn." Alia gave me a hurt look. *"But I still missed you. You never even came to visit me."*

I sighed. I knew how much Alia had missed me by the things she had written in her letters. And she was right: my visits to New Haven over the years had been mainly to see Cindy.

"It's been more than twenty years, Adrian," Alia said gently. *"Don't you think it's time you let it heal?"*

I narrowed my eyes. "Is this what you called me out here to say?"

"No."

"Ed Regis, then?" I asked. "I'm not staying here, Alia."

"No, Adrian, it's not about Ed. I know you're not coming back."

We looked at each other for a moment. Alia silently sipped her orange juice.

"I'm sorry about not taking the job," I said, "but this is your home, Alia, not mine."

"I know," said Alia. *"Anyway, it's okay. I've asked Ed to find his own replacement, and I think he has a few people he can trust with my life."*

I couldn't help smiling. Alia's sarcasm had grown subtle over the years.

"You look tired," I said, noticing her slightly sunken eyes. "Job getting you down?"

"I've had better months," admitted Alia. *"The Angels are pushing much harder now that we don't have Cindy's protection here anymore. The Meridian and the Avalon Union are causing lots of trouble too."*

"The Avalon can't be a major concern," I said, happy to be on a less personal topic. "They haven't had a unified offensive force since the Angels pounded the hell out of them four years ago."

"They're recovering," said Alia, who looked very conflicted about that news. *"And they're feeding the God-slayers with enemy intelligence."*

"You're kidding!" I said, surprised. "That's not very sporting of them."

Alia agreed. *"Slayers don't care where the information comes from as long as it's accurate. If the Avalon keep doing this, other factions might start doing it too."*

I raised my eyebrows. "And you?"

"Never ask a politician a question like that!" said Alia, laughing nervously.

"You are going to do it, aren't you?" I pressed.

After a moment's hesitation, Alia nodded. *"We're considering it."*

I gave her a wry smile and said, "Permission to speak freely, Ms. Gifford?"

"Always."

"It was a mistake for you to accept this position," I said carefully. "A member of the Council I'd understand, but not at its head. It's not in your nature to fight, Alia. You care too much."

"That's why the Council can overrule my decisions," Alia said sadly. *"And they often do."*

"This war is going to get dirty again," I said.

"Very dirty," agreed Alia.

"Are you up to it?"

"I will do what I have to."

I grinned widely. "Then why don't you stop dragging your feet and tell me why you had Laila Land of all people kidnap me in the middle of my gardening. You didn't bring me all the way out here to scold me for not keeping in touch."

Alia chuckled. *"Well, that was part of it. And I had a feeling Ms. Land would get a kick out of you, too."*

"You resent my peaceful lifestyle, don't you?" I said jokingly.

"I envy it, Adrian, but I still had to get you here in person."

"Then tell me why."

Alia took a moment more to sigh, and then said slowly, *"I had you brought to me because I know you don't want to live in New Haven, and I need someone on the outside that I can trust."*

"No more missions, Alia," I said flatly.

I was about to stand up, but Alia stopped me, saying, *"This isn't a mission, Adrian. It's more important than that."* She shook her head a little and added quietly, *"This one's personal."*

"What's going on?" I asked, suddenly curious.

"We found it," Alia said with a frown. *"We finally found it and shut it down."*

"Found what?"

"Site-B."

Alia and I had escaped the Psionic Research Center Site-A, an underground prison where the Wolves sent captured psionics to be experimented on. Site-A had been completely destroyed when we escaped, but we had later learned about the existence of a Site-B from Ed Regis's database.

Alia explained that her Lancer Knights had stumbled across the government-run research center and shut it down permanently a little over three weeks ago.

"Site-B wasn't just a research facility," said Alia. *"They weren't just studying psionics there."*

I looked at her questioningly.

"It was a…" Alia's telepathic voice trailed off. She gulped once, and continued, *"It was a genetics lab, Adrian. They were making people there."*

"A soldier program?" I asked.

Alia nodded. *"Composite psionics. They were using the data collected from Site-A and B combined."*

"What did you do there? I mean, what did the Lancers do?"

"They destroyed it," said Alia, looking downcast. *"They destroyed the whole building, and the research data, and the experiments. Everything."*

I shook my head. "You're hiding something."

Alia stood up from the table. *"Come with me."*

She led me to our old bedroom. It had been refurnished and redecorated as a guestroom.

It was occupied too.

The guest, currently fast asleep and hovering two feet above his bed, was a very small, dark-haired boy.

"The youngest experiment," explained Alia, her eyes blinking furiously as she watched the boy hover. *"He's only two years old. The Lancers couldn't kill him, so they brought him back to New Haven and I took him in."*

"You're just like Cindy, Alia," I said, chuckling. "Looking for lost kids to save."

"He's not lost, Adrian," Alia whispered into my head. *"He's home."*

I stared at her in astonishment.

Alia nodded. *"He's ours."*

Technically, this sleep-hovering child wasn't just ours. He was a genetic mix of Alia, me and several others who had been locked up in the PRC. Furthermore, the doctors at Site-B had done something to him that not only made his powers come early, but allowed him to gain many more powers than was common for psionics. At two years old, the child was already a flight-capable telekinetic, a spark and a telepath. Alia explained that he would probably also acquire healing, hiding, delving, puppeteering and perhaps even teleporting as he grew up.

As I watched, the boy's body rose a few more inches until he reached the full length of the tether that Alia had attached to his clothes to keep him from drifting away. I telekinetically guided the boy back down onto his bed. His eyes opened slightly when he touched down on the mattress, but then he went back to sleep.

"He's our child, Adrian," Alia said again. *"He didn't have a name, so I call him Richard. But there are already some people here that suspect what he is."*

I frowned. "You mean he's a master?"

"He's a boy, so he won't become a master," said Alia. *"But he carries the blood of Havel. Your blood."*

We stepped back out into the hallway. Alia quietly closed the door on the sleeping child.

"What do you want me to do?" I asked, though I already suspected.

Turning to me, Alia said, *"I want you to raise him outside of New Haven. If my people find out that Richard has master controller in him, they might kill him, or worse."*

"I don't mind hiding him for a few weeks, Alia," I said uncomfortably, "but I don't know about raising him."

"Why not?"

"Well..." I said, cringing, "I'm sure you do remember that I was never a very good parent..."

"I remember," said Alia, suppressing a smile. *"But I wasn't exactly the easiest kid to take care of either."*

I laughed. Alia started laughing too, and for a while we just stood there and laughed without reservation. It felt good to laugh with her like this again. It had been many years since I had a good laugh.

When we finally stopped, Alia looked into my eyes and said pleadingly, *"Just watch over him, Adrian. Watch over him as you once watched over me."*

"Are you sure, though?" I asked seriously. "I mean, what makes you think I won't kill that boy myself?"

In reply, Alia slowly reached down into the front of her shirt and drew out her other pendant. She looked at the amethyst thoughtfully for a moment before taking it off and carefully placing it around my neck. Then, with her right palm, Alia pressed the pendant to my heart as she whispered, *"I just know, Addy."*

I agreed to take the child home. He had my sister's eyes.

I can't tell you how my story ends because I simply don't know. Not even the Historian can tell the future. We all live our life stories without knowing where they will lead us, or when or how they will end. I suppose that is the only true fairness in life, as maddeningly unfair as it is.

Someday, when Richard is old enough, I will let him read these pages. His life will be his to lead, but at least he should understand how important his choices may turn out to be. And, in time, perhaps he will even add a few pages of his own. Perhaps Richard will live to know how some of our stories conclude.

But for the time being, allow me to suggest, in lieu of a more dramatic and less common ending, and in the spirit of blind optimism, as well as the possibility that it may even be true, that at least some of us really did live happily ever after.

AFTERWORD

The total number of words comprising the five books of my *Psionic Pentalogy* are roughly equal to that of Tolkien's *The Hobbit* and *The Lord of the Rings* combined, just a chapter or two shy of Tolstoy's *War and Peace.* If you are reading this afterword, I can only assume that you have read the entire series from *Wild-born* to *Guardian Angel.* I thank you from the bottom of my heart for sticking with this story and its characters through thick and thin. I hope you have enjoyed reading it as much as I have enjoyed writing it.

This is the first time I am writing in my own voice, that is, the voice of the author Adrian Howell (pen name) as opposed to the narrator Adrian Howell. I figure that if you've come this far, you just might be interested in knowing a few additional details about the characters, some background information about this story, and how it all came about. From here on in, everything I write will assume that you have already read all five books, so if you haven't, stop reading this afterword now.

Where to begin...

Wild-born is actually the first full-length novel I ever wrote in English. *The Tower* was the second, and so forth. I had written a number of short stories in my youth, as well as a full-length high fantasy novel in Japanese that will never see the light of day, but the *Psionic Pentalogy* was my first major series project in any language.

I can no longer remember exactly when I started writing *Wild-born,* but I think it was sometime in mid-2008. After nearly a decade of teaching full time at an EFL school in Tokyo, I had decided to open my very own private English school—right in my own house. With no business training, absolutely no experience in anything aside from teaching, I quit my stable job and took the plunge into self-employment. I converted my first floor into a classroom and lobby area, put up a sign, paid for a little advertisement, and waited for the phone to ring.

It was a leap of faith which ultimately (and very fortunately) resulted in success: by the second year, I had enough students to keep me fed and clothed, doing a job I love, with the added bonus of being my own boss and having my own bath and shower in my workplace.

But that first year was no picnic. With only two classes a week, and required to stay at home manning the telephone all day long, waiting for it to ring, wondering if it would... The mixture of boredom and anxiety was driving me insane.

So I started writing to keep my mind off of things.

I wrote the first two chapters of *Wild-born* (originally simply titled *Psionic*) thinking that it would be a standalone novella, but by the end of the third chapter, I knew what kind of monstrous project I was dealing with. Still, I figured that I'd write just one book and see how I felt at the end of it. There was no pressure to complete the project, so I took my time, occasionally stopping for a week or more between writing. Months later, when I finished the last chapter of *Wild-born,* I do recall it was that very evening that I wrote the first chapter of *The Tower.* I was hooked. It would become a pentalogy after all.

But that didn't mean I had mapped out the entire storyline over the next four books. Far from it. I knew very basically where I wanted to end up with these characters, but I took the journey with them, much like a reader would, not knowing what was going to happen until it actually did. Truth be told, I wasn't even sure until halfway through *The Quest* that Cat really was the master controller that Adrian would have to kill. I had been toying with the idea, of course, but it was still possible to make Randal Divine the final objective. At least, that's what I thought until I got to the Historian. I realized then that if Randal really was the master and Adrian's journey was that of killing this king and saving his first sister, then the whole story really would be a simple black and white fairytale. I couldn't live with that.

But I'm getting way ahead of myself here. Back to *The Tower.*

In 2009, as I continued to write *The Tower,* I was busy looking for a literary agent to represent *Wild-born.* Back then, e-books were still in their infancy, and I knew nothing about self-publishing. I was still of the mindset that a book could only get published if it was accepted by a traditional publisher. I sent my *Wild-born* manuscript to a long list of agents across the United States, and some of them were even kind enough to reply that they weren't interested. (It wasn't helping my situation that I was sending my query letters from Japan, but that probably wasn't the only reason.)

But by the time I was getting these polite rejections, I too was having second thoughts about releasing *Wild-born* so soon. I was halfway through writing *The Tower,* and I had hit a problem with the storyline. In the original version of *Wild-born,* psionic finders could in fact find non-psionic people as long as they were relatively close. But that didn't work for a part of my planned plot in *The Tower,* specifically the puppeteer's inability to lock onto Terry. So I went back and changed the rules of the world, rewriting a section of *Wild-born* to fit what I wanted to do in *The Tower.* In short, I cheated, and I couldn't have done that if *Wild-born* had already been published. Thus I concluded that I would stop trying to get published until all five books were completed.

For several reasons, this was probably the best decision I ever made in writing my books.

For starters, it gave me free reign over my world, allowing me to edit anything I wanted in my previous books whenever it suited the larger story arc. As I said earlier, I really wasn't sure until the end of *The Quest* whether Adrian and Cat were of master-controller blood. But if you go back to the second chapter of *Wild-born,* you will notice Ralph Henderson calling Adrian "Havel" by accident. That part was added in as I wrote the last chapters of *The Quest,* a full three years after I originally finished writing *Wild-born.* In fact, by the time I finished writing *Guardian Angel*, so many fixes had been made to the first four manuscripts that I almost felt like I had written an extra book.

Second, pre-completing the series meant that readers wouldn't have to wait a year for the next book. For me, the single most frustrating thing about reading a series in progress is having to wait for the release of the next installment. I didn't want my readers to have to wait around not knowing when (or if) the next book would ever be completed. It would be better, I decided, to have all five books ready before releasing any of them, thus allowing readers to set their own paces. And I really don't like writing to a deadline: That feels too much like work. I write because I enjoy writing, so I only write when I want to. The muse comes and goes.

Lastly, because I delayed all publishing issues for several years, by the time I got around to it, the e-book industry had taken off, allowing me to avoid the hassles of working with traditional publishing houses altogether.

I am very particular about my storytelling, and entirely unapologetic. I suspected when I wrote *The Tower* that some readers would find the first half of that book slow-paced. There are slow sections in the other books too, and I imagine that a traditional publisher's editor would have required me to tighten up the plots because modern audiences want more frequent action. But for my part, I see the *Psionic Pentalogy* as one large story first and five separate novels second. The pace picks up in the last two books (as would be expected of any story as it approaches its climax), and if certain sections of the first three novels did not have the mass-appeal speed and action that traditional publishers would require, I nevertheless felt these slower chapters entirely necessary for fully developing the characters and setting up the main story. Would readers agree, or at least be forgiving of my eccentricities? Do I really know my readers better than a traditional publisher's experienced editor? Perhaps not, but in the interest of preserving my own storytelling style, I was willing to take that chance. When it finally came time to publish my series, I knew that indie was the only way for me to go.

Thus I self-published all five books of my *Psionic Pentalogy* in approximate two-week intervals starting in December 2012.

There are downsides to this route, of course. Without the backing of an agent and publisher, the author is responsible for every aspect of the publishing process from proofreading to publicity and everything in between. I spent months editing the manuscripts and weeding out typos. I created my own book covers, which were crude and unappealing to say the least. I could have (and, in retrospect, probably should have) hired out for these services, but going into this business as an amateur, I had decided that my books would have to pay their own way. That is, I would only spend money on promotional materials such as advertisements and proper covers if the books sold enough to pay for them. A bit of a catch-22, I know, but it made sense to me because writing is my pastime, not my career. I wasn't about to invest lots of money in a new and untested endeavor.

Predictably, the books sold very, very slowly. Even so, initial reception was surprisingly positive, and in late 2013, *Wild-born* was announced a Science Fiction and Fantasy category finalist in the Kindle Book Review's Best Indie Book Awards Contest. No, it didn't win, but being in the top five was honor enough for me. And by then the series had sold just enough to afford professional cover art and occasional paid advertisements, so I decided to take things just a bit more seriously.

As a result, sales did pick up some, but not in a best-seller-list kind of way. In fact, three years since its release, the *Psionic Pentalogy* still remains largely unknown to the world. As my fellow indie writers often say, it takes a long time for an unknown author to get known, and most books only move a handful of copies, if any. Thus I am grateful to each and every reader like yourself who is willing to take a chance on a nameless self-published author, and I am additionally hoping that you will help spread the word, not just for my books, but for any that you enjoy.

But enough about the world of self-publishing. Let me move back to the *Psionic Pentalogy* world now and talk about a few of the characters. In this, I would be tempted to write a paragraph or two about every single one of them, but that would be far more than "a few," so here I will limit myself to just the characters that appear in *Wild-born* and *The Tower,* starting of course with my narrator, Adrian Howell.

You can easily see that my temperamental protagonist is no superhero, neither in power nor in moral character. Call me a cynic, but even as a child, I never really believed in the idea of an incorruptible hero. And while stories of all genres are replete with antiheroes, as a reader I have always felt that, far too often, we didn't get to directly see how these characters became flawed in the first place.

I believe that while nature may dictate our predispositions to some extent, nurture is what truly shapes us. Thus in the first book, Adrian is very much the victim, running from powerful, terrifying enemies. But over the years, various encounters with hostile forces rub off on him in all the wrong ways. By the end of the series, Adrian is the hunter. Still well-meaning in his own way, and not without his many regrets, nevertheless Adrian is a ruthless killer with a personal agenda. As much as he is a champion of freedom, he is also, by his own free admission, an agent of chaos. But if you were appalled by Adrian's lack of moral principles in *Guardian Angel,* at least you know how he lost them.

Next, Cat. To my mind, Catherine Howell, like her brother, is a victim of circumstance and environment. Her life was far more similar to Adrian's than Adrian would ever admit. She saw her brother kidnapped and tried to save him. She watched a war destroy her family and tried to put an end to it. She wanted nothing more than to bring peace and order to a world of turmoil. I never wanted the *Psionic Pentalogy* to be about a battle between good and evil, but rather a battle between conflicting ideologies. I wanted my readers to consider that perhaps the world really would be better off in the hands of the Angels. Would Cat really have been so terrible a dictator as Adrian imagines?

Alia. Though this was one of the most difficult characters for me to write, it was also one of the most rewarding because, in sharp contrast to Adrian's disagreeable transformation, Alia's journey is a process of growth and self-healing. This emotionally unstable introvert with attachment issues is nevertheless one of the most heroic characters in the entire series, and even Terry admits in the end that Alia had always been the tougher of the two. From the very beginning, I had intended Alia to become the future leader of the Guardians, and the *Psionic Pentalogy* is as much Alia's story as it is Adrian's.

So, a bit more about Alia's character.

Adrian's difficulty in getting Alia to mouth-speak in the first part of the series is actually very loosely based on my own real-life experiences as an English teacher in Japan. Children here, when not confident about their pronunciation, often resort to whispering and mumbling to hide their flaws, thus hampering their improvement and fueling my frustration as their instructor. Getting kids to speak aloud sometimes really does feel like pulling teeth, and I'm sure they wish as much as I that we could just converse telepathically and avoid the horrible mouth-movement practice altogether. Meanwhile, Alia's use of silent times to recharge her emotions is, though somewhat exaggerated, how I have always dealt with stress and long weeks. Sometimes I really do spend half a day staring blankly off into space. And yes, I take long baths too.

Cindy. Someone needed to nurse Adrian through his infancy as a psionic, and to bring Adrian and Alia together. Cindy served that purpose, and though she disappears from view after the third book and only reappears briefly at the end, she is nevertheless Adrian's driving force throughout his final battle, much as Adrian is Cindy's driving force during her own. In *The Tower,* Cindy states that she doesn't miss being a convert because her life "already has meaning." Though Adrian blames himself for destroying Cindy's mind, I feel it is important to note that, in the end, Cindy made a choice too.

But why did Cindy adopt Adrian in the first place? After all, as a skilled finder, no doubt she had sensed other wild-borns over the years and didn't go out of her way to help them. When she first brings Adrian into her home, Cindy explains to him that she wants to help him but also wants his help in taking care of Alia. In reality, however, it was primarily the latter reason that first led Cindy to seek out Adrian. Cindy had been at her wit's end with Alia's aversion to human contact, so when she sensed a wild-born child psionic off in the distance, she saw it as an opportunity to finally give Alia a playmate her own size who could help her get over her phobias. I can only imagine Cindy's initial surprise and disappointment upon discovering Adrian on that rooftop. Cindy had been hoping for someone younger, preferably the same age as Alia, and even more preferably a girl. But once she had found him, she couldn't just leave him there. You know the rest.

Mark Parnell. From the start, I knew that the God-slayers' deadly cult religion would play an important role in Adrian's story, and I didn't want to let the pentalogy become a one-sided diatribe against religion. I myself am an agnostic like Adrian, but I deeply respect the power of faith and the good (and not-so-good) that it can bring out in people. Mark is there to stand for the better half. My reason for bringing him back as the co-leader of the New Haven resistance was primarily to add a familiar face for both Adrian and the reader. Despite being tainted by the war, Mark remains one of the few moral characters in the series, and Adrian's final private conversation with him, highlighting both the differences and similarities between their worlds, is one of my favorite scenes in *Guardian Angel*.

Ralph Henderson. Unlike with Adrian, we don't get to witness the specific events that made Ralph the unpleasant man he is. Ralph's story is told almost entirely in the background, through other characters such as Terry, Mr. Baker and the Historian. But in terms of having a life and worldview shaped by painful decisions, Ralph and Adrian are clearly very similar. Ralph often sees a bit of himself in Adrian, and predicts early on that Adrian would end up becoming just like him. He's wrong, but not entirely. It wasn't an easy decision to kill off such an important character midway through the series, but I needed a proper conclusion to the battle between the Guardians and Queen Larissa Divine before the story could shift to Adrian and Catherine. Ralph's end was the end he would have wanted, and perhaps the one he deserved.

Dr. Kellogg. As far as I'm concerned, Adrian and Alia's surrogate father at the PRC did in fact know that Adrian was lying when he claimed to be whispering fairytales to Alia. He suspected that the research center would be attacked, and when it was, his first priority was to help Alia escape. When Adrian changes his identity at the end of *Guardian Angel,* he adopts the surname Kellogg. For the record, however, "Andy" is neither Dr. Kellogg's first name nor the name of his deceased son. It's just another name that begins with an A, which is easier for Adrian to use.

Major Edward Regis. I already knew when I wrote *Wild-born* that I wanted Adrian to cross paths with this man again when Adrian was both older and less innocent. I knew from the start that Ed Regis would return as companion as opposed to adversary. But why would I let someone like this live and kill off James Turner and Terry Henderson? Would it not have been better to let Ed Regis die the hero's death like Ralph, perhaps while defending Adrian and Alia? Unfortunately, that would have been too simplistic for me. Ed Regis spends the rest of his days serving Alia and the Guardian Council. I figured that would be enough.

James Turner. Though James only makes a very brief appearance in *The Tower* before becoming a major character in the latter part of the series, I actually didn't write the Frisbee scene into *The Tower* after the fact. James really was in the very first draft of *The Tower*, and when I needed a new character to join Adrian's team in *The Quest*, there he was, all ready to jump right into the fray. In the first half of the series, we see Adrian struggling to become a fighter, but once he had come full circle, I wanted to have another character that followed in his path. But James is everything Adrian is not: a veritable knight in shining armor out to rid the world of injustice. Perhaps a bit naive, James is nevertheless a natural fighter, focused, driven and as honorable as one can hope to be in such an imperfect world. Thus, to my mind, his death was inevitable. James is one of the very few true hero characters in the series, honestly believing in fighting and dieing for a greater cause, and so I felt that it was only fitting to let him do just that.

Last but certainly not least, Teresa Henderson. By the end of *Wild-born*, Adrian is semi-burnt-out and in no mood for more adventures. Understandable under the circumstances, but as they say, the show must go on. Terry was my solution: a wild, sharp-tongued warrior girl who could bring the adventure to Adrian whether he wanted it or not. By turning Adrian into Terry's sidekick, I could take him just about anywhere I wanted to, but more than that, Terry was just a ton of fun to write. The oft-friction-filled interaction between Terry and the other characters allowed for a fair bit of comic relief in an otherwise dark tale.

But did Terry really need to die in the end? I'm sure I upset more than a few readers by ending her life so pathetically: a death that is mentioned almost as an afterthought. In sharp contrast to James's heroic sacrifice, Terry is killed in her sleep. She doesn't even get the chance to fight for her new master. I am sorry about that, but please believe me when I say that Terry is one of my favorite characters, and it was no easy task to write her end. It is precisely because of my love for Terry that, after everything she had survived and accomplished, after all that she had done for Adrian and Alia, her death had to be the most meaningless one. Yes, I know that's crazy. But in storytelling, sometimes you just have to follow what you feel to be true in your heart.

Now, I am very tempted to write a little about Laila Brown, the Historian and Randal Divine, but they only appear from the third book, so moving right along…

Regarding the climax of *Guardian Angel*, and by extension the entire pentalogy, I knew that I would end up disappointing some readers who were expecting an epic battle scene, a final, bloody showdown between Adrian and Randal, with Terry and Catherine thrown into the mix. I certainly agree that such a climax would have been more common to this genre, and I apologize if that is what you had been hoping for. For my part, however, I wanted Adrian's final battles to be internal. I wanted to show (and in doing so, discover for myself) exactly how far Adrian was willing to go in order to complete his mission, especially now that he was no longer tethered to Alia. Adrian's final confrontations with Catherine and Cindy, in which he is forced to make hitherto impossible choices that lead to both his victory and his demise, felt to me like a more compelling climax than any action sequence I could write. After the rooftop scene with Cindy, I really couldn't imagine Adrian going into much detail on how he blew up his childhood home to end Cat's life.

For better or for worse, the ending to Adrian's long journey was always going to be, at the very best, bittersweet. As I wrote the final chapters of *Guardian Angel*, I suspected that readers would be dismayed at the sheer amount of collateral damage, at the loss of such important characters like Cindy and Terry, and even Catherine. I knew that it would be hard to watch Adrian distance himself from Candace and Alia. Again, I'm sorry. The truth is that I too would have preferred a more uplifting, feel-good end to Adrian's long journey. But I also felt that after everything that had happened, throwing pies into the sky would have been a disservice to my characters and readers alike. Adrian, never the hero, wasn't going to ride off into the sunset. At best, he could only limp off into it. But I still wanted some form of closure for Adrian. Thus, in the final chapter, having Adrian agree to raise Richard as his son was my way of ending this series on the hopeful note that Adrian might still redeem himself in the latter half of his life, and in doing so, perhaps mend his relationship with Alia as well.

But enough with the excuses. Now for a bit of trivia.

Readers familiar with terminology related to psychic abilities may know that "psion," not "psionic," is the more commonly used singular noun form of one who possesses psionic powers, while "telekinesist" is the correct noun to describe a person who has telekinetic abilities. In the *Psionic Pentalogy* world, however, both "psionic" and "telekinetic" are used as countable nouns in addition to adjectives, much like the word "psychic" is used as both noun and adjective. I consider the choice of these less common forms to be within the bounds of artistic license, and hope that readers will accept them as such. I have seen "psionic" used elsewhere as a countable noun, so I'm not the first to use it this way, and let's be honest here, "telekinesist" is a real mouthful.

Though a far cry from Adrian's misadventures in the psionic world, the years I spent writing these books were, for me, an amazing journey in itself. I am a firm believer in authenticity even for a paranormal fantasy, so I ended up doing a fair bit of research.

One simple way that I strove for authenticity was by directly linking the entire story to a period of five actual consecutive calendar years. If you carefully match up the dates and weekdays mentioned throughout the series, you could probably discover exactly which year each story occurs in. In terms of research, this means that whenever I was writing a scene where Adrian looks up at the night sky, any descriptions pertaining to the stars or the phases of the moon were made correct to the calendar. The story takes place in the northern hemisphere, and I always used planetarium software to "look" at the sky as it would have appeared to Adrian. Thus, as much as I might have wanted a full moon in a particular scene because it would have set the stage better, if it was a half moon that night, then a half moon it was. Period. I'm stubborn that way.

I also read up on everything from tattoo removal to the long-term effects of persistent vegetative state. For *Wild-born*, stopwatch in hand, I repeatedly acted out Adrian's every motion (within reason) during the auto-destruct countdown sequence to make sure that it could all happen within the allotted timeframe. I also researched lucid dreaming in a very hands-on way. That was truly fun. There are several how-to guides to be found online, and following them, I did manage to gain awareness inside several of my dreams. I still do from time to time.

But the most memorable research I did was in learning to cope with blindness. I spent much of one summer vacation wearing a blindfold and learning to get around my house. I purchased a Braille writer online and taught myself to read and write Grade Two Braille. I visited a Braille library and finger-read the first chapter of *Harry Potter and the Philosopher's Stone.* I can still probably sight-read Braille, though it's unlikely to stay with me since I don't use it regularly.

Regarding the gadgets that appear in *Lesser Gods,* while talking compasses and Braille watches with lift-up covers are real, Adrian's head-mounted proximity sensor, to the best of my knowledge, cannot be found in the world today. I consider it a theoretical possibility, however, based on existing "laser ruler" technology.

And speaking of technology, I'm sure some readers were wondering why psionics don't wear Kevlar body armor which, after all, is a synthetic material and would be the perfect non-metal protection from blasts and bullets.

To this, I will answer here that while the setting for the *Psionic Pentalogy* is based very closely on our modern world (night sky and all), it is nevertheless set in a parallel universe within which, at the turn of the 21st century, the internet is still in its infancy, and certain technologies, including Kevlar, smartphones, projectile Taser guns and advanced, brain-controlled prosthetics have yet to be invented. These omissions (and others) were entirely deliberate: I figured that if other superhero stories set in parallel universes of present day Earth could have hyper-advanced technologies, then the *Psionic Pentalogy* universe could be the opposite, a world from which certain common technologies are absent.

Even so, in the *Psionic Pentalogy,* modern technology has already surpassed the combat capabilities of most paranormal powers. While I enjoy an overpowered superhero story as much as the next guy, for this series, I really wanted to even the playing field between psionics and humans. Thus I did a fair amount of research on military hardware and terminology, studying, among other things, the range, magazine capacity, rate of fire, and accuracy of various pistols and rifles. I have some limited experience with guns from back when I was in the United States, but Japan has a near-blanket ban on all firearms, so most of my research was done online.

Yet despite my research, you will have noticed that Adrian never once specifies what kind of firearms he and his team uses. He always says "pistol" or "automatic rifle," without ever naming their exact models. Adrian is, of course, fairly well-versed in military tech thanks to his time with Terry, but as far as Adrian is concerned, a gun is a gun. It goes bang and people get hurt. As a writer, I preferred this style too: readers who didn't know much about guns wouldn't be bogged down by unnecessary jargon, and readers who did know and cared could insert whatever their personal favorites were for those scenes.

In case you're wondering, none of the locations mentioned in the *Psionic Pentalogy* are based on actual cities, towns or mountain ranges. That part is fiction. But if you ever find a place just like New Haven, with the park, condominium towers, the river and forest beyond, I'd love to hear about it. As to where the Historian lives, for my money, it's somewhere east of Europe.

And now a note about the Guardian call signs. This is my personal little jab at superheroes' secret identities. I, and by extension Adrian, think many comic-book heroes are a bit childish in their names. I parody these worlds of secret supers with call signs like Cookie, Dizzy, and Hansel and Gretel. But each call sign does in fact have a background.

Proton, whose call sign is mentioned just once in *Lesser Gods* (when Alia shouts at him) and later appears as the leader of the Resistance in *Guardian Angel,* is a former science teacher. Does this matter to the story? Of course not, so it's not mentioned. Just one of many details that never made it into the series due to the first-person-narrative nature of the storytelling.

There was no way for readers to know about Proton's pre-psionic profession, but I wonder how many people got the joke behind Raider's call sign. Raider is one of my favorite side characters in the whole series. His Guardian call sign is based on the fact that he is a total *Indiana Jones* freak to the point that he actually named his daughter Marion after the heroine in *Raiders of the Lost Ark*. One of my many joys as a writer is that I can bury little details like this into a plot just for the fun of it.

And so long as we're on the subject of secret identities, a quick note about my pen name before I finish.

During the years I spent writing this series and for a long time following its publication, I told no one, not even my immediate family, what I had written. The primary reason for my secrecy was sheer, stubborn pride: I really wanted to see how my series would fare standing on its own two feet, and as such I didn't want my very first readers to be family and friends. And I don't care for biased reviews, however glowing. I love my family very much, but regarding this series, I wanted only pure, honest feedback from readers who, like yourself, enjoy the genre enough to find the books on their own. (So if you haven't left any reviews yet, please take a moment to do so—and time permitting, leave a review on each book of the series.)

As to why I specifically chose "Adrian Howell" as my pen name for this series, that is pretty simple: Any pen name was as good as another, but using my protagonist's name allowed my first-person narrative to read more like an autobiography. I just thought it would be more fun that way for my readers. Confusing, perhaps, but fun.

Do I share any other traits with Adrian the character? A few, actually. I share his lack of spiritual direction as well as his dislike of coffee and firearms. I don't watch television. And I do wear the amethyst. I have for most of my life and will probably wear it till the day I die. But my reason for this is very different from Adrian's. What that reason is, exactly, is strictly need-to-know. Sorry.

Aside from those details, however, I am very different from Adrian the character. Whereas Adrian is mildly vertically challenged, I'm a fairly big guy. I am the younger of two brothers. And though I lived for a time in the kind of suburbia that Adrian begins his journey in, by his age, I was already living in Tokyo. I am an educator by trade, and as such I would like to think that I am a more principled person than Adrian becomes in his latter years. But he's the better cook.

Adrian Howell (pen name)
One Rainy February Day, 2015
Tokyo, Japan

About the Author

Born of a Japanese mother and American father, Adrian Howell (pen name) was raised for a time in California and currently lives a quiet life in Japan where he teaches English to small groups of children and adults. Aside from reading and writing fiction, his hobbies include recumbent cycling, skiing, medium-distance trekking, sketching and oversleeping.

Send comments and questions to the author at:
adrianhowellbooks@gmail.com

Visit the author's website at:
http://adrianhowell.com/

A Plea for Word-of-Mouth

The *Psionic Pentalogy* is an independently published work. Consequently, it does not have the big financial support of traditional publishing houses to promote the books, and instead relies much more heavily on reviews and word-of-mouth by readers such as yourself. If you have enjoyed this book, please tell your friends about it. Please give it a mention on any social networking sites you use such as Facebook, Twitter or Pinterest. Please also consider leaving a review on your bookseller's online site. Even if it's only a sentence or two, it would make all the difference and would be very much appreciated.

Adrian Howell's PSIONIC
Book Five: Guardian Angel
First Edition

38139005R00181

Made in the USA
Middletown, DE
13 December 2016